N

New Orleans

Atlantic Ocean

Gulf of Mexico

Tampa

Boca Grande

Miami

Marathon

Nassau

The Bahamas

Key West

Havana

Lee Stocking Key

Veracruz

Cuba

Great Inagua

Cancun

Hispaniola

Cayman Islands

Jamaica

Kingston

Caribbean Sea

San Jose

San Andrés

Jaco

Golfito

Colon

Maracaibo

Coiba Island

Panama City

Pacific Ocean

Track Chica

SALT CREEK JUSTICE

A Novel By

WILLIAM VALENTINE

Published by
Shutterplank Publishing LLC
6860 Gulfport Blvd. Suite 107
South Pasadena, FL. 33707

Designed by Vince Pannullo

Printed in the United States of America by RJ Communications.

ISBN: 978-09894754-0-2

DEDICATION

To Slim

Thank You

A huge thank-you to all my fishing, hunting, and sailing buddies
(You know who you are!).
This novel could not have been written without you.

A special thanks to my editor William Greenleaf, and to
the publishing team of Phil Whitmarsh, Jacki Lynch, and
Vince Pannullo

CHAPTER ONE

ST. PETERSBURG, FLORIDA-FRIDAY, JULY 21, 2001

A S Beau Stone drove north on I-275, through the humid St. Petersburg night, his hands sweated on the steering wheel and his heart pounded in anticipation of what he had gotten himself into. Beau's mind drifted back to the events that had led him to this critical point in his life. His gambling problem had gotten worse over the past year. He had lost all his savings, his waterfront house in Pass-a-Grille, and he still owed $50,000 to two Miami bookmakers. He had continued to gamble after being blacklisted by the Tampa mafia and the Internet casinos. His credit cards were maxed, and when he paid the interest each month, he barely had enough money to pay his rent and buy groceries.

A gambling buddy had turned Beau onto the two bookie brothers in Miami, Hector and Luis Fernandez. It hadn't taken long for Beau to be into them for $75,000. Beau had lied to his older brother Seth, who was his business partner in Stone's Boatworks in St. Petersburg, telling him that he'd sold his home to speculate on beach condos with the equity. Just lately, he had borrowed $25,000 from their company on the premise the loan was for a down payment on another "can't miss" condo deal. He had sent that money to the Fernandez brothers in hopes they would reopen his credit line. Hector and Luis knew a loser when they saw one and pressed Beau for the $50,000 balance. Finally, at rock bottom, Beau made a conscious decision to never gamble again and offered to pay the debt off over eighteen months.

The Fernandez brothers had countered with a much different proposal, a proposal that they had planned for him from almost day one. They drove up to St. Petersburg late one night and showed up at Beau's apartment at the beach. Luis rang the doorbell, and when Beau answered the door, they forced their way into his apartment with their guns drawn.

Once in the door, Hector quickly identified himself and said, "We have come up with a payment plan for you Beau … one that will benefit all of us. So, sit down and listen."

Beau sat down with no argument. The Fernandez brothers were large and menacing looking. They were both over six feet tall and weighed better than two hundred and fifty pounds. Both were dark-skinned, swarthy, and had beards like Pablo Escobar the Colombian drug lord. He sat on his living room couch and tried not to look as scared as he really was. This was the first time Beau had actually met Hector and Luis in person, and he was a bit intimidated by their size and the evil look in their eyes.

Hector said, "We need you to participate in a robbery we have planned. It will be dangerous, but the rewards will be worth the risk. If you don't agree, or foul up during the robbery, we will kill you. What do you say, Beau?"

Considering the alternative Beau was reluctantly receptive, and answered with a weak, "Yes … but you've really given me no choice. It seems like either way I might die. Is there something in it for me other than not being killed?"

"Of course," Hector explained, while running his right hand through his oily slicked- back hair. "If the robbery is successful, your debt will be forgiven, and you will receive $150,000 of the robbery proceeds."

Beau was now more receptive, as this sounded like a way to solve his financial problems.

"How do you plan to pull this robbery off, and where do I fit in," asked Beau?

Hector and Luis went on to explain that they had a cousin, Ricardo Cabeza, who lived in Tampa and had worked for the Tampa mafia family for twenty-five years. His job was at the family's central money-drop in the Cuban and Italian populated Ybor City district in Tampa. All of the money from the family's illegal Florida enterprises was collected there. The drop was located in a building next to the famous Columbia Restaurant, a Tampa landmark since 1905. The current mafia boss, John "No Nose" Cipriano, owned that entire city block and had a piece of the Columbia as well. The Ybor City section of Tampa was a very busy place. There was a constant flow of traffic in the parking lot behind the Columbia from dawn until closing. Food and beverage trucks, employees, and customers came and went at all hours. Most of the Ybor nightclubs were open until almost dawn. The traffic in and out of the money-drop appeared to be part of the normal Columbia restaurant traffic.

The mafia had divided the building next to the restaurant in two. The front half was leased to a Cuban cigar company. The back half was used for the money-drop. Its back door was right next to the Columbia's back door. There was no access from the cigar company to the back room just a solid brick wall. The money-drop was divided into three small rooms. The back door was steel, and was built like an old speakeasy door. There were no windows in the money-drop at all. When a money runner arrived he rang a doorbell. An armed guard opened a small hatch in the door, and the runner gave him a password that changed every day. The guard then let him into a small anteroom and took the bag of money. A man in the counting room, who watched on a closed circuit television, buzzed the guard through the second door. Then the guard passed the money through another locked door to the counting room and waited for a receipt for the runner. The guard would let the runner out only after checking outside. Only one runner at a time was let in. This system had worked flawlessly for over seventy years. The only updates were the closed circuit television, electronic calculators, and electronic door locks. These improvements allowed the drop to operate with only one guard and two accountants.

"What will your cousin do to help us with the robbery?" asked Beau.

"Our cousin, Ricardo, is the accountant who watches the closed circuit television and controls the doors. He will let you in the counting room after you take care of the guard," said Hector.

"Take care of the guard! No way am I doing this," said an agitated Beau.

Hector pulled out his Glock and pointed it at Beau's forehead and said, "Is that your final decision?"

Beau dropped his head and quickly said, "No ... no, I didn't mean it, I'll do it ... I'll do it!"

"Then let's get back to business, Beau, and if you interrupt me one more time you'll wish you hadn't. You don't have to kill the guard; you just take his gun and tie him up. Now keep your mouth shut and listen."

Hector went on to explain that the drop also had an emergency escape route if another money runner showed up outside the steel door during the robbery. A brick tunnel had been built under the remaining stores in the building. It ended under a storeroom behind a Cipriano-owned olive oil distributorship located in the last store in the block and Ricardo had the keys to everything.

Hector said, "Ricardo has worked long hours, seven days a week, for over twenty-five boring years. He's counted hundreds of millions of illegal dollars for the mafia over those years. He knew the money was gleaned from drugs, loan sharking, prostitution, gambling, hijacking, smuggling, extortion, computer, and credit card theft, because he was involved in all of those things early in his mafia career. Ricardo has a gift for numbers and it landed him in the counting room. He's well paid, but he's tired and wants to retire. When he asked, he was told he could retire when he died. He figured that meant he would either die on the job or be killed if he quit. That's when Ricardo called Luis and me, and proposed the robbery plan. He said that at any time there could be more than three million dollars at the drop. Every morning the money is loaded in an armored truck, along with the receipts from the Columbia restaurant. It's taken to a bank controlled by No Nose Cipriano. When it gets to the bank the mafia money is diverted to a secret vault. Then the Cipriano family launders as much of the illegal cash through their legal enterprises as possible."

"Any questions so far, Beau?"

Afraid to open his mouth, Beau just shook his head.

"Ricardo knows he will have to disappear after the robbery. He also realizes that Luis and I have to remain anonymous. We are well known to the Cipriano family and pay them a monthly tribute to run our book in Miami. Luis and I have also participated in some freelance drug deals over the years and have always paid the Tampa family a percentage. So we have "good earner" status with the family."

"Here is how you will fit in, Beau. We need an unknown front man to pull off the robbery. The robbery has to look like a conspiracy between Ricardo and an unknown accomplice. You're the perfect man for this job, because of the money you owe us. We knew we could make you an offer you couldn't refuse."

"Now here's Ricardo's plan," said Hector with a crooked smile on his face. "You will wear a full beard disguise along with sunglasses and a baseball cap. You'll never be identified. We'll use an untraceable rental for the getaway car. We will give you a bag, with a few thousand dollars in it in case the guard checks it, to take to the money-drop. After getting through the steel door with the pass-word supplied by Ricardo, you'll shove a gun in the guard's back as he is buzzed through the second door. Then you'll disarm the guard, zip- tie his hands and feet, and duct tape his mouth. Ricardo will buzz you into the counting room and you'll both tie up the second accountant. You and Ricardo will bag all the money and leave together. We know that No Nose will try to hunt Ricardo down. But if he has a million dollars, he can hide somewhere in the world. He doesn't want to die in that little room full of money. He wants to live the good life and enjoy himself a little before he dies. At any rate, he's more than willing to take the chance."

"Any questions Beau?"

"How do Ricardo and I get away?" asked Beau softly. "And how do we get the rest of the money to you and Luis?"

"Good question. Luis and I have spread a story among the Miami under-world that we're going to Mexico for a couple of weeks to work on a drug deal. We know that after the robbery you and Ricardo will never get out of Florida by car, plane, or train. The family has so many connections in law enforcement and on the street, that you would be quickly found. So we came up with an escape plan that plays to your boat background strengths. With your guidance, we will purchase a large, fast, seaworthy, yacht under an assumed identity. We'll dock the boat in Tampa, ditch the rental car, and all four of us will motor down Tampa Bay immediately after the robbery. We'll run to Mexico with a fuel stop in the Keys. We figure you know Tampa Bay like the back of your hand and can get us out to the Gulf of Mexico at night. What do you think, Beau?"

"I think navigating out of Tampa Bay, at night, will be the easiest part of this whole scheme, Hector."

"How many days will it take you to get the boat to Cancun," asked Luis.

"Well, if you get me a fifty-footer that'll do twenty knots in good weather, I'd say about four days. But we'll need some extra drums of diesel in case we run into some bad weather. What do we do when we get to Mexico?"

"We'll list the boat for sale with a broker in Cancun under our assumed name, split up the robbery money, and then fly out to our respective destinations," said Hector while looking very pleased with himself. "What do you think, Beau?"

"If I survive the robbery, I think it's doable."

"Then find us the right boat, Beau, and let's do it!"

Hector and Luis finally left a badly shaken Beau. Hector turned on his way out the door and added, "You made a smart decision, Beau. If you had refused … you'd be dead now."

Beau Stone sat all alone on his second-hand couch, at 2:00 a.m., in his shabby little apartment. He sat there until the sun came up and ran it all through his head over and over. His gambling had finally ruined him and robbed him of everything. Even of his morals and own self-respect. Should he kill himself … *no way*, run for it … *no money*, or go to the police … *with what?* He decided to take the gamble, and promised himself that if he somehow got through this that his gambling days would be over.

The next day Beau found a nice Bertram 54 sportfish for sale in Naples on the Internet. That model Bertram was a good sea boat, large, comfortable, and it had enough fuel capacity to make the four hundred mile trip from the Florida Keys to Mexico. Beau instructed Hector what to offer and had him call a good surveyor to check the boat and its engines before buying it. Hector convinced Beau that he had enough boating experience to pilot the boat the hundred miles from Naples to Tampa Bay.

So the plan was started in action. Beau sent Hector a nautical chart on which he had marked the route to Tampa. He included marker-by-marker instructions for the trip with distances and compass headings. He also furnished Hector with a detailed list of the equipment and spare parts they would need for the trip. Hector and Luis were supposed to call Beau when they arrived in Tampa and were fueled up. Beau had made them a slip reservation at the Imperial Yacht Basin in south Tampa earlier that week for Thursday and Friday.

Thursday came and went and the brothers had not called Beau; nor could Beau get anything but voicemail on Hector's cell phone. Their cousin Raul, who was running their book in Miami, answered Luis's cell phone. All he knew was that they had left for Mexico. Beau had rented a car the day before with a stolen credit card and driver's license that Hector and Luis had supplied. Two weeks ago he had sent Hector a small head-shot photo of himself along with the nautical chart, and a few days later the credit card and forged license was delivered to Beau by mail.

Beau arrived at the boatworks for work the next morning not knowing if the robbery was on or not for that Friday night. About an hour later he was absolutely flabbergasted when he saw the Bertram 54 moving across Charley Parker's boatyard, which was immediately east of Stone's Boatworks, suspended in Charley's travelift. He spotted Hector and Luis standing off to the side and walked over to find out what had happened.

Hector sheepishly admitted that he had run the Bertram aground in Tampa Bay late the afternoon before. His cell phone battery was dead because he had forgotten his charger. They had spent all of last night on that sandbar and called Sea Tow at dawn on the VHF radio to tow them off. Being towed to Charley Parker's yard by Sea Tow was an unfortunate coincidence, but Beau was livid. The propeller blades were bent, and the whole plan was going to be screwed up from the start. Beau told Hector the deal was off. Hector reminded him of the consequences. Beau quickly calmed down and made an alternate plan. He told them to ask Charley to straighten the props and launch the boat the next morning no matter what the cost. He told Hector and Luis to take a cab to the St. Petersburg Rainbow Resort on U.S. 19 and to call him on his cell phone from there. He would have a room waiting for them. Beau would outline where to be the next morning with the boat, and Hector could give him the money drop password at the same time. He reemphasized that they were to throw money at Charley Parker until he agreed to fix the propellers overnight. Beau was leaving just as Charley walked up to the boat.

He said hello to Charley, who was an old high school friend, and Charley asked, "Do you know these gentlemen, Beau?"

"No, I thought this was a Bertram that I fished on once in the Bahamas. I came over to say hello to the captain, but it's not the same boat."

Beau looked over his shoulder towards the two Cubans as he started to leave and said, "You're in capable hands, gentlemen. Charley will do a first rate job for you." Beau turned on his heel and continued towards the gate.

Beau got his call from Hector later that morning and he confirmed that Charley would have the boat ready to go first thing in the morning. He also relayed that tonight's password at the Tampa money drop was "watermelon" and the robbery was back on schedule. Hector started complaining about the $2,000 towing bill and the $3,500 boatyard bill.

Beau just laughed and said, "Welcome to the big time, Hector." Beau then told Hector, "Pick up the Bertram at 8:00 a.m. and pay Charley in cash, then motor out of Salt Creek and Bayboro Harbor and turn north past the city airport. Turn west into the opening to the city marina about a mile north, and go to the Marina Point fuel dock inside the breakwater and fill up with diesel. Ricardo Cabeza and I will arrive at the fuel dock at 10:00 a.m., hopefully with a large sum of money. I will call you at your room after the job is done tonight. Did you check in using your Ronald Santos alias?"

"Yes", said Hector. "But, I already replaced my cell phone charger so call us on my cell … we'll be waiting,"

Beau left the boatworks without checking out with the office. He hoped to be back in a week apologizing for going off on another one of his benders. Paying back the $25,000 he had borrowed would definitely help his re-entry. The robbery was on for 12:00 p.m. tonight. Beau tried to nap, but he was so nervous he just dozed in and out of sleep. He fiddled with the .38 caliber snub nose pistol Hector had given him during their initial meeting. The serial numbers were filed off. Beau knew it was untraceable, but he wondered what other crimes the gun had participated in. He watched The Weather Channel on his T.V. and the marine weather forecast was good for the next few days. Beau hoped a tropical storm or a hurricane didn't pop up in the next five or six days. So far this season they'd been lucky. But sooner or later one would rumble up the gulf.

Finally it was time to go. Beau looked around his small, cramped, apartment and thought … *with any luck I'll be condo shopping when I get back.* He started the rental car and headed for Tampa on I-275. His destination: the mafia money-drop and a date with destiny.

Beau's mind snapped back to attention as he drove across Tampa Bay and the Howard Franklin Bridge. Traffic was light on I-275, late that Friday night, and he turned off on the Ybor City exit ten minutes later. Beau cruised by the Columbia Restaurant's parking lot a couple of times and then turned down a dark side street and parked. He checked his watch and it read 11:35 p.m. He noticed that his hands were shaking, so he took a few deep breaths to help calm him down.

Ybor City was hopping as usual. The streets were filled with young people enjoying the Friday night nightclub scene. Beau could hear the whole area pulsing with the big boom bass sounds emanating from the open doors of Ybor's bars. He would make his move to the Columbia's parking lot and the mafia money-drop at 11:50 p.m.

CHAPTER TWO

SETH Stone stood on the fly bridge of his vintage 46 foot Hatteras sport-fish *Tar Baby* and looked down Salt Creek as the sun came up in the east. It promised to be a beautiful Friday morning, and even for July it felt less humid than usual. Seth was readying his boat for tomorrow's trip down to Key West to fish in the Drambuie on Ice - Marlin Tournament that started the end of the following week.

Salt Creek looked picturesque in the morning light. It was quiet now, but soon it would bustle with boatyard workers and boats coming and going. The sounds of the travelift and forklift engines would start, accompanied by the high-pitched whine of air- powered sanders and grinders.

Seth's mind digressed to a time when there were only a few businesses on the creek. He thought of the many hours that he and his younger brother, Beau, used to play in little homemade boats along the banks of the creek.

Salt Creek was located sixteen city blocks south of the center of down-town St. Petersburg. It was a small oasis of moored and stored boats, working boatyards, and fish-houses in the middle of a growing metropolis. The creek flowed east under several bridges towards Bayboro Harbor and Tampa Bay. From the last bridge, called "Thrill Hill" because of its severe hump shape, the creek's water-related businesses were located along both banks about a mile from Tampa Bay.

Seth had spent most of his years with the creek at the center of his life. He had worked nearly forty years at Stone's Boatworks. His father, Robert E. Lee Stone, had started the yard in 1946 after returning to St. Petersburg from World War Two service. His dad had built Stone's into a Florida west coast institution. The boatworks had grown over the years from a small marine mechanics shop into a large full service boatyard. It continued to grow as St. Petersburg grew from a sleepy winter health resort into a post war boomtown.

Seth had grown up in this slice of paradise sailing and fishing in Tampa Bay and the Gulf of Mexico. He had excelled in sports and academics at St. Petersburg High School as had his younger brother Beau. He never realized what a paradise he had grown up in until he left St. Petersburg to go to college at the University of Virginia. He accepted a football scholarship there because he wanted to see more of the country. The cold winters and the fast pace of the eastern seaboard were a rude awakening for a boy who had sailed downwind through the first eighteen years of his life.

Seth had gone to Virginia against his father's wishes. After a stellar sports career in high school, where he garnered all city and all state honors at defensive halfback, he had offers from Florida, Florida State, and Miami Universities. Robert E. would have been happy with any of the three, although he considered Miami "Yankee" territory. He finally consented to Virginia only because it had been the home of his namesake, Confederate General, Robert E. Lee.

Robert E. had named both of his sons after confederate generals. It was a family tradition started by his father Rhett Butler Stone, who had also named Robert E's sister, Scarlett Anne Stone. Seth was named after General Seth Maxwell Barton, a confederate general, coincidentally from Virginia. His brother Beau was named after General Pierre Beauregard. Their younger sister, Scarlett Elisabeth, was named after her aunt. Seth had carried on the tradition by naming his only son, James Ewell Brown Stone, after the famous Confederate General Jeb Stuart.

Seth had run Stone's Boatworks for the last twenty-five years, since the death of his father. Robert E.'s will had stipulated that Seth would receive a fifty-one percent share of the boatyard, and Beau would own the remaining forty-nine percent. Beau had married in his senior year of high school to a girl he had gotten pregnant. She later had a miscarriage and they divorced. After graduation, even though he had good grades and was a promising athlete, he passed up college for the military. Beau had gone to Vietnam with the Airborne Rangers and had a distinguished career. Seth had also served in Vietnam as an officer in the Rangers, after ROTC at the University of Virginia.

But Beau's high school experiences had set the tone for his relationships with the opposite sex. In total he had been married and divorced three times, thankfully, with no children. He hadn't been married in the last ten years, but he always had plenty of girlfriends. Beau had dark good looks, was humorous, and loved to have fun. Like Seth, Beau had grown up working at the boatyard.

He could do any job in the yard: mechanic, carpenter, rigger, travel lift operator, electrician, manager, or boat captain. But Robert E. had recognized that Seth was the steady one. Beau was a free spirit and lacked Seth's discipline. After Beau returned from the Vietnam War, he developed drinking and gambling problems. He had unexplained absences from the boat works, sometimes for days at a time. Robert E. had always forgiven him and believed Beau when he would promise to straighten up. Seth had forgiven him also, knowing that Beau was struggling with some inner demons that were rooted in his war experiences. Seth was realistic in knowing Beau would probably never change. But no matter what he did he was still family.

Robert E. had made a good decision. The partnership worked fine and Beau was actually relieved. Seth was the backbone and Beau added talent and good work despite his occasional indiscretions. The two of them continued to build up Stone's Boatworks over the years making it bigger and better.

But on this day Seth was again concerned about Beau. His friends had confided in him that Beau had some serious gambling debts. The word around town had it that Beau was into the bookmakers for big money. On top of that, it was rumored that the Internet casinos had also cut off his credit. Seth had agreed to lend Beau some money from the company the month before to speculate on a beach condo. Now he wondered if that was the truth. Seth knew the Tampa mafia was nobody to fool with. They controlled drugs, illegal gambling, prostitution, titty-bars, loan sharking, labor unions, and extortion across the whole state of Florida. They were also reported to control the Internet gambling out of Central America. Beau could possibly be into some life-threatening trouble.

Seth had questioned Beau about his gambling problem many times. He always got the same answer, "It's a small-time problem," "It's nothing serious," "I'm handling it, and it's nothing you have to worry about."

But Seth was worried. It was one of the things that had ruined Beau's marriages, along with his drinking and womanizing. The truth was, even with his talent and intellect; he would never have been able to hold his job at the boat works if he hadn't been family. No one had ever been able to change him, so Seth tried to think more positive thoughts.

He would be leaving tomorrow for the Key West Marlin Tournament. He had fished it for the last two years. Seth preferred the marlin fishing in the

Bahamas, but he couldn't bring himself to go back there since the death of his wife, Lisa, three years ago.

He had been married to Lisa for thirty-two years. Lisa had caught her first marlin just off of the Hopetown lighthouse six years ago and had caught "marlin fever". Each spring they returned there to fish and relax in the Abaco's. Until her untimely death, she had caught at least one or two, and sometimes four or more marlin each year they went. Most of the time, just the two of them fished for the big blues. They both loved to fish on their old Hatteras 46, and they had learned that four trolled lines and a couple of bridge controlled teasers worked best for them. When they hooked a big one, Seth was able to clear the two teasers and the other rods quickly and help Lisa work the fish with the boat. Each year they handled larger and larger marlin. If they hooked a really big fish they would double-team him by changing positions in the chair and at the wheel. Seth was in total awe of how proficient his 110 pound wife had become at big game fishing.

The two of them had grouper and tarpon fished for years while bringing up Jeb. Jeb had been a natural fisherman from an early age. He loved to fish the flats near the family house and became an expert at catching snook, redfish, and trout. But tarpon fishing became Jeb's favorite, especially after catching his first tarpon close to the beach in Boca Grande when he was twelve.

Seth had raced sailboats for twenty years, with success, up and down the Florida coast. Jeb raced dinghies all over the south with the St. Petersburg junior team. His team had done well enough to race nationally and internationally. After college, at University of Florida, and a stint in the Air Force, Jeb married his long-time girlfriend Lynne. They moved to California and both went to work in the computer industry. One day about two years later, Seth got a call from Jeb. Jeb said he and Lynne missed Florida and wanted to come home. He wondered if there was a place for him at the boatworks. Seth said he would talk it over with Beau and call him back later that night.

Jeb's decision was well received by both Beau and Seth. Seth wanted to slow down and semi-retire. Beau had never wanted to run the boatworks, as he was happy down in the yard. Jeb had solved both of their problems. He came on board, and after a couple of years of phasing in became the new yard manager. He excelled at running the yard and Stone's Boatworks became his future. It wasn't long before Lynne was expecting and Seth was looking forward to becoming a Grandfather.

Seth missed Lisa every day. He thought he would never get over the lost feeling he had developed since her sudden death. Her heart attack surprised him, as she had always been fit and active. He only had good memories of their thirty-two years together. But, he hadn't been back to the Bahamas since her death. He knew the memories there would be overwhelming. Their favorite place in the Bahamas was Elbow Cay, and they had always stayed at Sea Spray Marina in White Sound. Lisa loved the laid-back atmosphere and friendly people. They had made friends there and had their favorite restaurants and bars. They both enjoyed quaint little Hopetown. Seth called the Abaco's "an orderly place in paradise." Even the days they got skunked fishing in "The Pocket" or out on "The Bridge" were still great days on the water. At any moment you had the chance to catch a monster fish. They relished the passages, good and bad, across the Gulf Stream from Stuart and back through the Florida Keys. Seth tried to put these memories out of his mind, but he thought about her every day and knew he probably always would.

Seth looked eastward down the creek and he remembered again what it had looked like thirty years before. Now there was a huge High and Dry storage complex where a small fuel oil company once was. Four more boatyards were crowding the creek, and the old fish house, at the mouth of the creek, had been shut down. A new restaurant and bar sat across from Stone's. People ate and drank 100 feet across from the sanding, grinding, and painting that went on all day in the various boatyards. The patrons didn't seem to mind at all, even when the wind blew from the south. Developers had started to knock on the doors up and down the creek. People seemed to love the waterfront, no matter how small or industrial it was.

Stone's had been tendered several offers to sell, but he and Beau were not interested, especially since they had Jeb to run the boatworks into the next generation. They had bought a larger, wider, travelift the year before to accommodate the larger boats that were appearing on the west coast of Florida. Seth worried that the creek would eventually go condominium and that the developers would tear down the boatyards, then build condos, along with restaurants and bars where the marine businesses had been. The creek that had launched and maintained thousands of boats would be replaced by a nautical illusion. Salt Creek would probably be renamed after some cliché from a Jimmy Buffet song. Wealthy retiree's would replace the local mariners and fishermen, sporting green and red pants while navigating picnic boats up and down the creek's storied banks.

Where would the boats go to be maintained? Perhaps they would be ignominiously hauled inland on hydraulic trailers to former tomato fields across the bay in Ruskin. Seth hoped that with his and Beau's help Jeb could weather all this. But for now, the boatworks, sailboat racing, and Seth's former married life were becoming part of the past. Marlin fishing had become his passion.

Seth checked his rods and reels. He had put his 30, 50 and 80 pound combos aboard. Next he checked his tackle station and tackle boxes. He went through his medium to large lures. Seth checked his gaffs and filed their points. When he was satisfied he had everything he needed, he checked the Hatteras's engine and generator fluids. He topped off the transmission oil and then checked over the engine hoses and v-belts. Everything looked good. Later that afternoon, he would load the galley with provisions and stock the cockpit freezer with frozen bait.

Seth had called a fuel truck yesterday, and the boat would take on five hundred gallons of diesel that afternoon. *Tar Baby* would burn about 350 gallons on the run to Key West tomorrow. Seth had installed a new 10.4-inch GPS map on the bridge just for this trip. It was the newest and largest display available. Seth was thrilled that he could read the seamless electronic charts without his reading glasses. He had already called and confirmed his tournament crew the day before. They would meet him in Key West a couple of days before the tournament started.

He called his delivery crew, Annie Hart, from up on the fly bridge on his cell phone. Seth had asked Beau to ride down to Key West with him and to stay and fish. Beau had told him he had a couple of commitments and couldn't go at all. He had suggested Annie who sometimes varnished for them at the boatworks when she was needed. She and Beau had been friends for a long time.

Seth connected with Annie and confirmed a 6:00 a.m. departure tomorrow morning. He would put Annie on a plane back to St. Pete once they arrived in Key West and pay all of her expenses. Beau had said she wouldn't take any pay for the trip. She told Beau that she just wanted a boat ride.

During the phone call to Annie, Seth noticed Beau standing next to a large sportfish in the boatyard just east of Stone's. He was talking to two large Hispanic men who had slicked-back black hair and wore loud Hawaiian shirts. The boats name was *Pescadora* and it looked like a Bertram 54. Charley Parker owned the yard next door. He was a good operator and good competition. Charley and Beau had been friends as far back as high school.

Beau and the two Hispanics, Seth guessed Cubans because of their size, were having an animated conversation. Seth noticed *Pescadora's* hailing port was Naples, Florida. Seth suddenly had a bad feeling and wondered what was going on … *why was Beau in Charlie's yard? Maybe Charley called him over for a second opinion? They sometimes did that on a problem job.* Seth looked at his watch. He had better get to Publix supermarket and get provisions for the trip, as he was starting to run out of time.

Seth came back two hours later just as the fuel truck was pulling out of the gate, and stocked the provisions in the galley. He was ready to leave at dawn. He looked around the yard for Beau, but couldn't find him. He found Jeb in his office and asked him where Beau was. Jeb was a strapping, good-looking, young man with blond hair, blue eyes, and a ready smile.

Jeb said, "I don't know, Dad, I haven't seen him since before lunch."

"Can I do anything for you? I'm leaving for the Keys at dawn tomorrow."

"No, everything is under control. Why don't you come over for dinner tonight? Lynne and I would love to have you."

"Thanks, Jeb, but I think I'll pass this time so I can get to bed early tonight. Have Beau call me on my cell when you see him, o.k.? I'll be back a week from Monday. If you need me my cell phone will be on the whole time. I should be bringing the boat back up from the Keys a week from Sunday, weather permitting."

"O.k., Dad", said Jeb, "catch the "Big One" this year."

Seth gave Jeb a hug and left for home. He was very proud of him. He had been doing a great job of running the yard, and Seth knew he would soon be running it even better than he had. He and Beau would be set for retirement without having to sell the boatworks, and Jeb and his family would have a secure future. Seth was glad he had made Jeb do every job in the boatyard no matter how hard or nasty. Jeb had the respect of all the employees and could step into any situation there with confidence.

Seth drove the rest of the way home hoping Beau was not heading out on one of his disappearing acts. Their custom was to always check out up in the office when they left the boatworks for any reason. Seth arrived home ready to pack a duffel bag for his trip to the Keys. Seth was still uneasy about Beau's unexplained absence from the boatyard that afternoon and called Beau on his cell phone. He got no answer, just voicemail. Seth left a message for Beau to call him, and reminded him he'd be in Key West if he needed him. Beau had always been worrisome, but lately Seth was inwardly concerned that something bad was going to happen to Beau because of the gambling.

Seth had sold the family home in northeast St. Petersburg after Lisa's death because of the many memories that were everywhere in the house. He had moved to the beach and bought a town house on the Intracoastal Waterway. It was quiet and the neighbors were nice and not over friendly. The new location came with new restaurants to try and many unfamiliar sights. Seth was beginning to like the casual atmosphere at the beach and was getting used to the ever-changing tourist population. The property values out at the beach seemed to be increasing almost daily, and Seth wished he had invested in two of the town houses. He finished packing, then grilled a steak, and poured himself a glass of Pinot Noir. He sat out at the table on his second floor porch overlooking the waterway. He never got tired of watching the boats idle by.

When Seth finished his dinner he cleaned up the dishes and went upstairs to go to bed. He turned on the bedroom television to the Channel Nine News to get a weather report and climbed into bed. Even though Beau was still heavy on his mind, Seth fell fast asleep before the weather ever came on.

CHAPTER THREE

B EAU sat in the getaway car on the dark Ybor City side street and checked his watch every minute or so. The minutes went by like hours. He checked the cash Hector had sent to him and put it into a Publix bag. Beau glanced into the rearview mirror and it gave him a start. The full beard disguise really had changed his appearance. Beau had purchased it at a costume rental store up on Haines Road in St. Pete. The spirit-gum adhesive burned his skin a little, but he had put plenty on to hold the beard firmly in place. Hector had told Beau that Ricardo was medium height, about 150 lbs., and looked Cuban like him. Ricardo told Hector that the other accountant was short, weighed close to 300 lbs., and was Italian.

At 11:50 p.m. he made the move to the Columbia parking lot. He pulled in and parked next to the railroad tracks that bordered the back of the parking lot, just as two waiters came out of the back door of the restaurant. Beau waited until they passed, adjusted his hat and sunglasses, and then patted the .38 revolver in his pocket as he got out of the rental car with the bag of money. He took a deep breath to calm his nerves, walked up, and rang the doorbell. The little hatch in the center of the steel door opened.

Although nervous, Beau said evenly, "watermelon."

The guard opened the door and let him in. Beau handed the guard the bag full of money after he closed the door. The guard was short and stocky with thick, slicked-back hair. His head was small compared to the rest of his build. *A gym rat* ... thought Beau as he looked at the guard's Glock in his shoulder holster. The guard turned, walked towards the inside door, and was buzzed through. As he started to open it, Beau took a deep breath, pulled his pistol, and stuck it in the guards back.

"Put your hands on your head," said Beau as he pushed the guard through the door.

"This must be a joke," said the guard. "*Nobody* robs the family."

"Keep your mouth shut and you won't get hurt," said Beau as he relieved the guard of his Glock.

Beau pulled out two large tie wraps and cuffed the guard's hands behind him. He used the other one around his ankles. He took a small roll of adhesive tape out of his pocket and tore off a piece and put it over the guard's mouth.

Beau pushed the guard to the floor and said, "Stay put and you'll be all right."

With that done, Ricardo Cabeza buzzed Beau into the money room. Beau went in with his .38 leveled at the other accountant and said, "Hands up!"

The two accountants weren't armed, but there was a gun rack on a sidewall that held four sawed-off shotguns.

Beau handed Ricardo Cabeza the guard's Glock and said, "Tie him up, Ricardo."

Ricardo duct taped his officemate to his chair saying, "Sorry, Carmine, I'm retiring tonight."

Ricardo duct taped Carmine's mouth shut before he could say anything. Then he turned Carmine toward the wall and started helping Beau load the money in the mob's own black canvas duffel bags.

Beau had never seen so much money in one place. They were literally covered up in money. They loaded it up in four duffels and Ricardo took the first two out the door with Beau right behind him.

As Ricardo stepped thru the door, a shot rang out. Ricardo dropped the bags, clutched his right arm, and slumped to the floor. Beau threw down one of his duffels, held the other in front of him, and came out shooting. His first shot hit the stocky guard in the chest and his second finished him as they struggled to the floor. Beau got up and touched his hand to his stinging left cheek. He was all right, but his beard had been torn off on that side and his sunglasses lay shattered on the floor. He pushed the beard back up to his face, stuck it back on, and straightened his hat. Ricardo had struggled back up and was holding his arm.

Beau said, "Wrap it up with something, Ricardo, and let's get this money out of here."

Ricardo got a towel from the bathroom and Beau tied it around his arm. They moved the money duffels to the steel door and Beau looked out through the hatch. The lot looked mostly empty of cars and there was no movement anywhere.

"Stay here, Ricardo, and I'll back the car up to the door."

He walked outside and backed the car to the steel door, then got out and opened the trunk. Ricardo opened the steel door and Beau loaded the duffels. Ricardo got in the passenger side, at the same time Beau slid in behind the wheel. Beau took a deep breath and then slowly drove the rental car out of the parking lot. He made sure the lights were on and then eased into the Ybor City late night traffic and headed for I-275. Beau had learned to stay cool and blend in during his covert action training in the Airborne Rangers. Ricardo, however, was in a lot of pain and looked like he might go into shock.

Beau ran the car up on I-275 and drove a couple of miles, and then exited at Dale Mabry Avenue. His heart rate was slowly returning to normal and he knew he was lucky he hadn't been killed. He pulled into a Seven Eleven and bought a six-pack of Budweiser and a bag of ice. He had Ricardo drink a cold one while he looked at his wound.

"It's a flesh wound, Ricardo. You're not going to die; the bullet went all the way thru. Put some ice in the towel and wrap it back over your arm, and drink another beer when you finish the first one."

Ricardo seemed to bounce back, and he was drinking his second beer as they crossed back over the Howard Franklin Bridge to St. Petersburg. Beau couldn't figure out how the guard had gotten loose. Possibly he had a knife and gun hidden in the second room. Maybe he was a contortionist. Either way he obviously had access to another gun. They had been lucky on their timing, as the guard must have reached his second gun just as Ricardo started through the door. Perhaps Beau's luck was changing for the better.

The biggest downside now was that Beau's beard had been yanked half off during his brief scuffle with the stocky guard. His heart raced, and he broke out in a cold sweat as he wondered if he would be identified from the video cameras.

He asked Ricardo. "Is there a tape record of the surveillance cameras?"

"Yes," answered Ricardo, "They're recorded in another building somewhere, but I don't know who looks at them."

Beau figured he better count on being recognized, and now he needed to figure a new happy ending.

Beau decided to drive by his apartment to pick up some painkillers for Ricardo. Obviously there was no doctor in Ricardo's short term future. He drove around the block twice to make sure he was not being followed. Then he parked behind the apartment and cautioned Ricardo Cabeza to stay in the car. Beau went in and retrieved an old Percocet prescription and an out of date bottle of amoxicillin. He took a couple of t-shirts for Ricardo and a roll of gauze from the medicine cabinet. Beau returned to the rental car and drove back over the Bayway and started north on U.S. 19.

On the way he had Ricardo take two Percocet's and one antibiotic with his third beer. Beau drove by the Rainbow Resort and continued north on U.S. 19 another three miles. He pulled into a hot sheet motel called The Sandman and checked in. He paid cash and signed his name C.O. Jones. No questions were asked. Beau drove around to the room and parked. Ricardo had nodded off, so Beau woke him and helped him into the room. Beau took the four duffels into the room. They looked just like luggage. He couldn't chance leaving the money in the car in this neighborhood, as it was full of drug addicts and thieves.

Beau checked his beard in the motel bathroom's mirror. It still looked pretty good. He would need it in the morning at the fuel dock in case someone who knew him was there. He went back in the room and checked on Ricardo and then cleaned and bandaged Ricardo's wound. Ricardo was soon sleeping like a baby.

Beau started counting the money. He got through the first two duffels in about two and a half hours. At that point he figured there was about three million dollars in the four duffels. A plan started to formulate in Beau's head. He took the two duffels he had counted and put them in the trunk of the car. He locked the room, started the car, and headed for the boatworks which was twenty minutes away.

During the drive Beau's mind raced. He reviewed the situation: *the guard is dead, his disguise was compromised, and Ricardo is wounded.* Beau realized he could never come back to Florida or the United States. A change of strategy was definitely in order. He needed some insurance, big time. He had already figured that even if everything had gone smoothly, that the Fernandez brothers would probably kill him once he got them safely to Mexico. He also figured the brothers would kill Ricardo Cabeza. That should totally insulate the two of them from the Cipriano family ever finding out their involvement. Beau had to either kill the Fernandez brothers and Ricardo, or figure out some other way to insure his safety. By the time he pulled into the boatworks parking lot he had come up with a viable plan.

As Beau approached the main gate the boatyard Rottweiler's appeared and started to bark. *The beard* … Beau thought, so he said, "Good dog, Max, good dog, Gretchen", and the dogs instantly recognized his voice, stopped barking, and started wagging their short tails.

Beau unlocked the gate and walked in locking it behind him. He carried the two money duffels in and let himself in thru the shop door. He entered the building but didn't turn on the lights. He felt his way to the storage cabinets and found what he was looking for. He took the heavy-duty garbage bags to a workbench and put the money duffels next to them. Beau found a flashlight and covered it with a white cotton wiping cloth. It gave him just enough light to see. He divided the money between six garbage bags. Beau twisted the bags shut and double tied them, then folded the ends and taped them with shrink wrap tape. He put the garbage bags back in the duffels and took two crescent wrenches out of his toolbox. He turned off the flashlight and put it in his pocket with the tools.

Beau went out the door and headed for the fence that separated their yard from Charley Parker's. He carefully set a ladder on each side of the fence and climbed over after throwing the duffels over before him. Beau picked up the duffels and headed for the travelift slip and *Pescadora*.

She gently swung in the slings in the mild easterly night breeze. Beau threw the money duffels up in the cockpit and climbed a work ladder onto the boat. He lifted up the cockpit hatches and exposed the fuel tanks. He set the flashlight on the starboard tank, and removed the eighteen-inch diameter clean out hatch after wrenching off the eight nuts holding it on. The tank looked about 2/3 full of diesel. Beau slipped three garbage bags full of money down in the starboard tank. He checked the gasket and reinstalled the cleanout lid. Beau repeated the process on the port side tank and then put the cockpit sole hatches back in place. The boat would now hold less than its advertised fourteen hundred gallons, but each side would still pump equally. Two weeks ago, he had arranged for four plastic 55 gallon drums to be waiting for them at the Oceanside Marina fuel dock on Stock Island in the Keys. Their capacity would more than make up for the decrease in tankage caused by the moneybags, but Beau would have to watch his fuel closely.

Beau opened the salon door and walked down to the guest head. He was supposed to have thrown the .38 snub nose pistol off the Howard Franklin Bridge, but now he hid the loaded gun behind the motor cowling on the Raritan head. He might need it later. Beau went back over the fence and stowed the ladders. He stashed the two empty black canvas duffels under some trash in the dumpster. Max and Gretchen just sat and watched him, then ran up so Beau could pet them. Beau would miss them. They were very gentle with all the regular employees, but if an intruder ever jumped over the fence when they were out at night … God help him.

Beau went back into the shop, dropped off his tools and went up the stairs to the office. He kept the cotton cloth over the flashlight as he moved around the office. He took two envelopes out of the supply cabinet and two sheets of paper. Then he sat down and wrote a short letter to John No Nose Cipriano, the Tampa mafia boss, outlining the Fernandez brother's participation in that night's robbery, put it in an envelope, and sealed it. Next he booted up Jeb's computer and went on the Internet. He typed in "Tax Assessors records, Hillsborough County, Florida", and hit search. He typed in John Cipriano's name and a long list of properties appeared. Beau picked the Palma Ceia, 25 Golf View Street address and wrote it on the sealed envelope along with John Cipriano's name. The tax rolls listed an acre of land, 7800 square feet of house, a swimming pool, and a pool house. *Who says crime doesn't pay* … thought Beau?

Beau then wrote a second letter to his old Vietnam War buddy, Gary Anderson. Gary practiced law in Cincinnati, Ohio and could be trusted. Beau had saved his life in Vietnam after their transport helicopter had been shot down behind enemy lines. Beau and Gary were the only survivors. Gary was shot in the legs, and Beau carried him out of the jungle on his back. It took five days of hiding during the daylight hours and moving only at night. Beau instructed Gary not to open the letter to John Cipriano, but if he didn't hear from Beau within thirty days of the date he received the letter to mail it. He wrote that he was in a tight spot and hoped the letter would keep him alive. Gary was to disregard any reports of Beau's death before the thirty days was up and was not to mail the letter, under any circumstances, before the thirty days had elapsed. Beau promised him he would fill him in with more details when he called him. Beau found a stamp and sealed the outer envelope. He locked up and left the boatworks, petting the dogs on the way out. He would miss never seeing the boatworks, his friends, and family again, but there was no time to look back now. Beau started to choke up, but he forced himself to get into the car and go on. He drove back to the motel fighting his emotions and stopped only to mail the letter at the post office on First Avenue North.

He pulled into the motel, parked the car, and checked the room. Ricardo Cabeza was still asleep and snoring loudly. Beau went to the motel lobby and called Hector Fernandez from an outside pay phone. Hector answered his cell and sounded groggy and irritable.

"Hector, its Beau."

"Where the fuck have you been, Beau?" Hector yelled into the phone. "We've been sitting here going crazy. How did it go?"

"Well, we got the money. *But* ... Ricardo got shot and I had to kill the door guard."

"Holy shit! How bad is Ricardo?"

"He got shot through the arm. The guard somehow got loose and had another gun. Ricardo's sleeping now, and the bleeding has slowed down considerably. I stopped and got some Percocet for him."

"Where did you get the Percocet?"

"I made a quick stop at my place. Don't worry, I was careful and no one saw us."

"Where are you now?"

No way, I'm telling them, they might come over and kill Ricardo and me and take the money now ...thought Beau. "We're in a motel and nobody will find us, answered Beau. But, I did have my beard partially pulled off by the guard before I shot and killed him. They may be able to identify me."

"Fuck me!" whined Hector. "We are fucking, fucked!"

Beau said, "Calm down, it will take days for them to identify me and we'll be long gone by then. I didn't leave any prints and they might not ever ID me from the camera. You just get the boat from Charley Parker's yard and make sure you are fueled up by 10:00 a.m. I'll be at the fuel docks then with the money and Ricardo, ready to go."

"Okay" said Hector, breathing a little easier. "But, Luis and I want to know something else."

"What, Hector," said Beau impatiently?

"Why did you put us in a hotel full of *maricons*? Everybody in this fucking hotel is a flaming faggot. We have not left this room for nothing."

"That was the whole point", said Beau. "I didn't want anybody to even remotely have a chance to recognize you. Just check out in the morning and go pick up the Bertram."

Beau hung up and had to laugh to himself. He had booked them a room at the largest gay resort in the south. The Rainbow Resort had two hundred and fifty rooms, two pools, three bars, two restaurants, and a disco. The action was nonstop seven days a week. He was sure the macho Fernandez brothers had been uncomfortable there, but it was a great cover.

Beau went back to the room and tried to go to sleep, but his brain was on double overload. He had not wanted to kill the guard or anyone else during the robbery. But, when the first shot was fired, and his life was threatened, he instinctively reverted to his Ranger-special ops training. The Rangers had trained Beau for clandestine special-ops missions in Vietnam and Cambodia. He was conditioned to kill without remorse. Each situation was looked at as kill or be killed. He had been trained to embed himself far behind enemy lines, targeting high-ranking military and political enemies of the United States. He had used explosives, sniper rifles, knives, and even his bare hands. After a few missions his emotions almost ceased to exist. After the war, many of his compatriots joined the C.I.A. or mercenary security forces. Beau just wanted his life at the boatyard back. When he felt the inevitable nightmares closing in on him he would escape into alcohol and gambling. Beau wondered how many other government trained killers walked among us every day. He tried to sleep as Ricardo Cabeza continued to snore like a bear throughout the remainder of the night. The Percocet's had really knocked Ricardo out cold. Beau finally dozed off close to daylight and slept fitfully.

CHAPTER FOUR

S ETH woke up at 5:00 a.m. the next morning with the television still on. He groped for the remote and changed the channel to The Weather Channel from Atlanta. He didn't have to wait long for the local boat and beach forecast. The weather looked ideal for a trip down the Gulf to Key West. The next few days were forecasted at five to ten knots of wind from the southeast with no rain except for a chance of thunderstorms in the late afternoon. There was a big high-pressure ridge over Florida, and no tropical activity was headed towards the Gulf of Mexico.

Seth turned off the tube and jumped into the third-floor shower. Seth looked into the mirror as he toweled off. He was glad he still had most of his sandy blond hair, although he guessed he had shrunk an inch or so from his younger six-foot height. But happily, he was only ten pounds above his college football playing weight of 185 lbs. He brewed a pot of coffee in the second floor kitchen and poured it into a thermos. Seth went down stairs and walked into his two-car garage. He turned off the main water valve and flipped off the water heater breaker. He threw his duffle bag in the back of his Yukon, backed out of the garage, and headed for the boatworks and *Tar Baby*.

Seth always had to chuckle when he thought about the classic Uncle Remus story about Brer Rabbit and Brer Fox, and the Tar Baby. It was a story about getting the last laugh. Brer Rabbit was outsmarted by his nemesis Brer Fox. But, although hopelessly stuck in the Tar Baby, he still tricked Brer Fox into throwing him into the briar patch.

Seth loved the line where Brer Rabbit tells the Tar Baby, "You better answer me or I'm gonna knock your head clean off!" "And the Tar Baby", said Uncle Remus. "He don't say nothin."

He had painted the hull of his Hatteras jet black with a white boot stripe and black bottom paint. The boatworks sign painter had painted *Tar Baby* in large white letters on the transom, with a small artist's rendering of the Tar Baby at the end. Seth noticed that everyone who walked by either smiled or laughed when they glanced at his transom.

These days a 46 foot sportfish was one of the smaller boats on the marlin tournament circuit. Most of the competitor's boats were 65 to 85 feet. But the lucky thing was the fish didn't know what size your boat was, so smart fishing and luck could still win out over the big money programs.

As Seth pulled into the boatworks parking lot it was just starting to get light. Seth noticed that *Pescadora*, the big Bertram sportfish that he had noticed Beau standing next to yesterday, was in Charley's travelift poised over the water out on the travelift runway. Just seeing the Bertram brought all his apprehensions about Beau flooding back into his mind. If he hadn't already paid the entry fee for the tournament, and part of his crew wasn't flying in from out of state, and all of them weren't looking forward to it so much, Seth would stay home and track Beau down. The truth was that Seth hoped he might just be on another bender.

Charley's launch policy was the same as Stone's, *cash or no splash*. Seth imagined *Pescadora* would be paid for and launched soon after Charley opened at eight a.m.

Annie was waiting for Seth in the parking lot and grabbed her duffel from her jeep and headed for the front gate. Annie was a good-looking, athletic, beach girl with a great tan and sun-bleached hair pulled back in a ponytail. She reminded Seth of the female volleyball players he saw on television.

"Good morning, Annie", said Seth. "Looks like smooth sailing today."

"That's great," said Annie. "I'm looking forward to not varnishing for a couple of days, and some suntan time."

Seth opened the gate and let Annie in, then relocked it behind him. He shooed Max and Gretchen, the yard's Rottweiler guard dogs, into their kennel and headed for the Hatteras. Seth had started using Rottweiler's twenty years ago when the boatworks started having break-in problems. St. Petersburg had grown into a full-fledged city over that time complete with the problems that occur with growth. Since introducing the guard dogs at Stone's Boatworks they had never had another break-in, but the surrounding yards and businesses continued to have problems. Seth had been through six dogs over the years, losing three to old age and one to a ten-foot alligator. That alligator's head was hung up on the office wall with a bronze plaque beneath it that read, "Don't get mad, get even".

Seth opened up *Tar Baby* and checked the engine room and fluids one more time. Annie chamoised the dew off the flybridge enclosure and rolled up the clear eisenglass. Seth started the Cummins diesels and the Onan generator. He checked the refrigerator and the freezers, and then they cast off the mooring lines. Seth started down Salt Creek past the bothersome *Pescadora* hanging in Charley's lift slip, then past the high and dry, and the other yards along the creek. He turned east at Bayboro Harbor, idled past the Coast Guard cutters, and finally was out in Tampa Bay. He hoped, almost out loud, that what he witnessed yesterday was Beau helping out Charley and not the start of another Beau situation. He had a premonition about Beau and the two Cubans, but put it out of his mind and hit the throttles. As the *Tar Baby* got up on plane Seth silently thanked his father, Robert E. The business he had left to his sons had really been good to them. Here he was in a beautiful sportfish on his way to a week of marlin fishing in the Keys. He remembered what his father had told him just before he died.

Robert E. said, "Son, the only thing you have to do to be successful in business is to do what you say you're going to do."

How simple, but how true that was. Seth turned the Hatteras south and soon the boat was gliding along at twenty-four knots. Seth lined her up with the Sunshine Skyway Bridge, eight-miles south, and switched on the autopilot. The sun was rising on the eastern shore of the bay and the water sparkled with a red glow. The cool morning breeze blew through his hair and the vibrant sound of the twin diesel engines made Seth sure that life was worth living.

Seth piloted the Hatteras through the Skyway Bridge and down the bay toward Passage Key Inlet. He ran west out the unmarked inlet past the northern tip of Anna Maria Island about a mile, then turned south and set a course for Key West. He double-checked his engine gauges, and then engaged the autopilot. The Gulf only had a light chop, so the two hundred mile trip to Key West's North Channel would take about nine hours. Seth poured himself a cup of coffee from his thermos and settled back in the helm chair. Before long they had passed Bradenton Beach and Longboat Key. Seth could see the condos looming to the southeast in Sarasota and Siesta Key. Annie brought him up a warm Danish pastry from the microwave in the galley and then disappeared below. Seth was happy that the *Tar Baby* was running perfectly and was headed somewhere exciting.

The higher the sun got the hotter it became, and the more beautiful the gulf water looked. Sarasota, Siesta Key, and Venice were now off the transom and the *Tar Baby* was starting to lose sight of land.

Seth thought about the early days of fishing the beach from Venice to Boca

Grande for tarpon. In those days he had a 30-foot express with a casting tower, which was ideal for beach fishing migrating tarpon. They would move it down to Uncle Henry's Marina in Boca Grande for the April, May, and June tarpon season. Almost every weekend Seth, Lisa, and Jeb would drive down to Boca Grande after work on Friday for a weekend of fishing. They would sleep on the boat at Uncle Henry's. The express had a nice double in the v-berth, and the settee made into a bed for Jeb. The boat had a Pullman galley and was air-conditioned. Jeb would have fished off the marina docks for snook all night if they would have let him, and during the day they'd all fish for tarpon and occasionally grouper off shore. After fishing, they'd shower at the marina and drive into downtown Boca Grande to eat dinner at one of the island's excellent restaurants. On Saturday and Sunday morning they'd get an early start out of Little Gasparilla pass and prowl the beach close to shore looking for schools of tarpon to cast to. Once located, Seth would motor out ahead of their path and shut the boat down. Then he would cast three rod's out and hand down two to Jeb and Lisa. They used live crabs or pinfish rigged under corks for bait. It took patience and perseverance, but when they hooked up a tarpon, it was worth all the effort. The tarpon were large, 75 to 125 pounds, and were game fighters. Once hooked they made spectacular jumps and many times they threw the hook. Seth would work the hooked fish away from the beach and into deeper water, bringing them boat-side to release them. The family spent many idyllic weekends pursuing tarpon up and down those beaches.

Seth missed Lisa and didn't know what to do to fill that void. At a time in his life when he should be happy and fulfilled, he felt empty. Even when he was marlin fishing it didn't mean as much because Lisa was not there to talk to him about it.

Boca Grande Pass was another story. It was a naturally deep inlet, with two very large, deep, holes in it. One was forty-five feet deep and the other was seventy feet deep. These holes held thousands of tarpon during the season, almost like a natural aquarium. The swift current provided by the Gulf and Charlotte Harbor exchanging tides kept hordes of bait moving over the holes. Local professional guides, whose skills had been passed down from generation to generation, had fished the pass for years. The guides drifted their clients over the holes while barking instructions to them concerning placement of their live bait. The line was marked with a red and a green thread and the guides would alternate colors from the reel to the rod tip to keep the bait at the optimum depth during the drift. The pass was not an easy place to fish, but the guides were masters at it. But it only took one out of control amateur, who didn't understand the drift, to ruin it for everybody. The swifter tides brought more bait and more action and that made the boats even harder to control. The guides would tolerate amateurs if they followed the same etiquette and drift pattern that the guides adhered to, and that had worked for almost a hundred years. The occasional interloper who wouldn't conform was roundly chastised and sent packing. When the tarpon were biting there would be fifty to sixty boats in the pass, day and night.

There was a few times during the season, however, that almost anyone could catch a tarpon. The locals called them full moon or "hill" tides, and this was when the water moved the fastest. At the height of those tides, huge numbers of crabs would be swept down the bay and out of the pass. The tarpon would move out of their deep holes and move east up into the twelve-foot deep bay, slurping up crabs in a feeding frenzy. Even novices could net the swimming crabs and drift back down the bay with them free lined on a hook and almost be guaranteed to catch a few tarpon.

Boca Grande pass was truly a unique place in the fishing world. It was the only location in the world where you knew exactly where the tarpon would be every day during the season. But Boca Grande and Gasparilla Island had changed radically over the past twenty years. The island had changed from a quaint fishing destination, where guides inhabited the town, to an exclusive retirement village for people from the north. Large homes crowded the once pristine beaches and shorelines. Even the interior of the island was bought up and developed. The fishing guides and trades people, who had lived there for generations, were suddenly faced with wildly escalating real estate prices and were subsequently taxed off the island. This scenario had been repeated all over Florida and seemed to be the price of living in paradise. The guides and former town's people were economically forced off their island and were replaced with colorfully garbed retirees. Most of them only looked at the water, and never fished or boated on it.

But the tarpon fishing continued on and a new type of *pass* fisherman had shown up. Hordes of flats boat fisherman patrolled the pass with light spinning tackle and breakaway jig rigs. Whenever the tarpon in the holes came up to roll and replenish the air in their buoyancy sacs, the flats boats roared in and fired their jigs down into the school. They had been very successful in catching the tarpon with this method, and it appears there was little or no learning curve. Of course, the sheer number of the flats boats and the lack of adherence to the live baiting drifting etiquette had caused chaos in a once orderly system.

There was also a growing debate as to whether the breakaway jig was eaten by the tarpon or whether it merely snagged them. This situation had caused some confrontations, and the state fish and wildlife agency had been called in to try and settle it. Seth felt the whole tarpon scene, both up and down the beach and in the pass, was over-fished and that many of the tarpon had moved to other less pressured locales.

Seth had never regretted his decision to get a bigger boat and pursue bigger fish. Boca Grande was fun during its heyday, but moving on to new frontiers should be even more rewarding. He was glad that he spent the time there over the last twenty-five years, and he would never forget the great times he and his family had enjoyed. Especially up and down the beach.

Annie came out of the cabin from her mid-morning nap and brought Seth a sandwich and a diet coke.

She asked if she could do anything else for him, and he answered, "No, not at the moment."

Annie stretched out on the fly bridge settee and starting reading a novel. She had on a baggy tee shirt and a very small bikini bottom. Seth felt a slight stir in his fishing shorts, but quickly shifted his thoughts to his fishing strategy for the upcoming tournament.

Seth had reserved a slip at A&B Marina in Key West harbor next to the Galleon Marina. *Tar Baby's* cockpit freezer was full of pre-rigged mackerel, bonito's and some backup horse ballyhoo. He was counting on his crew to pick up fresh ballyhoo in Marathon on Vaca Key on their way down to Key West. His crew would meet him there on Monday. Then they all would practice fish the Tuesday and Wednesday before the tournament which started on that Thursday. Bobby Sanders, Gene Johnson, and John Harvey had fished with Seth in countless kingfish, dolphin, sailfish, and marlin tournaments over the years.

Bobby lived in Silver Springs, Maryland and had played football with Seth at Virginia. After a career in the Army, where he had been an intelligence officer,

Bobby currently owned a large, international, security business in Washington D.C.

Gene Johnson was from St. Petersburg and was a detective, retired from the St. Petersburg Police Department. Seth had gone to high school and played football with Gene.

John Harvey was a dermatologist from St. Petersburg and was a great sailor and all around sportsman. He also came in handy if you needed a prescription or stitches.

Seth had ordered a Roff's chart to be faxed for each day they were scheduled to fish. Roff's was a service that analyzed currents, sea surface temperature, and bottom contour information and predicted areas where fish would congregate. They would prepare a daily chart that would overlay the bottom contours with current and temperature data supplied by infrared satellites. Then they would supply GPS co-ordinates of likely fish concentrations. Seth would meld this information with his knowledge of the Wood's Wall drop-off twenty miles south of Key West. If Seth could locate the main bait schools in that area, then that is where he would also find the marlin. Seth hoped to find the bait schools during the two days they would scout and practice fish.

Seth checked his GPS map and saw that Florida Bay was just ahead. The light wind they had this morning was giving way to dead calm. The sea around them was now flat and glassy. Seth asked Annie to sit at the helm and lookout while he went below. He checked the engine room, checked the engine's mechanical gauges, and relieved himself while he was below. He climbed back up to the fly bridge and took a look around. He could see only water in all four directions; no waves, no boats, just calm, beautiful, blue water.

Annie got out of the helm chair and said, "I think I'll get some sun." She climbed down into the cockpit and took the canvas cover off of the fighting chair.

Seth studied his first Roff's chart that had been faxed to the boatworks the day before. The rest would be faxed to A&B Marina's office starting Tuesday. They were fifty dollars each, but if you caught the big one, they were worth every penny. Seth read Dr. Mitch Roff's interpretation of the satellite images and it looked like the bait was concentrated at the west end of Wood's Wall. That would change some by tournament time. The whole length of the wall showed the clear dark blue water that pelagic fish like. Seth was glad he had ordered the charts.

Seth turned to ask Annie to throw him up another diet coke from the cockpit cooler, but he never got the words out. Annie had taken her baggy tee shirt off and sat topless in the fighting chair. Her full breasts were tanned golden brown and Seth found it hard to look away. He finally looked back at his Roff's chart and then checked his GPS map again. They were only about three hours out of Key West. He heard Annie call his name and he turned and looked down at the fighting chair again.

Annie said, "Seth, will you come down and put some suntan lotion on my back? I want to turnover and lay out on the fish cooler."

Seth stammered, "O-o-ok, Annie" and climbed down to the cockpit after pulling the throttles back to idle and shifting the gears into neutral. He couldn't take his eyes off her beautiful breasts.

Annie turned and handed him the bottle of suntan lotion saying, "Really, Seth, these can't be the first pair of breasts you ever saw … just do my back, will you?" Seth laughed and started to lather the suntan lotion all over Annie's back.

"I'm sorry, Annie," said Seth. "It's just … been a while." As Seth rubbed in the lotion on her back he noticed Annie had changed into a thong bikini. He took a deep breath and exhaled slowly as he admired her tanned and muscled backside.

Annie stepped away when Seth had covered her back with the lotion and turned to face him.

"Thank you," she said. "Do you think you could help me with one more thing, Seth?"

"What's that, Annie?" said Seth, whose head was beginning to feel a little light as he tried to concentrate on her face.

"Well, I've always had this fantasy about getting it on in a fighting chair in the middle of the Gulf of Mexico, what do you say Seth?"

"Ah … Ah … Annie," stammered Seth. "Like I said, it's been a while."

Annie looked at the growing bulge in Seth's fishing shorts and said, "C'mon Seth, it's just like riding a bicycle."

Seth laughed and thought … *What the Hell! It was going to happen sooner or later.*

He pulled Annie to him, and she kissed him hard on the lips. Seth fondled her lotion slippery breasts, and it wasn't long before he felt her hand find him.

Annie backed away, took off her bikini bottom, and then pulled Seth's fishing shorts off.

He took off his t-shirt as Annie positioned herself on the fighting chair.

Annie smiled expectantly, and then exhaled sharply as Seth entered her. They sparred for a moment and then settled into a rhythm that matched the large diesels that pulsated beneath them. Seth cradled Annie's ample breasts up under his armpits while they continued to move to the beat of the big engines. Seth finished a little sooner than he would have liked to, but Annie didn't seem to mind.

She whispered in his ear, "Thank you, Seth, for making one of my fantasies come true."

She pulled him close and gave him a long kiss, then wiggled out from under him, and disappeared inside the boat with her bikini bottom trailing in her left hand.

Seth wondered what other fantasies Annie might not have yet fulfilled as he pulled back on his shorts and t-shirt. He got an ice-cold diet coke out of the cooler and climbed back up to the fly bridge. He put the *Tar Baby* in gear and pushed the throttles up to planing speed. He checked the course, took a deep breath, and sat back in the helm chair.

"Well, next stop Key West," said Seth aloud.

As he reflected on what had just happened with Annie, he said to himself … *I can't say it was like being in love, but I certainly feel much more alive.* He knew that there was not going to be a lasting relationship with Annie. He also knew that casual sex would not fill the large void he felt within himself. He just didn't know if he would ever find someone who could truly fill that void. He really didn't know where to look, so for the present he would try to enjoy the moment and try not make too much of it.

Seth punched up the stereo on the fly bridge remote and found his favorite Eagle's CD. He turned up the volume and sang along with Glen Frey as he started singing, "I'm running down the road, trying to loosen my load. I have seven women on my mind."

Seth's first stop when he hit dry land would be a drugstore, as these days everybody needed protection. He hoped he'd been lucky and he wanted to be prepared for a next time.

Seth also knew that when he got to Key West he was going to have to remember to wipe the shit-eating grin off his face.

CHAPTER FIVE

BEAU woke up at 6:00 a.m. and looked around the worn out motel room. Ricardo Cabeza was still snoring loudly. Beau wasn't sure which was louder, the ancient air conditioning unit or Ricardo. Beau felt tired, distressed, and fearful about leaving his hometown behind. But, he was also somewhat elated that he had not been killed, actually pulled off the robbery, and had set up a survival plan last night. He got out of bed and slowly stretched. He was still more than a little sore from the scuffle the night before. Beau took a hot shower and toweled off. He was careful not to get his fake beard wet and felt much better after the hot shower.

Ricardo grunted as Beau shook him awake.

Beau asked Ricardo, "How is the pain this morning?"

"It still hurts like a motherfucker," said Ricardo.

Beau handed him two more Percocets and another amoxicillin and said, "We need to taper off to one pain pill every six hours, if you can stand it, or we're going to run out in a few days, Ricardo."

"I'll try, but it hurts really bad, Beau," whined Ricardo.

Beau cleaned Ricardo's wound, rebandaged it, and handed him one of the t-shirts he had retrieved the night before.

"Give me your shirt with the blood on it, Ricardo, and we'll ditch it on our way out," said Beau. "Let's go get some breakfast."

Beau reloaded the duffels into the car and he and Ricardo drove up U.S. 19. He correctly guessed that Ricardo was so zonked on the Percocets that he wouldn't even notice they were missing two duffels. They stopped at MacDonald's for a takeout breakfast. When they finished, Beau put the bloody shirt in the trashcan along with the McMuffin wrappers. Then they drove to a nearby Hampton Inn and had a bellman call them a cab. Beau gave the bellman a twenty-dollar bill and the keys to the rental car and asked him to turn it in for him. The cab arrived and Ricardo, Beau, and the two duffels full of money headed for the Marina Point fuel dock in downtown St. Petersburg. Beau glanced at his watch, and it was 9:30 a.m. They should arrive at the fuel dock a few minutes before 10:00, right on time.

Beau pulled the duffels out of the cab and paid the driver. He and Ricardo walked around the ships store building and out to the fuel dock where the Bertram was fueling. Ricardo and Beau climbed aboard and went immediately into the salon without even acknowledging Hector who was busy pumping the fuel. Beau had only noticed a dock boy, who he didn't know, standing by the diesel pump. Luis was waiting for them inside. He hugged Ricardo and asked how his arm was.

"Not good, it hurts like hell," answered Ricardo.

"Well, go lie down in the right side cabin. You look very groggy."

"It's the Percocet," said Beau. "He's in a lot of pain."

Ricardo went forward and Luis turned towards Beau. "Where's the .38 pistol," he asked.

"I threw it off the Bayway Bridge last night," said Beau. "I didn't want to stop on the Howard Franklin with Ricardo being shot and all, so I threw it out the car window and over the side on the Bayway."

Luis patted Beau down, made sure that he was clean, and then went outside to help Hector shove off. Hector finished fueling, paid for the fuel, and started up the diesels. He had left the generator running to power up the refrigerator and air conditioning while they took on fuel. Luis threw off the lines and Hector idled away from the dock and started out of the marina. When the Bertram cleared the rock breakwater, Beau came out of the cabin, climbed up to the fly bridge, and took over the helm. Hector immediately went below to join Luis who had all ready started to count the money.

Beau was still irritated that Hector had run the Bertram aground. But, Beau had a bigger problem to solve. In two hours or so, the Fernandez brothers would discover that half the robbery money was missing. Beau ran the Bertram south towards the Skyway Bridge. He would set a course from the bridge to the northern tip of Anna Maria Island and enter the Gulf of Mexico through Passage Key inlet, an unmarked channel used only by locals. Beau knew Seth had probably left at 6:30 or so this morning for Key West and the Marlin Tournament. He wished he were with him and not in the predicament he was in now. Beau had set Seth up with his friend, Annie Hart, as delivery crew. Annie was definitely a free spirit, but what Seth didn't know was that Annie had always had the *hots* for him. He knew Seth would have an interesting trip down to Key West.

Beau's plan was to run south and anchor off Marathon and Vaca Key tonight. The next morning they would exit Florida Bay, via Moser Channel, under the Seven Mile Bridge, and continue down Hawk Channel on the Atlantic Ocean side to Stock Island which is just above Key West. There they would fuel up at the Oceanside Marina fuel dock located on Stock Island. Beau had arranged for the dock master to have four plastic 55 gallon drums waiting there for them. This was not an unusual request as many yachts used Stock Island and Key West as their jump-off points to travel to Mexico or the Bahamas.

They should arrive near Marathon about 8:00 p.m. tonight, just before dark. *Pescadora* would anchor a couple of miles north of the Faro Blanco Marina light. Beau had instructed Hector to order a new transom name graphic from the Boat U.S. store in Fort Lauderdale. Tonight Beau would peel *Pescadora* and Naples, Florida off the transom, and apply the Bertram's new name, *Chica*, from Ft. Lauderdale, Florida on the transom. Hector had the selling broker apply to change the name and hailing port with the Coast Guard documentation office, under his Ronald Santos alias, so it would be legal. That would break any ties with the boat being recognized as being in Naples or the Tampa Bay area. The following morning Beau would pilot the newly christened *Chica* west to Stock Island. Once there, Beau would send Hector and Luis to Publix for provisions for the trip and then to Wal-Mart and West Marine for some traveling clothes and a pair of boat shoes for him. Beau cleared the northern tip of Anna Maria and ran due west about a mile before turning south toward the Keys. He tuned in the autopilot and switched it on. Their next stop would be Marathon.

Beau settled back in the Bertram's helm chair and took a deep breath. The next few hours would be critical to any chance he had to survive this situation. He still had the .38 revolver hidden behind the head cowling in the guest cabin. But the two Cubans were armed and the odds were definitely against him. He went over his plan in his head again. He had to get out of the United States and needed to disappear into a foreign country. Costa Rica was the logical choice. He had created some life insurance by sending the Cipriano letter to Gary Anderson. He had control of a million and a half dollars from the robbery and he would play to the Fernandez brother's greed. He doubted they would kill him with the money hanging in the balance and the likely possibility that he was not bluffing about the letter addressed to No Nose Cipriano. The plan seemed like a good gamble.

Beau called down to the salon on the intercom and asked Hector to come up on the fly bridge.

Hector came right up and said, "What do you want, man?"

"I want to check the engine room over and take a look around the boat," said Beau. "Did you get all the spares and the oil I asked for?"

"I got everything on the list, including the new name."

"We'll put that on tonight, Hector, after we anchor," said Beau as he climbed down the ladder. "Watch out for crab trap buoys, keep the helm on auto pilot, and use the dodge buttons if you see any in our path."

Beau opened the salon door and walked in. Luis was counting the money and recording it on a legal pad he had brought in his luggage. It didn't look like he had gotten very far, but there were piles of money stacked all around.

Luis said, "Ricardo told me how you handled the guard after he got loose during the robbery; not bad for an amateur."

Beau wanted to tell him about his airborne ranger training and his high school wrestling experience, but he said, "I just got lucky, Luis."

If Beau couldn't negotiate a new deal, it might come down to *Mano y Mano*, and Beau wanted the brothers to be overconfident. Beau got a cup of water, went into Ricardo's cabin, and woke him up. He moaned and then yelped when Beau touched his wounded arm.

"Time for more Percocet and antibiotics, Ricardo," said Beau, slipping the pills into Ricardo's good hand. "Take these and keep resting." Ricardo took them and rolled over and went back to sleep.

Beau checked out the engine room and all the spares. Everything was in ship shape. He was glad he had put earmuffs on Hectors list, as the Detroit's twelve cylinders were so deafening no one could stand to be in the engine room with the engines running without wearing them. Next, Beau checked out the galley, and unfortunately the Fernandez's had only brought minimal provisions. Beau found beer, soft drinks, snacks, and six large Cuban sandwiches in the refrigerator. Beau took half of a sandwich, and a diet coke, and headed back up to the bridge. Hector climbed back down to help Luis count the money as Beau settled back into the helm chair. They were just passing by Sarasota to the east and Beau could see the crowded beach at Siesta Key as they ran past Big Sarasota Pass. Beau checked the course on the GPS map; they should be passing the Boca Grande sea buoy in a little over an hour and a half. The Bertram was running along smartly at twenty-four knots and that should put them just north of Marathon before dark.

Beau figured Luis and Hector would finish counting the money in another hour or so. He ran his options through his mind again. Worse case, he would spend the rest of the trip as a prisoner. He wouldn't be killed until they got to Mexico because the Fernandez brothers needed him to navigate and run the boat. His ace in the hole was the gun he'd hidden behind the motor skirt at the base of the guest head. He knew even a hardened criminal would not watch another man use the head. If Hector and Luis didn't buy Plan A, Beau would launch Plan B from the guest head with the .38 pistol in his hand.

Beau hoped he could sell Plan A. If he could get to Costa Rica with a new identity and a new stake, he could get a fresh start. He had finally come full circle with his gambling problem. He no longer was gambling for just the money; he was now gambling for his life. If he won this one, he was through with gambling. If he lost, well it wouldn't matter anymore, would it? Beau had been to San Jose, Quepos, Golfito, and Flamingo over the years to fish for billfish and tuna. He remembered the Costa Rican people as being friendly, honest, and hard working people who were very proud of their country. Costa Rica had little in the way of natural resources, but the country was an ecological wonder. The country had countless rain forests, beautiful beaches, waterfalls, rivers, live volcanoes, and abundant wildlife. It was close enough to the equator so the climate was virtually the same all year round. There were scores of different ecosystems in the mountain ranges and on the plains. You could pick the average temperature you wanted to live in by choosing a height above sea level. The country also had the Pacific Ocean as its western border, and the Caribbean Sea as its eastern border. Costa Rica was a democracy, had no army, was politically stable, and had strict environmental and conservation laws. The economy, except for coffee and banana exports, was dependant on tourism. As a result, the country had an almost endless array of excellent hotels and resorts. Beau thought it would be a great place to start over.

The Bertram was somewhere between Boca Grande and Naples, and Beau had just dodged a line of crab traps, when he felt the salon door slam shut and heard feet clamoring up the fly bridge ladder. It was Hector and Luis and they did not look amused.

"Where's the rest of the fucking money, Beau?" shouted Hector, his chest heaving from the climb up the ladder.

Luis pulled his gun and held it to the back of Beau's head and said, "There should have been at least three million dollars at the drop. What the fuck did you do with it?

"We only counted one million-six," Hector added. "You better tell us now, or we'll blow your fucking head off and feed you to the sharks."

Beau stayed outwardly calm, even though his heart was racing, and replied, "There *is* more than three million dollars, Hector, but if you kill me you'll never find the other million and a half. I've hidden it in St. Petersburg, in a safe place, so both of you calm down and listen to what *I* have to say. Luis, put the gun away, you're making me nervous."

Luis lowered the gun and looked over at Hector and shrugged.

Beau continued talking, "Ever since the two of you forced me to do this job I never really thought you'd actually come through on my end of the deal. I figured that when I got you within sight of Mexico you would feed Ricardo and me to the fish. With both of us out of the way there's nothing to tie the two of you to the robbery. No Nose would look in vain for Ricardo Cabeza and his mysterious accomplice, while you two deposited the three million in a Mexican bank, listed the boat in Cancun with a yacht broker, and then flew safely back home to Miami. The broker would communicate with Ronald Santos through your P.O. Box in Fort Lauderdale, and then he would finally wire that money to your Mexican bank when the boat sold."

"From my standpoint, after having my disguise half ripped off, I have to figure I'll eventually be identified. There's no way I can go back to the United States … so even if you didn't welch and kill me, that leaves me in Mexico with only a hundred and fifty thousand dollars. So I bought myself some insurance last night. While Ricardo was zonked out on Percocet at the motel, I counted the money and hid half of it. There was over three million dollars. Now all I want is an equal share and you two still get two million. Ricardo is already a dead man, and if No Nose ever found him all three of us would go down."

"I also mailed a letter last night to an old friend of mine who will not betray my trust. Inside that envelope is another sealed envelope addressed to Mr. John Cipriano's Tampa home. My note to my friend asks him to send that letter to No Nose if he doesn't hear from me in the next thirty days. I also told him to disregard any bad news he may hear about me before the thirty days are up. I don't think I have to tell you what information my letter to Mr. Cipriano contains. When I am safe, and you are back in Miami, I will send a letter addressed to

Ronald Santos at the Fort Lauderdale P.O. box telling you where the money is hidden. I will then contact my friend to tell him not to mail the letter to No Nose."

The Fernandez brothers looked at each other in utter disbelief. Their tan faces had turned a little gray. It was obvious that they hadn't expected this raggedy-assed boatyard owner, alcoholic, and gambling sucker to get the drop on them.

Hector recovered first and said, "How do we know we can trust you?"

"That's easy," said Beau. "At this point and in the future, I have no interest in having John Cipriano trying to find me. The two of you and my trusted friend will be the only three people who will know that I'm alive. My friend will be kept in the loop and he will expect a call from me every three months for as long as I live. When we get to Key West … I have a plan to stage my own death in a very public way. Ricardo will also die in Key West, and we both will be identified. Once that information has been made public the Cipriano Family will stop looking for us."

"The next change of plans is that I don't want to go to Cancun … I want to go to Costa Rica. It will take about ten days longer, but I can disappear among the thirty-five or forty thousand Americans that live there. I can use the Ronald Santos passport and social security card that Hector used to buy the boat. Hector and I look a lot alike except he's seventy-five pounds heavier. I'll grow a beard like his and tell customs I went to weight watchers."

Luis seemed to be getting the drift of the new plan better than Hector and asked, "Well, how do you plan to whack out Ricardo and yourself?"

"Tonight, we'll anchor up off of Marathon and change the boat's name and hailing port. Tomorrow, we'll head down to Stock Island to fuel up, buy provisions, and some clothes and boat shoes for me. We'll run through Moser Channel, at the Seven Mile Bridge, and then motor west down Hawk Channel to Stock Island. Once there, we'll fuel up at the Oceanside Marina dock where they have our extra fuel drums waiting. While I fuel the boat you and Hector will buy the provisions and my clothes. I'll give you a list of the clothes I need and you just need to double the original provisions list. After you return, we'll motor around and anchor on the west side of the Key West Channel, off of Sunset Island, and lay low. I'll give Ricardo two Percocets on the ride around and that will put him asleep. When we've anchored I'll garrote him while he's sleeping. At three in the morning, we'll motor the boat across the channel to the Key West

Aquarium docks and tie up. Then, we'll carry Ricardo to the shark tank and feed him to the sharks. Hector will cut off two of my fingers and shove them down a bonito's throat and then feed it to the sharks."

"Where do we get the bonito, Beau?" asked Hector.

"At the Stock Island fuel dock, Hector," said Beau. "The marlin fishermen use them for bait. We'll put my watch and t-shirt in another bonito and then throw my old boat shoes in the tank for more evidence. The sharks will bolt down the bonitos and the shoes and shirt will get cut up in the feeding frenzy. The police will cut open the sharks and find Ricardo's wallet, both watches, my fingers, and what's left of Ricardo. They'll DNA test the human tissue for positive identification, to confirm the wallet's ID. It will look like a Mafia hit and No Nose will save some face, although he'll wonder if someone killed us for his money. But, he'll stop looking for Ricardo and me. Then we take the boat to Costa Rica, and you and Luis fly to Cancun and then to Miami. You pay No Nose his drug deal commission out of the robbery money and your alibi stands up. A couple of weeks later, my letter will be in your Fort Lauderdale P.O. Box and you can go get the million and a half in St. Petersburg. I call my buddy with the Cipriano letter, and he sits on it for another three months. What do you think, Hector? I don't think there are any loose ends."

"What choice do we have?" said Hector. He and Luis just shrugged and looked lost.

"Well, I have another question for you, Hector," Beau continued. "Who is, or was, Ronald Santos?"

Hector explained, "Ronald was a young Cuban exile who had worked for our father, Manolo, as a runner for his numbers business. He participated in the Bay of Pigs invasion along with him in nineteen sixty-one. They trained, along with hundreds of other Cuban exiles, at a CIA camp on Useppa Island on the west coast of Florida. *Beau had been to Useppa Island. He'd stayed in the marina there on a friend's boat while tarpon fishing in Boca Grande pass. Useppa was four miles south of the pass. It was a former home of Baron Collier, who was once Florida's largest landowner, and was now an exclusive island club.* The exiles trained there in secret, being flown on and off the private island. The heavy foliage on the island masked the activity from the passing boaters. The two of them met there in the late fifties and became friends during their training. By the time the invasion began, Ronald had become a naturalized American citizen and Manolo's associate.'

'The Bay of Pigs Invasion turned out to be a disaster for the Cuban exiles and the American government. The CIA had promised artillery and air support from the U.S. Navy ships that had delivered them to the beachhead. Fidel Castro's intelligence in Miami had learned of the exact time and place of the invasion. For weeks before the attack date, Castro rounded up all sympathizers and resistance suspects and held them in the baseball and soccer stadiums. His forces lay in wait when the exiles hit the beach. The exiles were pinned on the beach by Fidel's artillery up in the mountains above. President John F. Kennedy ordered the navy ships to leave without firing a shot and withdrew promised air support. He was fearful that the Soviet Union would escalate the situation into a nuclear war. So, the CIA left the exiles stranded on the beach.'

'Ronald Santos and many other brave Cubans were killed on that beach. Most of those remaining were captured and put in jail in Cuba. My father took Ronald's identification and hid in the adjacent swamp for four days, eluding all the search parties. He and a small group of his compatriots made their way to Mariel and then back to the Florida Keys, stowed away on Cuban fishing boats. After our father returned to Miami, and resumed his numbers business, he maintained Ronald's I.D.s. eventually passing them on to Luis and me. He knew that someday the I.D. could be useful if one of us got into some deep trouble. His judgment was good, as we have been able to obtain some things with Ronald Santo's clean slate, which our own police records had made impossible." *Real, firsthand, history, from a different perspective … thought Beau … and it looks like they're buying into the new plan.*

The *Pescadora* anchored up two miles north of Faro Blanco light on Vaca Key about an hour before dark. Beau watched the sunset west of Spanish Channel. As the shimmering red ball slid behind the horizon, it almost looked like the water around it was boiling. Beau blinked as the last part of the red sun disappeared and looked for the famous "Green Flash". No such luck tonight, although Beau had seen it once many years ago on his way in from fishing the Gulf Stream loop current located 120 miles west of St. Petersburg.

As soon as it was dark, Beau and Hector cleaned the transom and peeled off the name *Pescadora* and Naples, Fl. After cleaning the transom again, Beau applied the new graphic, *Chica* from Ft. Lauderdale, Fl. He backed up on the swim platform as far as possible and surveyed his work. It looked straight in the glow of the flashlight, and *Pescadora* had just disappeared into thin air.

Beau went below and woke Ricardo up. He gave him two more Percocets and an antibiotic.

Ricardo complained about the pain and Beau said, "This should hold you for tonight, I'll give you two more in the morning."

Fifteen minutes later, Ricardo was feeling a little better and said he was hungry.

Beau said, "Why don't we all have a Cuban sandwich and a cold one?"

The beer put Ricardo right to sleep, and the Fernandez brothers weren't far behind him. Beau lay awake in his bunk and felt good that he had the Fernandez brothers under control. Well, at least he did for now, anyway.

No Nose Cipriano paced back and forth alongside his swimming pool that overlooked the Palma Ceia golf course. Saturday's sun was just starting to set in the western Tampa sky. He seethed with anger as he thought about the robbery of his Ybor City money-drop the night before. His Tampa capo, Luigi "Wall-to-Wall" Scuzzi, had informed him that it was an inside job involving Ricardo Cabeza, a long-time and trusted associate, but no one knew who his accomplice or accomplices were. The Tampa mafia had marshaled all their statewide resources to monitor airports, hotels, and credit card use. Luigi had put the word on the street, in every corner of the state. No Nose was confident that his organization would find Ricardo and whoever else was involved, quickly. When they were found he would make an example of them that was so horrific, that no one would ever steal from the Tampa mafia again.

CHAPTER SIX

T**AR** *Baby's* GPS put Seth right on top of the Key West northwest channel
sea buoy. He altered course to avoid running over the buoy and then turned
to starboard and ran between the day buoys that marked the cut through the reef.
As Seth turned back towards Key West and the south, he could see the town
sparkling in the sun. The northwest channel was long and wide, and he still had
a few miles to go to reach the harbor at Key West Bight. He was full of anticipation for the upcoming marlin tournament. Seth knew it would be fun for him
and his buddies to compete in a tournament with seventy-five to one hundred
entries. Seth looked east and west at the concrete jetties that the government
had built to calm the channel for the Navy. He thought about the history of
Key West and of how its economy had always been dependant on the reefs that
surrounded it.

The original settlers of Key West were major ship wreckers, with a minor
in commercial fishing. They would move the navigation lights that marked the
treacherous reefs at night to lure unsuspecting passing ships to their doom.
Then the wreckers would salvage the wrecked ship's cargoes. Many of the old
houses in Key West were built with the wood left from the ships that had been
wrecked on the reefs. A good number of Key West's settlers came from the
Abaco Island's in the Bahamas where many British loyalists had fled the new
United States after 1776, to save their necks. They started filtering into Key West
in the early 1800's. The Key West Founders Park displayed bronze busts of these
prominent wreckers and pioneers. In the early eighteen hundreds the wrecking
trade had made Key West one of the wealthiest towns in the United States.

The reefs still supported Key West to this day. The only continuous living
reef in the continental United States drew people in droves to fish and dive
it. With only eight square miles of area, Key West had also become one of
America's premier party destinations.

Seth ran the Hatteras past newly named Sunset Key (formerly Tank Island)
and up toward the Key West Bight rock breakwater. He called the A&B Marina

dock master on the VHF radio and got his slip assignment on the east side of the marina. He preceded past a row of docked sportfish boats and backed the *Tar Baby* into its slip. Annie had the lines ready and secured them to the forward pilings. Seth stopped the boat at mid-slip, climbed down the fly bridge ladder, and tossed the stern lines to the waiting dock master. Seth shut the engines down at the cockpit station as Annie made the aft spring line fast.

"How are you, Seth?" asked the dock master. "Good trip?"

"It couldn't have been better. How have you been, Don?"

"Well, I'm still here!"

"Have a big crowd coming in for the tournament?"

"We're full up as usual," smiled Don.

"That's good news! I'll turn off my generator, hook up the shore power, and come up to your office later to sign in," said Seth as he handed Don a twenty-dollar tip. "Thanks for the help."

Don thanked him and walked back down the dock. Seth hooked up the shore power and turned the air conditioning back on after switching off the diesel generator. He and Annie scrubbed and hosed off the boat. She had a flight back to St. Petersburg early tomorrow morning, so Seth was curious how this evening would go after their encounter in the fighting chair that afternoon.

As Seth walked down the dock to the marina office he saw several large sportfish boats he recognized from Miami, Palm Beach, and Stuart. A lot of big guns were already here for the tournament.

Seth signed in with Don and asked, "How's the fishing been the last few days?"

"Well, the charter boys have been catching a lot of dolphin."

"Was there any size to them?"

"Some went 25 to 35 pounds."

"Any billfish caught?"

"They catch an occasional sailfish and maybe a small marlin or two in a normal week. But nobody's been targeting them. Some of your competitors have been fishing out at Wood's Wall this week, but the professional captains have been tight lipped as usual."

"Well that's normal," replied Seth. "My crew is coming in Monday after-noon, and we'll scout for a couple days before the tournament starts Thursday."

"Good luck to you, Seth, it's nice to have you back."

Seth walked back out the dock and looked around the Bight. The Bight's five marinas were packed with sportfishing boats. The waterfront bars were overflowing as were the four restaurants that now lined the Bight. Everybody Seth passed had *that smile* on his or her face. It was a smile that you saw in only certain cities, like Las Vegas, New Orleans, Rio de Janeiro, or Cancun. It was an expectant smile signifying that we are here to party. Walk up Duval Street any night of the year and you will see *that smile* on almost every person's face. Seth stepped back on the *Tar Baby's* swim platform, and walked through the open tuna door into the cockpit. The boat was clean, and he could hear Annie running the vacuum inside.

Seth went in and Annie asked, "What do you want me to fix for dinner, Seth?"

"Annie, I've got a treat for you tonight. Why don't we go up the hill and have dinner at the Seven Fish restaurant tonight?"

"I've never heard of that restaurant, Seth, but I'm up for it."

"It's a little local place. Most people have never heard of it. It's way off the beaten path and has a local clientele, but the food is really good and they have a nice wine list."

"Sounds good to me, I've already showered, so I'm ready when you are."

Seth took a quick shower in the forward head. The hot water felt good on his back muscles after eleven hours in the helm chair. He dried off, shaved, slicked back his hair, and padded across his cabin with his towel around him. He thought … *why am I being modest now and feeling foolish about it?* He put on clean shorts, a new light blue fishing shirt, stepped into his flip-flops, and was ready to go. Annie had changed into a Hawaiian print silk shift that accentuated her every move. He and Annie walked down the dock and caught a cab on Front Street next to the A&B Lobster House restaurant. They arrived at Seven Fish ten minutes later. The restaurant was crowded, but Seth had called ahead so they were seated immediately. Seth ordered a bottle of Seghesio Red Zinfandel. The waiter brought the wine, opened it, and poured two glasses at the table. Seth and Annie clinked their glasses together and toasted their successful passage. He asked Annie if she had a busy week coming up.

Annie said, "Yes, every week is busy. I'm maintaining the varnish on over twenty yachts. Jeb and Beau are responsible for getting me all of them."

Seth and Annie made small talk throughout a dinner of fresh snapper, new potatoes, and fresh green beans. Neither one of them alluded to their encounter in the fighting chair, but it was obviously on both of their minds. The dinner

and the wine were excellent, and they talked on laughing about different characters they both knew from Salt Creek's past and present. Salt Creek had its own
quirky personality, and the people that lived and worked on the creek definitely
followed suit. Seth finished his second glass of wine and paid the bill. He had
enjoyed having dinner with Annie. She was easy to be with and didn't seem to
have an agenda. They caught a cab that was dropping off another couple and
took it back to the marina. They walked back to *Tar Baby* and stepped into the
cockpit. Seth put his key in the salon door and opened it for Annie.

As she passed him on her way into the salon, she stopped and kissed Seth
on the cheek and said, "Thank you for the lovely evening. It was a perfect ending
to a perfect day."

"Good night, Annie. I've got a cab coming to take you to the airport at 6:30
in the morning. If you're not up, I'll wake you."

Seth turned out the salon lights and they headed for their respective cabins.
He stripped off his shirt, shorts, and underwear and climbed into his queen size
berth. Seth set the alarm clock just in case and was asleep, literally, before his
head hit the pillow.

Very early the next morning Seth woke with a start. The cabin was pitch-
black, but Seth felt something moving in his berth. It was Annie, and she was
naked. She had slipped in behind him and was gently pressing her generous
breasts against his back.

She whispered, "I woke up and was lonely. Do you mind, Seth?"

"Not at all," replied Seth, trying to keep his voice from cracking. "I was just
in the middle of a dream."

Annie reached over him with her right hand and found that he was all ready
aroused.

"Were you dreaming about me, Seth?" she giggled.

Actually, Seth had been dreaming about backing down the *Tar Baby* on a very
large marlin, and at the moment he had a major piss hard-on. But the situation
called for him to say, "Of course", with a slight chuckle. Annie nibbled on his
ear while she gently stroked him.

She whispered in his ear again saying, "It's my turn to be on top, Seth."

Annie rolled Seth over on his back, and mounted him. She moved slowly at
first and then faster and faster. Seth cupped his hands on her rounded bottom
and pulled her in tighter. Annie was breathing hard and started to moan. Her
pendulous breasts brushed against his chest and her hard, protruding, nipples

found his lips. She came with a little shriek and then collapsed on Seth's chest. Seth was out of breath, too, and he finished within a few seconds of Annie. They lay spent and silent. Annie recovered first and rolled off.

She leaned back, kissed Seth softly on the lips, and said, "Way better than my fighting chair fantasy, Seth ... way ... way, better!"

She slipped out of bed, and before long Seth could hear the shower running.

He looked over at the alarm clock and it read 5:30. Like old Robert E. had always said, "Timing is everything." When Annie was through in the shower, Seth relieved himself, brushed his teeth, and took a shower. He put his shorts back on, and found a fresh t-shirt in his top drawer.

Seth took his cell phone off the charger and called the cab company just to make sure they were on schedule. A few minutes later, he walked Annie and her duffel down to the cabstand in front of A&B. he gave her a hug and a kiss, put her in the waiting cab, and shut the door. He gave her a wave as the cab pulled away, and then turned and walked over to the Deli behind A&B. He ordered breakfast and sat outside. By the time he had finished his first cup of coffee his mind had fully returned to marlin fishing. He had a lot of work to do before his crew came in the next day.

Seth was glad to see that the marina Deli had added a wine, liquor, and package store since his last trip here. He and his crew would drink a lot of beer and wine in the week they were here. The Deli would make it easy for him to restock. Seth kept the beer and soft drinks that weren't in the cooler stacked up on the dock behind the boat. In all the years he had done that, no one had ever touched even one can. The only thing he could ever remember missing, were two "nutty buddy" ice cream cones from a small freezer he had put up on the dock during one trip to the Bahamas. Not being a Captain Bligh type, he didn't start an investigation.

After breakfast Seth went back to the boat and loaded the Roff's information in the GPS. Roff's had pinpointed four locations along Wood's Wall where the marlin would most likely be found. Once that chore was finished he decided to stretch his legs and get a little exercise. He walked down Front Street towards Duval and passed a shop that had a large red pirate flag hanging outside. Seth had one exactly like it on his boat. Lisa had taken a fancy to it years ago during a trip to Key West. She had seen it first at the old Bight Bait Store and wanted to fly it off one of the outriggers during the Gasparilla Pirate Invasion in Tampa. *Seth's mind wandered to Gasparilla days past...*

The annual Gasparilla Day Parade is in February and is great fun. The Tampa Krewe, made up of a couple of hundred of Tampa's most prominent social scion's, dress up like pirates and invade the city on their pirate ship. They sail up Seddon Channel from Tampa Bay and land in downtown Tampa. They are accompanied up Seddon Channel by a chaotic flotilla of private yachts. Many close calls and a few collisions always ensue due to the condition of the alcohol-fueled owners piloting the private yachts. The boats jockey for position near the pirate ship and throw beads and water balloons back and forth. Many of the women passengers get topless to attract more bead throwers.

After the pirate ship docks, the pirates get off and man a fleet of motorized pirate floats that make their way to city hall where the mayor surrenders the key to the city to them. Along the parade route the same bead throwing and "show me your tits" games continue to the delight of the huge parade crowd, especially when some of the more comely wenches are kidnapped from the crowd and put in a rolling cage behind the pirate floats to be taken to the post-parade party. It is considered an honor to be chosen, but rumor has it that few of the wenches have ever actually delivered. At any rate, a good time is had by all. Local convention says that the Tampa Krewe and Gasparilla Day originated from the southern Mardi gras pre-Lent tradition.

When the Gasparilla memory faded, Seth found himself walking up Duval Street. As the Conch Train passed, he crossed the street and walked past the Hog's Breath Salon, Sloppy Joes, Rick's, and the Bull and Whistle, until he was finally standing in front of Fast Buck Freddy's Department Store. He had wanted to buy a new Hawaiian shirt and this was the place. Fast Buck Freddy's was a very trendy store, with an owner who had a wonderful, offbeat, sense of style. Seth went in and in a matter of minutes found a great looking shirt. He bought it, and walked around the rest of the store looking at the unusual merchandise.

Seth finally headed back down Duval and slowly walked along the crowded sidewalk. Walking towards him were two large tanned and oiled body-builders wearing matching stars and stripes Speedo bathing suits, head bandanas, and sneakers. They were holding hands, and nobody but Seth even gave them a second look. *Welcome to Key West* ... thought Seth. The hawkers were on every street corner selling dive trips, fishing trips, pookah beads, parasail rides, sunset cruises, scooter rentals, and you name it. Seth wondered what Ernest Hemingway would think about Key West today?

He had gone out to Hemingway's house in Cuba on one of his clandestine fishing trips to Havana a few years ago. Hemingway's home in Cuba was fifteen miles outside of Havana, in Cohi Mar, and far from his favorite bars in old Havana. So Ernest stayed overnight in Havana, at a hotel where he had a permanent room, when he drank at the *Floridita* and his favorite mojito bars downtown. Maybe he had learned something when he was in Key West and lived only eight blocks from Sloppy Joes. He was forced to navigate home, alone, every night no matter how inconvenient it might have been. His Havana plan was much better for a world-class carouser.

Hemingway had also kept his sportfish *Pilar* moored, at Cohi Mar, near his house. Seth had looked up Hemingway's famous captain, Gregorio Fuentes, while in Havana. He was 102 years old and still living in Cohi Mar. Captain Fuentes was considered the inspiration behind Hemingway's novel "The Old Man and the Sea" and would autograph your copy for a small remembrance.

As Key West continued to evolve, it had always been incomprehensible to Seth that an eight square mile island that was populated by a majority of redneck shrimpers and commercial fisherman could peacefully co-exist with the legions of gays who now lived and worked in Key West. There were forty art galleries, countless gay hotels and bars, and numerous gay nightclubs. But somehow these two diametrically opposed cultures made it work. Add to this the Israeli owned T-shirt industry, and you really started to stir the pot. T-shirts are big business in Key West. Where else could you buy a t-shirt that proclaimed, *Honk, if you want to blow me* or *I'm not a gynecologist, but I'll take a look.*

The newest ethnic entry seemed to be the influx of eastern Europeans. Rumor also had it that the Russian Mafia held a toehold in Key West. They had taken over the staffing of the restaurants and the titty bars. Every waiter and waitress had a Czech or Polish accent, and all the topless dancers were stark white and sullen looking. They only smiled when they saw green. If they didn't see enough green they said, *you no like me?* Seth thought Key West should be called the world's smallest melting pot. No matter, he still liked it there because it was fun.

Seth walked past Sloppy Joes and turned right on Greene Street. He walked past the new Crabby Bill's restaurant and turned left at the Conch Republic. He was impressed with the way the Key West city fathers had reinvented the Bight Harbor. They had torn down the old fish plant and turtle kraals. They leveled the shrimper bars and moved the old bait shop off the water. In their place three new restaurants and two bars were built. The docks were rebuilt and a pedestrian walkway was created from the existing Galleon and A&B Marina complex, past the Conch Republic, then five blocks north to the new Conch Resort and Marina. The municipal marina was updated and a waterfront supermarket and shops were added. The commercial fishing and shrimping interests were relocated to Stock Island. This redevelopment ultimately resulted in increased tourist business for all of Key West. They were getting some amazing mileage out of their eight square miles.

The new docks had attracted two large wooden sailing ships, the 139 foot schooner *America* and the 130 foot *Western Union*. There were also scores of smaller charters from 65 foot catamarans to P.T. boats. Key West was definitely a happening place. Seth thought he might check out Stock Island and the relocated shrimper bars. He had always enjoyed the fresh shrimp served in the local bars, and Key West "Pinks" were definitely the tastiest shrimp in the world.

Seth walked over to the new supermarket across the walkway from the municipal marina to complete a mission. So far he was "O for two" in condom usage. He knew in these uncertain times he needed to be more careful, but he hadn't used a condom since he graduated from college and was married. Once inside the market he found the nonprescription drug section and bought a dozen Trojans; *maybe a little optimistic, but better safe than sorry* … he thought. He was a little embarrassed at the checkout counter but the checkout girl didn't even look up. Seth wound his way back to the *Tar Baby* and went aboard. He was ready for a little nap before dinner tonight. Seth dozed off wishing his crew was all ready there, and that they were ready to start fishing tomorrow.

CHAPTER SEVEN

THE next morning Beau woke up at about 6:00 a.m. The Bertram's cabin was dark, and it took him several seconds to realize where he was. He quickly reviewed yesterday's events in his mind and was fairly certain that the Fernandez brothers had totally bought into his program. He was glad he had the presence of mind to build his insurance plan. Hiding half the money was strong, but the Cipriano letter that his friend Gary was holding was stronger. If it were just the money, Hector and Luis would have tortured the location of the money out of him and then killed him.

Beau got up and wished he had a toothbrush. He scrubbed his teeth with a little soap and his index finger and then took a quick shower. He put on his last clean t-shirt and went up to the galley. Beau took a diet coke out of the Sub-Zero refrigerator and found a leftover Cuban sandwich. It didn't look quite as good as it did last night. He drank the coke and opted for some pretzels instead of the Cuban sandwich. Then he went outside to the cockpit and climbed down into the engine room. He checked over the engines and their oil levels. The generator was running smoothly, and there were no fluid leaks. The bilge had a little condensate water from the air conditioners in it, and the shaft stuffing boxes were dry. Beau lifted the bilge pump float switch with his finger and pumped the bilge dry. He was satisfied everything was in working order in the engine room, and climbed back up into the cockpit.

Beau opened the transom tuna door and stepped out on the swim platform. The new name looked straight on the transom, and the new hailing port covered any shadows from the old one. He faced south toward Vaca Key and the city of Marathon. The water looked pink and pastel blue, reflecting the rising sun. Beau made his way back inside to wake up Hector and Luis. He found them in the galley eating what was left of the Cuban sandwiches.

Luis greeted Beau with a sarcastic, "Well, partner, this promises to be quite the day that you've planned for us. Let's get started."

Beau just smiled, because in reality he hadn't left them much of a choice.

Beau went forward and woke up a snoring Ricardo and gave him two more Percocets and an antibiotic. Ricardo felt hot like he had a fever, and he was sweating heavily. He also complained that he had a splitting headache. It was looking like Ricardo's wound was probably infected. Beau didn't feel sorry for what was going to happen to him; the truth was that Ricardo was a dead man the minute he pushed the button that opened the counting room door.

Beau climbed up to the fly bridge and started up the Bertram's engines. It looked like it was going to be another beautiful day. The NOAA weather channel on the VHF predicted five to ten knots from the southeast, with possible late afternoon thundershowers. He nudged the boat forward as Hector pulled the anchor line in with the windlass. After the anchor was secure and Hector had gone aft, Beau put *Chica* up on a plane and headed for the Seven Mile Bridge and Moser Channel.

They had a smooth run down Hawk Channel passing Big Pine Key to starboard and the reef towers and Loue Key to port. Loue Key was one of the prettiest spots in the Key's reef system. It was a spectacular place to snorkel and Beau had done just that many times over the years. He was saddened that he probably wouldn't ever see it again. They continued past Newfound Harbor and were approaching Summerlin Key when Beau called Hector up to the fly bridge on the intercom. Hector came up the ladder with his usual, *what? ... look.*

Beau told Hector, "It's time for you to take care of Ricardo Cabeza. We can't chance him being seen at the Stock Island fuel dock."

"Why do I have to do it?" whined Hector.

"Look, Hector, I shot and killed the guard in Tampa, besides you're a professional and I'm an amateur. I gave him two Percocets only an hour ago, so he should be sound asleep. He'll never know what happened."

Hector went down the ladder and came back up twenty minutes later.

"It's done. Luis helped me wrap him in the shower curtain before we propped him up in your shower stall." Then Hector asked Beau, "Why are you still wearing the beard disguise?"

"Remember," answered Beau. "I'm suppose to die tonight and I don't want the fuel dock personnel to recognize me if there are any pictures of me in the newspapers later." It wasn't long before the Stock Island Channel markers loomed ahead of them.

Beau turned the Bertram into the Stock Island Channel and slowed down as he approached Oceanside Marina. The marina was full of sportfish boats that were there for the Key West Drambuie Marlin Tournament. All of the marinas over in Key West Bight would also be full, including A&B where Seth always stayed. Key West would be jumping this weekend. Beau hoped Costa Rica would be as much fun as Key West, but unfortunately not many places were. He pulled the big Bertram alongside the Stock Island fuel dock. There was a large shrimp boat already fueling forward of him. The dock master handed Beau a fuel hose and asked him how many gallons he needed.

Beau said, "Somewhat less than 1000 gallons". "Do you remember I called you last week and ordered four, 55 gallon plastic drums?"

The dock master said, "Of course." Then he sent one of his dock-boys scurrying to get them. Beau and the assistant dock master lashed the drums in the forward part of the fishing cockpit.

Beau had asked Hector to buy a manual drum pump and some stout line at a tractor supply store located outside of Naples on Route 41. The pump and line were stowed in the aft cockpit lazarette.

While Beau tended to the fuel, Hector and Luis took a cab to the Publix on Roosevelt Boulevard with Beau's doubled up provisioning list. They would also stop at a pharmacy for first aid and toiletry supplies and at West Marine for shorts, shoes, shirts, hats, and foul weather gear for Beau. A quick stop at Wal-Mart would take care of some underwear and some extra towels. The washer and dryer combo across the companionway from the guest cabin would allow them to travel light.

Beau asked the assistant dock master, "Do you have any Deezol fuel conditioner here?"

They did, so Beau bought a case. As they traveled down the islands, the fuel quality would deteriorate. The Deezol would help the fuel burn better and cut down on the exhaust smoke. Hector had also stocked a case of Racor fuel filters, at Beau's request, in case they took on any contaminated fuel along the way. Beau had filled the main tanks and was almost finished with the four 55 gallon drums, and the brothers were not back yet. Maybe they had chickened out and were on their way back to Miami. *No way … thought Beau … would those two leave this much money.*

He asked the dock master, "Can I wait in a holding slip until the crew comes back?"

The dock master said, "Sure," and helped him move around the north corner of the fuel dock where Beau retied *Chica*.

He paid for the fuel, the drums, and the Deezol with cash from the stash. The bill for the 820 gallons of diesel, four plastic drums, and a case of Deezol came to $1780.00. Beau tipped the dock master and his crew a hundred dollars.

Beau asked him if he could stay until about 7:30 p.m. and the dock master said, "Of course." He then asked Beau, "Where are you headed?"

"Down island," answered Beau.

He thanked the dock master for his help and went into the salon to avoid any more questions. Beau took a fifty from the cash stash and walked over to the bait store next to the fuel dock. He bought three large frozen bonitos, brought them back to the boat, and put them in the cockpit sink. Hector and Luis finally pulled up in an airport van. Hector walked down the dock pushing a dock cart full of groceries.

"We couldn't fit everything in a regular cab," said Hector smiling. "So they sent a van from the airport."

They spent the next couple of hours packing away the drinks, food, and other provisions. Beau brushed his teeth with his new toothbrush, but he didn't change his clothes, that would come later. He filled the boat's fresh water tank and then made himself a fresh sandwich.

At 7:30 Beau fired up the engines, cast off the dock lines, and eased the boat back out to the Stock Island Channel. The sun was getting low in the western sky as Beau ran the boat toward Key West Channel. He wanted to arrive at Sunset Island just after sunset when the visibility was poor. The sun was just beginning to dip below the horizon as they came around the southwest point of Key West. They glided by the old fort and the submarine pens while passing through a gaggle of tourist filled sunset cruise boats. It was just getting dark as they idled across the channel in front of Mallory Square.

Beau looked at the large crowd of tourists on the wharf. They were watching fire-eaters, trained cats and dogs, jugglers, mimes, and tightrope walkers. They had all come to see the famous Key West sunset. There were rows of vendors selling trinkets and art. It was definitely much ado about nothing. But in Key West, where the weird turned pro, it was a big deal. Beau piloted *Chica* west and continued across the channel in front of the Key West Aquarium, which was just closing. He anchored the Bertram in front of Sunset Island. The sunset sailing cruises passed by them on their way back to the bight, and the large schooner *America* doused her sails right in front of them. It was an impressive sight. The rest of the cocktail cruisers straggled by, and another day in paradise was done.

The revelers on Mallory Square headed towards Duval Street to fill the waiting restaurants and bars. In less than thirty minutes Mallory Square was deserted.

Beau went below and suggested that they cook some dinner then get some sleep. He set the alarm clock radio in the main salon for 2:30 a.m. They would make their move on the aquarium at 3:00 a.m. Luis cooked up some *arroz con pollo*, and Beau made a salad. They all had a glass of Yellowtail Shiraz and turned in.

Beau's alarm clock went off at 2:00 a.m., and he immediately got up and woke Luis and Hector. They were sound asleep, but Beau got them both up and moving. He had thoughts about grabbing the .38 pistol in the head, shooting both of them, and disappearing with the three million. But the specter of No Nose Cipriano hunting him down made him stick to the present plan. He took a Percocet and two amoxicillin's with a half finished coke he found in the galley. He hoped the Percocet would take the edge off of what he had to do to his fingers in the next half hour.

Hector and Luis didn't look to enthusiastic about participating in the job they were about to do at the aquarium. Beau figured they both had a bully mentality. As long as they had the upper hand, and they didn't have to do any dirty work, they were happy. Now it was time to get down in the dirt, and they didn't like it. But the promise of millions and the thought of No Nose Cipriano's possible revenge spurred them on.

Beau felt safe starting up the Bertram's engines in the early morning along the Key West Channel. The cruise ships had left around midnight, and various fishing and government boats arrived and left at odd hours all night. The Bertram moving at this hour would not attract any unusual attention. Beau eased the darkened Bertram across the channel at idle speed and backed in next to the Aquarium pier. The outside fish pens were dark and quiet. Beau backed in so anyone passing in the channel would not notice the Bertram's name on the transom or see any movement in the cockpit. Hector tied the Bertram to the dock with a couple of lines. Beau's heart was pounding as he climbed up on the dock and took a quick look around. The lights were out, and the large wooden doors that led to the inside of the Aquarium were latched like barn doors, but were not locked. The old door creaked as Beau opened one and looked inside. The only light was from the wall aquariums, and it cast an eerie glow across the center shark tanks. The large floor level shark tank was quiet, but Beau saw a ripple as a large fin broke the surface and continued around the outside perimeter of the tank. Sharks had to keep moving twenty-four hours a day to keep water moving through their gills or they would die. It was no wonder that they were hungry all the time.

Beau went back to the boat and told Hector and Luis to get Ricardo Cabeza. He was worried that the brothers might panic and start shooting if something went wrong. As they went below, Beau got the three bonitos out of the cockpit sink. He stuffed the Rolex that he had won crewing with Seth, down one of the bonito's throats. It was inscribed with the regatta name and date and would help identify him eventually. He took his shirt off and stuffed it in another bonito. He kept his wallet in his pocket because he didn't want to be identified too quickly. He wanted Seth to be back in St. Petersburg and himself to be in Costa Rica before the police figured out his identity. The DNA testing would take that long, and the watch would confirm his identity when Seth eventually got involved.

Beau pulled a serrated fillet knife out of the tackle center. The knife was razor sharp, but the serrations were the key. This type of knife would cut through a tuna or wahoo's backbone like butter. Beau decided to do the job on his fingers himself, because he didn't trust Hector. He poured some rum over the knife and his fingers, and took a deep breath. He laid the last two fingers of his left hand on the cutting board on top of the tackle center and lined the knife up just below the second knuckle. Beau took another deep breath and made a strong, clean, cut across the two fingers completely severing them. He thought for a moment he would pass out, but he caught himself and hung on. He cried out only once, clenched his teeth, and steadied himself. He poured more rum on the fingers, and then wrapped them tightly with gauze and adhesive tape from the ships first aid kit. Right now the two missing fingers didn't feel any worse than a bad cut, and the gauze had staunched the blood flow. Beau was glad he had taken the percocet. He picked up the two fingers and shoved them down the throat of the third bonito with his right hand. He put the three bonitos in a plastic grocery bag he had saved and climbed up on the dock feeling a little light-headed.

The Fernandez brothers were just starting out of the salon door with Ricardo, and both of them were huffing and puffing. Beau had to laugh, Ricardo weighed only a hundred and fifty pounds or so, and both of the brothers were well over two hundred and fifty pounds. It was obvious that they weren't in very good shape. They swung Ricardo up on the dock and climbed up after him. They picked him back up and followed Beau inside the Aquarium. Once inside, Beau told the brothers to hold on a minute. The two of them were breathing hard, and they looked like they could use a rest.

Beau threw the first bonito in the center shark tank. That tank was about eight feet deep and protruded up from the floor about three feet. It had been designed for people to watch the sharks close up. As soon as the bonito hit the water two fins sliced through the dark water and the bonito was gone. Beau threw in the other two with the bloody fingers and the Rolex in them. The tank erupted in fins, tails, and wicked-looking teeth.

"Throw Ricardo in now!" shouted Beau over the sound of the thrashing water. Ricardo was tossed into the frothing tank and all hell broke loose. Beau took off his old boat shoes and threw them into the tank. Blood and water was being splashed everywhere.

Beau pushed the shocked Fernandez brothers away from the shark tank and said, "Let's go, now!"

The three of them turned away and left the grisly scene. Beau closed the creaky back door, and followed Hector and Luis back to the boat. They jumped back down into the Bertram, and Beau started the engines. Hector uncleated the lines and they idled south out of Key West Channel. Beau turned on the navigation lights and pushed the throttles up to twelve hundred RPM's when they reached the ships channel. He headed *Chica* south to the sea buoy, then east by northeast, at ten knots. They ran the rest of the night at ten knots and stood their watches as planned.

Beau took another Percocet and started his watch as the sun came up. He wondered how his brother would take his death when he was told a week or two from now. Beau also hoped nothing else would go wrong, and he really did end up dead. He didn't like the cold, evil look that was always in Hector and Luis's eyes. Beau was smart enough to know there was no honor among thieves. But, on the bright side, they were on their way to Costa Rica by way of the Bahamas.

Determined to get the three million dollars back and prove himself to Cipriano, Luigi Scuzzi had called all the other Cipriano capos in Florida on Saturday. They all would scramble to get their intelligence networks operating overtime. The underworld population, including police and customs personnel on the mafia's payroll, knew if they could find the information leading to the capture of the robbers they would be handsomely rewarded.

By 10:00 Sunday night Luigi nervously paced the floor before making the call to No Nose. He wished he had something positive to tell the reclusive mafia Don, but he didn't. No new information had come through all day. Finally he set up a meeting with No Nose by satellite phone and drove over to the Golf View Street mansion to relay the bad news.

Luigi was escorted out to the veranda where No Nose was watching a Yankees game on a huge T.V. He explained that no one had seen Ricardo or his partner yet. No Nose calmly said, "Ricardo and his accomplice must be holed up somewhere in Hillsboro or Pinellas County. But we know they can't stay hidden forever. Keep the pressure on, Luigi, and when they make a mistake we'll be on them like a pack of blind, starving, dogs."

Luigi nodded and hoped the mistake would happen sooner than later.

CHAPTER EIGHT

SETH woke up from his nap and looked at his watch. It was 6:00 p.m. and he felt rested. He got up, brushed his teeth, and ran a comb through his hair. *Still no gray hair, pretty amazing ...* thought Seth, looking in the mirror. He still had plenty of time to have dinner and take in the sights at Mallory Square. He walked down Front Street towards Mallory to eat dinner at *El Meson de Pepe's*, the best Cuban restaurant in Key West. It was still early so he had no problem getting a table on the porch overlooking the entrance to Mallory Square and the Key West Founders Park. Seth ordered a glass of *vino tinto* and *arroz con pollo* with a side of *frijoles negro*. The dinner came with a tasty salad that had Spanish olives in it. The early Mallory sunset crowd was just beginning to filter down the alley.

Seth looked over into the Founders Park and as usual it was full of chickens. Actually Key West was being overrun by chickens, as they were almost everywhere you looked. The roosters made quite a racket every morning when the sun came up. Seth had read in the St. Petersburg newspaper that the Key West city council was considering thinning them out a bit. Of course, that met with anguished outcries from various animal rights groups even though almost everyone eats eggs and chickens. The fact was that these wild chickens were not easily caught. Seth noticed several inept tourist children trying to catch the chickens. It wasn't even close because these chickens were lean and fast.

Watching the tourist children reminded Seth of the last time he had been in this restaurant, many years ago, with Lisa and Jeb. They had been staying at A&B for a week of fishing and relaxation. Seth had brought them here for lunch one windy day when they didn't go fishing. Jeb had been chasing the chickens in the park while Seth and Lisa waited for their lunches to arrive. Jeb hadn't come close to catching one of the chickens. Finally, Seth called him back up to the restaurant porch when their lunches arrived.

Jeb said, "Those chickens are just too fast for me, Dad! I can't even get a hand on one."

"Now, Jeb, they're really a lot like the fish we catch. What do we do to get the tuna, snapper, or kingfish bunched up and biting?"

"We chum them up, Dad."

"Right," said Seth. With that said he stood up and grabbed the loaf of Cuban bread that the waiter had brought to the table. He broke it in pieces and started throwing them over into the park. The chickens made a rush for them. Seth threw some more into the alley and made a trail to their table.

Lisa said, "Seth, please sit down, you're embarrassing me."

"Oh, come on, I'm just having some fun."

Within a minute, several chickens surrounded the table. Lisa and the waiter glowered at Seth. But Seth, Jeb, and the rest of the restaurant patrons all laughed. When the bread was gone the chickens quickly exited and no harm was done. Jeb had learned a valuable lesson. If you want to catch something elusive just learn what kind of chum they like. It works on people, too. The waiter didn't ask us if we would like more bread.

Seth chuckled to himself, finished his dinner, and paid the bill. He strolled out to Mallory Square just as the sun was going down. The jugglers and fire-eaters were giving it their all as the sun sunk below the horizon. Seth walked over to the edge of the wharf. He could see the tall sailing schooners tacking up the channel. They were a beautiful sight in the fading light. In amongst all the marine traffic he noticed a Bertram 54 with a swim platform crossing the channel towards Sunset Island. He strained to see the name on the transom; it read *Chica*, Ft. Lauderdale, Fl. "I must be going buggy," said Seth out loud. "It looks just like the one I saw in Charley's yard Friday, same outriggers, same swim platform, and no tower. But that one was named *Pescadora*." *There must be at least ten or fifteen of them just like that in Florida* … thought Seth … *I wonder what set that alarm off in my head.* He answered his own question … *Beau and the two Cubans had hardly been off his mind since Friday.* He retraced his route out to Front Street and walked by Pepe's on his way back to the A&B docks.

Seth poured himself another glass of red wine on the boat and climbed up into the fly bridge to enjoy the languid night breeze. He could hear the sounds of a Jimmy Buffet cover band coming from the Schooner Bar across the bight. He took a sip of wine and was glad he was in Key West. He laughed out loud when he thought about the cemetery tour Lisa had talked him into going on some years ago. Key West's cemetery turned out to be all above ground crypts, and it was right in the middle of town. Just like the rest of Key West it was crowded and bizarre. But what amused Seth the most were the inscriptions on the tombstones.

"Sloppy Joe" was buried there and his tombstone read, "Died while fishing with Ernest Hemingway."

On the grave of B. Pierce Roberts was the inscription, "I told you I was sick."

On the grave of a philandering husband was the inscription penned by his long-suffering wife, "At least I know where he's sleeping tonight."

Another one that tickled Seth was the headstone of a woman who died in 1986; it read, "A devoted fan of singer Julio Iglesias."

Seth laughed to himself and thought … *they ought to change the name of this island to Key Weird.*

Seth stretched out on the forward fly bridge bench seat and propped a throw pillow behind his head. He was enjoying the Jimmy Buffet cover's singing; he really sounded like the real thing. He yawned, closed his eyes, and listened as the strains of "Mother Ocean" lilted in the breeze. Seth couldn't remember when he had felt this relaxed.

Seth woke up the next morning at dawn, still up in the fly bridge. He had obviously dozed off and slept straight through. He got up, retrieved his half full glass of wine, and went below to relieve himself. Once below he brushed his teeth, showered, and shaved. Today his crew was coming in, and tomorrow they would go fishing.

Seth walked off towards downtown and stopped for breakfast at the Two Friends restaurant on Front Street. He planned on busying himself the rest of the morning setting the drags on his 50 and 80-pound Penn International reels. He always used a 15 pound strike setting on the 50's and 30 pounds on the 80's. When trolling, Seth had his anglers set the drag down to an 8 to 10 lb. mark. He felt his hook-up ratio was better at that lighter setting. While he was eating his sausage and scrambled eggs he heard sirens further down south on Front Street. He got up and looked down the street as a fire engine and an ambulance turned south on Front Street, and then turned west towards Wall Street. He wondered what could have happened so early in the morning down there. It was too early for any drunks to be street diving yet. Seth sat back down, finished his breakfast, and then went back to the *Tar Baby* to work on his fishing reel drags.

Around 10:00 a.m., Don the dock master walked by and asked, "Did you hear what happened down at the Aquarium last night?"

Seth said, "No, but I saw there was quite a commotion down on Wall Street while I was eating breakfast earlier down at Two Friends. What happened?"

"Well, it appears that two people somehow ended up in the shark tank last night and the sharks ate them. It's all over the local radio station this morning. The report is that the police are going to open up the sharks to try and get enough of the victims bodies back for DNA testing and to also find anything else that might help identify the victims."

"I guess anything is possible in Key West."

"You got that right!" laughed Don.

Gene Johnson and John Harvey planned to leave St. Petersburg at 6:30 a.m. on Monday. Seth figured they should arrive around 3:00 in the afternoon. They were driving down in John's Escalade, and it would serve as the crew's wheels in Key West. Seth always kidded John that he looked like a Mexican drug dealer riding around in his black Escalade with the chrome kiddie wheels. He guessed his Yukon was almost as bad. Bobby Sanders would fly in from Maryland on U.S. Air and would arrive at Key West Airport at 7:10 p.m. Seth and the other St. Petersburg boys would pick him up at the airport and then drive to Louie's Backyard Restaurant for drinks and dinner. Seth liked the view and the ahi tuna at Louie's.

Louie's location also had some fishing history. Before Hemingway moved himself and his marlin tournament to Havana, Cuba, the tournament's headquarters had always been at Louie's. Also, years before while Seth was on spring break in Key West, from the University of Virginia, he had seen a young country and western musician named Jimmy Buffet perform there one night. Jimmy wrote and sang his own songs about sailing, fishing, drug smuggling, and the Key's rollicking lifestyle. Seth had been a fan of his music from that point on, and he considered Jimmy as one of his generation's best songwriters. Louie's was more of a beach bar and restaurant in those days. Now it had gone upscale, just as Jimmy Buffet finally had. Most of the old time salt water people in Florida, that Seth knew, still liked to listen to the old songs that had made Jimmy famous and wealthy. But many of them, including Seth, had discontinued their support of the "Save the Manatee" Club that Jimmy and Governor Bob Graham founded in 1981. They also were surprised that the onetime Key's troubadour had virtually disappeared from the Keys and now lived in Palm Beach and in the Hampton's on, Long Island, in New York. Seth had read in a recent Marlin magazine issue that Jimmy was the proud owner of a new 42 foot walk-around express sportfish built by Rybovitch Boatworks in Palm Beach, and had named it *Margaritavitch*. He hoped Jimmy didn't run over a manatee with it, as you could only imagine the field day the media would have with that one.

Seth had never seen a West Indian manatee around St Petersburg until he was about forty years old. He guessed they couldn't stand the cold water during the winters. Their appearance on the south and central Florida coasts coincided with the building of several large power plants in the major metropolitan areas. The power plants discharged millions of gallons of hot process water into the bays and rivers every day, along Florida's east and west coasts, year around. Those same power plants were where you could find the entire manatee population all winter.

The "Save the Manatee" Club had started as a noble cause. The heightened awareness and reduced speed zones, especially around the power plants in the winter, had dramatically decreased accidental manatee deaths each year. Unfortunately, Seth felt the Club now seemed to have a monetary and political agenda. They lobbied against almost all public water access issues, dock and marina permitting, and the recreational boaters access to the waterways. Seth had read that the Florida Wildlife Commission had been conducting their own manatee herd counts on a yearly basis for a number of years and the herd counts were steadily increasing. The preliminary herd counts taken that past winter around the power plants were substantially the highest in recent history. This year's manatee count as published in Florida's newspapers was high enough to take them off the endangered species list, which was the "Save the Manatee" Club's original goal. Seth hoped this would officially happen soon. His real hope for Florida's future was that the manatee herd and the recreational boaters could continue to coexist and that both would continue to grow in numbers.

Seth had watched "Radar," a full-grown manatee with a yellow radio beacon attached around his neck for state tracking purposes, grow up in busy Salt Creek. He had returned each spring for the past ten years. He surfaced near the docks whenever the employees were washing a boat, just looking for a drink of fresh water from the hose. He had that cute manatee face that everyone loves, and had made friends up and down the creek. It was a testament to his resilience that "Radar" could survive in boat traffic laden Salt Creek and the adjoining industrial Bayboro Harbor.

The day flew by as more boats and crew arrived at the A & B docks. Finally John and Gene walked down the dock pushing a dock cart full of duffels and coolers. It was 3:15, and they had made good time.

"Howdy, Seth," chortled Gene. "How's it going buddy?"

Seth shook hands with both of them and slapped them both on their backs.

"Man, I'm glad to see you guys, c'mon aboard and stow your gear."

John piped up and said, "Seth, we stopped in Marathon at World Class Bait and Tackle and got four dozen fresh horse ballyhoo. They're nice and firm and their beak tips are bright red."

"Good job, John. They might be just the ticket, you never know. Put them in the bait cooler and sprinkle some rock salt over them. It's under the galley sink. The brine will toughen them up and they'll run longer."

John took care of the ballyhoo and then they all cracked open a cold one.

"Ah! There's nothing like an ice cold *cerveza* after a long drive," said Gene. "What's the plan for tonight, Seth?"

"Well, we're going to pick Bobby up at the airport around 7:00 p.m. and then we'll head over to Louie's for dinner."

"Sounds like a plan," said Gene.

"We're going to go fishing tomorrow to scout out the bait pods along Wood's Wall. I've got a fresh Roff's chart coming tomorrow morning and every day after that."

"So, what's going on in Key West?" asked John.

"The strangest thing is; the dock master told me that two people were eaten by sharks in the shark tank last night at the aquarium."

"You've got to be kidding me."

Seth laughed and said, "I'm as serious as a heart attack. We'll have to grab a newspaper in the morning and read the story."

"Only in Key West," said Gene rolling his eyes.

The boys stowed their gear and then they all had another cold one. An hour or so later they showered, dressed for dinner, and headed for the airport to pick up Bobby. On the way out to the airport they caught up on family news and talked about retirement. Gene was doing a little security consulting for Publix to keep busy, and John had taken a partner on in his dermatology practice. He had cut back to three days a week so he could go flats fishing, and play more golf. None of them really wanted to retire altogether. Seth had always thought that dermatology was the best field for a doctor to be in. John had a life outside his practice and seldom had an emergency. Gene's family was doing fine; one of his boys was a lawyer, the other had followed him into the police department. They pulled into the airport and walked to the U.S. Air gate to wait for Bobby. The terminal had grown a little over the years, but it was still small and very informal by any standards. Bobby's plane finally arrived, and he was the last person off the plane. He had carried on his duffel, so after a round of backslapping they were back in the Escalade directly. John pulled back out on Roosevelt Boulevard and they headed for Louie's.

They left the SUV with the valet in front of Louie's and the four friends headed for the outside deck bar after checking in with the maitre d'. The view of the Atlantic Ocean was stunning. The water was flat calm and they watched two jet skis running back and forth as they enjoyed their drinks. It wasn't long before they were seated and ordered another round of drinks. They kidded each other and laughed at themselves as they retold their favorite stories recalling their previous fishing trips. Seth and Bobby told a couple of funny football stories about some of the unbelievable characters they had played with in college. When they were finished with dinner they headed back towards A&B.

John suggested that that they park the car in the A&B lot, and then go on a "Duval Street crawl". Nobody objected so twenty minutes later they started at the Hog's Breath Saloon on lower Duval. The Hog's Breath was crowded with tournament fisherman who had arrived for the Drambuie. The boy's had a round of beers and then headed up Duval to Rick's. They went upstairs to check out the titty dancers.

John ordered four beers for the crew and said, "It looks like girls night out in Bosnia."

Seth laughed and said, "Times have changed since only Cuban girls danced here. They only spoke Spanish, but I'm not sure what language these girls are speaking."

They went back downstairs and backtracked for a round at Sloppy Joes. Then they walked down Greene Street and stopped for a nightcap at Schooner's on the Bight. Twenty years ago the boys would have made it all the way up one side of Duval and back the other. Now, they couldn't decide if they were wiser or just older. They found a table by the boardwalk and ordered one more round of cold ones. It was a hot night in Key West and the water misters and fans were going full blast. The misters actually did cool you off some. Seth had thought about installing two in the fishing cockpit of *Tar Baby* to cool the crew on those long hot Florida afternoons when the fish weren't biting. But, he decided he didn't need another gadget to maintain. The same Jimmy Buffet imitator came back off break and sang a rousing rendition of "Cheeseburger in Paradise".

Seth told the boys, "Let's get up at 6:00 and leave the dock about 8:00 a.m. tomorrow. We can eat a leisurely breakfast down the street at Two Friends and be out at Wood's Wall by 9:30. I want to check out the west crack and the mid-crack."

Everyone nodded and Gene said, "Drink up boys; it's almost midnight and time for us to hit the rack."

6:00 a.m. came early on Tuesday, but Seth was already wide-awake with anticipation. Everyone rolled out of bed and headed for the showers and the marina deli.

"Let's skip breakfast and get some coffee and donuts here and go fishing," said John.

They all agreed and started back to the boat. This is what they'd come for and they couldn't wait to get started.

Seth lit off the diesels and the generator. The crew disconnected the shore power cords and in less than five minutes they were on their way out of Key West Bight. "Tar Baby" cleared the rock breakwater and Seth headed her south towards the southwest channel. As he passed the aquarium he looked to port and could see yellow crime scene tape all around the aft docks of the aquarium. He wondered what had gone on back there. When they cleared the rocky point past Fort Zachary Taylor, Seth put *Tar Baby* up on a plane. He called down to Gene in the cockpit to bring up this morning's copy of the Key West Citizen and read it to him on the way out. Gene climbed up in the fly bridge and sat down in the passenger chair next to Seth. He found the shark tank article on the front page. The headline read "Shark Attack on Wall Street."

Gene read on from there, "Early Monday, evidence that was found at the Key West Aquarium indicated that two persons had entered the indoor shark exhibit tank and had been consumed by the sharks in the tank. Bits of clothes, shoes, and personal effects have been recovered from the largest sharks' stomachs. Key West police have sent the human remains that were discovered to the FDLE for DNA testing. Some of the personal effects indicate that the victim's were males, but no information will be forthcoming until the police have a positive ID and have notified the next of kin. Key West Chief of Detectives, Troy

Baggett, stated, 'at this time we have no reason to classify this case as a homicide or a double suicide. We have no leads or suspects, but we will continue to investigate and process the forensic evidence'."

Seth said, "I remember taking Jeb to that aquarium a few times over the years. There are a lot of big sharks in that tank."

Gene said, "I worked on some crazy cases in St. Pete, but nothing like this."

"Well, stay tuned Gene, it's just another normal day in Key West, I guess."

Seth glanced up at *Tar Baby's* GPS. They were fifty-eight minutes from the west crack in Wood's Wall. The weather continued to be ideal and there was a short chop, which is better for billfishing than a flat calm. Seth had decided to fish six, 50-pound wide, 2-speed, rod and reel combos. The crew would have an 80-pound wide, 2-speed, combo ready, with a dead bonito or mackerel bait attached, to pitch at any large marlin that might come up behind the teasers. They would run two jumbo teaser lures (no hooks) off the bridge teaser reel, a mirrored bowling pin daisy chain off the left transom corner, and a Mylar ballyhoo dredge off the right transom corner. John Harvey would be the designated pitch bait angler.

Tournament fishing was fun, but it could also be grueling. The boats left the dock at 7:30 a.m., with lines in at 8:30. The crew stayed on station and was alert all day, continually changing baits and lures almost hourly in the hot sun. Lines came out at 4:00 p.m. and the boat was back at the dock at 5:30. The boat and gear was scrubbed, the crew took a shower, rushed to the cocktail party at 6:30, had dinner at 7: 30, and then everyone fell into bed exhausted by 9:00 p.m. Then they got up at 6:00 a.m. and did it all over again. Three days on that schedule would take its toll.

But as Robert E. always said, "A bad day of fishing is better than a good day at work."

Seth arrived at the first west crack waypoint and slowed down as the crew let down the outriggers and set out the spread of lures and teasers. He adjusted the Hatteras's speed to seven and a half knots and started zigzagging down the edge of the crack drop-off. They were finally fishing.

CHAPTER NINE

BEAU checked *Chica's* position on the GPS, and it showed that they were in the Gulf Stream moving north by northeast. The waves had increased about a foot in height and now were two to three feet. The wind held steady out of the southwest at seven to eight knots. The sun was beginning to climb in the sky but all Beau could see in every direction was dark blue water. The GPS put them sixty-seven miles southwest of the Orange Rocks where they would enter the Bahamas Bank north of Andros Island.

Beau had made this same crossing to get to a marlin tournament at Chub Cay ten years ago in twenty to twenty-five knots of wind from the southwest. The waves had been six to eight feet in the Gulf Stream. The boat could only make thirteen or fourteen knots in the pounding seas. The entire crew, except for Beau, was seasick the whole way, but they made the tournament on time.

When the sun rose a little higher and the visibility improved, Beau put the Bertram up on a plane and ran at twenty-four knots. His severed fingers felt surprisingly good, most probably because of the Percocet. Skippers that ran over ten knots at night were cooking up a recipe for disaster. If the boat hit a floating log, or a packing crate lost overboard from a freighter, while running fast, it would sink like a stone. Within two and a half hours the Orange Rocks came into view. Beau changed course for the run across the Great Bahama Bank to the Northwest channel, past Chub Cay, and then thirty-five miles across the top of the Tongue of the Ocean to the port of Nassau on New Providence Island. There they would refuel for the run down through the Exumas' to Great Inaqua Island at the very end of the Bahamas chain. Nassau would be their first stop to clear customs in a foreign country. Beau thought they would be less notice-able fueling up and clearing customs in a port that had eight or ten fuel docks clustered between Nassau and Paradise Island. They could have stopped in Chub Cay, but they only had one fuel dock and one customs agent. A large sportfish there might attract some gawkers. Beau planned on anchoring out off Nassau that night, and then making the long run down to Great Inagua with a one-night remote anchorage stop along the way. The less people that saw them the safer they'd be. He had to remember he was now Ronald Santos, and he had started having Hector and Luis practice calling him Ronald.

The Bertram was running across the shallow bank comfortably in a slight chop. Beau checked the course and turned on the autopilot before turning the helm over to Hector. Then he went below to check the engine room and bilges. Everything checked out okay, and Beau moved on and checked the fuel gauges. Fuel usage was about what Beau had anticipated. He checked the 55 gallon fuel drums in the cockpit, and they were secure. Beau headed for the guest head and removed the fake beard carefully. He cleaned the spirit-gum adhesive off his face with alcohol. His own beard had grown into thick, black, stubble while he wore the disguise, and he decided it made him look more like the picture of Hector on the Ronald Santos passport. He took one more look in the mirror and then went back up to the fly bridge.

Beau took back the helm from Hector and piloted *Chica* south through the sparsely marked Northwest Channel. They passed an empty freighter and a fifty-five foot Viking sportfish that were headed north. He ran by Crab Cay and Chub Cay and navigated back into the deep blue ocean water towards Nassau. An hour and a half later, New Providence Island loomed on the horizon. He headed for Nassau and the east breakwater at Paradise Island. Beau throttled *Chica* down as he passed the end of the breakwater and idled east towards the HarborView Texaco fuel dock. It was the furthest from the two high-rise bridges he had to pass under. He didn't want anyone crossing the bridges to notice the boat as they refueled and waited for customs to arrive. They passed by the entrance to the Atlantis Marina on Paradise Island, and Beau thought he'd like to have all the money back he'd lost in that casino. Even though Beau had gambled poorly there he still should have enjoyed the world-class hotel and grounds at Atlantis. He wished he could just enjoy places for what they were. Sadly, when he was gambling he was oblivious to his surroundings.

Beau called Harborview Marina on the VHF radio, as he passed by Hurricane Hole and Nassau Yacht Haven Marinas. Harborview's dock master was waiting on the dock as they pulled in. Beau put up *Chica's* yellow quarantine flag and asked the dock master to please call customs for him. He had also found a Bahamas courtesy flag along with the quarantine flag and had it ready to put up after they cleared. The only trip the previous owner had ever taken was probably to the Bahamas.

They were half way fueled when the customs officer arrived. He was a jolly-looking rotund man, and he wore a crisp khaki uniform. His name was Percy Lightbourne, and he looked very official. His Government Issue uniform was seldom seen in the out islands and then only at the airports. Beau, as captain, filled out the forms and showed him all of the passports.

"Where is your final destination in the Bahamas," asked Percy.

Beau lied to cover his trail, "Our destination is Staniel Cay in the Exumas."

"Do you have any firearms to declare?"

"We have no firearms, Sir."

Firearms were not illegal on vessels visiting the Bahamas, but customs wanted the serial number and manufacturer recorded on your visa. They also required that you keep the weapon and it's ammunition under lock and key. Percy would not have found any weapons unless he had frisked the Fernandez brothers, because the .38 was too well hidden.

Percy really didn't seem to be interested in searching the boat and charged *Chica* the standard three hundred dollars for a cruising permit and fishing license which was good for six months and two reentries. Beau thanked him and gave Percy a fifty-dollar cash donation to BASRA, the Bahamas Air Search and Rescue Association.

Beau wondered if the Association would ever see the fifty. Outside of Nassau and Freeport one seldom saw any kind of police presence anywhere in the rest of the Bahamas. Percy stamped the passports and bid them a polite good day. Beau took down the quarantine flag, put up the Bahamas courtesy flag, and finished pumping the diesel. He paid for the fuel with cash from the stash, tipped the dock master fifty dollars, and prepared to leave.

Earlier, Beau had taken the time during the passage across the bank to hide the robbery cash in black plastic garbage bags under the spare parts and five gallon buckets of spare engine oil. He kept less than ten thousand dollars up in the cabin.

The dock master asked Beau, "What happened to your fingers, Mon?"

Beau looked down at the blood soaked bandages and calmly replied, "The cockpit lazarette hatch fell down on them."

The dock master winced in mock pain.

Beau asked him, "Have you seen a weather report."

"Yes, there's a category two hurricane heading northeast of us toward

Bermuda, they named it Gail. Our weather and south of here should be five to ten from the southeast with afternoon thundershowers for the next few days."

Beau thanked him and motored *Chica* back out the channel towards the west and ran around to Lyford Cay. They tucked into the West Bay anchorage for the night and prepared to anchor up. There were five or six sailboats anchored closer to shore, and Beau could smell one of their stern rail barbeque grills cooking something that smelled mighty good.

The run down to Great Inagua would cover about 350 nautical miles. Beau planned to take it easy and cut the trip into two legs. He didn't want to run at night at any speed in the Exumas. The danger of hitting an unmarked reef or coral head was very real. They would start to run tomorrow morning in fifteen hundred to five thousand feet of water, but halfway through the day they would pass over the shallow yellow bank. Beau would carefully pilot *Chica* through the narrow cut at Highborne Cay, and then head down Exuma Sound. He would take his time and not push the Bertram hard as they headed for remotely located Lee Stocking Island, where they would anchor overnight. Once anchored, they would transfer the fuel from the four drums in the cockpit into the main tanks.

The following day they would run down the length of Long Island, past Acklin Island, then through the Mira Por Vos passage and on to Matthew Town on Great Inagua Island. There they would refuel and anchor out for another night's sleep. Hector and Luis had settled into the daily routine pretty well. Each brother was standing his watches with Beau, and their eyes were acclimating better to the water each day. Beau would really need them for the 370 mile overnight trip from Great Inagua through the Windward Passage to Jamaica. Then again for the almost 450 mile, day and a half, continuous passage from Kingston to San Andres Island which was located a hundred miles off the Nicaraguan coast.

Beau prayed that the weather would hold. If the weather turned on them during the San Andres leg they would need every drop of fuel they had to make it. The next stop after San Andres Island would be the city of Colon and the Panama Canal. Although that leg was only 275 miles it could be treacherous in bad weather because of a counter current. A twenty-knot wind from the south could turn it into a thirty-five hour passage in ten to twelve foot seas. Beau hoped that his luck had really changed, since he was gambling for his life and not for money.

Beau and Hector got *Chica* anchored behind Lyford Cay, and then they settled in for the night. Luis cooked pork tenderloin in the convection oven with spicy cooked onions and sliced carrots. Beau had frozen enough Cuban bread in the bait freezer to keep the two brothers happy for the rest of their trip.

During the run across the Bahamas Bank Beau's kill or be killed instinct made him decide to ultimately eliminate Hector and Luis. He did need them to get the boat from here through the Panama Canal, but once they were through the canal he could run the boat to Costa Rica by himself. He knew he would have to set their elimination up carefully, as the two brothers carried their handguns twenty-four hours a day. Beau still had plenty of time to concoct a plan and invent a way to divide the two of them and take them out. Even though he had the insurance letter with Gary up in Ohio, Beau doubted if his new partners would forget him and the million dollars he had extorted if John Cipriano met with an untimely death. His training told him he'd never be safe while they were alive. Once they were eliminated Beau hoped No Nose would think the Fernandez brothers had disappeared with his money and would look for both of them in vain. When he sold the boat and had all the money he would buy a new identity, and Ronald Santos would also disappear. That really would be the end of the game. Beau went to sleep that night thinking about the possibilities three and a half million dollars could make possible.

Beau motored *Chica* out of the anchorage at Lyford Cay the next morning as the sun came up. He had a genuine smile on his face for the first time in a long while. As old Robert E. would have said, "He had planned his work, now he had to work his plan." It was a beautiful morning with scores of birds working the bait pods that broke the surface of the lagoon. He put the Bertram up on a plane and steered southeast towards Exuma Sound. They were finally headed down island. Beau was glad to leave the crowded Nassau area, as he headed for the sparsely populated Exumas.

As the Bertram ran effortlessly through the sea, Beau thought about living in Costa Rica. Once he established a new identity he would set up an annuity in the Cayman Islands to meet the guaranteed income requirements for a Costa Rican retirement residency. Beau would deposit most of the balance of the money in Panamanian and Costa Rican banks. He would then live out his life in Costa Rica enjoying, *la pura vida*, the pure life. He hoped he could contact Seth and talk him into visiting him from time to time. But first he had to figure out his plan for the Fernandez brother's demise and complete his voyage. Beau turned his attention to the task at hand which was navigating down the Exuma Sound to Lee Stocking Island.

After a good day's run Beau had Lee Stocking in site. They had only seen a few other boats on the trip down, mostly sailboats around the Staniel Cay area. Beau cut in at Adderley Cay and continued around the inside point in about twenty feet of water leaving Normans Pond Cay to starboard. He idled past the small airstrip, which was visible from the flybridge, into about eight feet of water and had Hector drop the anchor. The island was covered with scrub vegetation and a few palms. They had the anchorage all to themselves. After dropping the hook, Beau immediately started pumping the fuel from the drums into the main tanks. As dusk fell Hector grilled three steaks on the electric barbeque. The only sound in the anchorage was the whoosh from *Chica's* generator exhaust. Luis and Hector sat outside in the cockpit after dinner smoking cigars. Beau sat up in the flybridge looking at the stars above and wondered how Seth would take the news of his death in the shark tank. He knew Seth would be devastated and hoped his plan would work so he would get the opportunity to explain everything someday soon. Even thought he couldn't go back, he wanted Seth to know the truth. He wanted Seth to understand the circumstances that he had to overcome. Beau had no pity for the Fernandez brothers. He knew they were sociopaths, and Beau knew they would kill him in an instant, without any remorse, if the situation changed. Hector and Luis finished their cigars and the three of them turned in. They were all asleep by 10:00 p.m.

Beau was up by 6:00 a.m. and checked out the engine fluids and v-belts. He checked the generator, which was running smoothly, and found no leaks. So far the air conditioners were working perfectly, and the interior of the Bertram was nice and cool. Hector and Luis were up by 7:00, and after some toast and coffee they were all ready to leave. Beau motored out of the anchorage exactly the same way he came in. He was through the cut and out in fifty feet of water in a matter of minutes. The boat planed up faster and ran better with the cockpit fuel drums emptied. Beau sipped his coffee and surveyed Exuma Sound from the flybridge.

"What a beautiful place to cruise if you have the time," he said out loud to no one.

The water was as clear as gin, and the hundreds of small cays and coves were utterly deserted and beautiful. Beau followed a course south towards Acklin Island. Soon they were through the Mira Por Vos passage and in water nearly nine thousand feet deep. Beau adjusted his course and throttled up to twenty-five knots so they would make Matthew Town in time to fuel before dark. Hector was starting to get the hang of navigation and was full of questions. Given sea time and some instruction he probably could have been turned into a decent boatsman. He had aptitude and wasn't as lazy as Luis. Beau sent Hector into the engine room telling him what to check and what to look for. He had Hector write down all the mechanical gauge readings for the engines and generator. Beau wanted Hector to learn some basics, as there might be times that Beau wouldn't want to leave the helm.

Halfway from Acklin Island to Great Inagua is Hogsty Reef. Beau pointed out the large freighter that was shipwrecked on Hogsty to Hector as they passed southwest of the reef. The lesson is what can happen to experienced professional skippers and crew at night or in bad weather. If the GPS craps out and you haven't been marking your position on a paper chart every half hour or so you really don't know exactly where you are. A pro will always mark a chart so he can immediately start to dead reckon for wind, tide, and current drift, along with forward progress. The freighter sitting on top of Hogsty Reef was a stark reminder of the perils of the sea.

"Captain Ron" was right when he said, "If it's gonna happen, it's gonna happen out there."

The wind had picked up some after passing Acklin Island. The swells had become larger and larger and were probably a good preview of the open ocean where they would be headed tomorrow. The beamy Bertram handled the increasing sea state at twenty-five knots of speed with no problem. At 3:30 p.m. Beau could see the radio towers on Great Inagua. The GPS read twenty-seven minutes to their destination at Matthew Town's sea buoy. Beau had been to Matthew Town once before when Robert E. had taken him on a delivery from Florida to Jamaica. The town was protected from the sea only from the east and southeast, so it was safe most of the time in a prevailing wind. Beau remembered a small rock jettied basin that boats could use when the wind picked up from the wrong direction. The wind was brisk out of the southeast, so Beau was going to anchor north of Matthew Town in Man of War Bay. He would rather anchor up under its high bluffs than be in the small crowded basin with a bunch of other boats.

Matthew Town was a big town compared to other Bahamas out island towns. The Morton Salt Company had a large presence there and exported millions of tons of salt each year from Great Inagua's extensive salt ponds. Beau radioed ahead, and then pulled *Chica* up to the large Texaco fuel dock. Beau fueled up the tanks and drums while Hector and Luis stretched their legs in the ships store. Beau asked the dock master for a weather forecast and was told it would blow fifteen to twenty from the southeast the next two or three days because of a small upper level disturbance. There were no tropical storms headed their way according to the dock master. Beau thanked and tipped him, paid for the fuel, and then motored up to Man of War Bay.

The bay had a little surge running, but the water flattened out when Beau got up under the bluffs. Once anchored, Beau listened to the single sideband radio and corroborated the weather report he had gotten at the dock. Luis cooked up a dinner of black beans and yellow rice with a Cuban salad. They all turned in early anticipating the long, open sea, passage that they faced the next day.

CHAPTER TEN

SETH followed the west crack drop-off on *Tar Baby's* GPS map. The chart showed the bottom detail and depth in color. As he zig-zagged the boat back and forth across the drop-off an electronic arrow followed the boat's course on the chart. He could also monitor the depth recorder that changed from eight hundred feet to over twelve hundred feet and vice-versa as he crossed over the drop-off. Over the years Seth had learned that seventy-five percent of the strikes he got happened as the boat moved over drop-offs or structure.

What Seth wanted to accomplish on their two days of pre-tournament scouting was to identify where the large concentrations of baitfish were holding. The game fish would be where the baitfish schools were schooling. When they ran over bait it would show up on the depth recorder as a cloud of tiny arches. A large fish would show up as a large arch. Seth planned to work both sides of the west crack and record the position of any large bait schools he saw. When that was completed they would troll east along Wood's Wall to the mid crack and start checking it out. Seth consulted his newest Roff's chart for its input of thermoclines and confluent currents. Theoretically, where they interplayed with the wall drop-off should be the best spots to fish. But it didn't always work like that, so that's why Seth was doing his homework.

About twenty minutes into the first hour of trolling two of the outrigger clips went off, and the boys had two nice size dolphins on. They released them several minutes later, guessing the weight of the bull at twenty-six pounds and the cow at nineteen pounds. The crew all high fived each other, and everyone was smiling and laughing. Seth had marked the large bait school, on which the dolphins had been feeding, on the GPS. The crew put the spread back out and started happily chatting back and forth. They had been quiet, but now that the skunk was off of them they livened up. Bobby was a Democrat and the rest of them were Republicans, so the boy's started kidding him about how Florida had sunk Al Gore in his bid for President and what a bunch of sore losers the Democrats were.

Bobby took it good naturedly and finally Gene said, "Bobby, you *do* know what Bill Clinton's biggest problem was, don't you?"

Bobby just rolled his eyes and said resigningly, "No, Gene, what?"

"Well, Bill thought harass was two words!"

Even Bobby had to laugh at that one and so the rest of the day went. The crew all got into the routine of fishing, but they enjoyed needling each other and poking fun at themselves. Two more dolphins, about the same size as the first two, were caught and released. No billfish showed themselves, although Seth recorded the position of three large concentrations of bait. If it had been tournament day, Seth would have worked those areas exclusively. Instead he worked *Tar Baby* east down Wood's Wall towards the mid crack. He had counted ten or eleven boats fishing the west crack and had not noticed any prolonged fight or boat backing down all day. Seth called lines out at 3:30 in the afternoon and headed back to Key West.

The boy's straightened up the cockpit and put the rods up in the fly bridge holders. Then they cracked the first cold one of the day. Gene and John went inside the air-conditioned cabin for the ride in and Bobby climbed up on the fly bridge.

He slid into the passenger chair next to Seth and said, "Pretty slow out here today. I hope it picks up by tournament time."

Seth said, "I marked some nice bait pods holding tight on the wall. There has to be some fish there, or maybe they're all sitting on a temperature break somewhere. Tomorrow we're going to check out the mid-crack and the east crack. If we don't see something more promising we might just run out to the "Hooters" on tournament day."

"Where and what are the "Hooters", Seth?"

"They're two underwater mountain peaks about twelve miles further south from the mid-crack. The water might be a little colder out there, and there's an upwelling. I don't know, but it's just another option."

"Maybe you should use your old James Brown grouper trick on the marlin tomorrow," said Bobby with a smile. "We'll put "I Feel Good" on the stereo and crank up the volume."

Seth laughed and said, "I've never tried it on billfish, Bobby, but you never know."

Years ago during a slow summer grouper trip, twenty-five miles off of St. Pete Beach, Seth had cranked up James Brown on the stereo to relieve the boredom. To everyone's surprise the grouper suddenly came alive and literally jumped all over their bottom rigs. Since that time it had become standard procedure when the bite slowed down, and most of the time it worked. He figured that the grouper came out of their hidey-holes to check out the booming bass sound and couldn't pass up a free meal when they saw the bait.

Seth could finally see the radio and cell towers on Key West looming on the horizon. He got on his cell phone and made a call to Roff's in Miami to remind them he wanted an updated chart faxed each of the next four days. He ran in the ship's channel and stayed on plane all the way to the old submarine pens before he throttled back to idle. He backed *Tar Baby* into her slip and the boys tied her up. After they scrubbed and hosed the boat and equipment they all cracked another cold one and headed for the showers.

One by one the crew came back to the boat all cleaned up and dressed in fresh clothes. They sat on the cockpit gunnel, opened another beer, and relaxed.

When they were all back Seth said, "Tomorrow we are going to just fish big lures. So we don't need to rig but a few ballyhoo on the way out in the morning. We'll rig a 30-pound spinning rod with one in case a white marlin or a little sailfish comes up in the spread. I think the big lures will bring the marlin up."

The boys all nodded their approval and Bobby said, "Let's go over to the Schooner bar and check out the talent."

Seth laughed and said, "O.K. Bobby, but remember we have 8:00 p.m. reservations at Seven Fish tonight and we leave the dock at 8:00 in the morning tomorrow."

"No problem," said Bobby with a smile. "I'm just looking."

Before they left for Schooner's, Seth went over the tournament format and rules with everyone. The Key West Marlin Tournament was an average cost tournament as marlin tournaments go. $1200, got the boat and two anglers entered in the marlin and billfish division. $200 covered the cost of each additional angler. Another $300 entered the boat in the fun fish division, which had a cash prize for the largest dolphin of $5000. The largest wahoo and tuna each brought $750, each.

The overall tournament winner won $25,000, second was worth $10,000, and third place $5,000. If a boat caught a marlin over 600 pounds and brought him to the scales they got a point a pound. If the marlin weighed less than 600 pounds they got zero points. If anyone caught and weighed a marlin breaking the Key West record of 784 pounds, it was worth $100,000. There was also a

$100,000 prize for breaking the Key West dolphin record of 64 pounds during the tournament. Usually two marlin and three heavy fun fish or a sailfish release worth 50 points would win this tournament.

Seth explained that I.G.F.A. rules were in effect. They also must get time-dated photos of every release, and only the angler who hooked the fish could touch the rod during the battle. The leader had to touch the rod tip, or a mate had to touch it for a release to be legal. A marlin release was worth 400 points, while white marlin and spearfish counted for 200 points. Tuna, wahoo, and dolphin had to be over twenty pounds to weigh, but its gross weight counted for points, and you could only weigh one of each species per day. They'd all been through it before in other tournaments, so it didn't take Seth long to finish his instructions.

Then they all walked over to Schooners bar for another cold beer. The bar was packed, but they found a spot on the rail overlooking the boardwalk and ordered up four beers. The water misters and fans were still going full blast and so was the cash register. The crew watched the constant ebb and flow of the tourists walking past the bar. Many of them were making their way to the different sunset cruise boats moored along the bight's boardwalk. Seth thought he'd like to go out on the big black-hulled schooner *America* sometime. It looked very impressive at the dock and under sail. The boys had another round, and then they drove up to Seven Fish in the Escalade.

All of them had yellow tail snapper and lightly braised asparagus, and they were back at the boat by 9:30. Seth went aboard first and went directly to the forward head to get rid of all the beer he had consumed in the past two hours. As he was zipping back up he wondered how asparagus could taste so good but make your urine smell so bad? After a full day on the water in the hot August sun, they were all ready for a good night's rest. Seth told them they would leave the dock at 7:00 a.m. and put the lines in at 8:30. They all went to sleep thinking about the 800 pound marlin they hoped to catch during the tournament.

The next morning they were all up before 6:00 a.m. A big breakfast was forgotten again, and they got coffee and donuts from the deli at the dock. At 7:30 *Tar Baby* cleared the breakwater and five minutes later the Hatteras was running at twenty-five knots towards the mid-crack of Wood's Wall. Seth pulled the throttles back at 8:25 and at 8:30 the lines all went in.

They had slowed about a half a mile from one of two numbers Seth had punched in off the new Roff's chart that had just been faxed in. Fifteen minutes later Seth located a large bait school within six hundred yards of the first number, holding tight on the mid-cracks east wall. He made two passes over the bait with no luck, but on the third pass across the drop off, the right long rigger was knocked out of the clip. Something had hit the black, orange, and white soft-head Moldcraft lure.

Seth turned the boat into a port turn while the crew shouted, "Right rigger! Right rigger!" and in a matter of seconds the fish came back and literally jumped on the lure. The 50-wide reel began to scream as line peeled off it a high rate of speed.

Seth shouted down at the crew in the cockpit … "Blue Marlin!"

He pulled the throttles back to dead slow, but left the engines in gear. As boat slowed down to idle speed the marlin broke the water with a spectacular jump about a hundred yards behind the boat. Seth guessed that he was 200+ pounds. John had taken the rod out of the holder and switched the clicker off. He eased the drag lever down a little as the fish took more and more line off the reel. When the marlin stopped stripping line from the reel, John settled in at the transom and began pumping and reeling whenever the fish wasn't taking more line out. Gene put a rod belt around his waist being careful not to touch the rod. The marlin started taking line again at a pretty good clip, as Bobby and Gene reeled in the other lines. Seth brought in the bridge-controlled teasers reeling the overhead double pancake reel as fast as he could. When Bobby and Gene pulled the dredge teaser in over the transom everything was finally cleared. Seth then put the boat in a starboard turn and started to run up parallel to the fish.

He yelled down to John, "Get ready to reel in some line; we're going to run up on him."

Seth throttled up a little and John started gaining on the fish. Seth kept going until the boat was parallel to the marlin and then slowed. John had reeled in almost all the line, so Seth turned off to port and put the fish off the transom again. John pumped and reeled and it was obvious that the marlin was tiring. He made a series of jumps and then tried to sound.

"Let's back on him, John, before he sounds on us," yelled Seth as he put *Tar Baby* in reverse.

Seth throttled up until water was splashing over the transom and into the cockpit. John was gaining on the tired fish and soon Seth could see the marlin thirty feet off the transom. He was lit up and looked fluorescent blue. When the fish saw the boat he made one more valiant jump and tried to surge away from the boat. Seth put the engines in neutral, and John put more pressure on the marlin by pushing the drag lever back up a few pounds while pumping him up with a series of small jabs.

Bobby put on the leather gloves to handle the leader and moved to the transom. John soon had the Dacron wind-on leader past the tip and on the reel, and Bobby grabbed the 300 pound test monofilament leader. He led the fish up the side of the boat, reached over, and grabbed the marlin by his bill. The fish thrashed while Gene took his picture and then calmed down. Bobby held the fish's bill in his left hand, worked the hook loose with his right hand, and gently released him.

The crew's emotions exploded in a series of high-fives and end zone antics! They were definitely on a marlin high. Seth had recorded the lat-long location of the hook-up with a stroke of a key, and he checked the machine just to be sure he had it. He then told the crew he wanted to go up to the east crack and check it out. The less attention they drew to the area they just fished the better it would be the next day. No other boats were in that area yet, so no one was the wiser. Seth put *Tar Baby* on plane and headed for the east crack while the crew straightened up the cockpit. John changed the wind-on leader and hook on the Moldcraft "Red Bailey" lure that got the hook up.

By the time they got to the east crack there were six boats already fishing it. They were all spread out and trolling over a square mile area. There were a few flocks of swirling birds working some small surface bait pods. Roff's service had mentioned that they thought there would be current movement over the east crack. Seth slowed and had the crew put the spread in the water. He watched the fish finder closely as he moved *Tar Baby* back and forth over the drop off. In the back of his mind he hoped no one scouting the mid-crack found the large ball of bait where they had hooked the marlin. He finally marked some bait after two hours of trolling, and they hooked up a couple of 20-pound black fin tuna. Seth told John to keep one so they could have a sashimi appetizer back at the dock, so they released the second one. They kept trolling until 1:30 and then headed for the dock. Seth had to check in at the tournament desk at the Conch Republic Restaurant before 4:00 p.m.

Everyone was in good spirits for the ride in, and Seth felt good about the pre-fish. He thought they had a good shot at an early marlin at the mid-crack tomorrow morning. He told the boys not to talk to anyone about the marlin they had released.

He had Gene put the tuna flag up on the starboard outrigger and said, "Boys, tell anybody that asks where we caught the tuna."

An hour later they were back at the dock, and Seth and John went over to sign up while Bobby and Gene cleaned up the rods and boat.

"Let's get that tuna filleted and on ice, Gene," said Seth and he walked off the boat. "We'll be back in about thirty minutes for some thin sliced raw tuna and wasabi sauce."

Seth recognized several of the captains who were standing in line waiting to sign in at the tournament desk. He had seen them before at different Florida and Bahamas tournaments. He waved and shook hands as he was recognized. The core of the billfish tournament circuit was a close-knit group of professional captains who moved the boats from tournament to tournament for their owners. John gathered up the crew t-shirts, duffels, and other give-aways while Seth signed in. Many fishing gear companies helped sponsor these tournaments and took the opportunity to put samples of their products into the hands of the very anglers they wanted to buy their products.

"Hey, Seth!" someone called from behind.

Seth turned and recognized Mike Rouse, the long time captain of *Really Reel*, a Hatteras fifty-two. Seth had met Mike at a B.B.C. tournament in the Bahamas about four years ago.

Mike shook Seth's hand and said, "Good to see you, Seth. I heard you fished today, anything biting?"

"Well, we picked up some nice tuna over a big bait pod at the east crack this morning."

"See any billfish?"

"Not yet," Seth lied, hoping he wasn't turning red.

Mike patted him on the back and said, "Thanks, Seth, and good luck."

"Same here … catch'em up, Mike."

Mike would start at the east crack in the morning and so would every other captain Mike talked to tonight. Tuna in an area meant bait, and sometimes a marlin would show up to pick off the smaller tuna. But Seth would rather take that chance than have a bunch of boats at the mid crack tomorrow morning. *Just a little gamesmanship … thought Seth … and so much for free advice.*

The tournament kick-off dinner was always lots of fun. Seth and his crew ran into a lot of people they knew and the energy level at the kickoff was very high. Around 9:00 p.m the captains and crewmembers started heading to their boats for the night. Everyone was looking forward to the Gran Prix start out in front of Mallory Square in the morning. *Tar Baby* would not be among the fastest boats, as many of them could run thirty-five knots, but Seth knew exactly where he was headed and at twenty-four knots he would be on his spot for the 8:30 a.m. lines in.

Seth and the boys had a nightcap back at the boat, and then tried to fall asleep so the next morning would come quickly. Sleep didn't come fast for Seth, however. He was worried about Beau's situation, and Seth tossed and turned for a good hour before he finally fell asleep.

CHAPTER ELEVEN

BEAU was wide-awake before first light. He looked at the alarm clock on his way to the head and saw it was 5:30. After pulling on his shorts and a shirt, he checked out the engine room and all the fluid levels. There were no signs of any oil or coolant leaks. The v-belts on the engines and generator looked fine. Robert E. had taught Beau that as long as a v-belt had no age cracks in it, and stood a little proud at the top of the sheave, that it was still good. As soon as it showed age or wore down into the sheave, it should be replaced. The bilges had stayed nice and dry. Beau was beginning to gain some confidence in the big Bertram 54. He climbed back out of the engine room and went into the cabin.

Hector was already up and had made a pot of coffee. He was just putting some breakfast rolls in the convection oven as Beau walked in. Beau must have awakened him when he ran the electric head earlier. Hector was definitely the more alert of the two brothers, as he seemed to be aware of where Beau was at all times.

"Time to get Luis up, Hector," said Beau as he approached the galley to pour a cup of coffee. "This leg is going to be the roughest yet, and Luis will do better if he's up from the beginning."

Beau took a roll and his coffee and headed for the fly bridge. Once there, he started the engines and then punched three new waypoints into the GPS. They would need them to navigate to Kingston, Jamaica, which was close to four hundred miles away.

Beau had been impressed with the Furuno network navigation system that had been installed on this Bertram. It integrated the radar, global positioning system, and the depth sounder onto one screen. The captain could use the whole screen for any one function, pull up any two functions, or see all three at once. The system also allowed a customized on screen information box containing a digital format that included speed over the ground, distance, time to go to a destination, and an almost limitless list of other useful data. Beau liked to have the GPS map on half of the ten-inch screen, and the radar on the other half set at twenty-four miles. Within that setup he had programmed in a small box along the port side of the screen containing, digital depth, speed, time and distance to destination, the course to the destination, along with the actual compass heading, alternator output, and the time of day. If something of interest popped up on the radar screen, he could push a button and fill the whole screen with the radar and still have the digital information. The radar was capable of tracking any targets speed and direction, giving warning of a potential collision course. Beau was glad he had it because he knew there would be heavy freighter traffic in the Windward Passage tonight.

As *Chica* left the island of Great Inagua behind, Beau pushed the big Bertram up on plane. He started running south at eighteen knots in three to four foot seas with a twelve-knot southeasterly breeze aft of his beam. Later that day, after he had cleared the eastern tip of Cuba, the wind backed into the east and freshened to twenty to twenty-five knots. Beau was then able to steer a more southwesterly course and put the larger waves on his port aft beam. The big Bertram rolled as she surfed down the swells. Beau turned the gain down on the autopilot, and pulled the throttle back until the boat was moving at fifteen knots on top of the swells and twenty knots surfing down them. After a while the three of them got into the rhythm of the yaw and roll and the ride wasn't that bad. At 8:00 that evening they had covered nearly two hundred miles. Beau slowed down to eight knots, just before dark, and transferred two drums of fuel into the tanks.

Later that night they passed the Navassa Island Light off the north coast of Haiti and were then able to steer a more westerly course for the ride around the Morant Point Light on Jamaica's eastern coast. Once they made it around Morant Point, with the Bertram running at ten knots downwind, they should be within an hour or two of Kingston when the sun came up.

Beau continued running thru the night and he set up two-hour watches with the Fernandez brothers. The wind continued to be brisk out of the east-southeast all night as they cut across the Windward Passage. The moon shone on the water as it played in and out of the passing clouds and accentuated the phosphorus wake that *Chica* was leaving behind her. The big radar screen showed a number of large ships moving north and south in the passage throughout the night, but none came close enough to cause alarm. Beau got a couple of hours sleep and had instructed Hector to wake him if a ship came within six miles of them while he was off watch.

Beau took the helm back at first light. The GPS had them forty miles from the Kingston sea buoy. The seas were still running five to seven feet, so Beau pushed the Bertram back up to fifteen knots as the visibility improved. An hour later, as the sun climbed, Beau could see the mountains of Jamaica. They were a beautiful sight in the morning light. In less than two and a half hours Beau spotted the Kingston sea buoy. The GPS had put them right on it. He could see Port Royal Point ahead of them and he had Hector fly the yellow quarantine flag from the starboard outrigger.

Beau hadn't been to Jamaica for a good many years. He had helped his dad deliver a brand new 46 foot Hatteras sportfish, like Seth's, to Jamaica back in the seventies. He vaguely remembered a marina and an old white wooden hotel right around Port Royal Point. He thought it was called Morgan's Landing, and he recalled the wealthy British owner waiting for them on the dock dressed in a white linen suit and a Panama hat. He had welcomed them with a big smile and spoke English with a clipped British accent. Beau had cleaned the salt off the boat as the new owner and Robert E. concluded their business. After that they took the new owner for a sea trial to familiarize him with his new vessel. Beau remembered being oddly uncomfortable the whole time he was in Port Royal. They stayed in the hotel that same night and flew back to Tampa the next morning through Miami.

Robert E. hadn't delivered many boats throughout his long career in the marine business, and he especially didn't care for long ones like the one to Jamaica. Beau suspected that he took the job so he and Beau could spend the time together, and he could have Beau's undivided attention. Beau remembered that he was gently lectured during the whole trip. He needed lecturing because he was all ready displaying the bad judgment that would plague his personal life later. Robert E. was working him hard at the boat works and he knew his performance there wasn't up to expectations. He was drinking too much and was running with a fast crowd. He knew that his father was concerned. Even though Robert E. didn't get through on the personal issues, the trip helped hone Beau's boat handling and navigational skills. As he thought back, Beau loved Robert E. for trying.

The Port of Kingston was first and foremost a working harbor full of freighters and tankers. It was one of the largest natural deep-water harbors in the world. Kingston thrived on commerce, not tourism. There were no yacht basins or marinas along the Kingston waterfront. Beau's only hope for a marina berth was in Port Royal. He hoped Morgan's Landing was still in business. He piloted *Chica* around Port Royal Point and there was the white hotel and marina. Nothing looked like it had changed in the last thirty-some years.

Beau looked across the large harbor towards Kingston, five miles in the distance. The Kingston waterfront had grown five-fold. Scores of docked container ships and large cranes dotted the shoreline. Beau hoped Morgan's had diesel fuel, so he wouldn't have to go to one of the large bunker docks over in Kingston. He hailed Morgan's on the VHF and inquired about a slip for tonight and fuel. The dock master answered affirmative to both requests, and Beau breathed easier.

The dock master was waiting for them at the fuel dock. Beau pulled alongside, tied up, and shut down the engines. The dock master introduced himself as Avery.

Beau said, "Avery, my name's Ronald and this is my crew, Hector and Luis. I'm wondering what the custom's drill is? It's been more than thirty years since I've been here."

Avery answered in his lilting Jamaican accent, "You can clear customs at the airport, and it's only ten minutes down the road, Mon."

"Can we fill up the fuel tanks first and then put her in the slip?"

"Of course you can, and then I'll call you a cab to take you to customs. How many gallons do you anticipate needing?"

"I'm guessing about a thousand gallons, including the two empty drums."

Beau handed Hector the pump nozzle, and Avery turned on the diesel pump.

Beau gathered the passports and the ships papers. When Hector was finished fueling Beau started *Chica's* engines and backed her into a slip over by the swimming pool. Avery helped them tie up and hooked up the shore power. Beau turned off the generator, which had been running non-stop since they left St. Petersburg. He would check it over thoroughly before they left the next day.

His plan was to check in and out of customs today, rest up, have a nice dinner tonight at the old hotel, and turn in early. They could stretch their sea legs in the quaint, historic, town of Port Royal, and maybe take a swim in the pool. Tomorrow, they would leave at first light on the longest and potentially most difficult leg of their trip. The passage to San Andres Island would take them across over more than four hundred miles of open Ocean and past some dangerous banks and shoals. They would run all night, and depending on the sea state they might be at sea for close to thirty hours. It would take almost all the fuel in their tanks, plus the 220 gallons in the four plastic drums. Their destination was a four-mile wide by eight-mile long speck of rock in the Caribbean Sea. Beau had never been there, but it was reported to be a beautiful island. San Andres was located about 120 miles east of the Nicaraguan coast. Strangely, the island belonged to Columbia which was 350 miles to the southeast.

Avery had called a cab for Beau, and he started up the dock to catch it. As he left *Chica* he cautioned Hector and Luis not to leave the boat until he came back. In each port it was the captain's duty to clear his crew through customs, and they were not allowed ashore until he did. Beau got into the cab and was at the airport before he even got comfortable in the cab's backseat.

The customs agents weren't busy when Beau arrived at the customs and immigration area at the airport. The agent gave him all the necessary forms and Beau filled them out. The agent wanted to know their next destination, and Beau told him San Andres, Columbia.

He asked if he could prepay the twenty-seven dollars per person exit tax, and the agent replied, "No problem, Mon."

The agent filled out the exit forms and Beau gave him eighty-one dollars in cash. The agent stamped the three passports and handed them and the visas to Beau.

Beau thanked him and went outside, hailed a cab, and rode back to Port Royal. As Beau rode back to the marina in the cab, he got the same déjà vu feeling he had felt when he pulled around Gallows Point in the Bertram this morning. He felt he had been here a long, long time ago. When he got back to the marina he went directly to the boat and took the quarantine flag down. He suggested to Hector and Luis that the three of them go to the hotel for lunch.

Hector said, "Looks like a dull little town, Beau!"

"Well, that's the idea, Hector. We're here to fuel up and get some rest. You'll be back at sea before you know it. After lunch we'll take a walk around Port Royal and stretch our legs. I know it's hard to believe, but over three hundred years ago Port Royal was one of the wildest party towns in the entire world."

Hector and Luis looked at Beau like he had lost his mind.

A few minutes later they settled into their chairs in the dockside restaurant that overlooked the harbor.

Beau said to Hector, "Remember to fill the fresh water tank when we get back to the boat." The tank held 250 gallons and Beau was guessing they would be lucky to have 50 gallons left.

"So Beau, tell us about this party town," said Luis with a laugh.

Beau smiled and said, "Well, over the years, Port Royal has been home to some of the nastiest and most famous pirates in the whole Caribbean. Henry Morgan and Blackbeard were both here. The fort you saw on our way in was built by the British in the sixteen hundreds to protect their possessions in the area. They let the pirates headquarter here as long as they didn't bother British shipping. In turn, the pirates acted as a deterrent to the French and Spanish. More and more pirates moved their ships here, and the town rapidly grew around the fort. The pirates always had plenty of gold, and they needed materials and stores for their ships and crews. Merchants moved in and set up shop, and the town kept expanding.

By 1675, Port Royal had over six thousand residents. Henry Morgan had reformed and was appointed Governor by the King of England. He helped the British Navy, as they started to eliminate the pirates in the Caribbean after England signed treaties with Spain and France. The population here supported numerous taverns, drinking houses, and houses of ill repute. At Port Royal's pinnacle, over half the residents were pirates and prostitutes. Besides them, there were shipwrights, riggers, sail makers, and merchants of all kinds. The tavern and innkeepers grew wealthy. Over two hundred ships a year passed through Port Royal. The town counted over two hundred buildings on the fifty-acre spit of land. Many considered Port Royal as the richest town in the New World. Others considered it a moral cesspool full of cut throats, thieves, whores, and despicable pirates."

"A lot like Miami, huh, Luis?" laughed Hector.

"Well, it doesn't look like fifty acres now," said Luis.

"Actually you're right, Luis," answered Beau. "Early one morning in 1692, in less than one hour's time, Port Royal was hit by an earthquake and a huge tidal wave. Two thirds of the town disappeared under the sea and over four thousand people were lost. The sunken part of the town is right out the window in front of you. But it's fifty feet under water. The God fearing people, who were left alive, figured God had destroyed Port Royal because of the rampant wickedness and sin. The British Navy took full advantage of the situation and eliminated the remaining pirate population. Lord Nelson was dispatched to Port Royal early in his career to clean out the few pirates that remained, and by 1725, most of the pirates had been hanged or were hiding out far from Jamaica. The sight of pirates left to hang for months out at Gallows Point, until their flesh was gone and the sun bleached their bones, was quite a deterrent. We'll take a walk up to the fort after lunch."

"So, you've been here before, Beau?" asked Hector.

"Yes," answered Beau. "A long time ago my father and I stayed at this marina, after delivering a Hatteras here from Florida. The boat's owner took us for a tour and filled us in on the towns checkered past."

Suddenly, Beau had a flashback and the sunken portion of the town rose out of the water right before him. It receded as fast as it had appeared, but it left Beau shaken.

"Beau, you look like you saw a ghost!" said Hector. "Are you O.K., man?"

"Yeah, I'm all right. But I *do* think there are lots of ghosts in this town," replied Beau as he tried to regain his composure.

They ordered lunch and when they were finished the three of them walked around the fort and what was left of the town of Port Royal. Beau was certain that he had been there before. Not just on the trip with Robert E., but in another life. Everything in the old town looked and felt so familiar. When he gazed out over the water where the sunken part of the town now was, he instinctively knew where each street was and what buildings had been on it. Whenever he walked anywhere near Gallows Point the hair on the back of his neck stood up. Maybe he had the soul of a pirate. That certainly would make some sense.

Beau finished the town tour with Luis and Hector and exclaimed, "I'm going back to the marina, and I'm going to take a swim in the pool. Why don't you two scrub down your boat and then join me for a drink poolside? *Chica* could use a good hosing to get the salt off."

Hector mumbled something under his breath and Beau reminded him that it was their boat, not his. He walked back to the boat and fetched a towel. It was the last one in the guest head. Beau gathered up all the dirty towels and sheets in all three cabins and loaded them in the washer/dryer combo located in a locker forward of the crew cabin. He also threw in his dirty t-shirts and fishing shorts. Beau asked Hector and Luis to bring him any dirty whites they might have, and once the load was complete he dumped in some Fab and turned the combo on. The load would be clean and dry by the time he finished his swim. Hector and Luis were busy swabbing the foredeck as he left the boat and walked towards the pool.

It had been almost eight days since the robbery in Ybor City and Luigi was dreading tonight's upcoming meeting with No Nose.

There had still been no leads concerning the whereabouts of Ricardo Cabeza and his unknown henchmen. They, and three million dollars, had virtually disappeared into thin air. Unless something broke soon, Luigi knew it wouldn't be long until he would start to become No Nose's whipping boy.

CHAPTER TWELVE

DAWN broke to another perfect day in Paradise. The *Tar Baby's* crew were all out of their bunks before 6:00 a.m. and ready to go at 7:00. The prevailing southeast breeze was right at ten knots. Seth started the engines and the Hatteras left the slip at 7:15. As Seth cleared the breakwater he could see thirty or forty boats already milling around in the channel near Mallory Square. He looked behind him and counted a like number coming out behind him. The Grand Prix start at 7:30 promised to be thrilling and maybe a little dangerous. With this in mind, Seth jockeyed *Tar Baby* into position on the west side of the channel where there was more depth and room to bail out if it became necessary. There was no room for that on the Mallory Square side … just docks and rocks. The committee boat was anchored right in front of Mallory Square, where a crowd was forming to watch the start.

At precisely 7:30 a.m. the committee boat fired a shotgun in the air, and the tournament had officially begun. Seth picked an open spot in the fleet and quickly put the Hatteras up on plane. There were several large sport fishes to his portside, and they all pulled ahead within the first two to three minutes. Seth fought over their wakes and moved a little eastward as the fleet cleared the rocky point below Fort Zachary Taylor. Some of the boats continued south into the ship's channel, and others broke more westerly towards the wide southwest channel to take them to the west crack. Seth stayed a little west of the ships channel, running in six to eight feet of water, opting for less traffic. There was plenty of water for *Tar Baby*, as she only drew four feet. By the time the fleet cleared the ships channel sea buoy the old Hatteras had been passed by two-thirds of the fleet. At that point the remaining fleet started to fan out with better than half of the boats heading towards the east crack. The rest looked headed for the mid-crack area. As the boats spread out further, the concentration of stern wakes decreased, the ride became smoother, and Seth's heart rate dropped back to normal.

Tar Baby had been rolled by five or six sportfishes over 65 feet, traveling at thirty knots or better. Seth wondered when these wealthy owners would start having 100 footers built for them that ran that fast or faster. Was the size and speed necessary to win tournaments, or was it all an ego thing? It would be interesting to compare a 100 foot sportfish's ability to fight a really large marlin against a Merritt 37 or 43 which are arguably the best handling sportfishing boats ever built.

The ride out to the mid-crack was over before Seth knew it. At 8:30, they were only about a mile from the spot where they caught the marlin yesterday. Seth ran another half of a mile, and then pulled the Hatteras off its plane and slowed to eight knots. The crew put down the outriggers and deployed the exact same lure and teaser spread that they had used the day before. Seth let the bridge teasers out until they ran on top of the first stern wave. Fifteen minutes later they ran over the spot on the mid-crack ledge where they had hooked up yesterday morning. Seth checked the spread behind the boat, and he liked the way the lures were smoking and popping. He scanned the area from his vantage point on the fly bridge and noticed several boats working the west side of the mid-crack about a mile away. There were more boats further south out on the Wood's Wall drop off but for now they were alone and over their spot.

Seth turned back to the west and worked the boat back over the drop-off. On the next zigzag back to the east, Seth picked up the large bait school he had been looking for on the fish finder. The radio had been quiet, so nobody had caught a billfish yet. *Tar Baby* cleared the drop-off and Seth swung south and west back toward the drop-off continuing his zigzag pattern across the bait and the drop-off. As the boat crossed the drop-off Seth turned his attention to the lures trailing the boat. He saw a large dark shape trailing the right rigger lure.

The shape made a quick move forward and Seth yelled, "Marlin, right rigger!" just as the line came out of the outrigger clip with a loud pop.

The dark shape disappeared and Seth put the boat into a port turn and headed back east. The marlin had come up on the same Moldcraft "Red Bailey" lure that had worked the day before. As Seth brought *Tar Baby* out of the turn the marlin came back up under the accelerating "Red Bailey" and literally pounced on it.

The 50-wide Penn reel began to scream as the marlin peeled line off of it.

Seth yelled, "Fish on, right long rigger!"

He pulled the throttles back to idle, but left the engines in gear.

He shouted down to John, "Get on that rod!"

The rest of the crew had all ready started to bring in and clear the other rods. Seth wound in the bridge teasers with his overhead double pancake reel. Bobby started pulling in the transom teasers when he and Gene had finished clearing the rods.

John pulled the rod from the rod holder and was in the chair in almost one motion. He flipped off the clicker and settled into the chair for the fight. Line was still coming off the reel at a fast clip, but it was beginning to slow some as the fish angled away from the boat.

Seth grabbed the VHF radio mike and hailed the committee boat saying, "This is *Tar Baby*, one blue marlin hooked up at 9:07, comeback."

The committee boat acknowledged and issued him a release number. Seth settled down and started fighting the fish. Gene had stationed himself behind the fighting chair to move it as the fish or the boat changed direction. Bobby stood by to handle the fish when it got to the boat. Seth took the port engine out of gear and the line stopped coming off the reel. The marlin came really tight and John started to gain back line, as the big blue jumped three times about two hundred yards behind the boat.

"Reel, John, reel," yelled Seth from the bridge. "It's a nice fish, about two hundred and fifty pounds."

The marlin wasn't big enough to weigh in, so Seth would work to release it as quickly as possible.

"Get ready to reel fast, John," Seth called down. "I'm going to run the boat up alongside of the fish."

Seth pulled the starboard single lever control back in reverse and started to spin the boat, then moved forward towards the fish, slowly at first, then faster as John gained more and more line back. When the reel's spool was full again he turned off to port, and then left only the port engine in forward gear at idle speed. John had the marlin twenty yards behind the boat and he kept the pressure on. The marlin surfaced, all lit up, and jumped four or five more times. The boys whooped and hollered with each jump. John kept the fish tight and reeled him closer to the transom.

Bobby put on the leather gloves to handle the leader and the fish's bill, and moved to the transom as the leader reached the rod tip. Gene had gone into the cabin for his camera and was already videotaping the fish in the water. Bobby took the leader and led the marlin around the port side of the transom. He grabbed the fish's bill and held the release number card over the marlin's head while Gene took some more video shots as the marlin thrashed at boat side. Seth got a few digital camera shots from the bridge, while Bobby was removing the hook, just for insurance. Bobby made sure that water was running through the tired marlin's gills as the Hatteras idled forward and then he released him. The marlin glided slowly away and then with one powerful flick of his tail disappeared into the deep blue ocean.

Seth radioed the committee boat saying, "This is *Tar Baby* reporting one blue marlin release … right now!" He glanced at his Rolex and noted the time was 9:22.

The crew was high fiving and dancing around the cockpit like they were on "Soul Train." Seth was grinning from ear to ear. The committee boat came back on the air with their congratulations and a confirmation of a blue marlin release at 9:22 a.m. *Tar Baby* had the first marlin release of the tournament and was in the catbird's seat. Only one weighed marlin over 600 pounds, or two released marlin, could beat them. The next boat that released a marlin would be in second place.

Seth calmed the crew down and they quickly put the lures back out so they could continue fishing. Seth knew that this early in the tournament they were probably only as good as their next fish. Of course, the marlin battle had not gone unnoticed. Within ten minutes of the hook up there were eight boats moving in and around them. They were all very courteous and had kept their distance during the fight. But now they all were feverishly crisscrossing the area where the fish had been caught.

Seth settled himself down and brought up the waypoint for the second bait school they had found in this area yesterday. *Tar Baby* slowly zig-zagged south along the mid-crack towards it, leaving the newcomers behind.

As they closed in on the second number Seth noticed two large sportfish boats working near his waypoint. He joined the large boats and they crisscrossed each other, and the bait school, for about two hours. *Tar Baby* caught two nice dolphin around 25 pounds, but none of the boats raised a billfish.

Off to the west Seth watched a 58 foot Carolina built sportfish, named *Stinger,* drift live baits under two kites. During the two hours he kept his eye on them, he saw them catch one small sailfish. It was getting close to mid-day when Seth had the crew pick up the spread so he could head to the west crack for the afternoon bite.

On his way to the west crack, Seth pulled up three GPS waypoints that had held large bait concentrations a couple of days earlier. He headed for the one where they had caught a couple of nice dolphin during the pre-fish. Large marlin also liked to feed on big dolphin. Seth slowed the boat as they got close to their destination and the boys put out the trolling spread. He immediately started marking bait on the fish finder. Seth noticed a cluster of boats about a mile away, indicating someone had caught or was fighting a fish. They trolled the west crack area the rest of the afternoon and saw a lot of bait, but they could muster only a few 10 to 15- pound dolphin.

The radio had crackled on and off all morning and afternoon, and Seth knew of two other marlin releases and several sailfish releases. They pulled the lines out at 4:30 feeling they were off to a great start but were being hotly pursued. After a brisk ride in, the crew cleaned the boat while Seth turned in the marlin release video and picture and had their largest dolphin weighed.

After a hot shower and a change of clothes, they all headed for the open bar and fish fry at the Conch Republic. They got there just as the results were being posted and they were indeed in first place in the marlin division. Three other marlins had been released later in the day, so *Tar Baby* was in first on time. In the fun fish division, the boats that had fished the east crack had caught plenty of tuna in the 25 to 30-pound class. Add to that, a couple of 40-pound wahoo and several 30+-pound dolphins, and the leading fun fish boats had 50 to 65 points.

Seth liked his team's position. If they could catch and release another marlin, and add a couple more respectable tuna, wahoo, or dolphin in the next two days, they had a chance to win the overall tournament.

There was a lot of chatter and back slapping at that night's fish fry. A great deal of inaccurate information was also exchanged amongst the participating captains and anglers. When dinner was over and the leader board was checked again, most of the participants went back to their boats or hotel rooms to get some sleep in anticipation of another long day on the Atlantic. Seth and his crew turned in before 10:00 p.m. They were exhausted but happy.

Tournament day two dawned much like the day before, but the air was more humid and the temperature was forecasted to be 94 degrees. The wind was still light and prevailed from the southeast. Seth and the boys ran out the main ship's channel after leaving the dock at 7:00. Seth reviewed in his mind what he had learned at the fish fry the night before. They had caught the only marlin at the mid-crack. The other three were caught on Wood's Wall near the west crack. Seth decided to give the mid-crack another shot, so he ran *Tar Baby* almost straight south. He looked for bait in vain on the depth recorder and trolled all morning with no signs of fish. The radio crackled with reports of a white marlin and three sailfish being caught and released to the west of them. *Reel Crazy*, an Albemarle 32, had caught the white marlin. They also were one of the four boats that caught a marlin on the first day. That put *Reel Crazy* in first place, although a white marlin was worth only two hundred points.

Seth stuck to his plan and fished the mid-crack numbers the rest of the day. They caught a 35 pound wahoo in the afternoon, along with a few small dolphins. The crew was not as effusive as the day before on the ride in, but they knew they were still in the hunt. Two blue marlin releases had been reported to the committee boat during the day, but they were first marlin for those boats. Seth thought *Tar Baby* was probably in second place after day two.

The fish fry was again at the Conch Republic restaurant, but tonight it was a "Pirates of the Caribbean" theme party. All the crews had known this in advance and dressed in headscarves, pirate hats, and eye patches supplied by the tournament committee. The restaurant staff was also dressed in pirate costumes and joined in the fun. There was much pirate lingo heard in the evening conversations, such as, "Arghh", and "Aye, matey". The tournament chairman, who was dressed in full pirate captain regalia, even quoted a famous line from "Long John Silver" during his recap of the overall tournament scoring. He fabricated a fictitious weather report, citing unusually rough seas and high winds for the third and last day of the tournament, adding that, "Them that dies will be the lucky ones." He also offered a short prayer before he opened the buffet line and ended it with, "Arrr-men." In reality the weather was co-operating, although a few large thunderhead clouds that formed offshore during the afternoon had threatened the fleet. During the banquet, one came ashore and opened up over Key West and drenched the island with a forty-five minute torrential downpour. Late afternoon and early evening thunderstorms are a way of life in Florida and the Keys in the late summer season, and they also serve as a reminder that it's Hurricane season.

Seth made the rounds at the pirate bash and found out that both blue marlins had been caught in the west crack area. Also, a second white marlin had been caught there that afternoon. Seth knew the west crack would be crowded with boats the next day, but he had no choice. The common sense rule is to fish where you know the fish are, and to also cover your competition.

Seth looked around at the tournament crowd all dressed up like pirates. They were all having a wonderful time. The band was rocking out an Eagle's tune, while John and Gene were talking and laughing with a group of guys from St. Petersburg. Bobby was at the bar making time with a chesty barmaid who was dressed up like an English wench. Seth hoped he and his friends could continue to fish and have fun at these tournaments in paradise for a long time to come. Then Jeb's latest phone call crept back into his mind.

Jeb's cell phone call, just after they had tied up at the dock that afternoon, had been a disturbing intrusion on his mid-tournament, positive, mindset. He had asked how the tournament was going, and Seth had filled him in about the marlin they released and his strategy for tomorrow. But Jeb's call had really not been about the tournament results. He told Seth that Beau had not shown up at the yard all week. Jeb had called Beau's apartment and left messages to no avail. He had finally ridden out to the beach yesterday, after work, and had found Beau's apartment undisturbed. There were no signs that Beau had been there, and Beau's truck was parked and locked in the parking lot. He wondered if he should report Beau missing to the police. Seth told him not to worry at this point, as Beau could be off on one of his escapades. After all, he'd been gone a week or more before and had never had the decency to let anyone know where he was. They decided that they would let everything slide until Seth got home Sunday, and Seth would handle it from there.

Seth was worried, though. The picture of Beau talking to the two large Cubans kept running through his mind. The Bertram 54 he had seen the other night, while at Mallory Square, was still bothering him. *How many Bertram 54's have a swim platform and Schaefer outriggers …* he thought? Seth wondered if he was being paranoid, and it was all just a coincidence. Beau would probably show up at the boatyard on Monday, with a sheepish grin on his face, and blame it on some woman he had met in a bar and too much Mount Gay rum. But the bad feeling Seth felt in the pit of his stomach persisted.

Seth walked over to where Gene, John, and the St. Pete crowd were talking and joined the conversation. On his way across the room he dodged a couple of Ernest Hemingway look-a-likes. Seth had to laugh to himself, everywhere you went in Key West this time of year you saw Ernest Hemingway. At the fish fry, the night before, there were seven of them together at the bar. The

Ernest Hemingway look-a-like contest always coincided with the Key West Marlin Tournament. There were at least fifty Hemingway doubles around town all week. That contest would be decided tomorrow afternoon while the boats were out fishing, and the Hemingway winner would present the winning trophy at the tournament banquet tomorrow night just as the real Hemingway had done years before.

Seth finally decided he'd had enough partying and started back to the Hatteras. He was tired, but he knew he would have a hard time falling asleep. Tomorrow's fishing strategy was on his mind, and Beau's disappearance was also bothering him more each day. Seth got back on *Tar Baby* and walked forward to his cabin. He was just climbing into his bunk when he heard John and Gene come in.

About an hour later he heard Bobby slip in alone.

CHAPTER THIRTEEN

BEAU walked directly to the pool bar at the Morgan's Landing Hotel, ordered a Mount Gay rum and coke, and then set it on the edge of the pool. He dove into the crystal clear water and swam back to his drink. The water felt fresh and cool on his weathered skin. He was alone except for two tourist couples that were sitting in the water at the shallow end of the pool. Their accents gave them away as British, and they were obviously on their third or fourth rumrunner. Beau finished his drink in the cool pool, and then he climbed out to get another. He sat with it at a table under some large shade palms and relaxed. Before too long, Hector and Luis showed up and went to the bar. They ordered two mojito's and then came over and sat down with Beau.

Hector looked at Beau and said, "Luis and I, we could use some women."

"This is neither the time nor the place, Hector. Wait until we get to Panama or Costa Rica. Right now we can't risk being detained and chance losing this good weather window we have. Remember, you have to get back to Miami before you arouse any suspicion among your mafia associates. This is no time for the little head to be thinking for the big head."

Hector thought about it and grudgingly agreed.

He quickly changed subjects and asked Beau, "When you sell *Chica* in Costa Rica, how will you send the money to us? Remember, we paid $580,000 in Naples for her."

"Hector," said Beau patiently. "When we get to Los Suenos Marina in Jaco, I'll list her with the H.M.S. brokerage office there. When she sells I will subtract the expenses for fuel, maintenance, dockage, and the ten percent brokerage commission from the selling price. Then I'll wire the remaining money to whatever account number you give me in Florida. You know … maybe you should set up an account in the Caymans or Mexico. It would be a lot safer for both of you. Does that all sound fair?"

"What choice do we have?" said Luis. "We have to trust you."

"Luis, our partnership is dependent on you two keeping me alive and me keeping you two happy."

"Yeah, but you have the upper hand," chimed in Hector.

"Look," said Beau. "As long as No Nose Cipriano doesn't suspect you two, and thinks I'm dead … all three of us prosper. You two get to go back to the United States, and I don't. I think that makes us kind of even."

Luis started to order another round, but Beau declined saying, "I'm going to check out the engine room now that it's cooled off and then take a shower. Why don't we have dinner about 7:00 and turn in early. This next leg could be tough and we need to be at our best. I'll check the weather forecast with the dock master now."

Beau stopped in at the office on his way back to the boat and asked Avery for a forecast to San Andres. He typed in a request on his weather fax system.

While they waited for the fax Avery asked Beau, "What happened to your fingers?"

Beau had taken off the gauze bandages and Band-Aids now covered the stub ends. They both were healing, but were still very sensitive.

"Oh, I had a hatch drop on them," answered Beau without hesitation.

"Well, they look like they're healing quite well," said Avery winching at the thought of a heavy hatch pinching off your fingers.

A couple of minutes later the fax came through.

"Looks like moderate to rough going the first half of the trip," said Avery. "But if you leave right at dawn tomorrow the approaching low should stay off your stern. Tomorrow night and the following day, as you arrive at San Andres, the wind should be fifteen knots from the northwest with four to five foot seas. If you wait until the next day to leave, you'll have two days of north-northeast wind at twenty plus knots with a six-foot sea. There's also a tropical depression moving west across the Virgin Islands, but you'll be below the hurricane latitudes by tomorrow night."

Beau thanked Avery and gave him a "Big Ben" for a tip saying, "We'll be leaving at first light."

At seven, the three partners sat down for dinner in the Morgan Hotel dining room. Dark wood paneling and old colonial style furniture surrounded them. The service and food both turned out to be excellent. Beau ordered a filet mignon, medium rare with béarnaise sauce, asparagus, and garlic mashed potatoes. Hector and Luis both ordered roast pork, peas and rice, and a salad.

The waiter suggested a Spanish Rioja wine that turned out to be very good. The dinner progressed with little conversation. The brothers seemed relegated to, but basically unhappy with, their present situation. Beau did not trust them at all, and he was all the more resolved to eliminate them after they cleared the Panama Canal. He had checked behind the electric motor cover on the Raritan Crown head, and the loaded .38 was still there. Hopefully, it would not be found if customs searched the boat in San Andres or the Panama Canal. Hector and Luis would have to hide their guns or declare them and hand them over for safekeeping when they transited the Panama Canal. Considering their considerable bulk, they might get away with keeping them in their waistbands with their Hawaiian shirts covering their lumps and bumps. It would be good for Beau if the Panama Canal customs agents found the brother's guns and confiscated them, but the chances of that happening were slim.

They finished dinner and Hector and Luis each ordered a Cuban cigar and a snifter of brandy. They smoked the cigars and spoke to each other sporadically in Spanish. When they finished the brandy, Hector paid the bill with money from the stash. Beau also settled up at the front desk for the slip, fuel, and other charges. They were ready to shove off at dawn for San Andres Island. The trio walked back to the boat in silence, split up in the salon, and went to their respective cabins for the night.

Beau woke up with a start, and realized he had been dreaming. He awoke just as the trap door had opened up under him, out on Gallows Point, pulling the noose tight around his neck. He was bathed in sweat, was out of breath, and his heart was racing wildly. *Thank God, it was only a dream …* thought Beau. Still, he checked his neck for the rope which did not exist. He got up and went to the head and splashed cold water from the faucet on his face. He was wide-awake and full of adrenalin from his imagined close call with death. Even though it was only a dream, his body had reacted as if it were real. Beau decided to take a walk to shake it off. He pulled on his shorts and a t-shirt. Then found his boat shoes with his feet. He slipped out of his cabin, opened the aft salon door, and quietly closed it behind him. He stood in the cockpit for a moment and looked around. *Chica* and the all the other boats in the marina were pulling at their lines in the freshening trade wind breeze. The full moon bathed the marina in an eerie white light, as low moving clouds skidded across the face of the moon. There definitely was some heavier weather moving this way.

Beau silently got off the boat, walked down the dock, and past the old white

hotel. He glanced at the moon and figured it was 3:00 or 4:00 in the morning. He
walked through the deserted streets to the fort and climbed up the steps to the
ramparts. Beau looked out over the wall at a moon-lit sea that was tossed with
whitecaps. He at once felt an affinity and revulsion for this place. He wondered
what might have happened to him here. His next thoughts were that his imagina-
tion was either running away with him, or maybe he was actually losing his mind?

He heard a sound behind him and as he turned, a large shape came out of
the shadows at him. Beau reacted instinctively with a Judo move that he had been
taught in the Rangers. He tossed the large assailant over his hip and the attacker
landed flat on his back with a thud. Beau started to finish the move with a blow
to the man's throat, but pulled the punch back as he realized it was Hector.

"What the hell," said Beau? "What are you doing sneaking up on me like
that?"

"Damn-it, Beau," said Hector, a little hoarsely. "I couldn't sleep either and I
was just trying to catch up with you."

"I thought you were someone who was trying to mug me."

They both laughed nervously, as Beau helped Hector to his feet. But Beau
didn't buy it for one moment. Hector had been tracking Beau in case he was
trying to pull something. They didn't trust Beau anymore than he trusted them.

"Where did you learn to handle yourself like that, Beau?"

"I was lucky you didn't fall on top of me, Hector, you must have lost your
balance," lied Beau. "Let's go back to the boat; the sun will be up in a couple of
hours."

As they walked back to the boat Hector rubbed his shoulder and his back in
silence. Beau knew that he had given away the fact that he could handle himself
against a much larger man. Unfortunately, he had lost one element of surprise.
He knew that Hector would be on his guard around him now, and would never
buy into Beau being just lucky.

When they climbed back on *Chica* Beau told Hector, "Try to get a couple
hours sleep, we still are leaving at dawn."

Hector nodded and went to his cabin. Beau climbed back into his bunk, but
he couldn't go back to sleep. He watched the clock until 6:00 in the morning
and then got up and started to ready the boat for the next leg. He put the new
waypoints in the GPS on the fly bridge and entered them in the hand-held back
up. If the ship's twelve-volt system ever failed he wanted the AA battery powered
backup to work immediately.

Hector and Luis were up and ready to go by 6:30 a.m. Beau had Hector stow everything that was loose and latch all the cabinets. This leg of the trip promised to be the roughest yet, although Beau expected the wind and waves to be aft of their beam as the low pressure passed behind them. Beau started the engines and the generator, while Luis disconnected and stowed the shore power cords. He climbed up to the bridge as Hector slipped the lines and stowed them. Beau piloted the Bertram out of Morgan's Marina and around Gallows Point. He had the same uneasy feeling that he had when he came in yesterday. The hair on the back of his neck stood up until he cleared the Kingston sea buoy. He vowed to never come back to Port Royal or Jamaica, if he could avoid it.

Beau took a deep breath and pushed the throttles up to planning speed. The sea looked black and was covered with whitecaps and long streaks of foam. He set the autopilot at 230 degrees and backed off the throttles a couple hundred revolutions. He adjusted the trim tabs to bring the bow up a few degrees and settled in. *Chica* was riding the swells nicely and he noted the boat speed at twenty-two knots. He looked back one last time at the mountains of Jamaica as the morning sun broke over them. He was frankly confused by the flashbacks, dreams, and the feelings he'd had in Port Royal for the past twenty-four hours. He decided it was best to put it out of his mind and better to focus on the trip to San Andres.

He glanced at the paper chart in front of him and traced the course he had drawn to San Andres. He began memorizing the shoals and rocks they had to avoid. Soon he had formed a mental picture in his mind of the planned course. When he visualized San Andres he anticipated a high rocky island surrounded by beautiful, clear, azure colored water. He had never seen a picture of the island or been told what it looked like by anyone. On the chart the island was just one of four small yellow specks, a hundred miles off the Nicaraguan coast. *What it looked like didn't matter ...* thought Beau ... *what did matter was that it was their next fuel stop.* Beau rechecked the engines gauges and settled in for the morning watch.

Luigi Scuzzi was elated. He had just received a call from one of his news desk informants at the Key West Citizen detailing the bizarre death, and subsequent identification by police, of Ricardo Cabeza in that city. He had no other details, except that an unidentified person had died along with Ricardo in the Key West Aquarium's shark tank. *Killed by a shark in a public aquarium* ... thought Luigi ... *now that was bizarre!* But, he was relieved; at least he had something positive to report to No Nose Cipriano. Now the mafia's dragnet could be pulled in tighter and they would soon be closer to recovering the $3,000,000. Wall-to-Wall speculated that Ricardo and his unidentified shark tank mate were probably double-crossed by some additional accomplishes. He was also surprised that they had made it to Key West undetected. At any rate, he was finally off the hot seat.

CHAPTER FOURTEEN

EVERYONE in Key West Bight seemed to be up and on the docks at dawn on Saturday morning. The anticipation of a big finish was on every tournament crew's mind. Seth woke the crew at 6:00 a.m. and then headed for the marina showers thinking … nothing *like a hot shower to get the cobwebs out of your brain.*

The crew wolfed down a quick breakfast at the marina deli and was back at the boat rigging baits and checking tackle before 7:00. Seth left the slip at precisely 7:30 and hooked up the engines when they cleared the breakwater. He ran the boat out towards the west crack at full speed knowing he needed to get there as close to the faster boats as possible. Every fishing minute might count as the tournament wound down towards lines out at 3:30 this afternoon. The Hatteras ran through the two to three foot chop on top of the long Atlantic swells smartly. The wind had increased to ten to fifteen knots and that would favor the larger boats over forty feet.

Seth would continue running large lures, but he had John take two 30-pound class spinning rod combos out of the rod locker. John rigged them with circle hooks and naked ballyhoos. The rods would be kept at the ready in the cockpit with the rigged ballyhoo on ice in a small cooler. If a white marlin swam into their spread, Gene and Bobby would quickly reel in the lures and teasers, while John would cast a rigged ballyhoo to the white. White marlins were finicky eaters and they were seldom fooled by the large blue marlin lures. When the white marlin made a move and took the ballyhoo, John would leave the bail open on the spinning reel and let the fish take the bait with no resistance. Six or seven seconds later, he would close the bail and let the fish come tight as he swam away with the bait in his mouth. This method had proven to be the surest way to hook up the wary white marlin.

Even at *Tar Baby's* top speed, the newer, faster boats were starting to pull away already. Seth wasn't happy with the situation. But you had to go where you thought the fish were, even if there was going to be a crowd of boats. Gene came up the fly bridge ladder with that day's copy of the Key West Citizen. He read Seth the latest news bulletin about the aquarium victims, as they ran to the west crack.

"Wait till you hear this," said Gene as he started reading. "The Key West Police Department's Chief Detective, Troy Bagget, revealed today that they have positively identified one of the shark attack victims as Ricardo Cabeza of Tampa, Florida. Mr. Cabeza has been further identified as having ties to the Cipriano crime family and has a long arrest record. Other details of his death are being withheld, as this is an ongoing investigation. The other victim has not been identified at this time."

Seth said, "Sounds like maybe some Tampa wise-guys crossed some of the Russian mafia down here. But what a novel way to whack them out; using a shark as a murder weapon. If that's the case, it will probably start a turf war down here."

"The Cipriano's are tough customers," said Gene.

"I guess that shoots the gay lover's double suicide theory," laughed Seth.

An hour later, *Tar Baby* arrived at the west crack. There were already sixteen boats there, but Seth didn't see *Reel Crazy*, the Albemarle 32, who he had been sure would be there. Seth throttled back to eight hundred r.p.m.s, and the crew quickly dropped the outriggers and put out the spread. He had John change both long rigger rods to 80-pound combos. Seth headed the Hatteras for the crack drop-off and the GPS number where the largest bait concentration had been seen earlier. Seth marked clouds of bait below them, and birds worked the water all around them. Seth continued to zigzag the boat across the drop-off moving south and away from the other boats working the area. About fifteen minutes later, Seth spotted some debris about one hundred yards to starboard. He called down to the crew to be alert as he worked *Tar Baby* over toward it. The debris turned out to be a small piece of an old wooden dock with a large piece of rope trailing behind it. Seth could see some small dolphin under the wood, and they quickly came out and hit the passing lures.

Only one dolphin got hooked on the large lures and Seth yelled, "Pull that dolphin in quickly, I'm going back to circle the wood again."

He put the boat in a starboard turn and started a tight circle around the debris. He was just coming out of the turn when the left rigger went off, and the reel began to scream. Seth shouted down to John to get in the chair and steered the boat out of the tight turn before pulling the throttles back to idle. Gene and

Bobby started clearing the other rods as John picked up the screaming rod and reel. John switched off the clicker, but he still couldn't start to reel because the fish had not slowed down. John headed for the fighting chair, and Gene hooked him up in the bucket harness. Ten seconds later the blue marlin broke the surface three hundred feet behind the boat with a spectacular series of jumps. The crew stood and watched almost dumbstruck. This was a very large marlin. She might be the Key West record fish they had all dreamed of catching. The huge blue resumed taking out line at a steady pace.

Seth spun the boat 180 degrees to starboard and started after the magnificent fish. He pushed the throttle up to fifteen hundred r.p.m.s, as the big marlin greyhounded, and John started taking line back on the reel. Seth throttled back to one thousand r.p.m.s, as they got closer, but kept after her.

He fumbled for the VHF mike with his right hand, found it, and called the tournament committee boat saying, "Tournament committee this is *Tar Baby* reporting one blue marlin hook up at 9:43," while taking a quick look at the Rolex on his left wrist down at the steering wheel.

Seth caught his breath, as the committee boat confirmed his transmission and assigned them a release number. Meanwhile, John continued to recover line from the marlin. Seth needed to get another look at this marlin to see if it had a chance to break the Key West record of 784 pounds. If it did, that fish would be worth $100,000 and they would easily win the tournament. But, if it were smaller than six hundred pounds, they would lose the four hundred points a release was worth and the fish would be worth zero points. Seth continued to pursue the fish hard and fast so it would not sound. He had fought three and four hundred pound marlin that had sounded in deep water and had either lost, or killed those fish while planing them up.

John had gotten back most of the 80 pound line, so Seth throttled back to idle and turned the bow away from the big fish. John eased the drag up to about 20 lbs. and started pumping her from the fighting chair keeping his legs straight and reeling himself up off the chair over and over. The line started coming up and away from the transom ten yards at a time. Seth and John worked in perfect concert to keep pressure on the big fish. The fish was coming up to the surface. The big blue jumped again fifty yards off the transom. Gene got some nice videotape of the jumps and Seth started to back the boat down on the fish as John retrieved more line.

Seth had gotten a good look at the fish on her last series of jumps and called down to the cockpit, "She's not big enough to weigh boys, but let's get a fast, clean, release on her, and I think she'll win us the tournament."

After the second look Seth had refigured the marlin at about 500 to 550 pounds. He continued to back the boat down hard on the fish as John wound her closer and closer to the transom. Soon he could see the dark outline of the marlin coming up from the deep, and next the double line was coming out of the water. Seth stopped backing and went into forward just to keep the fish off the transom a bit. He could see the fish clearly now. It was all lit up in fluorescent blues. Gene was taking video, and Bobby was pulling on the leather gloves to handle the leader when it came up.

As Bobby leaned over the transom in anticipation of grabbing the leader, the big fish surged away towards the port transom corner and leaped skyward. Her jump took her high enough that Seth made eye contact with her huge right eye at the apex of her jump. It gave Seth the chills and almost stopped his heart for a second. The marlin came down and missed the port transom corner by just inches. She proceeded to swim under the boat, which pulled John, who was clipped into the bucket harness, out of the fighting chair, across the deck, and finally crashed him into the port gunnel. The only thing that kept him from being pulled overboard was the six-foot safety strap attached from the reel to the fighting chair stanchion. John hit the gunnel with a loud thud. Seth hit the throttles to clear the fish aft, but he was too late. The monofilament line broke when it touched the running gear under the boat, and the great fish was gone. That split second when the fish had looked Seth in the eye had transfixed him at very moment that he should have been moving the throttles forward.

Seth shifted the levers into neutral and slid down the fly bridge ladder, his feet never touching the steps. Bobby and Gene were unclipping John and the rod and reel from the harness and straps.

John looked dazed and Seth checked his ribs while asking, "Are you o.k. John?"

"I think so," he said as he moved his arms and legs. "Everything seems to work. I think I just had the wind knocked out of me."

He had a strawberry mark on his left knee. Also, his left shoulder had taken a hard blow to the gunnel and was all ready starting to show a bruise. If *Tar Baby's* cockpit gunnels hadn't been padded, John probably would have broken his shoulder.

"I thought that fish was coming right into the cockpit with us," said Bobby.

"I'm glad I didn't get a chance to grab the leader, that fish was way greener than we thought."

"Thank God she didn't come down in the cockpit," said Seth. "It could have been much worse than just losing a nice fish! I'm thankful for that."

Gene was standing next to the tackle center in the back of the cockpit, looking at his video recorder.

"I got the whole thing on tape, John," he said excitedly. "It really scared me more the second time I watched it!"

Seth turned to John and said, "I think we should go in and have you checked out at the emergency room, John."

"No way, Seth, I'm O.K., I didn't hit my head and I might be a little sore later, but I'm all right. Let's fish on!"

Seth just laughed and said, "You guys would fish on unless you were unconscious. Well, if that's your decision, let's reload and get the spread back out there. Gene, there's an extra 80-pound rig in the salon. Bring it out and put another black and green Moldcraft wide range on it."

Seth climbed back up into the fly bridge and put the boat back in gear. He radioed the committee boat and reported that they had lost the marlin. He could almost hear the competition's collective sigh of relief. That marlin probably would have won the tournament, and Seth felt responsible for losing her. He had frozen when the marlin had looked him in the eye. The fish seemed to have an understanding of what was happening, and it was like she was communicating ... *not this time, Captain!* Seth was disappointed that he'd lost the marlin, but at the same time felt lucky that things hadn't ended tragically. Most of all, he was full of respect for the magnificent marlin.

Tar Baby resumed fishing, and the lures were soon chugging and popping behind the boat. Seth found the drop-off and continued to follow it south. In consideration of the pounding John had just taken, Seth had the crew switch positions in the cockpit. Bobby would be the designated angler, Gene would wire, and John would handle the camera and clear rods.

There were still almost six hours to lines out, so this tournament was far from over.

CHAPTER FIFTEEN

THE voyage to San Andres was going smoothly. The seas were four to five feet, and Beau felt fortunate that they were running down wind in the brisk breeze. After his watch was over, and he had prepped the Fernandez brothers for their watch, Beau checked the engine room and bilge pumps. He planned to double watch Hector and Luis during the day so he could rest enough to pilot *Chica* all night. They would be running past a number of unlighted reefs and shoals during the night. They passed the marked and lighted Pedro Bank about 9:00 a.m. At 2:00 in the afternoon, Hector woke Beau as they approached the New Bank, which rose from seventy-five hundred feet to within ten feet of the surface. Beau checked the course and their location on the GPS, and then he located the breaking waves through the ship's binoculars. *Chica's* course left the bank a safe mile to starboard. The wind had switched into the northeast quadrant and the sea swells were increasing in height and moving closer together.

Beau slowed the boat to eighteen knots as he adjusted the course for the 120 mile run between North Cay and the Serrana and Quita Sueno banks. There was twenty-five miles of deep water separating them, and his course ran directly between them favoring North Cay. It would be dark when they got there, and *Chica* would be running at ten knots as they passed within a couple of miles of North Cay. Beau would also have to navigate past Low Cay which was unlit and Providencia Island just below it, sometime before dawn. If all went according to plan, they should arrive off San Andres at 9:00 or 10:00 a.m. that morning.

As night fell, Beau slowed the Bertram down to ten knots, and he and Hector transferred all four drums of diesel fuel without incident. Beau washed the diesel off his hands and climbed back up on the bridge. He coached Hector on the course and then catnapped on the fly bridge bench seat, instructing Hector to wake him if he was sleeping when they neared any of the rocky cays. He knew he would be instinctively awake as they neared these hazards, but better safe than sorry. Nighttime passages played tricks with novices, with the lights looking either closer or farther away than they really were. Any slight bit of fog or haze in the air just made it trickier. Beau remembered the story Robert E. used to tell about a skipper coming into a jettied inlet in a light fog at night. He lined up with what he thought was the red flashing sea buoy light and only after he was high and dry on the jetty's rocks did he realize it was a gas station sign, a block inland, with a tree branch moving with the wind in front of the lighted sign.

Hector awakened him in the middle of the night to deal with a passing fishing trawler he had spotted on the radar. Beau stayed awake from that point on.

"Hector, go down to get some sleep, and send Luis on up to the fly bridge. Ask him to please make me a sandwich and some coffee."

Later that morning, he located the flashing light on North Cay through the binoculars. It was easy because the GPS precisely located it for him. Beau continued to mark *Chica's* location on a paper chart every thirty minutes in case he lost the GPS for some reason. He would need that information if he were forced to dead reckon to his destination using the compass, speed, depth, tide, and wind direction to figure his course. Mariners had navigated this way for centuries also using the sun and stars for additional help in finding their position at sea. Unfortunately most new skippers these days didn't mark a chart as they progressed along a route and had never practiced dead reckoning. They were totally dependent on their Global Positioning Satellite devices.

As dawn neared, Beau navigated past Low Cay leaving it to starboard. He could hear the surf pounding on its rocks as he passed, but he could only see the flashing light ahead on Providencia Island. It was unsettling to hear breaking waves in the middle of an ocean, but he could, however, see the rocky cay and the island clearly on the ship's radar.

Beau punched in his last waypoint, which was for San Andres Island, as he worked past Providencia. He zoomed out the GPS chart until San Andres appeared on the screen, some fifty miles away. The dotted course line had *Chica* passing fairly close to Providencia Island which they also had to leave to starboard. The island had a beacon and was easy to see on the radar, but Beau was glad dawn would soon be breaking. He had not seen any ship traffic since the fishing trawler, and the radar was set for a twelve mile range. Beau set the radar alarm for six miles and settled in for the rest of the ride.

Beau had the time and the quiet to think about his exit plan for Hector and Luis. Luis was asleep on the bridge bench seat and Hector was asleep below. He needed to invent a way to surprise the brothers now that they knew he had

training in hand-to-hand combat. Beau suddenly remembered an old movie that
he had seen on late night television, the Bogart classic, "Key Largo". The movie
starred Humphrey Bogart, Lauren Bacall, and Edward G. Robinson. A ruthless
mobster (Edward G.), who had been deported to Cuba, had brought himself
and a large sum of counterfeit money to Key Largo, both illegally, in a chartered
sportfish. He planned to sell the counterfeit bills for a price to the Miami mafia,
collect his money, and motor back to Cuba on the chartered sportfish.

An unexpected hurricane had interfered with his plans. The mafia contacts,
the mobster, and his men from Cuba were trapped in Key Largo by the hurricane. They all had checked in at the Old Key Largo Hotel, which was owned
by an old man and his young daughter (Bacall). They had just hired a returning
World War Two veteran (Bogart) to captain the hotel's sportfish. All three of
them lived on the premises. As the hurricane approached the Cuban sportfish's
captain spooked and fled with his boat in the middle of the night. The local
deputy sheriff then became suspicious of the gangsters during a routine pre-
hurricane check of the hotel. When he doubled back to confirm his suspicions
the gangsters ultimately shot and killed him.

The payoff arrived from Miami just before the hurricane made landfall, and
the money was exchanged. The deported gangster shanghaied the hotel's boat
captain and boat, and threatened to kill the hotel owner and his daughter if he
didn't cooperate. Immediately after the hurricane passed, they set out for Cuba
in the hotel's sportfish. Bogart knew as soon as he got them to Cuba he was a
dead man. There were three armed gangsters on board; the boss, and his two
henchmen. The boss and one henchman went below, while the third stayed in
the wheelhouse holding a gun on Bogart.

When the boat arrived at the Gulf Stream, about ten miles off shore, the sea
got rougher, and there was a lot of Sargasso weed and debris in the stream from
the hurricane. Bogart worked the starboard throttle back and forth like something had wound up around the propeller. He continued to work the throttle
while putting the shift in neutral, explaining to the gangster in the wheelhouse
there must be weeds or something wound around the shaft and prop. He asked
the gangster to go back and look over the transom to see if there was anything
streaming out behind the transom. The mobster didn't hesitate and walked aft
and leaned over the transom. As he leaned over, Bogart gunned the boat forward
and the momentum threw the gangster over the transom and into the water.
Bogart scrambled to the transom to pick up the gun that the mobster dropped

on the deck as he was catapulted over the transom. Then he climbed quickly up onto the boat's hardtop. The two gangsters below had been thrown to the floor when the engine was gunned and when they recovered the boss sent his other henchman up to see what happened. Bogart shot him dead through an open hatch in the hard top. Bogart then exposed the boss as a coward and tricked him into coming up into the wheelhouse with a promise of a money split. A hand-to-hand fight ensued and the gangster pulled a hidden gun during the struggle. The gun went off as the two men grappled and it was the mobster that was shot dead … end of story.

Beau decided to get rid of Hector with the "over the transom" trick while he was on watch with him and Luis slept below. Then he would shoot Luis from the bridge, with the gun he now had hidden in the head, when Luis came out of the salon door to check out the sudden commotion. Beau would move the hidden gun from the head to under the fly-bridge helm during their passage through the Panama Canal or at his first opportunity. Any plan was dependant on some luck, but this one had possibilities if the brothers hadn't seen the old movie. Beau was betting his life that they hadn't.

Luis was still asleep and snoring loudly on the bench seat in front of the helm. Beau looked down at the GPS, and it showed they were well clear of Providencia Island. About an hour after first light Beau could faintly see the island of San Andres looming off the port bow. As the sun rose in the sky, he could see that the island's rocky coast stood fifty to seventy-five feet out of the most beautiful blue water he had ever seen. He could see no beaches, just rocks and cliffs. Their course had them heading for the main harbor's red and white entrance buoy. The closer they got to San Andres the more beautiful the water became. There were at least five or six distinct shades of blue. Beau had never seen anything like it anywhere. When they finally ran up close to the sea buoy, Beau slowed *Chica* to an idle. He picked up the VHF mike and called the fuel dock in the harbor on channel sixteen.

"San Andres fuel dock, this is the motor vessel *Chica*, come back."

The radio crackled back, "*Chica*, this is Nene's Fuel Dock, go to channel fourteen, *Senor*."

Beau switched to channel fourteen and requested permission to come to the fuel dock for diesel, and asked about the Columbian customs procedure. He was told to call the Serena Custom's Agency on channel sixteen and to proceed to the fuel dock in the inner harbor. The agent on duty was named Rene Cardoza, and he agreed to meet *Chica* at the fuel dock in thirty minutes to handle customs for them. Hector put up the yellow quarantine flag on the way down the well-marked channel into the small harbor's turning basin. Beau idled up to the fuel dock where he and Hector began pumping diesel into the Bertram's fuel tanks and drums. Rene Cardoza arrived and checked them in and out of San Andres for a $40 fee. Beau asked him if he knew anything about the Panama Canal transit requirements.

Rene replied, "Yes Sir," and started to rattle off a long list of regulations and requirements. When he was finished he added, "It would be smart to engage an agent in Panama to assist you with your passage. You also need to call ahead at least forty-eight hours ahead of your arrival in Colon, if you want to start the transit process the day after you arrive there."

Beau asked Rene if he could recommend and call an agent for them in advance. Rene suggested an independent agent named Fonda Johnson. Rene said she spoke perfect English and had been educated in the United States. Beau asked Rene to call her as soon as possible, and wondered how long a canal transit usually took.

"What I hear from yachts coming in from the Pacific side is two or three days for the paperwork, and then ten to twelve days waiting for an apprentice canal pilot to take you through. The passage can be done in a day in a yacht such as yours. If you are in a hurry and are willing to pay $2250 U.S. dollars, you can hire a senior canal pilot, and retain an agent, like Ms. Johnson, who can do the paperwork in one day. Then you can transit the next."

"That sounds like the answer for us. Please contact Ms. Johnson and arrange it for us."

"I'll call her immediately, Mr. Santos, but there's more you should know. The fee for your yacht is $850 U.S. dollars, and you will need two additional line handlers at $55 a day, plus you will have to rent four, 125 foot, 7/8 inch diameter lines, and tire fenders. They only take cash or credit cards."

"None of that will be a problem. Please call Ms. Johnson and tell her we'll be in Colon the day after tomorrow. Beau handed Rene a crisp one hundred dollar bill and asked, "Will this cover the call?"

"*Gracias, Senor,*" replied Rene.

"Just two more questions, Rene. Can you ask her where we should tie up and refuel in Colon, and please get her cell phone number for me?"

"No problem, *Senor*," answered Rene as he headed towards his car. "I'll be back here in thirty minutes."

Beau finished fueling the boat and the four drums. They wouldn't need the extra fuel for the next leg, but the Columbian diesel was so inexpensive he couldn't pass up the bargain. He paid for the diesel and asked the dock boy where they could stay overnight. He recommended the Club Nautico and gave Beau directions. He had to go back out the inner harbor channel and then turn to port after marker ten and follow the deeper water in the lagoon between the shore and the reef. The dock boy assured Beau the clear water was easy to read.

Rene arrived a few minutes later, and announced, "You are all set with Fonda Johnson and here is her cell phone number. She suggested that you dock at the Panama Canal Yacht Club in Colon. She will advise them you will be arriving the day after tomorrow. Call her when you get there and she will pick you up and take you through customs and the port authority process. She will arrange today for a canal pilot for the day following your arrival."

"Thanks for your help, Rene," said Beau while shaking his hand.

"Have a safe voyage, *Senor*."

Beau started the engines and Hector cast off the fuel dock lines. He eased the Bertram out of the channel, and then turned to port between markers ten and twelve. He stayed in the deeper water along the shore line and nervously watched his depth finder as he idled *Chica* towards the distant docks and buildings he could see further down the lagoon. The water never got shallower than nine feet.

Halfway to Club Nautico Beau realized that the hair was standing up on the back of his neck. He was having another déjà vu event in this beautiful lagoon. He suddenly realized that San Andres Island looked exactly as he had pictured it in his mind's eye back in Jamaica.

He quickly put the feeling out of his mind and set his sights on the Club Nautico. It was an impressive sight, built out over the water with a transit dock around it. Beau called the dock master and got permission to tie up alongside for one night. There were several sailboats anchored in the lagoon seventy or eighty yards off the dock. Beau was all ready looking forward to another dinner in a restaurant and a soothing swim in the club's swimming pool.

The plan was to sleep late tomorrow and not leave for Panama until the afternoon. They would run hard until dark, and then travel at their customary ten knots all night. As soon as they could see in the morning they would pick it up to twenty-four knots and arrive in Colon about 9:00 or 10:00 a.m. If they were able to follow that plan, they would have enough time to clear customs and the Port Authority and be ready for the transit through the canal the next day. Beau was counting on Ms. Johnson to cut through the red tape.

Beau coasted *Chica* up to the club's dock, and the dock master asked him to moor in stern first, as he had more boats coming. Beau put Hector on the bow, with the anchor at ready, and pivoted the Bertram around. He eased the bow out about two boat lengths from the dock and had Hector drop the anchor. He called for Hector to make it fast to the bow about a half a boat length from the dock. The anchor caught, and *Chica's* transom stopped just short of the dock. Luis tossed the two stern lines to the dock master, and he crossed and tied them to the dock cleats.

"Well done," said the dock master, as Luis handed him the 50-amp shore cord to be plugged in.

Beau came down off the bridge and placed a fender between the transom and the dock saying to the dock master, "What is your name, *Senor*?"

"Orlando," answered the young dock master.

He was a handsome, olive-skinned, man with a large grin and flashing dark eyes.

"Welcome to Club Nautico. Where did you come in from?"

"Port Royal, Jamaica," answered Beau. "We ran all night."

"Port Royal is a famous pirate town. But, did you know that Henry Morgan and Blackbeard were reputed to have buried their treasure on this island? There are people here still digging for it now."

Beau just rolled his eyes and thought … *I guess I must have been here before, too.*

Then he said to Orlando, "You know it might be close to this exact spot."

Orlando laughed, "You're probably right, Senor, this island is only thirty-two square miles. Let's get you signed in. I'm sure you're tired after your long voyage."

Beau signed in showing Orlando their customs paper work and checked on the dining room hours. He came back to the boat to find that Hector and Luis were all ready hosing the salt off the boat. Beau was pleasantly surprised; maybe these two were trainable after all. After lunch, a swim, and a couple of cervezas, the three of them showered and had a nap in their cabins.

Beau woke up about 6:00 p.m. and in turn, woke Hector and Luis saying, "How about dinner at the Club Nautico, tonight? Orlando says they have the best seafood on the island."

Beau radioed the office and made reservations at 7:30. The brothers mixed up a couple of Cuba Libras and sat in the salon smoking their ever-present cigars. Beau went up on the fly bridge to escape the smoke and plotted tomorrow's course on the GPS.

After a nice dinner of local snapper, rice and beans, and fresh broccoli, Luis announced that he and Hector were going to look around town.

Beau said, "Why don't you wait until tomorrow morning and, we'll rent a taxi and tour the island for a couple of hours?"

Luis said, "No, we want to look around the town, tonight."

Beau laughed to himself, he knew they wanted to check out the hotels and bars for some local pussy.

"Well, go ahead, and I'll stay here. I want to read the Panama Canal information that Orlando gave me when I checked in."

Beau paid the dinner check and waited a good fifteen minutes at the bar after they left in a taxi before going back to *Chica*. He went straight to the guest head and retrieved the snub nose .38 from behind the head cowling. He found a roll of duct tape in the utility cabinet in the galley and headed for the fly bridge. Beau carefully taped the pistol under the helm, just above the access door, with two narrow pieces of tape. He secured it to the metal hydraulic tubing connected to the helm unit. He doubted anyone would find it in a search, and it would afford him quick accessibility when he needed it.

With that done, he settled in his cabin and began to read the Panama Canal transit rules and regulations. About two hours later he heard Luis and Hector come back aboard the boat and go into their cabin. He turned off the reading light and almost immediately fell asleep.

CHAPTER SIXTEEN

SETH took a deep breath to clear his head. He put the lost marlin behind him and concentrated on the task at hand. The marlin battle had attracted a number of boats to their area … eleven to be exact. *Tar Baby* trolled in that crowded situation for another hour before Seth decided they needed to make a decisive move. He glanced at his Submariner and saw it was after 11:00 a.m. The radio had not reported any more hook-ups, so Seth made a decision.

He called down to the crew in the cockpit, "Boys, I have a hunch that if we run out to the "Hooters" we might get one more shot at a marlin before lines out. But, we've got to pick up and run out there now so we're in position if there's an afternoon bite."

There was no discussion, and Bobby said, "Let's go for it!"

The crew pulled in all the lines. Seth reeled in the bridge teasers and pulled up and secured the outriggers. He then put the boat up on plane and headed for the "Hooters" at twenty-four knots. He could tell from the cockpit chatter that the fight had come back into his crew. They arrived at the "Hooters" just before noon and were trolling again with the full spread out in five minutes. Seth had the crew change the transom teasers to two holographic Mylar strip fish dredges. Hopefully they would look as much like a bait school to the marlin as they looked to Seth and the crew.

They trolled the "Hooters" for two hours with no success. He checked his watch often, knowing that lines-out was at 3:30 the last day of the tournament. They also had only until 5:30 to make it back to the dock in the event of a late hook up. Seth searched the area incessantly with his binoculars looking for weed lines or bird action. Finally, he saw some birds working about a mile away. As he trolled towards the birds, he could see a weed line and some floating debris. He also noticed a boat approaching the area on plane from the north.

As Seth maneuvered the Hatteras along the weed line, he noticed a couple of small dolphin underneath, but they didn't come out. All of a sudden the radio barked, "Committee boat, *Cracker Boy* … hooked up!" Seth had been concentrating on the weed line so hard, that the radio message made him jump halfway out of the helm chair. *Cracker Boy*, a Bertram 50, had released a blue marlin on day two, and if this was a blue, and they caught and released it, they would probably win the tournament. Seth had no luck with the first weed line so he continued on to the second where the birds were working. Seth glanced behind him, and he immediately recognized *Reel Crazy*, the Albemarle 32, getting out her spread on the other side of the first weed line. Seth wondered if it was just a coincidence or was *Reel Crazy* covering his competition. Seth hoped the little dolphins under the first weed line would keep the newcomers busy for a while.

Seth got closer to the working birds, and was carefully running the left rigger lure a few yards off the second weed line. Then he saw a dark shape come out from under the weeds. The fish knocked the left rigger out of the outrigger clip and continued across to the right long rigger lure and started to trail it. Seth knew it was a white marlin because of its small size and extra large pectoral fins.

"White marlin, right long!" yelled Seth. "Bring in the long riggers and drop back a rigged ballyhoo."

Gene and John reeled in the long rigger lures, and the marlin followed them toward the transom and lit up like a neon sign. Bobby free-spooled the spinning rod, rigged with a naked ballyhoo and a circle hook, back toward the advancing marlin. When the incoming lures came past the free spooled ballyhoo, Bobby stopped the advancing line with his index finger and held the rod tip up high to make the ballyhoo skip on the surface. The lit up white marlin saw it and made an aggressive move and picked up the ballyhoo in his mouth. Bobby let him eat it, with no drag pressure and the rod pointed right at him for about six seconds, as he swam away. Then he closed the spinning reel's bail and let the fish come tight. When the marlin came tight the circle hook set itself and the fight was on. The white marlin jumped and tumbled as he raced away from the boat. But the circle hook had embedded cleanly in the corner of his mouth and held fast. Bobby kept the pressure on the acrobatic white as he jumped time after time. He was a nice one at about sixty or seventy pounds. Gene and John cleared the other rods and pulled in the strip tease dredges. Seth wound in the bridge teasers after he called in the hookup to the committee boat and got a release number.

Ten minutes later he called the committee boat back and reported, "One white marlin release for *Tar Baby* ... right now!"

John had gotten a couple of good pictures of the white with Gene holding the release number card right on top of him. The gamble was paying off. Seth assumed *Cracker Boy* was still fighting the marlin since he hadn't heard that it pulled the hook or that they had successfully released it. *Reel Crazy* was still trolling, and was past them and into the third weed line. *Tar Baby* had about an hour left to fish, and the tournament was still up for grabs.

The crew put the lures and teasers back out, and Seth started trolling back towards the birds that were still working the second weed line. *Tar Baby* and *Reel Crazy* both continued trolling the weeds with no success. At 2:52 p.m., the radio came alive with the sound of *Cracker Boy's* captain calling in a big blue marlin release. That blue marlin put *Cracker Boy* in first place with little more than a half an hour to go. Seth continued scanning the area with his binoculars and finally spotted a piece of debris about a half a mile to the south. He couldn't pass it up, so he turned toward it and throttled the boat up to twelve knots to get there quickly.

He yelled, "Debris!" down to his startled crew.

Seth concentrated on the debris, and as it got closer he thought it looked like part of a roof. Finally he could see two or three rows of shingles protruding from the water.

"Must be hurricane debris from somewhere," Seth said to himself.

Before he could complete his turn and slow down to troll by the debris, the flat line that they trolled right behind the boat in the white water wake popped its rubber band. The reel started screaming as the fish took off. Bobby grabbed the rod and just held on.

Seth still wasn't sure what it was, as the crew brought in the other lines and cleared the teasers. The fish ended his scorching run after stripping over two hundred yards of line from the 50-wide Penn reel. Bobby put a Bimini belt on and started to reel and apply some pressure on the fish. The fish put up a stubborn fight stopping every minute or so to violently shake his head.

Bobby said, a little out of breath, "It feels like a big wahoo, Seth."

Seth agreed, and hoped it was a big one. A big wahoo would be worth a point a pound, and if it was the largest caught in the tournament, $750. Bobby soon brought the fish to the boat, and it was a large one, indeed. Gene made an excellent gaff shot on the fish as Bobby led the wahoo up the side of the boat. It took both of them to lift the fish into the boat. Seth estimated the wahoo at close to sixty pounds. Bobby and Gene put the wahoo in the fish box and covered it with ice.

Seth looked at his watch and it was 3:28. He found *Reel Crazy* with his binoculars and she was still trolling. He watched her stop and reel her lines in at 3:30, as the committee boat announced lines out on the VHF. It was over, and for the first time that day Seth felt exhausted and strangely relieved.

He called down to the crew, "Good job guys!" "I believe we've got a good shot at second place. It looks like *Cracker Boy* has won it with two blues, so let's go home and see what happens."

Seth pulled up the outriggers and headed the Hatteras north as he punched in the Key West ship channel GPS waypoint. Seth put the boat up on plane, and as he recounted the last day of the tournament in his mind, he was both elated and deflated. It had been quite a day. He felt sure they would place in the top three, but sometimes you miss a radioed in fish. He also had no idea what *Reel Crazy* might have in her fish box. He was proud of his friends for sucking it up after John had been pulled out of the chair, and he was thankful that John wasn't hurt badly or worse. Anytime you are hooked up to a huge fish there are any number of dangers present. He was over losing the fish, but he knew he would chastise himself for freezing for that one critical second for a long time. But, he was happy with himself for gambling on the "Hooters". He hadn't heard of any more billfish caught at the Wood's Wall, except for *Cracker Boy's,* since they left, and the "Hooters" had paid off with two nice fish. But mostly, he knew they had been very lucky all day.

The boy's cracked a cold one for the ride in, and they all came up on the fly bridge. Their admiration and friendship for each other was evident. It had been a good tournament for them, and they were stoked. After a second round of beers Gene started kidding Bobby about the bartender he had been pursuing the night before.

"Bobby," said Gene. "What was it that attracted you to her? Did you have similar political views or was it her huge tits?" Bobby, who had put on quite a bit of weight during the last few years, was never at a loss for words.

He offhandedly replied, "You know, Gene, I've been a tit man my whole life, but now that I have two of my own …. I'm really not that impressed."

Everybody got a good laugh and they started speculating on whether they were going to be second or third.

Soon the Key West radio towers loomed on the horizon, and *Tar Baby* joined the tail end of the parade of tournament sportfish boats making their way into the south channel. Fifteen minutes later they were back in their slip at A&B

Marina. Bobby and Gene washed the boat and the rods and reels, while Seth and John loaded the wahoo in a dock cart and headed for the weigh station. When they got to the Conch Republic, there were a few dolphins, wahoo's, and tunas in front of them. Seth took a look at the other fish, but none of them were half as big as their wahoo. Seth sent John over to the committee desk with the white marlin release picture and affidavit, while he waited with the wahoo. John seemed to have recovered from the fish fight; his shoulder and knee were just sore.

The weigh-in crowd cheered when the weigh-master hung *Tar Baby's* wahoo on the scale.

"59 pounds," shouted the weigh-master. The crowd cheered again and the weigh-master said to Seth, "Biggest one so far, captain."

Seth smiled as they took the wahoo into the kitchen. He left to look for John. John was all ready at the bar with Gene and Bobby, talking with the winner of the Ernest Hemingway look-a-like contest who was recognizable by the large crown on his head. He was surrounded by at least fifteen of the losers, and they all seemed to be pleasantly toasted. Seth wasn't sure if he was watching a dream or a nightmare. But, they all seemed to be having a great time and probably didn't realize how bizarre it all looked. It was classic Key West, where the next thing they might think up was a Liberace look-a-like contest. Seth didn't even want to think about that. He had one cold one, and then headed for the showers.

Seth felt tired, but the hot water beating on Seth's shoulders felt great. The shower gave him his second wind, and he was looking forward to finding out what place they had finished. He was feeling good about the situation, but then his mind strayed and a little reality crept in. Tomorrow he would run *Tar Baby* home with Gene, leaving at the crack of dawn. It would take about ten hours after fueling at 6:30 a.m. in the harbor. The weather forecast looked good; southeast winds ten to fifteen knots, with a chance of an afternoon thunderstorm. Once home he would have to deal with his brother, Beau. He was hoping Beau would surface after the weekend like he had so many times before, but Seth had a nagging feeling that this time there might be more to it.

The awards banquet was is full swing when Seth and the boys got to their table at the Conch Republic. The tournament organizer had brought a great old Key's band down from Islamorada, "Big Dick and the Extenders". They were playing Barrett Strong's 1960's hit, "Money", as Seth's crew sat down to dinner and drinks. Seth hoped he was eating his own wahoo, but no matter whose it was it was great. It was grilled on the rare side, with just a little limejuice on it. Bobby was already making a move on a Cher look-a-like, who was sitting at the next table with a group of Hemingway contestants and their wives. All of the Hemingway's looked totally toasted at this point. Seth wondered if the Hemingway couples ever got confused after a few drinks as to whose husband was whose.

"Big Dick" ended his first set of the night and turned the microphone over to the tournament chairman. The chairman rolled through his committee person thank-yous and then introduced Stosh Brzezinski, from Joliet, Illinois, who was this year's Ernest Hemingway look-a-like winner. Stosh would present the marlin tournament's trophies and prizes. The chairman announced the biggest dolphin award, first prize of $5,000 for a 42.9 pound fish. Next, he announced the tuna winner at 36 pounds, and a first prize of $750. Seth sat on the edge of his chair, as the chairman got ready to announce the wahoo winner.

"And now the wahoo winner, 59 pounds, and the $750 prize, *Tar Baby!*" Seth and the crew jumped up out of their chairs with their arms raised in celebration, and Seth sent Bobby up to collect the trophy and the cash prize. He noticed the Cher look-a-like enthusiastically clapping as Bobby held the trophy up on his way back to the table. The whole crew high-fived Bobby when he arrived at the table.

Then the marlin overall winners were announced. The committee chairman handed the microphone to Ernest Hemingway, and he read the results, "In third place and the winner of $5,000, *Reel Crazy*. Seth held his breathe as the announcer said, "in second place and the winner of $10,000, *Tar Baby*, and in first place, with two blue marlin releases and the winner of $25,000, *Cracker Boy!*"

Seth and the crew let out a whoop and headed to the stage to pick up the trophies and check. *$10,750* … thought Seth … *not a bad weekend,* as he strode up to the stage to pick up the check and pose for some pictures. He congratulated the captains of *Cracker Boy* and *Reel Crazy* and accepted the congratulations from the other captains and anglers at the banquet.

"Big Dick" cleared the stage and struck up the music again. The dance floor erupted with happy anglers and Hemingway's, and the party was on. The whiskey and beer flowed free, and the party promised to last into the wee hours.

After another hour at the party Seth reminded Gene that they were fueling and leaving at 6:30 the next morning. Then Seth drifted out of the Conch Republic and headed south down Greene Street past Crabby Bill's to Duval

Street. He passed Sloppy Joe's bar, which was cranking as usual and walked west on Duval. Key West was in the middle of another raucous Saturday night. Seth walked down past the Hog's Breath Saloon and then over to the aquarium. It was closed, but for some reason Seth got a chill as he walked by it. He shook it off and walked north past the Founder's Park to El Meson de Pepe. He walked up the alley and looked over at the bronze busts of Key West's founding fathers, shining in the streetlights. Pepe's was dark, as Seth knew it would be at this late hour, but he could feel Lisa's presence there with him. He could almost see her sitting at one of the empty porch tables. His thoughts turned to his casual encounter with Annie, and he at once felt guilty.

He spoke out loud from his heart, "Lisa, I miss you so much, and I still love you." Seth felt a tear roll down his cheek. "Don't hold whatever I do the rest of my life against me. I will never love anyone like I love you. I can only hope our souls will be together again someday."

He turned and walked back toward the boat feeling sad and alone on a night he should have felt ecstatic. Seth took a deep breath and felt thankful for the wonderful years he'd had with Lisa. He walked back down the dock towards *Tar Baby* who gently tugged at her mooring lines and beckoned him like an old friend. He slipped into his bunk feeling somewhat better, but knowing for sure he would never get over Lisa, or ever really want to.

Seth paid his bill at the A&B Marina dock master's office at 6:00 a.m. the next morning. They moved *Tar Baby* to the fuel dock and fueled up for the trip to St. Petersburg. He and Gene said their goodbyes to John and Bobby, and Seth reminded them of their next tournament, the Old Salts Loop Tournament, out of Longboat Key, Florida in mid-August. Gene and Seth shoved off for St. Pete, and John left with Bobby, in the Escalade, to drop him off at the airport on his way out of town.

Seth idled the Hatteras out past the breakwater and anchored boats before he put her up on plane in the northwest channel. Gene came up to the bridge with two cups of coffee and a copy of the Key West Citizen as the sun came up over the horizon. They passed several shrimp boats anchored up in the wide channel that were culling the catch they had caught the night before. Seth could see small blackfin tuna breaking the water in the slicks behind the shrimp boats.

"Nice tournament coverage in the paper," said Gene. "John must have been interviewed at the banquet. There are a few lines about the marlin that got away."

Seth laughed, "How big did John say it was?"

"Easily over 800 pounds," chuckled Gene.

"Well, they always get bigger after a few drinks," said Seth smiling. "It will be good press for the tournament."

Tar Baby cleared the northwest sea buoy, and Seth set the autopilot on a northeast heading towards Tampa Bay. Florida Bay was a beautiful blue green color with some pink streaking from the rising sun. The sky was clear and it promised to be yet another beautiful day in paradise. Seth and Gene passed the next couple of hours listening to the blues channel on the XM radio.

At 9:00 a.m., Seth called Jeb at home on his satellite phone. He filled Jeb in on the tournament details and then asked about Beau. Jeb answered that he still had not seen or heard from Beau, and had checked his apartment again. Seth told Jeb not to worry, as he would work on finding Beau when he got home.

After terminating his call to Jeb, Seth explained the Beau situation to Gene. Gene offered to help Seth and even offered to get his police buddies involved if necessary.

Seth turned the helm over to Gene and went below to check the engine room. Seth had installed mechanical engine gauges in the salon and they all read perfect. He put on his earmuffs and went down into the engine room. He flipped on the lights, found a flashlight, and gave the engine room a good once over look. He found no engine oil or water leaks, and the new graphite shaft packing's were running dry. He opened the front of the gen-set sound shield and everything looked fine in there. Seth closed up the engine room and made his way to the galley. He made a couple of sandwiches and took them up to the bridge. After lunch, Seth took a nap on the fly bridge bench seat while Gene ran the boat.

He woke up refreshed and said, "Thanks, Gene, now you take a break."

"Seth, I never get to go to sea enough, let me run the boat for you."

"O.k., Gene, just holler if you need a break."

At 8:00 p.m. that night, Seth and Gene hosed off *Tar Baby* at Stone's Boatworks and then drove to Harvey's Fourth Street Grill for a grouper sandwich. Harvey's, arguably, had the best grouper sandwich in Pinellas County. It was a hotly contested honor, as several other local restaurants also had great grouper sandwiches. Fully eighty percent of all the commercially caught fresh grouper in Florida came over the fish docks located at John's Pass in Madeira Beach, Florida. Thousands of pounds a week were caught, and the best of it went to the local fish restaurants.

Seth and Gene made more plans for the Old Salt's Marlin Tournament in August. Gene agreed to provision the boat for six anglers who would be fishing 125 miles offshore for three days. Seth would bring two more crew along because they needed to run two man watches all night while they drifted and slept. They would also fish for swordfish and yellowfin tuna on those nighttime watches.

Seth picked up the check at Harvey's and then drove to Gene's home in Barclay Estates in northeast St. Petersburg. He thanked him for helping to bring the Hatteras home and dropped him off. Then he headed for the beach and drove by Beau's on the way out. There weren't any lights on at Beau's. He stopped and knocked on the door, but nobody answered. Beau's truck was still there, so he just continued on home. Once home he called Jeb, told him he was home safe, sorted through his mail, and went to bed. His own bed felt good, so even with Beau's disappearance heavy on his mind he quickly fell asleep.

CHAPTER SEVENTEEN

B EAU was already up early the next morning, had gotten a weather report from Orlando, and was toasting a bagel when Hector stumbled out of his cabin.

Beau took a look at his red, bleary, eyes and asked, "Well, what was downtown San Andres like, Hector?"

"Better than you would have guessed," was Hector's answer. "There are plenty of Canadian tourists, so everything's cheap." Neither Beau nor the brothers brought the subject up again.

After a morning swim, Beau checked the engine room. He changed the generator v-belt and topped off all the fluids. He felt the boat was ready for the trip to Colon and the Panama Canal. Beau thought about the weather forecast, as he stood in the guest head's shower. His neck and back felt much better after the hot shower. The forecast looked good. The trough had dissipated, and there should be at least two days of good weather with ten to fifteen knots of wind from the southeast, three to four foot seas, and a seven to eight second wave moment. What potentially could have been the worst leg of the trip had turned into maybe one of the best. Beau dried off and put on fresh shorts and a fresh t- shirt. It certainly was nice to have a washer/dryer combo on board. He walked up to the dock master's office and paid *Chica's* bill. He tipped Orlando a "Big Ben", and then walked by the pool to collect Hector and Luis. The two of them were swimming in the pool. They could have passed as a couple of tourists from the mainland.

Beau called out to them, "Time to get going, we leave in an hour."

Forty-five minutes later they were on deck ready to cast off. Beau started the engines and generator and idled towards the anchor after Luis retrieved the stern lines from the dock. After Hector weighed the anchor, Beau piloted *Chica* out to the channel, picking his way along the shoreline of the lagoon. He had the same déjà vu feeling as when he came in. He instinctively knew where the deep water was. Once in the marked channel he headed for the sea buoy, and then set a course south toward Colon. As he pushed the boat up on plane, he couldn't help but notice the beautiful shades of blue all around him. The sun being directly overhead made the blues even more vibrant than they were when they arrived the previous morning. This group of islands was truly a paradise unto itself.

Chica had been running south about three hours when Beau noticed she was losing power in the port engine. The tachometer was beginning to fluctuate up and down 200 rpm's. Beau pulled the throttles back from 2400 rpm's to about 2100 and the engine ran steady again. Beau put Hector on the helm and headed below to check out the port engine. The first thing he did was shine a flashlight in the clear plastic Racor fuel filter bowls. As he had suspected the port bowl was mostly gray milky water, not clear amber diesel. Beau quickly retrieved a small plastic bucket and drained the water into it by opening the petcock in the bottom of the Racor bowl. He did the same to the starboard filter, but it didn't have nearly as much water in it. Both bowls were now both full of pure amber diesel. Beau went back up to the fly bridge after emptying the plastic bucket over the transom.

Hector asked, "What's up?"

"Water in the Racors," answered Beau. "We have a bad load of fuel."

Beau indexed the throttles back up to 2400 rpm's and both engines ran smoothly. Beau explained to Hector that he would go back down in the engine room in two hours and drain whatever water had accumulated in the Racors again, and would continue to repeat the process as many times as needed. Tonight, when they were running at ten knots, he would run on one engine, and then the other, while checking each of the filter cartridges for dirt and algae. He would change them if need be. He guessed they had been lucky that this was the first bad fuel they had encountered. Even the Deezol that they added at each fueling would not handle that much water. The fuel at Nene's had been inexpensive, but obviously it had not been filtered enough.

Like old Robert E. used to say, "A boat is like a whore with a bloody nose. If it's not one thing … it's another."

When they docked in Colon, Beau would change the secondary spin on fuel filters on both the engines just to be safe. They might have a little water in them, but he didn't feel that the injector pump or injectors had incurred any damage since the water hadn't stopped the engine.

Beau checked the GPS course made good and tweaked it up 2 degrees. He asked Hector to continue looking out so he could catch a catnap. He told Hector not to let him sleep more than two hours, so he could drain the Racors again. Beau lay down on the cushioned bench seat forward of the steering console and finally dozed off to the strains one of the brother's Gloria Estefan CD's.

Hector woke Beau up two hours later. Beau shook off his nap and headed for the engine room. The engines were still running smoothly, but Beau expected there would be more water in the Racor filters. Once down between the engines, he shone his flashlight on the port bowl. Beau let out a sigh of relief. The port bowl was only a quarter full of water. The majority of the water had been filtered out the first time and it would be all out in the next few hours. Beau would still drain it off every two hours until it was all gone. The starboard bowl had no water at all.

Beau went back up to the fly bridge and told Hector the good news. Then he asked Hector, "Can you get Luis to cook us up an early dinner? I want to get the nighttime schedule of watches set, so I can drain the Racors and open them to see if I need to change the cartridges."

"*Es arroz con pollo* o.k.," asked Hector.

"*Si, Senor*," answered Beau, who was getting used to Cuban food.

Darkness finally fell after a spectacular sunset, and Luis's chicken and rice dinner was delicious. Beau checked the radar out to forty-eight miles and saw only a few freighters; none were close enough to worry about. He set the radar intercept alarm at six miles and throttled *Chica* back until she was running at ten knots. He put Hector at the helm and shut down the port engine. When he checked the port engine fuel filter bowl it had only a few ounces of water in it. He took the top cover off the Racor after shutting the fuel valve and pulled the paper cartridge filter up and out. The filter was still clean with little debris on it, so he put it back in and resealed the top. He repeated this process on the starboard engine once the port engine was restarted and got similar results. The fuel was so hot he had to be careful not to burn his fingers, while handling the cartridges. Beau was pleased with the outcome of the Racor inspection, and didn't think there'd be anymore problem with the fuel. He returned to the bridge and settled back in the helm chair for the remainder of his watch.

The rest of the night was uneventful and Beau took over the helm at daybreak. After checking the, now water free, Racors first. He put the Bertram back up on a plane about seventy-five miles from the Colon sea buoy. Beau was glad he had chosen the route through the Bahamas, rather than running to Mexico and then down the Central American coast. They had been running with the wind aft of the beam almost the entire trip. If they had traveled the Mexican route the wind would have been on the nose most of the way. They had been lucky, and the ride had been fast and comfortable.

Within two hours, Beau picked up the Panama shoreline on the radar. Inside another hour he could see the city of Colon's skyline. The GPS had taken them directly to the Colon ships channel sea buoy. It would have been easy to find even without it, as huge freighters moved in both directions past it and several were anchored outside both sides of the, long, well marked channel.

When *Chica* cleared the Colon harbor breakwater, Beau radioed the dock master at the Panama Canal Yacht Club on channel sixteen. He received an immediate response and was given directions to the club docks. Hector put up the yellow quarantine flag and then readied the fenders and dock lines as they neared the Yacht Club docks. Beau stopped the Bertram in the middle of the wide commercial channel in front of the Yacht Club. The facility looked more like boat yard than a Yacht Club. There was a travelift and a haul out slip and seven or eight empty docks. On shore there were several boats blocked up ready to be worked on. A small one-story building, with a large covered patio, sat to one side of the property. A dockhand walked out on the dock and stood by one of the wider slips.

Beau maneuvered *Chica* over to that dock and backed her in. Hector threw the aft lines to the dockhand after securing the boat to the forward pilings. The dockhand, whose name was Manny, asked for the shore cord and plugged it in. Beau tipped Manny twenty dollars and asked if he would call Fonda Johnson's office for him.

Manny replied, "You'll have to do that in the office next to the bar, *Senor*. Jose, the dock master, will be glad to take care of that for you."

Beau thanked Manny again, and then turned to Hector and Luis and said, "Remember, you both have to stay on board until I return from customs and immigration. Hose the boat down and then relax. I'll take all the passports and check us through when our agent picks me up. Meantime, it would be smart to hide your guns in the salon air conditioner return vent. Unscrew the grate, put your guns in as far as you can reach, then replace the vent and the screws, that way a metal detector will look like it's just picked up the metal grate."

Beau shut down the generator and switched all the ship's systems to shore power. Then he walked up the dock with the passports and ships paper in search of the dock master. He entered the small building adjacent to the covered patio. The television over the bar inside had a soccer game on it. The bartender motioned him towards a door on the other side of the room when Beau asked for the dock master. The building was air-conditioned and it felt good. The temperature outside must have been ninety-five and the humidity had to be close to that number also.

"Are you, Jose?" asked Beau as he walked into the dock master's office.

The slender dark eyed man behind the desk replied, "*Si, Senor*, I am. How can I help you?"

"My name is Ronald Santos. I am captain of the Bertram 54 that just pulled in. I have two crewmembers on board, and I want to check us in. I also need to contact Fonda Johnson, the customs agent, to check us through customs and immigration."

"No problem, *Senor*, I'll call her right now, and here's a marina form for you to fill out. Will you pay with cash or credit card?"

"Cash," replied Beau as he started to fill out the marina form. Jose dialed the phone and handed it to Beau.

After four rings a women answered, "Johnson Agency, may I help you?"

"Yes," said Beau. "Is Fonda Johnson there?"

"Speaking," answered the woman.

"Ms. Johnson, this is Ronald Santos calling. May I call you Fonda?"

"Of course, Mr. Santos, I've been expecting your call. Did you have a good trip from San Andres?"

"Yes, we had a little water in the fuel. But it wasn't anything we couldn't handle, and please call me Ronald."

"Okay, Ronald, first we have to get you through immigration. It's almost right next to the Panama Yacht Club. Why don't you walk over there and get started with the forms. Do you have all your crews' passports and the boat papers?"

"Yes, I do," said Beau.

"Okay, I'll be down there in about twenty minutes and I'll meet you over there."

Beau hung up and thanked Jose and started to leave the office.

"Mr. Santos," said Jose. "It's all right to walk down to immigration during the day, but don't walk anywhere at night. There are local street *banditos*. Always take a taxi everywhere, no matter how close."

"Thanks for the tip, Jose. How's the food on the patio here at the Yacht Club?"

"It's good local food, *Senor*, especially the fish."

"I'll probably stay close. Which way is immigration?"

Jose pointed to his left and Beau headed for the front door. The Panama immigration building was clearly marked and Beau walked in. This time of year they weren't very busy, and Beau had finished the immigration process and was back sitting in the waiting area when Fonda Johnson walked in. She almost took his breath away.

She strode up to Beau as he rose from his chair and offered her hand, "Ronald Santos, I presume? I'm Fonda Johnson."

"Yes, Ms. Johnson … ah, Fonda," Beau stammered as he struggled to regain his composure. She was a knockout, five foot-eight, slim hips with nice breasts, olive complexion with electric blue eyes, thick jet black hair cut mid-length and pulled back in a ponytail. Beau guessed her age at around thirty-five. She was dressed in a light blue Columbia short-sleeved fly-fishing shirt with "Johnson Agency" embroidered over the left breast pocket, khaki shorts, and a pair of Sperry "Topsider" billfish boat shoes. She carried a leather briefcase, but no purse. Beau recovered his composure and they shook hands. Her handshake was firm and warm.

"Nice to meet you, Fonda," said Beau, not wanting to let go of her hand.

"The pleasure is all mine, Ronald. Have they helped you yet?"

"Yes," said Beau, finally letting go of her hand. "I was finished in fifteen minutes. What's next?"

"Well, I've called ahead, so we go to customs next, and the Canal admeasurer is waiting for my call to meet us at your boat. Do you have sufficient cash to pay the transit and pilot's fees or do we need to go to a bank?"

"I have $9,000 in cash with me now, and I have more cash available on the boat."

"That's more than enough, Ronald, and you won't have to pay the buffer deposit fee since I'm handling the transit. You'll pay the $2250 captains fee and the transit fee of $850 at the canal operations office. I'll be billed for the line handlers, lines and fenders, visa taxes, tourist cards, exit tax, etc. You'll pay me for that amount, plus my $350 fee. If all goes well tomorrow, you should be having a cold drink at the Balboa Yacht Club on the Pacific side by 5:00 in the afternoon. Your bill from the Johnson Agency should run about $1350. Your visa will be good for thirty days, but can be extended for ninety days if there are any mechanical problems."

Fonda whisked Beau through customs and then through the Canal operations office. When they had finished, she called the admeasurer on her cell phone and asked him to meet them at the Yacht Club so he could verify the *Chica's* size and weight. Beau requested a quick stop at a Bodega to replenish provisions, and then they started back to the boat in Fonda's Toyota Land Cruiser.

"Nice ride," said Beau as they rode through Colon.

"It works well for me everywhere in Panama," said Fonda with a smile.

"I have a question, Fonda. I have four drums of bad fuel from Nene's in San Andres lashed in *Chica's* cockpit. It has water in it and I wonder if there's any way to get rid of it?"

"I can do better than that. Jose has two, model 1000 Racors on a portable pump cart. Manny can clean your fuel in about two hours."

"Great. I'll ask him when we get back."

"Ronald, did you run the boat all the way down here from Florida?"

She turned and looked deeply into Beau's eyes as she asked the question.

"Yes, I'm going to take it to Los Suenos Marina in Costa Rica and fish it for a year or so."

He noticed that Fonda had no rings of any kind on her fingers.

"Have you ever been sport fishing, Fonda?"

"Yes, I have. My father worked for Canal operations for many years as a civil engineer. We fished on both coasts while he was still alive."

"Oh, I'm sorry," said Beau.

"He had a good long life, but now I take care of my mother. I haven't been fishing in a few years. I would like to hear about your trip down here, though. Did you come through the Yucatan Straits or the Windward Passage?"

"The Windward Passage," said Beau just as they were pulling into the Yacht Club parking lot.

Beau wanted this conversation to continue, so he took a chance.

"Fonda, would it be out of line for me to invite you to have dinner with me tonight? I'd like to finish telling you about the trip down here, but I'd also like to hear about your life here in Panama and how you became a canal agent."

"Your place or mine?" laughed Fonda.

Beau liked the fact that she had a sense of humor.

"Jose tells me that the food at the Yacht Club is good, and I'd like to keep a weather eye on the boat tonight. It looks like a rough neighborhood outside the gates."

"You're right about that. Will your crew mind if I join you?"

"My crew will head for downtown Colon the minute I give them their visas. That's one reason I'd like to stick around and I'd be grateful for your company."

"All right, we have a date."

They exited the Land Cruiser and headed for the docks and the Bertram.

The admeasurer was waiting on the dock and Fonda spoke to Beau as they walked toward him, "I'll go through the boat inspection with him and then to the bank with the cash you owe me. What time do you want to meet for dinner, Ronald?

"Say, 8:00, in the Yacht Club bar," replied Beau trying not to act like a schoolboy.

"I'll be there," said Fonda smiling.

The inspection went well, and Beau sent Hector and Luis up to the Yacht Club bar so they wouldn't be underfoot. When the inspection was over and the admeasure was on his way up the dock, Beau counted out $1350 for Fonda and she gave him a receipt and copies of all the Canal permits and documents. She said the Canal pilot and the line handlers would be at the boat, ready to go, at 7:30 in the morning. Fonda looked into his eyes again when he handed her the cash, and he recognized that she was also attracted to him. There was definitely some chemistry working between them.

She took the cash and put it in her briefcase and was on her way out the salon door when she looked back and said, "Until eight o'clock, Ronald."

Beau watched her walk back up the dock. He felt a pleasant stirring in his loins; it was a far better feeling than the puckered asshole he'd had for the last two weeks. He cleared his mind and called Jose on the VHF radio to ask him to send Manny down to clean the fuel in the drums. *Chica* had plenty of fuel to transit the Canal and they would fill all the tanks in Panama City tomorrow.

Beau walked up to the bar to retrieve Hector and Luis. He found them sitting in a corner booth, and gave them their passports and visas. Predictably, they headed back to the boat, showered, and changed into their street clothes. They announced they were going to have dinner and see the city of Colon and would be back later that night. Beau told them what Jose had said about taking cabs at night. But you'd pity the banditos that would try and mug those two.

Beau told the brothers that they were scheduled to leave at 7:30 a.m. and the two of them muttered, "No problem, man." Then they left for downtown.

Beau walked back down to *Chica* and checked out the engine room.

Everything checked out a-okay. He showered, while Manny continued to filter the fuel in the cockpit, and by the time he had shaved and dressed, Manny was gone. He changed the Band-Aids on the ends of his finger stubs and looked at the alarm clock. It was only 7:00 p.m. He passed some time reading a Canal locking procedure manual, and he reread the Canal rules and regulations. For the first time in quite a while, he couldn't wait for it to be eight o'clock.

CHAPTER EIGHTEEN

S ETH woke up with a start at 6:00 a.m. Monday morning. He had been so exhausted that he had slept straight through the night. His first thought was about his finish in the marlin tournament, but his elation was short lived as his thoughts immediately turned to Beau's disappearance and his premonition that something was really wrong this time.

The sun was just coming up as he stepped into the glass enclosed shower stall on the third floor of his townhouse. He could see the glistening Intracoastal Waterway through the glass portal in the master bath porch door. There was a light easterly wind making small ripples on the dawn pink water, and three dolphins were feeding a hundred yards out from the seawall below. The hot shower beat on his neck and shoulder muscles that were still sore from the eleven-hour boat trip home from the Key's. Seth was grateful for the good night's sleep, as he knew today was going to be a long one. He continued to look at the peaceful water as he dried off. One of the dolphins came to the surface and slapped the water with his tail. Most people thought the dolphins were playing when they did that, but Seth knew they did it to attract fish. Fish were naturally curious and would come out of their hidey-holes to see what the ruckus was all about. Many times their curiosity got them eaten.

Seth got dressed, went downstairs to the kitchen, and started the coffee. Then he went down to the ground floor and retrieved the morning paper off the stoop. When he walked back upstairs he put a bagel in the toaster and checked the sports page. Predictably, there was no mention of the Key West Marlin Tournament in the St. Petersburg Times. It had been the same when he was sailboat racing. For years, St. Petersburg and Florida had been home to many world-class sailing regattas and fishing tournaments, but the Times never covered those sports. They were more interested in providing the British soccer league scores to a handful of English beach tourists.

Seth finished his coffee and bagel. Then he poured himself a coffee traveler in a Styrofoam cup and headed for the boat works some twenty minutes away.

His mind reviewed all the events that pertained to Beau's disappearance as he drove. He tried to make them add up to something: the Cubans, the Bertram, the gambling debts, he just couldn't make sense of it all. But his instincts told him that the Cubans were the key. He arrived at the boatworks and waved to the men working out in the yard as he walked in. The travelift was moving off the lift slip runway with a Sunseeker 62 in it. Seth stopped in the carpenter's shop and gave George, the foreman, a quick fishing report, and then he continued up the stairs to the offices on the second floor. George was an avid fisherman and the two of them had traded fishing stories for many years.

"Hi, Dad," said Jeb as Seth walked into the main office.

"I'm going to work on finding Beau, Son," said Seth. "The first thing I will do is call the police department and report him missing."

He went into his office and called the police, and asked for missing persons. He was on hold for at least five minutes when an Officer Turley came on the line.

Seth introduced himself and said, "My brother, Beau Stone, has been missing for over a week. His truck is still parked at his residence and his apartment has not been disturbed. My son checked inside and all of Beau's clothes and traveling articles, including his passport, were there."

Officer Turley said, "Come down to the station, Mr. Stone, to help me fill out a report. Please bring a copy of any ID information you might have, along with a current photo of your brother."

Seth retrieved a photo of Beau standing in front of *Tar Baby* when it was hauled out earlier in the year. He wrote down Beau's social security number and took a copy of his driver's license that they had on file at the yard. He headed downtown and spent the rest of the morning filling out forms and answering questions about possible enemies, girlfriends, and behavior patterns. Seth was forthright and informed Officer Turley about Beau's gambling and drinking problems. Officer Turley was short, had his head shaved, and was muscle bound. He looked about eighteen years old to Seth. But Seth had to admit he was thorough and very professional. Of course, these days, everyone was beginning to look very young to Seth.

Officer Turley said, "Thank you for coming in Mr. Stone, we will make every effort to find your brother. I will put out an APB immediately and I will call you whenever I receive any kind of information."

Seth left the police station and stopped for lunch at George's Coney Island restaurant on Ninth Street North. He had been eating George's hot dogs with chili, mustard, and onions since his high school days. His Coney Island's still tasted as good as the first ones did over forty years ago.

When he got back to the yard he walked over to Charley Parker's yard to talk to him about Beau. He found Charley examining the bottom of a trawler he had just hauled out.

"Charley," said Seth as he walked up behind him. "I hate to bother you, but do you have a minute to talk to me?"

"Of course I do," smiled Charley. "I always have time for you, Seth … what's up?"

"Well, I have a problem. No one knows where Beau is, and he's been gone over a week."

"Maybe he ran off with one of those racy girls I see him with now and then," said Charley … laughing nervously.

"I don't think so this time. He was supposed to stick close to the yard and help Jeb since I was fishing the Drambuie in Key West last week."

"How'd you do?"

"Second place and we lost a big marlin, at the boat, on the last day."

"Too bad about the marlin … but a damn good showing Seth!"

"Thanks, but back to Beau. I've got a bad feeling about those Cuban guys I saw over here with the Bertram 54 from Naples. Did you ask Beau to come over to look at that Bertram?"

"No, I didn't ask him to look at anything, although we've all helped each other over the years. When I walked up, Beau acted like he might have known those Cubans. He was actually getting on their case about something, and then stopped talking when he saw me coming."

"How did Beau explain why he was there?"

"He said, 'Charley, I thought this was a Bertram I had fished on over in the Bahamas, so I walked over to see if the same captain was running it, but it's a different boat.' Then he turned to the Cubans and said, 'Charley will do a good job fixing these propellers for you', and walked back over to your yard. After he left, I asked the Cubans if they knew him and they said, 'No, he just came over to look for his captain friend.' I thought maybe he was mad that they didn't bring the boat to your yard."

"Honestly, I don't know anything about them or their boat, but I'd like to check them out if it's all right with you," said Seth with concern. "Could you give me the vessel ID numbers and the owner's name off your work order? There's something fishy about this whole deal."

"Sure Seth, no problem."

"Did they pay you with a credit card or check?"

"No, they paid cash."

Seth followed Charley into his office, and Charley ran a copy of *Pescadora's* work order and gave it to him.

"Anything else you can recall about the Cubans?" asked Seth.

"Mostly that they were in a big hurry, and were willing to pay extra for it. But they just didn't act like boat people. They weren't comfortable with boating terms or handling the boat."

"Thanks for the info, Charley,"

"Sorry about Beau," said Charley with a knowing look. "If I can do anything else for you, you know I will."

"Thanks again," said Seth as he walked out the door and back over to Stone's.

Seth sat down at his desk and studied the work order. The Bertram belonged to a Ronald Santos from Fort Lauderdale, Florida. *Pescadora* was a Coast Guard documented vessel, and the hailing port was Naples, Florida. Ronald Santos had given no address, only a P.O. Box in Fort Lauderdale, and he had not given Charley a phone number. So, what is a guy from Fort Lauderdale doing with a boat registered in Naples … *maybe a new purchase?*

Seth picked up the phone and called Gloria Rector in Tampa. Gloria ran a marine documentation and title service that many of the area's boat brokers used. He gave her the information he had and asked her to check it out.

Thirty minutes later she called back with some interesting information. A Marine Max broker named Captain Herman Herzog had sold *Pescadora* in Naples some three weeks before, to a Ronald Santos, from Fort Lauderdale. It was a cash sale, no mortgage. Additionally, the broker had filed papers with the Coast Guard, for the new owner to change the name to *Chica*, and the hailing port to Fort Lauderdale. Seth said, 'Thank you, Gloria, for your good work and prompt response." He asked her to send him a bill at Stone's Boatworks.

Gloria declined saying, "Thank you for all the business you have sent me over the years, Seth. The least I can do for you is a small favor like this."

"Thank you, again," said Seth, as he hung up the phone and bells and whistles started going off in his head.

He looked at *Chica* written on his note pad, and his mind flashed back to

Mallory Square; *Chica, and Ft. Lauderdale, FL*.... flashed through his mind. That was the name and hailing port that he'd seen on the Bertram that cut across the channel to Sunset Island, he was sure of it. Where did they have the name changed on the transom? Why did they go around the Key's through Key West if they were going to Fort Lauderdale? It would have made more sense to cut through west of Marathon at Channel Seven. Why would you buy a boat in Naples and then come north to St. Petersburg and then go south to the Keys?

Seth was starting to dial his friend Gene, to fill him in on the situation and ask him to help, when the boatworks receptionist called him on the intercom and said, "Mr. Stone, a Detective Baggett on line two for you."

Seth stopped dialing and picked up line two and said, "Seth Stone speaking."

"Mr. Stone, this is Detective Troy Baggett from the Key West Police Department. I'm afraid I have some bad news for you. Last week we found some initially unidentifiable human remains in one of the Key West Aquarium's shark tanks. One person has been identified by personal identification that we recovered and by dental records. His name was Ricardo Cabeza of Tampa, Florida. His identity was further corroborated by a DNA check. The other recovered remains DNA has also been crosschecked, and the FDLE computers have matched it to Beauregard Stone of St. Petersburg, Florida, a former U.S. Army Airborne Ranger Sergeant. You are designated as his next of kin. I'm sorry I have to be the one to inform you of his death"

Seth's emotions washed over him, and he could not speak. His heart raced, and he heard a roaring in his ears.

"Are you still there, Mr. Stone?" asked Detective Baggett gently.

Seth caught his breath and finally was able to answer, "Forgive me, Detective, but this is all too hard for me to comprehend at once."

"I understand, Mr. Stone," replied Detective Baggett. "Shall I call back at another time?"

"No sir," said Seth, the roaring in his ears subsiding some. "Please continue. I'm anxious to hear the details. He's been missing from St. Petersburg for over a week."

"Well, sir," continued Detective Bagget. "We only found two small pieces of your brother and they appeared to be fingers. But, we did find a Rolex watch in one of the shark's stomachs and it had an inscription on the back that read, *U.S. Yacht Club Challenge-Champions 1987*. We also found a pair of size ten Sperry boat shoes in another shark that would not have fit Mr. Cabeza."

"That's Beau's Rolex, Detective; we both crewed on the winning boat out in Newport Beach, California in 1987. Do you have any leads?" asked Seth, as he suddenly felt sick to his stomach.

"No sir, not yet, this is a strange one even for Key West," answered the detective.

Seth took a deep breath and choked back the bile rising in his throat. "I was in Key West last week. I read about the deaths in the Key West Citizen. I read about Ricardo Cabeza."

"What were you doing in Key West and where did you stay, Mr. Stone?" asked Detective Baggett, suddenly more interested.

"I fished my boat in the marlin tournament, Detective, and I stayed at the A&B Marina. I arrived in Key West on Saturday afternoon, and I was there all week."

"Was your brother there with you?"

"No, he was supposed to be working here at the boatworks with my son, Jeb. The last time either one of us saw him was a week ago Friday. I can't believe I was in Key West a few blocks from him when he died. So … you really don't have *any* leads?"

"No sir, we don't, but we believe the victims were brought in by boat. There were no visible signs of entry and the front of the aquarium was locked up tight, but the rear is always open to the water."

"This is all so hard to believe.

"There is one more thing, though," said Detective Baggett. "We ran a check on Ricardo Cabeza and he is connected with the Cipriano mafia family in Tampa. Did your brother have any contact with them that you know of?"

"Not that I know of," replied Seth warily. "But, Beau liked to gamble and drink and he led a very colorful life. So please keep digging. Anything could be possible."

"I'll ship you his remains, the boat shoes, and the Rolex if you'll give me your address, and, again … I'm sorry."

Seth gave him the address and asked him to just send the remains and the Rolex.

He hung up the phone and just sat at his desk for the next fifteen minutes, completely devastated. He thought about growing up with Beau: fishing, water skiing, and sailing. It was hard to believe that he was gone. The Rolex that identified him had been won after a week in Newport Beach, California where they'd competed against some of the best sailors in the country in the U.S Yacht Club Challenge. John Harvey had been the skipper, and he and the entire crew were presented with Rolex's for winning that regatta. That night, in the Newport Yacht Club bar, Beau had the large silver championship trophy cup filled with six bottles of champagne. He made the whole crew take turns drinking it until it was gone. The memories were overwhelming him, but it was all he had left of Beau.

Seth finally pulled himself together, went into Jeb's office and told him the bad news. Jeb broke down, and Seth gathered the strength to console him.

Jeb was both sad and angry and said to Seth, "I knew Uncle Beau was headed for something like this, he was just living to fast and loose."

Seth put his arm around Jeb and comforted him saying, "Son, your Uncle Beau always had a rocket in his pocket … even when he was just a kid. Let's just try and remember all the good times we had with him."

Seth went back to his office and wrote a notice to inform the employees of Beau's death. He called the St. Petersburg Yacht Club and booked the ballroom room for Beau's wake on Thursday night. Then he wrote an obituary, complete with a notice of Beau's wake at the Yacht Club, Thursday night, and faxed it to the newspaper. Seth knew all of Beau's friends, including his sailing and fishing buddies, would be there for his final sendoff. Seth and Jeb would scatter what little remained of Beau, in the Gulf of Mexico, off of Egmont Key, at a later date. That's where Beau always said he wanted to be when he was done. Seth wanted to be alone, so he gave Jeb one more hug and headed for the beach and home.

Seth sat out on his second story porch and started working on his best bottle of wine. He had been keeping the aged Caymus Cabernet for an occasion. Well, this was definitely an occasion. His little brother was dead. Seth called his sister Scarlett, in Atlanta, during his second glass of wine, and filled her in. She cried and said she'd be down for the wake with her family. As he hung up the Sunset began out over the Gulf.

Seth watched the boats glide by in the waning light and thought about Beau: a four sport athlete, soldier, craftsman, raconteur, sailor, big game fisherman, bon vivant, alcoholic, failed husband, and compulsive gambler. Well, seven out of ten wasn't so bad. He still couldn't believe it. Who had thrown Beau in that shark tank? He hoped Beau had been shot dead or knocked out with drugs before being attacked by the sharks. His killers must have surprised him because Beau had been trained in the airborne rangers to kill and not be killed. He had survived Vietnam and many dangerous covert missions. He didn't look the part but he had confided in Seth, after the war, that he had killed a number of enemy soldiers in hand-to-hand combat, and scores more in firefights and sniper missions. Seth's mind started to work again. The wine had dulled his grief and he was thinking again. There had to be more to this than gambling debts. If the Tampa mafia wanted to kill him they wouldn't take him to Key West and throw him in a shark tank with one of their own men. They would just kill him and drop him in the Gulf of Mexico fifty miles off shore.

Seth woke up in his Adirondack chair out on the townhouse porch the next morning as the sun was coming up. The wine bottle was empty and he couldn't decide if his head or his back hurt more. He limped inside and made a pot of coffee, then headed upstairs for a hot shower. Finally, he got dressed and drove down to the boat works to continue telephoning. He wanted to know why Beau had been killed and he wanted to know who did it. He knew in his gut that the Bertram 54 and the two Cubans were somehow involved.

When Seth got to his desk he pulled a stack of cruising guides out of his bookcase. He made a list of all the fuel docks from Marathon to Key West and started calling. He called all five of the fuel docks in Marathon and none of them remembered a Bertram 54 called *Pescadora* or *Chica*. He called the three fuel docks in Key West Bight with the same result. *Maybe I'm wrong* … thought Seth, but the image of *Chica* idling across Key West channel was still clearly in his memory. He called the fuel docks on Stock Island, just east of Key West on the Atlantic side. The second call paid off. The dock master at the Oceanside Marina fuel dock remembered a Bertram 54 named *Chica*. They had called and ordered four, 55 gallon, plastic drums a week before they arrived.

"Do you remember what day they fueled?" asked Seth.

"That'll be easy. Let me find the fuel and drum ticket," said the dock master. He came back on the line two minutes later and said, "Two Sunday's ago."

"What did the crew look like, and how many were there?"

"Let me think …. There were two heavy set Latinos, and the captain was an average sized white guy with a scruffy black beard.

"Did they say where they were going?"

"Down Island," answered the dock master without hesitation.

"Anything else you remember?"

"They were here for over a half a day. The captain fueled everything up and the two Latinos came back with a van loaded with provisions. The crew didn't look too sea worthy, but the captain handled the boat like a pro. He left us all a big tip, too."

"How did they pay for the fuel?"

"Everything in cash, even bought some bait."

"Thanks for your help. What did you say your name was?"

"Fred."

"Thanks, Fred, you've been a big help."

"If I had to guess, I'd guess that they went to Mexico," added Fred.

Seth thanked him again and hung up.

He sat back in his chair and tried to fit the pieces together, but he couldn't make it work. Fred had identified the two Cubans and a captain. He wondered which one was the owner, Ronald Santos? Sunday night was the night Seth saw *Chica* right at dusk in Key West. Were Beau and Ricardo Cabeza being held below in the boat? Who was the captain with the black beard, and where did they go next? The best thing Seth could figure out to do was to continue to follow the boat. The fuel drums certainly indicated a long passage. The Bertram 54 held 1400 gallons of fuel in her regular tanks, and the four drums would add over 200 more gallons. They could run to Mexico and still have fuel left over.

Seth picked the phone up and dialed the dock master at El Cid Marina, in Cancun. Seth had been to El Cid a couple of years before on a spring sail fishing trip to Mexico. He got a hold of the dock master and asked him if he had seen a Bertram 54 named *Chica*.

He said, "No, I haven't seen *Chica*, or any other Bertram 54 lately."

Seth made a note to call him back in a couple of days, to check again.

A call to Hemingway Marina in Cuba didn't turn up anything, so Seth decided they were headed for the Caribbean through the Bahamas. Seth closed the door to his office, settled down, and started compiling a fuel dock list for the Bahamas.

By the time he finished his Bahamas list it was lunchtime. It would make no sense to call the dock masters until after lunch hour. He didn't want to talk to any assistants; he knew the dock masters would remember details, since its how they make their living.

He grabbed Jeb for a quick lunch and filled him in on his detective work up to then.

Jeb said, "He's gone, Dad, can't you just let it go?"

"No, I can't, Jeb," answered Seth. "My gut is telling me there's more to this. Just humor me, and don't say a word to anyone. I'm going to play this out to make myself feel better. Who knows, I might find out who's behind it all."

"Its work for the police, Dad," reprimanded Jeb.

"Just humor me, boy!! It'll keep me busy if nothing else," replied Seth sternly.

"Okay, Dad. I'll field any calls that come about the wake, and any sympathy calls. But, if you come up with something, please give it to the police … OK?"

"We'll see, Jeb, we'll see," said Seth with a shrug.

CHAPTER NINETEEN

JOHN Cipriano sat on his porticoed veranda in Tampa, Florida overlooking Palma Ceia Golf Course. The veranda was fifty-eight feet long and was comfortably furnished with rattan furniture complete with overstuffed cushions. No Nose liked to be outside, but to make the veranda even more ideal he had heating and air-conditioning piped in all along its curved open-air length. Six ceiling fans distributed the controlled climate with balmy precision. He could look over the railing at the twelfth hole and still see his pool and waterfall spa in the foreground.

He had built this mansion in south Tampa after taking over the Trafficante mafia family in 1987. John Cipriano had been an all-city linebacker and Tampa golden gloves champion while at Robinson High in south Tampa. He had the ability to take a punch as well as deliver his own devastating right hand. He had always had a proclivity towards violence and distaste for authority. It had gotten him expelled from high school and estranged from his parents. Out on the streets and on his own, John soon fell in with the Trafficante crime family where he worked as a hi-jacker and enforcer. His handsome good looks were only marred by a proboscis that had been broken so many times that it appeared to be splattered all over his face. Hence the underworld's chosen nickname for him … No Nose. Besides being street smart, John was extremely intelligent, and he rose quickly in the Tampa Mafia. He had the good sense to marry one of Santo Trafficante's daughters. When the venerable old Don finally passed away, leaving no family successor, John Cipriano was the logical choice.

John's nickname was never used in his presence, nor was any reference to the absence of a protuberance in the middle of his face ever mentioned. His associates and enemies were all aware of the ferocity that boiled just below his otherwise calm, outward, demeanor. It wasn't long before everyone began calling the Tampa mafia the Cipriano family. No Nose had also legitimized the family business. He bought and ran an array of businesses and actually paid corporate and personal income tax on millions of dollars of profit. Of course, that was just a small part of his actual take each year. He laundered millions of illegal dollars through his legitimate companies. Most of his ill-gotten fortune had been smuggled out of the country and rested offshore.

No Nose had purchased an old rundown mansion on the Palma Ceia golf course. The large Victorian house had once belonged to a prominate shipping magnate. John had it bulldozed and built a new house. The new Italian villa style home was an elegant mix of: exotic wood floors, expensive fabrics, slate, granite, and marble. Large fireplaces were found in most of the rooms. He had: a walk-in wine cellar, a commercial grade kitchen, his and her showers and closets, a library, an office, a sauna and steam room, a gym, billiards room, a media room with six television sets, and an automatic backup generator. The windows facing the golf course were bulletproof glass. Clear Lexan panels, making them bullet and bomb proof, covered the windows facing the street. The house had a six-car garage and the sixth garage had an automatic opening door at each end. Visitors could drive in and drop the door, then exit the car unseen. When they left they'd use the rear garage door and drive out still incognito. The grounds were monitored by electronic surveillance equipment, and the front yard had a six-foot brick wall around it complete with an electronically controlled gate. The backyard had a six-foot chain link fence surrounding it, tastefully painted green. No Nose had two bodyguards on the grounds, twenty-four-seven.

He had been successful by studying the mistakes his crime boss predecessors had made. Al Capone didn't pay income tax, Paul Castellano had given his Capo's too much power, and John Gotti was too high profile and did not continually sweep his environment for listening devices. The list goes on and on. Except for the 7800 square foot house on Golf View Street, (which really didn't stand out on a street lined with mansions), No Nose tried to keep a low profile. He had a large sportfish boat in the Bahamas, captained by the famous Tony Fungello, but it was titled to one of his legitimate corporations. His cousin, Pauly Castellucci, who had no police record, was President of John's Florida banks. Pauly was also listed as the owner of a six bedroom house in Incline Village, Nevada, on Lake Tahoe. A Cipriano import-export company owned a Falcon jet.

John's wife, Teresa, was active in Tampa charitable circles, and he attended maybe two of those events a year. He was seldom seen in public in Tampa, except for maybe a round of golf at Palma Ceia once a week where he was known as John or Mr. C. He was not recognized by the patron's of Tampa's trendier restaurants, as he always dined in small private rooms at those establishments. When he traveled he rented an entire floor at whatever hotel he was staying in, so security was simplified. His low profile and attention to detail had paid off, as he had never been arrested or indicted for any crime.

No Nose had also studied and applied many of the successful practices developed by other Mafia bosses over the years. He never talked directly to anyone in his organization over the utilities telephones. He never used computers, cell phones, or voice mail. He only used face to face and Iridium satellite phone communication. A satellite phone could not pinpoint your location like a cell tower could. A satellite phone would bounce a call off a satellite that was in outer space and saw half a continent. He would only call another satellite phone, and they all rotated fictitious identity SIM cards daily. No Nose and his Capos also talked in a code language only they could decipher.

For example: "Did, "Two Shirts" bring you the four Yankee's tickets last night?"

"No, he only brought three."

"Well, get the other one from him tomorrow and if he doesn't have it, take him to lunch and tell him he can't go to the game with you." This translated to the following;

"Did Carmine bring us the forty thousand he owes us?"

"No, he only came up with thirty thousand."

"Get the other ten thousand from him tomorrow, and if he can't come up with it, whack him out to make an example of him." This technique had been successful for years, but No Nose and his capos had perfected it into a precise foreign language of their own, mixing in Italian and Spanish words to further complicate it. The risk of jail had been shifted to the rank and file, who had never spoken to John Cipriano or even seen him in person.

No Nose was furious over the robbery of his three million dollars at the Ybor City money drop. As each day passed, and there was no sign of Ricardo and his henchmen, he grew more frustrated with his organization's inability to find them. He had been pleasantly surprised on Friday night, a week after the robbery, when Luigi informed him of Ricardo Cabeza's death in the Key West Aquarium's shark tank. Luigi had gotten that heads up from a paid informant that worked on the Key West Citizen's police desk. But, he wondered how the "perps" had eluded his net and made it to Key West undetected. No Nose figured Ricardo's accomplices had killed him. He had wondered who the second body found in the shark tank might be.

The money drop guard had been a loyal soldier and had fought back gamely during the exchange of gunfire with the bearded thief. No Nose hated to lose good men. The surveillance cameras had revealed the shooter as a white male with a dark tan wearing a fake black beard. The guard had grappled with him after he was hit with the first shot and he had pulled the accomplice's fake beard partially off. The still photos were grainy and no one in the family, and none of the family's police contacts, could identify the robber.

No Nose suspected the Russian Mafia, who was operating out of Key West and Miami. Who else would have the balls to rob the family? He had let them operate in the Keys by allowing them to staff the restaurants and titty bars there with eastern Europeans. He had also allowed them to deal drugs at the street level in the Keys. They paid weekly tribute to the family, but No Nose could see that it was a mistake. They would grow stronger and always want more. Once he had recovered the three million and solved this puzzle; he would eliminate the Russian faction from the State of Florida.

This Monday morning, he had gotten some more interesting information from Luigi "Wall-to-Wall" Scuzzi, who was his Tampa Bay Capo. Luigi ran a large Cipriano family-owned carpet and flooring business with outlets all over Tampa Bay. After setting up a meeting by satphone, Luigi arrived at No Nose's home using the sixth garage to enter. He had gotten a call from a St. Petersburg detective who was on their payroll. A Key West detective had called their department earlier in the day to report the identity of the second person found dead in the shark tank with Ricardo Cabeza. He had been identified by D.N.A. testing, and his name was Beauregard Stone, a lifelong resident of St. Petersburg. The detective had also provided a background biography. Stone was a partner in Stone's Boatworks, located on Salt Creek in south St. Petersburg. He had graduated from Saint Petersburg High School, and had been highly decorated by the U.S. Army in the Vietnam War. He had worked at Stone's for thirty-four years. He had two D.U.I. convictions and one assault and battery arrest at Shadrack's Bar in Passe-a-Grille Beach, resulting from an altercation with a biker group. No conviction had resulted, as it was ruled self-defense. He had a very poor credit rating, and had filed for bankruptcy twice. His partner and older brother, Seth, was squeaky clean. The brother had filed a missing persons report early that morning. Luigi remembered that Beau Stone had owed the family a few large gambling debts, but that he had always paid them off. After the last one, his credit was suspended. Luigi had also pointed out that Ricardo was related to the

Fernandez brothers from Miami. They were two small-time bookies that also free-lanced large drug buys from time to time.

No Nose said, "Call Vincent in Miami and check them out."

Luigi left the room and dialed up Vincent on his satphone, and told him to start checking out the Fernandez's (Vincent Carlucci was the Cipriano's Miami Capo and his nickname was "Cadillac."). Cadillac made a few calls and called Luigi back twenty minutes later with some more information. Hector and Luis Fernandez had left Miami ten days ago for Mexico, after informing their mafia contact that they were going to arrange some large cocaine buys. Their cousin Raul was running their book while they were gone. They were expected to be back in a week or two. Luigi related this information back to No Nose out on the veranda.

No Nose did not seem alarmed and said, "Hector and Luis, and their father before them, have always sent us ten percent of their book's profits and twenty percent of any drug profits. They told our lieutenant that they were going to Mexico, so it sounds like business as usual. Have Cadillac keep his ear to the ground for any Cubans spending big money, though. You know … A new car, a new house, or a new boat."

"Right, boss," said Luigi. "I can do that research with no problem."

Luigi went back to the Dale Mabry carpet location of J.C.Carpet and called the family's contacts at the State titling office, asking for a computer run of any Hispanic names titling cars over $40,000, boats over $100,000, and houses over $500,000 in the last two weeks. An hour later he was faxed a list with twenty-seven names on it. Two homes over $500,000, fourteen Cadillac's, five Mercedes, two BMW's, and four boats to people with Latin names. He called Cadillac by satphone and gave him seven names and addresses in the Miami area and told him to check them out.

The next morning he got a call back from Cadillac.

"Two leads panned out, Luigi. Paloma Ortiz is Ricardo Cabeza's sister. She bought a new Cadillac Escalade a week before the robbery. She lives in Miami Lakes with her husband who is a concrete contractor. She says her brother sent her the money and told her to buy the car for herself. She was pretty broken up about her brother being killed in Key West. She said she hadn't seen him for years, but that he called her from Tampa every Sunday night. There's also another name on the list I need to check further, Ronald Santos. He used to run Manolo Fernandez's book with him back in the sixties, when I was just a kid and was hi-jacking trucks down here for Trafficante. But nobody's seen him in years. His address in Ft. Lauderdale is a P.O. Box, and he bought a $580,000 Bertram sportfish over in Naples from Marine Max."

"Thanks, Vincent, good work."

"You know, the Bertram and Ronald Santos smell fishy to me," added Cadillac. "Run it by No Nose, he might figure a connection."

"You might want to question Hector and Luis about Ronald Santos when they get back from Mexico."

"I'll do it," said Cadillac.

John Cipriano was not surprised about Ricardo's gift of the Cadillac Escalade to his sister. He had already asked Pauly to bring Ricardo's bank statement over to the house. Ricardo was only worth about $200,000. He had made a $190,000 withdrawal over two weeks ago.

"Don't hurt Ricardo's sister or brother-in-law, Luigi," said No Nose softly. "But have Vincent blow up the Cadillac in their driveway. It will send a message that we will always find out who steals from us. It will also alert our family and associates that we are dealing with a traitor. They may even think we threw Ricardo in that shark tank."

Luigi Scuzzi nodded and said, "I sent "Fat John" Conte to Naples this morning to talk to the Marine Max broker who sold the boat to Ronald Santos."

"Call Fat John on your satphone and tell him to get a good description of Ronald Santos from the broker. Also, find out what kind of car he drove and any other pertinent information that he can get. Then call one of our contacts at the Tampa Police Department to request an FBI computer check on Ronald Santos.

Wall-to-Wall made both calls on his way back to the carpet store, and then waited in his office for the return calls.

Fat John called two hours later from Naples. He had impersonated a Tampa Police Detective, badge and all, when he met with the Marine Max broker. He told Luigi that Captain Herman "Buster" Herzog remembered Ronald Santos as a Cuban who spoke perfect English. He had described a man with black hair, brown eyes, who was six feet tall, and weighed 250 pounds. Captain Buster thought it was odd that he and his similar looking sidekick always wore long pants, Hawaiian shirts, and street shoes, even when they came to pick up the Bertram. Ronald had paid cash for the boat and had given Captain Buster a Fort Lauderdale P.O. Box as his address. He introduced his companion as Jose Pinocha, and Jose never said a word either time he was there. Captain Buster said they came in a Hertz rental car to pick-up the boat. He knew this because he picked them up at the Hertz lot out on Route 41 and brought them back to the Marina when they turned the car in.

Luigi asked Fat John, "Did you check out the rental car office?"

"Yes, I have Ronald Santos driver's license number and the same P.O. Box number appears in the address box."

Luigi hung up and called the Florida Department of Motor Vehicles who corroborated that Ronald Santos had a current driver's license and that P.O. Box was his mailing address. The residence address turned out to be a vacant lot titled in his name. Luigi's State Motor Vehicles Bureau contact faxed him a copy of Ronald Santo's license. He in turn faxed a copy to Vincent Carlucci in Miami at his titty bar, The Pink Pony. Luigi called the Lauderdale Post Office and also represented himself as a Tampa detective, asking for the method of payment on Ronald Santos's P.O. Box. The clerk pulled up the records on a computer and came back on the line.

"All the bills have been paid by money order, Detective."

"Can you tell where the money orders originated from?"

"Yes sir," answered the clerk. "They are all from an Amscot office in Miami."

Luigi thanked her, hung up, and was wondering where this would lead when his satphone rang.

It was Vincent Carlucci, and he said cryptically, "Ronald Santos is Hector Fernandez."

"Are you positive?" asked Luigi.

"Does a hobby horse have a hickory dick?" was Cadillac's sarcastic reply. "The picture on Ronald Santos's drivers license is definitely Hector. No Nose is going to go fucking bananas when you tell him."

"Thanks, Cadillac, I'm sorry the scam is from Miami," said Luigi, softly.

"No problem, we'll get Hector and his brother and they'll pay dearly for their sins. A beheading now and then always keeps the other troops in line for a long time."

Luigi called No Nose and set up a meeting at the Golf View mansion within the hour. He pulled up to the front gate forty-five minutes later and waited for it to open. As he drove up to the garage he noticed that the sixth door was already open, and as he pulled in the door closed behind him. Anthony, one of No Nose's regular bodyguards was waiting for him inside of the garage.

Mr. C. is waiting for you in the billiard's room, Luigi. He's not in a very good mood today."

"Thanks for the heads up, Anthony," said Luigi as he exited the garage and made his way towards the billiard's room. Anthony followed him into the house and waited outside as Luigi walked in. No Nose made a complicated double bank shot just as Luigi stepped in the room.

"What did you find out?" said No Nose without looking up from the table.

Luigi recounted the facts he had learned from Fat John and then moved on to the P.O. Box and driver's license research. No Nose continued to study his next shot until Luigi said, "The picture on Ronald Santos's driver's license is Hector Fernandez."

John Cipriano looked up with a start and with one quick overhand motion broke his cue stick over the side of the pool table. He lapsed into several seconds of unintelligible Italian, before yelling in a rage, "Those, no good, ungrateful, mother-fucking, Cuban bastards! Do they think we're stupid? Now we're going to get the three million dollars back, plus the boat, and then we'll kill both of them … and their stinking cousin Raul. Shooting is too good for those fat fuckers. We're going to drag their fat asses down a gravel road behind a pick-up truck, piss in their cuts, then stake them out in the Everglades and let the Alligators tear them up while they're still alive. We need to make an example of them that nobody will ever forget."

"I think that will send the desired message, John. We'll get busy trying to find them immediately. They may be in Mexico buying cocaine to complete their alibi, or they may be aboard the Bertram somewhere. Let's have Cadillac stake out the Airport, in Miami, while we track down the boat. We should leave Raul out on the street for now in case the brothers check in with him. We don't want to spook them away from Miami."

No Nose was back to his composed self by this point, but Luigi had seen the cold rage within him. Luigi made a mental note to never, ever, cross No Nose Cipriano.

"Luigi, you're right. Put Cadillac on alert in Miami and let's gather our resources to check the Caribbean Islands, Cuba, and Mexico. We have contacts in all the customs offices from the U.S. through the Caribbean, and throughout Central and South America. There won't be too many Bertram 54's running around the Caribbean at the height of hurricane season," said No Nose. "Call Captain Tony, on my boat in the Bahamas, and get him on the trail of the Bertram. Give him Captain Buster Herzog's number so he can find out the name of the boat. They may have changed it before they picked it up. They'll have to fuel up sooner or later, and my Captain Tony knows every fuel stop from Tampa to Buenos Aires." As Luigi left, No Nose lit up a Cuban cigar that looked a foot long.

CHAPTER TWENTY

BEAU walked to the Yacht Club bar and ordered a cold beer. He prayed Fonda would show up on time. He looked at the clock behind the bar and it was 7:50. There were a few people at the bar and two couples sitting across the room in the booths. Beau looked out the window at the covered patio restaurant. It was about half full, and all the overhead fans were on helping make the humid, tropical, night air more bearable. At precisely 8:00 p.m. Fonda walked through the front door. She was wearing a white dress and white heels. Her dark hair was down in a flip, and she carried a small white purse over her right shoulder. She was absolutely stunning. Fonda walked over to Beau and kissed him on the cheek.

"Would you like a drink, Fonda?"

"Thank you, Ronald, a vodka and tonic with a lemon slice would be nice."

Beau carried it from the bar for her as they walked to the restaurant outside. They sat down at a table overlooking the harbor, looked into each other's eyes, and started talking. Fonda had gone to the American School in Colon and then to Miami University in Miami, Florida. After graduation she worked in Miami for a large worldwide import-export firm for a few years, but then returned to Colon to take care of her elderly parents. She worked in Colon as a shipping agent for the International Shipping Agency Ltd. After her father's death her mother received her father's canal pension and some hefty life insurance proceeds. Fonda then started her own agency so her hours could be more flexible, and she could better tend to her mother's needs.

Beau told Fonda that he was a successful businessman from Miami who had an English mother and a Spanish father. He had been in the military and then had gotten into real estate. He had ended up building and investing in condominiums up and down the east coast of Florida. He turned the conversation to a description of the *Chica's* trip from Florida to Panama. Fonda asked him what had happened to his missing fingers.

"Oh, the aft cockpit lazarette hatch fell on them, but they're just about healed," said Beau as Fonda cringed at the thought. Then Beau said, "How is it possible that a beautiful, intelligent, woman like you doesn't have a husband or a boyfriend?"

Fonda flushed a little but answered, "I really haven't met a Panamanian man that I could really connect with. They all have this macho thing about where a woman's place is in society. An independent woman, like me, is threatening to them. The single American canal employees are all very transient these days, and I wouldn't go back to the states since I have my mother to care for. I have a date now and then, but I really don't have the time for a relationship. Have you ever been married, Ronald?"

"Yes, a long time ago. We divorced, had no children, and I guess I got too busy with the real estate business and my fishing priorities to have more than casual girlfriends. But now I'm slowing down. I've made enough money, and now I'm going to enjoy life."

"Good for you, I hope to do the same when my mother passes on. She's in the first stages of Alzheimer's and requires a lot of attention."

"We all go through some tough times when our parents' health fails. I think we have to live life to the fullest when we're young enough to enjoy it."

"But we have to take care of our responsibilities."

"Right on," said Beau wondering if his nose was getting longer.

They talked about Miami, Florida, and America. Both of them seemed to agree about everything. They finally ordered dinner, and Beau let Fonda order everything. They talked on with Beau having another beer and Fonda another vodka and tonic. When dinner came, they were both very hungry. Fonda ordered sea bass, broccoli, and garlic mashed potatoes. Beau had never had better fish in his whole life.

When dinner was finished, Beau suggested they walk down the dock and sit up on *Chica's* fly bridge and have a nightcap. Fonda agreed, and Beau quickly paid the check. They walked down the dock hand in hand to the *Chica*. Fonda climbed up the ladder onto the fly bridge, as Beau went into the salon to mix a drink for her and retrieve a cold one from the refrigerator for himself. He balanced the drinks on one arm and climbed up the fly bridge ladder one handed. He handed Fonda her drink and then rolled up the Stratoglass curtains to let in the night breeze. They sat next to each other forward of the console and looked out over the harbor waters at the moon. They made small talk for another minute, and then Fonda turned and looked at Beau. He set his beer down and leaned over and kissed Fonda lightly on the cheek. Fonda put her arms around Beau's neck and pulled him toward her. They kissed gently at first and then more and more passionately.

Beau started to tell her how beautiful she was and Fonda whispered, "Don't talk, Ronald, just kiss me."

Beau kissed her hard, and he felt his alter ego begin to swell. Fonda pulled him closer and he slipped his good hand under her dress and caressed her buttocks. Beau realized she was wearing a t-back, and he went on full alert. Beau slowly slid his hand up between her silky smooth thighs. She didn't stiffen, just moaned softly, and let it happen.

Fonda whispered in Beau's ear, "Not here, Ronald, let's go below."

Beau got up and gave her his hand, then led her aft to the fly bridge ladder. He went down first and waited as she backed down the ladder. When she turned at the bottom, Beau took her in his arms and they kissed again, hungrily. Beau guided her thru the salon door and down to the guest cabin where he carefully took off her white dress. He kissed her, and then took her bra off with a one-handed move he had perfected in high school. She took his shirt off, and then Beau felt her hand find him. Beau scooped Fonda up and laid her on the queen size bed. He slipped out of his shorts, and took a long look at Fonda's body before getting onto the bed. She was magnificent! Her breasts and nipples were larger than he had imagined and her hips were perfectly proportioned. Beau took off Fonda's t-back, turned her over, and started to massage her back and legs. After a few minutes he rolled her back over and took her in his arms. They kissed and stroked each other until Beau moved between her legs and gently entered her. The rhythm started slowly and soon increased to a near frenzy. Fonda finished with a shudder and Beau followed seconds later. Neither one of them had wanted it to end. They both lay there trying to catch their breath. Beau's heart was beating so fast he could hardly breathe. He took a deep breath and slowly let it out.

Fonda kissed him on the cheek and said, "Well, what are we going to do on our second date, Ronald?"

Beau laughed and said, "Oh, we'll think of something, Fonda, no worry."

They lay there for a long, long time, not wanting to lose the afterglow.

Fonda finally broke the silence, "What do you think brought this all on, Ronald?"

"Chemistry, Fonda, pure … chemistry."

A number of Beau's failed relationships had started this way. But Beau hadn't been able to sustain them when the lust had worn off. Because of the circumstances he probably would never get the chance to screw this one up. Fonda kissed Beau one more time and then got out of bed and went into the guest head. When she came out Beau got another long look at her spectacular body as she dressed.

Beau's libido was starting to stir again as Fonda turned and said, "I don't know what got into me tonight, but I certainly don't regret it. Please make contact with me when you bring your boat back through the canal, or better still, call me when you get settled in Costa Rica. It's only an hour's flight either way. I really hate to leave, but I have to pick up the Canal pilot and deckhands at 6:30 in the morning to have them here at 7:30."

She walked back to the side of the bed and kissed Beau hard on the lips.

"Thank you for a lovely evening that I shall never forget."

She turned quickly and walked through the cabin door, up the steps, and left through the salon door. Beau felt like he had just awakened from a dream, as he faded slowly off to sleep.

Beau woke up the next morning and realized it had all been real. He could still smell her perfume on his pillow. He looked over at the alarm clock and it was 5:55 a.m. He got up, pulled on his shorts, and went to the galley to start a pot of coffee. He checked on Hector and Luis, as he hadn't heard them come in last night. They were both sound asleep and snoring like two hibernating bears. He could only imagine what they had been up to. He decided he would let them sleep another half an hour.

Beau took a quick shower, and the whole time thought about last night and Fonda Johnson. He had never met anyone even remotely like her. What terrible timing, but such is life. She might have been the one to keep Beau on the straight and narrow. Beau had to laugh at that last thought. He knew after all these years that only he could keep himself on the straight and narrow. Maybe if his plan worked out over the next few days he could pursue her from Costa Rica. He hoped he would see her this morning when she dropped off the canal crew.

Beau woke Hector and Luis at 6:30 and by 7:00 they were waiting for break-fast at the patio restaurant. There was still a little breeze, and the air hadn't gotten stifling hot and humid yet. They had ordered, and Beau went into the dock master's office to clear *Chica's* bill. He thanked Jose for his help, especially with the filtering of the fuel drums, and tipped him a "Big Ben". His *huevos revueltos* and *chorizo* were waiting for him when he got back to the table.

"Do you think we'll make Panama City today, Beau?" asked Hector.

"If everything goes smoothly it should be no problem. "How was Colon?"

"Colon was okay," answered Hector. "But it was kind of old and worn out."

"Did you have a good time?" chided Beau.

"We always have a good time in a big city," laughed Hector. "That's why I want to make it to Panama City tonight."

"Well, I want to make it there too," said Beau between bites of his scrambled eggs and sausage, because we have to keep moving. We need to make Jaco four days from now so you two can get to San Jose."

"How far is it from Jaco to San Jose?"

"It's an hour and a half drive over the mountains. From there you can fly to Cancun and then back to Miami. Was your cousin Ricardo originally from Miami?"

"Yes, he was."

"Then you should probably call your cousin Raul in Miami, and tell him that the Mexican drug deal will take a few more days. The Cipriano family is probably asking some questions in Miami, trying to figure out who else was involved in stealing the three million."

"Yeah, Beau, we'll do that tonight from Panama City."

"I'm curious," said Beau changing the subject. "How do you square a free-lance drug deal with the Cipriano's?"

"We just contact our Miami lieutenant after we sell it to the street dealers and give him twenty percent of the profit. We only act as middlemen and sell it either to the Haitians or Russians in a single deal, highest bidder."

"How do you smuggle it in?"

"We have lots of cousins everywhere," laughed Hector while looking at Luis. "Right now it is shipped to Miami hidden in P.T. Cruisers that are built and shipped from the Tampico, Mexico, Chrysler plant. It is vacuum-packed and shipped inside the spare tires. The drug dogs can't smell it because of the new rubber smell. We plan to give No Nose $100,000."

"So you're going to pay him a hundred grand of his own money," laughed Beau. "You two have large *cojones*."

"You've got that right," said Hector, with a grin.

"Yours are not so small either, Beau," added Luis smiling.

They all had a good laugh and Beau knew that when he hatched his plan in the Pacific, they'd never see it coming.

Fonda and our crew arrived at 7:30, just as Beau was paying the breakfast bill.

"*Hola*, Ronald," called Fonda with a wave as she walked down the hill to the boat.

Beau and the Fernandez brothers walked down right behind them.

When they all got down the dock to *Chica*, Fonda turned and said, *Buenos Dias*, gentlemen, this is Captain Miguel Rojas," and she introduced everyone all around. The two line handlers' names were Pepe and Julio.

Fonda said, "Ronald, you will work at running the boat with Miguel, but he is in charge and will make all the decisions. Hector and Luis, you will work with Pepe and Julio handling the lines and fenders in the locks; all four of you are required. You need to work together to control the boat when the water is fed into the bottom of the lock. The fenders will protect you if any other boats or tugboats are transiting with you, and they will also protect you from the lock walls. There is a considerable amount of water turbulence when they fill, and if you're behind a freighter when she pulls out of a lock the prop wash is dangerous. If you load the lines and fenders and leave now you have an excellent chance for a one day transit."

Fonda extended her hand to Beau and said, "Good luck, Ronald, and it has been a pleasure meeting you. Have a safe transit and thank you for allowing me to be your agent. If there are any problems Miguel can call me on his cell phone. I have secured a mooring for you at the Balboa Yacht Club on the Pacific side. You can take on fuel and fresh water at their dock, and the food in the club restaurant is very good." (When she said food, she gave Beau a little wink.) "Ronald, here is my address and phone number if you need anything else." She pressed a folded piece of paper in his hand with a squeeze.

"Thank you, Fonda, for everything."

He wanted to say more, but this was not the time. He reluctantly let go of her hand, and she turned and walked back up the dock. Just watching her spectacular backside disappear up the dock brought a tear to his eye.

Beau composed himself, jumped aboard *Chica*, and started the engines and generator. He then turned the vessel over to Miguel and stood by to help in any way he could. The crew carried the fenders and lines aboard, and Miguel motored away from the dock towards the Gatun locks. Miguel explained to Beau that the canal was less than fifty miles long, but it consisted of three sets of locks. Each direction had two sets of locks at each location. The lock chambers were 1000 feet long and 110 feet wide, and each end had two opening doors like barn doors. The locks were gravity filled with water from Lake Gatun through pipes in the floor of each chamber. The Gatun locks had a three-step chamber that would raise the vessels a total of eighty-five feet to the level of Lake Gatun. Miguel said it took fifty-two million gallons of water to get a ship through all the locks.

Miguel asked Beau, "Mr. Santos, what is *Chica's* cruising speed?"

"Twenty-five knots Captain."

Miguel throttled the Bertram up to twenty-five knots and headed for the locks.

"Do you take many yachts through the canal, as opposed to freighters and cruise ships?"

"I take mostly large commercial boats through, Mr. Santos, but occasionally I get a one hundred and fifty foot yacht. This is quite a treat for me to take a small, fast, and maneuverable sportfish like this through. I haven't done anything like this since I was a beginning advisor pilot years ago. Most of the smaller boats won't pay the twenty-two hundred and fifty dollar pilot fee, since the pilots in training are included in the yacht transit fee. But you might have to wait three weeks or more to get a trainee."

They were at the Gatun Locks before Beau knew it. The scenery had changed from tropical city to tropical jungle. Beau was taken aback by the sheer enormity of the four locksets. The western outboard bottom lock doors were open, and a freighter was moving into the lock and being cabled to the port and starboard locomotives that would power it through its three-chambers. Miguel was busy on his hand held radio speaking in Spanish.

Switching to English he said, "That is our lock, Mr. Santos, and we will be moving in behind that freighter in a few minutes."

Chica pulled in to the lock a few minutes later behind the *Dorian B*, from Amsterdam. It was flying the flag of the Netherlands. The professional line handlers buddied up with Hector and Luis to show them the ropes. They hung the tire fenders on the port and starboard hull sides. Then *Chica* headed for the starboard side of the enormous chamber, and the crew worked the lines into position. The aft doors closed behind *Chica,* and when they were fully closed the water started to bubble up from the lock bottom and the vessels started to rise. There was some turbulence and the lines strained a bit as the vessels steadily rose until they reached twenty-eight feet. Then the aft door opened to the next chamber, and the vessels moved into that chamber for the next step up. After the third chamber filled the forward door opened out onto Gatun Lake. *Chica's* lines strained tightly as *Dorian B* left that lock under her own power and her prop wash pushed against the Bertram. When *Dorian B* was clear of the lock Miguel told Beau that they would run *Chica* through the lake at twenty-five knots and rendezvous with another large ship over at the Pedro Miguel Locks in time to transit the locks with her. As *Chica* ran across the great expanse of Lake Gatun it became clear why Panama was chosen for the canal. The distance was less than fifty miles and they needed only three sets of locks. But in reality, the harsh topography and tropical climate had claimed thirty thousand lives during the building of the canal. Miguel mentioned that the locks were too small to handle the new "super" freighters that were three times larger than the locks would allow. Panama had committed to building new locks that would accommodate those ships along side of the existing locks. When they were completed both sets would continue to serve the world's shipping industry.

They had a nice run across the small yacht "Banana" Channel on Gatun Lake and then into the mountain cuts near Gamboa. There they encountered numerous freighters traveling in both directions and a few sailboats. Miguel didn't slow down for the sail boaters as he had a commitment at the next lock, and each sail boater either shook his fist or flipped him the bird as *Chica* passed them and they turned up into her wake.

Beau laughed and said to Miguel, "It's the same everywhere, the sail boats and trawlers that go six to eight knots think everybody else should go through life at that speed."

Miguel smiled and said, "You got that right, *Senor!*"

Beau marveled at the scenery changes as they made their way across the Isthmus. The expansive marshes gave way to lush rain forests around Gamboa and then to rocky mountain precipices in the narrow Culebra Cut that had been blasted out of rock to get the ships to the Pedro Miguel Locks. Gatun Lake itself had been the Chagres River until an ingenious Dam had been built to supply the canal with the enormous amounts of water the canal needed to operate.

Miguel slowed *Chica* as they approached the locks and maneuvered around a waiting freighter and deftly moved the Bertram into the waiting inboard lock behind a huge white cruise ship. It was *The Star of Norway* from Oslo, and the size and height of the ship was incredible. There was a look of complete disbelief on Hector and Luis's faces. They had seen many large cruise ships across from Rickenbacker Causeway in Miami Beach, but they had never been tied up under the stern of one and seen the top of a twenty foot propeller blade sticking out of the water fifty feet in front of them. The Panamanian crew took it in stride; it was just another day at the office for them.

After repeating the tie up procedure, the control tower opened the valves to let thirty-one feet of water out of the lock to level it with the Miraflores locks which were next and only a few miles south.

Beau had been through the Okeechobee Waterway locks, in Florida, many times over the years. He had thought those locks would have prepared him for the Panama locks, but those locks were minute compared to these giant locks. The Okeechobee Waterway connected Fort Meyers, on the west coast to Stuart, on the east coast. It saved over two hundred miles by eliminating the run down through the Florida Keys then back up the east coast to Stuart. The waterway covered one hundred and fifty-two miles. There were five locks and a thirty-nine mile run across Lake Okeechobee, which is approximately twenty feet above sea level. The locks were two hundred and fifty feet long and fifty feet wide. There was only one lock per location so only one direction could lock through at a time. It was efficiently run and maintained by the Corp of Army Engineers, and on a good day a twenty-knot boat could make it across the state in eight to ten hours.

The giant forward doors opened and the crew started to brace for the cruise ship's prop wash. The cruise ship started out and Miguel held *Chica's* position with some engine use, and then followed *The Star of Norway* to the last set of locks which would drop the Bertram fifty-four feet to sea level on the Pacific side four miles away.

Beau said to Miguel, "It looks like we'll get to Panama City by mid-afternoon."

"It should be no problem, *Senor*, if there are no delays at the Miraflores lock."

Beau noticed the terrain remained rocky, and the blasted out ditch they traveled in was even narrower. Lush green vegetation continued to cascade down the sheer rock walls on the way to the Miraflores Locks.

The last lockset went smoothly, and *Chica* again followed *The Star of Norway* out of the lock. The crew coiled the lines and stacked the tire fenders in the

Bertram's big fishing cockpit. Miguel put *Chica* up on plane and passed the cruise ship, whose decks were now lined with its passengers, waiting for a glimpse of the Bridge of the Americas that linked the two continents. Soon, Beau saw the famous one-mile long Bridge in the distance. They passed under it and then turned into the Balboa Yacht Club and idled to the main dock. There was a sizable mooring field outboard of the Yacht Club, and it appeared to be about half occupied. Miguel was on the radio to the Balboa dock master whose name was Roberto.

"Mr. Santos," said Miguel. "You have mooring number sixteen. I will land at the main dock so my crew and I can disembark with our equipment."

"Can you ask Roberto if we can fuel up before we go to the mooring?"

"It should be no problem, *Senor*. There is no one at the fuel dock now. I'll land there instead."

After they tied up the Bertram Miguel introduced Beau to Roberto, and Beau had Hector fuel the boat while he checked into the Yacht Club. He asked Roberto if he could take on fresh water and whether there was an AT&T pay phone available. Roberto's answer was "yes" to both questions. Beau followed Roberto to his office and filled out the Yacht Club registration form. He caught up with Miguel and his crew just as they were finishing loading the lines and fenders into a van.

Beau hollered, "Hold on a minute, Miguel!" He tipped Miguel a "Big Ben" and gave the line handlers an "Andrew Jackson" each. Beau asked, "Miguel, are you going back to Colon in the van?"

"No, *Senor*. The pilots have quarters at both ends of the canal. I will pilot a ship back through the canal tomorrow."

Beau shook hands with Miguel, said goodbye, and went back into the dock masters office to get a weather report.

Roberto said, "The Pacific looks good in both directions, but remember it's the rainy season. The winds should be five to ten from the east with thundershowers likely every afternoon and evening.

"Is there anything big out there?"

"There is a hurricane brewing north of Nicaragua, but it will be moving north towards Cabo San Lucas, Mexico, then west," Roberto cautioned. "Be careful near any of the river mouths up and down the coast because you might encounter floating debris, such as branches, logs, and whole trees. Some might be quite a ways off shore, so don't run at night at all, and pay close attention during the day."

"Can I pay you now for the mooring? I want to get an early start in the morning."

"Of course," answered Roberto, and he radioed the assistant dock master at the fuel dock, added that total to the mooring charge, and wrote up a bill for *Chica.*

"Is there a water taxi service at night?"

"Yes, it's 24/7, and costs five U.S. dollars per trip."

Beau paid the bill in cash and gave Roberto a "Ben Franklin" while thanking him for his help and said goodbye.

As Beau walked down the ramp to the fuel dock he noticed two haul-out railways just west of the Yacht Club. There was an old Hatteras 46 like Seth's up on one of the ways. His eyes clouded up as he thought about his older brother. Why couldn't he be like Seth, solid and consistent? Seth had always helped Beau through all his troubles. Beau didn't realize until this very moment how much he loved Seth. The shame was he might never see him again ... so he could tell him.

Hector was just tightening the water inlet cap on the gunnel as Beau climbed into the cockpit. He went directly to the fly bridge and started the engines. Hector cast off the lines, and Beau motored out to their mooring. When he shut down the engines it occurred to him that the fresh water passage across Panama had probably flushed the salt out of the engines' and generator's cooling systems.

He took a deep breath as *Chica* swung into the westerly sea breeze on her mooring. Beau was happy that they'd made it through the canal without a hitch, but tomorrow would probably be the most important day of his life and he was nervous. His plan to eliminate Hector and Luis had to happen tomorrow to make the whole situation work out for Beau. He was fearful of the task ahead, but he realized it was necessary to ensure his long-term welfare. With them out of the picture he could just disappear in Costa Rica and not have to watch his back every minute.

Beau composed himself, climbed down out of the fly bridge, and started to tell Hector and Luis about the water taxi.

Hector interrupted saying, "We know about the water taxi and we know there's an AT&T telephone up in the Yacht Club. I asked Geraldo, the assistant dock master, when we were fueling. I'll have Luis call Raul, in Miami, on our way out to Panama City tonight."

"I have plenty to do here. I need to check the engine room and set up our navigation from here to Costa Rica. I'm planning on leaving tomorrow at 7:00 a.m."

"No problem, Beau. Geraldo filled us in on the hot spots in Panama City, so we won't have to waste time finding them. We'll be ready to go in the morning."

Beau studied the charts while Hector and Luis showered and dressed for their night on the town. He plotted a course southwest, then west along the Azuero Peninsular for 125 miles. Then he would head northwest for a 130 miles to the Island of Coiba, which was still in Panamanian waters. He would anchor in a cove that was protected by a small islet called Granito de Oro. It would be a nine to ten hour run, if the weather held. The next day he would run further north to Golfito, which was a 150 miles from Coiba Island, at the head of the Golfo Dulce in southern Costa Rica. Beau had been to Golfito four or so years ago, and had fished out of the Banana Bay Marina. He could dock overnight there and fill up with fuel for his run to Jaco and Los Suenos the next day.

Hector and Luis appeared and Beau called the water taxi for them on VHF radio channel 10. Five minutes later they were gone, and he had the boat to himself. He finished plotting the lat-long numbers and decided to put them in the GPS on his way out of the channel in the morning. The engine room was too hot to go down into, especially with the generator still running, so he put that off until tomorrow morning when it would be tolerably cooler.

Beau went down to the guest cabin and undressed to take a much-needed shower. He took his wallet out of his pocket and felt the folded piece of paper Fonda had given him in Colon. He took it out and opened it to make sure her number was there. She had written a short note under her phone number; *Dear Ronald, I will meet you tonight at the Balboa Yacht Club at 8:00 p.m. and don't be late … Love, Fonda.* At once his heart started to pound, and Beau felt a little light-headed. He looked at the alarm clock on the dresser and it read 7:45. Beau showered, shaved, brushed his teeth, got dressed, and was ready to go in less than fifteen minutes. He called the water taxi and was walking briskly up the ramp to the Yacht Club at 8:05.

CHAPTER TWENTY-ONE

SETH came back from his lunch with Jeb, went into his office, and closed the door. He took the Bahamas fuel dock list out of his top desk drawer and got busy on the phone. His first call was to Chub Cay in the Berry Islands. The dock master was co-operative and checked his records for the last two weeks.

"Sorry, Mon," said the dock master. "We have no record of a Bertram 54 fueling. But you are the second call today about that boat."

"Who else called?" asked a very surprised Seth.

"A Captain named Tony, checking out a float plan."

Seth thanked him and asked if Captain Tony had left a call back number. The answer was no. Captain Tony, whoever he was, was ahead of him, but Seth would try to catch up. However, he wouldn't be leaving any name or call back numbers in case he called ahead of Captain Tony. Seth wondered if Captain Tony was a friend of Ronald Santos.

Seth called five more fuel docks up in the Abaco's with no results and then started on a long list of fuel docks in Nassau and Paradise Island. The answer was no at Hurricane Hole, no at Atlantis, no at Bayshore, no at Yacht Haven, but he hit pay dirt at the Harborview Texaco Starport. The dock master remembered a 54 Bertram named *Chica*. He also recalled that the captain had left him a nice tip when they left.

Seth asked, "What day was *Chica* in Nassau?"

"Monday, a week" was the reply.

"What is your name?"

"Ernesto."

"Ernesto, how many people were in the crew, and what did they look like?"

"The captain was very tan, had black hair, and hadn't shaved in a few days. The two crewmembers looked like brothers and were Cuban. The captain had injured his hand. I remember because it was bandaged and still bleeding. He told me a cockpit hatch had fallen on it."

"Which hand?"

"The left one,"

"Did he say where they were headed?"

"He didn't tell me, but they had four large plastic fuel drums in the cockpit. I'd say they were going some distance. They cleared customs here after they fueled. Agent Percy Lightbourne came to the boat, maybe you could check with him."

"Thank you, Ernesto," said Seth. "You've been a big help."

Seth didn't want to get involved with Bahamian customs or any other government agency. He didn't know enough about the situation to know if he should get any authorities involved at this point. But, he did know that he needed to double check the bleeding captain's left hand.

Seth called Fred back at the Stock Island fuel dock in the Keys. Fred answered and identified himself.

"Fred, I'm calling about the Bertram 54, *Chica*, again, which I talked to you about this morning. Do you remember anything unusual about the captain's hands?"

"No sir, nothing unusual."

"No bandages?"

"No, sir, I'm sure of that."

Seth said, "Thanks again, Fred," and hung up.

Seth leaned back in his desk chair and thought about what he had just learned. No bandage, then the next day a bloody bandage. Detective Baggett finds a watch, two shoes, and two of Beau's fingers in a shark's stomach. *Left hand ... Left fingers.* He was now sure Beau was still alive and captaining the Bertram. But, were the two Cubans forcing him? Seth wasn't sure. Fred had told him that the two Cubans had been gone to provision *Chica* for over two hours, and Beau was alone on the boat. So why was Beau doing this, and why did he cut his fingers off and fake his death? Seth decided not to confide in anyone and to find out for himself. He would continue to follow the boat until he could physically catch up with it and then find the answers. If Beau needed help he would help. If Beau had gone off the deep end, he'd deal with that when he knew the facts.

Seth resumed telephoning his Bahamas list and started to record a day-by-day time and destination log for *Chica*. He called Staniel Key and George Town in the Exumas with no luck. If they were headed in that direction, that would leave only Great Inagua or the Turks and Caicos. Seth walked downstairs to *Tar Baby* and pulled his big Caribbean chart from under the guest bunk. He liked to store his charts flat so he could fold them to use in the wind up on the fly bridge. He took it back to his office and plotted mileage against fuel usage and came up with two major possibilities; Matthew Town on Great Inagua or Providenciales in the Caicos. From those ports, they could run to the Dominican Republic, Haiti, the Caymans, or Jamaica. Haiti was a poor option, as was the Dominican Republic, because neither was user-friendly. Jamaica was a good jump off destination to go further south, and the Cayman's were an extremely user-friendly destination, but very small. If they wanted to run and hide, for whatever reason, further south made more sense.

Seth's phoning day was an hour from being over. He phoned the Turtle Cove Marina in "Provo" and got a negative answer. They hadn't been to the Caicos. Seth asked the dock master "Has anyone else called you about this boat?"
"No," answered the dock master. "I hope you find them."
Seth thanked him and hung up.

Next he called the fuel dock in Great Inagua. The dock master answered at the Matthew Town Texaco Starport and quickly confirmed that *Chica* had been there. Seth's Maptech cruising guide put all the marinas in the Bahamas, their levels of service, and their phone numbers, right at his fingertips. Seth asked if anyone else had called about the Bertram, and the dock master said no. Maybe Seth had pulled ahead of Captain Tony. Seth gave the dock master the same story about trying to intercept them to inform the captain of a family emergency.

He decided to call Jamaica next because his instincts told him they were probably heading for Central or South America. He pulled the Kingston, Jamaica harbor fuel docks up on the Internet using "Noonsight". There were three large commercial fuel bunker docks in Kingston, and Morgan's Marina across the harbor in Port Royal. It appeared that Morgan's was the only yacht marina in Kingston harbor.

Seth vaguely recalled that Robert E. and Beau had delivered a Hatteras sportfish to Kingston when Beau was just out of high school. Seth remembered the story, because Robert E. had told him he was taking Beau along to straighten him out. Robert E. thought a trip like that with just the two of them might turn Beau around. At least he had tried, but obviously to no avail. Seth dialed the three commercial docks, but got little co-operation and no one remembered any sportfish boats. Seth called Morgan's and the dock master answered identifying himself as Avery.

Seth asked about *Chica* and the dock master said, "I remember the boat and the captain. His name was Ronald."

Seth asked about the crew and Avery described the two heavy-set Cubans.

"When did they fuel up?" asked Seth.

"They came in last Friday morning, stayed overnight, and left early Saturday morning for San Andres."

"How do you know he went to San Andres?"

"Well, the captain asked for a weather forecast for that area, and he had the four plastic fuel drums in the cockpit filled with fuel.

"That's a long haul."

"Yes, it is, but it's the standard course to the Panama Canal from here. Many smaller boats, carrying extra fuel, go that way all the time. For this time of year the weather was very favorable."

"Was the captain medium build, black hair and beard?"

"Yes, I could tell he was an experienced seaman and a capable person. He also left me a most generous tip."

"Did he have a bandage on his left hand?"

"Just on his fingers, he said a hatch had fallen on his hand and sliced off two of his fingers."

"Thanks for the information, maybe I can reach him before he gets through the Canal," said Seth just before he hung up.

Seth looked at his watch and it was past quitting time in the Central time zone so he was done playing detective for today. Everybody was long gone from the boatworks, but Seth had been on such a roll that he had been oblivious to the exodus at 5:00 p.m. He sat back and slowed his mind down. He again tried to make sense of it all. He concluded that Beau was in big trouble, but what he didn't know was whether Beau was in it willingly or not.

He locked up the office and let the dogs out before he left for home. He stopped by the Yacht Club and checked with Robby, the club manager, about the details concerning Beau's wake on Thursday. Robby nervously relayed his condolences to Seth while he fidgeted with his stylish mullet haircut. Beau would be missed at the Yacht Club bar. Seth specified top shelf whiskey and wine. He also ordered hot and cold hors d'oeuvres to be served from 6:00 to 8:00 o'clock. A three-piece band would play, and as many of Beau's friends that wanted to come up to the microphone to eulogize Beau were welcome to speak.

Seth had decided not to call the wake off because of Captain Tony's interest in *Chica*. If Beau were trying to disappear, maybe a wake would help his cause. Maybe Beau was really dead and Jeb was right. Seth might be just kidding himself. Seth didn't think so. He would just play it out to whatever the final conclusion was, all by himself.

Seth stopped at Walt'z Fish Shack in Madeira Beach on the way home and had a grouper sandwich and two glasses of Shiraz wine. By the time he got home, he was really ready for bed.

Luigi Scuzzi got his first report from No Nose's captain in the Bahamas early the next afternoon. Captain Tony had information that a Bertram 54 had fueled up, the Saturday morning after the Tampa robbery, at the St. Petersburg Municipal Marina's fuel dock. There were two Latinos aboard and they paid in cash. The name of the boat was *Pescadora*.

Captain Tony had confirmed with the yacht broker in Naples that *Pescadora* was the original name on the boat sold to Ronald Santos (Hector Fernandez). The broker had also volunteered that the new owner had filed a name change form with the Coast Guard Documentation Office. The new name was to be *Chica*, with a hailing port change to Fort Lauderdale, Florida. Later in the day, after calling fuel docks down the west coast of Florida and throughout the Keys, Captain Tony had turned *Chica* up Sunday at the Oceanside Marina fuel dock on Stock Island just east of Key West. He reported that the boat had taken four extra drums of fuel aboard and had been heavily provisioned by the Hispanic crew. The assistant dock master, also remembered a captain with a full black beard, medium build, and Caucasian features. When questioned, he said they paid in cash and the captain had left a large tip for him and his dock boys when *Chica* finally got under-way near dusk.

Captain Tony thought that extra fuel, heavy provisions, and leaving late in the day, signaled Mexico. The boat's name had obviously been changed somewhere between St. Petersburg and Stock Island. Captain Tony called Cancun and Isla Mujeres, which is an island nine miles from Cancun. He checked six fuel docks and marinas and no one had seen *Chica*. He also called Hemingway Marina in Havana, Cuba, and they also had not been seen there.

Captain Tony called Luigi back, updated him, and said, "I will start calling the Bahamas marinas and fuel docks tomorrow morning. We've run out of time today."

Luigi had started Cadillac checking with the family's customs contacts in Mexico and the Bahamas, but that was a slower process and he wouldn't have anything from them until sometime tomorrow at best. The Stock Island, Key West, fuel stop proved that Hector and Luis had eliminated two partners at the aquarium, but who was the bearded captain and where were they headed with the three million?

Luigi called No Nose and drove over to Golf View Drive an hour later. No Nose's bodyguard was waiting in the garage and Luigi followed him out to the hot tub below the waterfall. Luigi filled No Nose in as the mafia Don sat in the hot tub smoking another one of those foot long Cuban cigars.

When Luigi was finished, No Nose said, "Well, some progress is better than none. I wonder where they got the captain. Those two morons couldn't navigate a boat that size across Tampa Bay. I know Captain Tony or Cadillac will come up with something tomorrow. Customs will be the only paper trail, because they are paying cash, my cash, for everything, even the fucking big tips. Have Captain Tony figure two or three possible destinations, so Cadillac can follow the customs trails. They could be headed for the Caymans to deposit my cash in one of the Cayman Banks. Hell, we've got millions hidden in those banks and the Bahamas banks, too!"

Luigi left No Nose to make the call back to Captain Tony for the possible routes. The captain promised to work on them that evening, and call him by eight a.m. the next day.

True to his word, Captain Tony called the next morning at 8:00 a.m. sharp. He gave Luigi three possible routes and said he would spend the day calling possible fuel stops along all three routes. Luigi arranged for Captain Tony to phone his son, Giorgio, at the carpet business to get him a list of the marinas Captain Tony wanted to call. Giorgio was a whiz on the computer and could probably look them up three times as fast as Captain Tony could. Once they were teamed up, Luigi called Cadillac in Miami and gave him the routes to check through the customs contacts.

Captains Tony's left ear was beginning to hurt from making call after call to the Bahamas. He had confirmed a fuel-up and departure in Nassau and was now canvassing the rest of the Bahamas looking for *Chica's* next stop. At least now he didn't have to look the numbers up on the stupid Internet. He wasn't complaining, but he hadn't spent his life becoming a top-notch fishing captain to turn into a computer geek. But, the money and the fringe benefits were better than good; and he knew enough not to ever cross Mr. C. Captain Tony wanted to catch fish, not sleep with them.

Tony had called about twenty-five more marinas in the Bahamas, including Hawk's Nest on Cat Island, Flying Fish on Long Island, and Riding Rock on San Salvador, before he tried the Texaco fuel dock in Matthew Town. Great Inagua was the end of the line in the Bahamas. He asked the dock master if he had seen *Chica*.

The dock master remembered the Bertram, and said, "Yes, they came in for fuel."

Captain Tony asked, "Did they stay overnight?"

"No, they didn't dock in Matthew Town; they fueled up and left immediately."

"Were there three men aboard and extra fuel drums?"

"Yes, there were three men aboard, and there were four plastic fuel drums in the cockpit. Why are you looking for this boat?"

"They're running late on their original float plan, but I should be able find them in the DR in a day or so. Thanks for your help."

"Glad to be of service," said the dock master.

Captain Tony ended the call and set the satphone down on the salon table. He had given Luigi possible route destinations to the Turks and Caicos, the Dominican Republic and the Caymans. Now he wanted to add Central America. He called Luigi to fill him in on Great Inagua.

"Luigi, they fueled up in Great Inagua last Wednesday. I want to add Jamaica, San Andres Island, and the Panama Canal as another possible route. If they go through the canal it opens up two or three more possibilities."

"Good work, Tony," said Luigi breathing easier. "I'll call Cadillac, and I know Mr. C. will be pleased. Is Giorgio working out for you?"

"Thanks, Luigi. The kid is feeding me numbers faster than I can call them. I feel like I've got this fucking telephone growing out of my ear."

Luigi laughed, hung up, and called No Nose. Thirty minutes later he arrived, delivered the update, and was glad that No Nose was beginning to smile a little.

"We're starting to close in on the bastards, Luigi. Keep the pressure on and keep me informed. I'm going to play golf this afternoon with Tommy "White Shoes" Gamino and a couple of federal judges, so if you get something don't call me until tonight."

Twenty-eight calls later, Captain Tony had eliminated Haiti, the major ports and resorts in the Dominican, and most important, the Cayman Islands. Tony had also called the marinas in Ponce, at the Mona Passage end of Puerto Rico, and all of the marinas from there around to San Juan. Having no success in Puerto Rico, he turned his efforts to Jamaica. He got lucky on his fourth call. Tony had been to Kingston two times over the years, and he had stayed at Morgan's Marina both times. He had all but forgotten about it until Giorgio gave him the Jamaican numbers. The dock master had left for the day, but his assistant remembered the Bertram being there almost a week ago. Captain Tony asked him to describe the crew, and the assistant described the black bearded captain and two "menacing" looking Latinos. Captain Tony thanked him and then called Giorgio. He filled him in and then asked Giorgio to look up all the facilities on San Andres, the Columbian Island, and the facilities at both ends of the Panama Canal. They both agreed they were done for the day and Giorgio promised the numbers at 8:00 a.m. the next morning.

Tony then called Luigi and gave him the latest report, including the *Chica* sighting in Jamaica. He asked Luigi to get Cadillac on the customs trail in San Andres and Panama. The family had good connections in both Columbia and Panama because of their drug trade. A tremendous amount of illegal drugs passed through both countries on their way to Florida. It would be hard for the average American citizen to understand that bribery and patronage was a way of life at all levels of those governments.

Luigi had another sit down with No Nose shortly after he had called Cadillac to get him started in Central America. It had taken two days for the Bahamian Customs contact to inform Cadillac that the Fernandez brothers and the captain using Ronald Santos' passport had cleared customs in Nassau. Everything moved very slowly in the Bahamas.

Thursday morning started early for Captain Tony when he got a 7:00 a.m. call from Giorgio giving him the phone numbers that he needed. He went out for breakfast and returned to start calling at 9:00 a.m. daylight savings time. His first call was to Nene's Fuel Dock in San Andres at 7:00 a.m. central time. It had turned out to be the only fuel dock in San Andres that could handle a diesel yacht. The dock attendant remembered the boat and the crew. In fact, he recalled, the San Andres customs official had called him a couple of days ago to tell him that the Bertram had experienced water intrusion problems with the fuel they had gotten at Nene's, but had arrived in Panama none the less.

"It happens from time to time," said the dock attendant. "We don't filter the fuel we get off the tankers."

Captain Tony thanked him, hung up, and called Luigi.

"I've got them in Panama, Luigi.

"We already know, Tony, Cadillac got a call at 8:00 this morning from our Panamanian Customs contact. He has *Chica* checking out on the Panama City side on Wednesday afternoon. So where do you think they're headed next?"

"If I wanted to hide down there on the Pacific side, I'd pick Ecuador to the south, and Costa Rica, El Salvador, or Guatemala to the north."

"Which is the closest?"

"Costa Rica. There's minimal crime, a stable government, and with enough money you can buy citizenship."

"Well, let's start there and if it doesn't pan out, we'll try the other countries."

"Okay, I'll have Giorgio pull up all the information, but *Chica* will spend at least two days traveling before she needs more fuel or checks into customs," counseled Tony. "My left ear could use a day or two of rest and we don't want to get ahead of them. If we tip our hand they may ditch the boat."

Luigi called No Nose and arranged a sit down for later in the day. Then he called Cadillac and asked him to put his Costa Rican customs contact on notice to alert them if Ronald Santos and the Fernandez brothers checked into Costa Rica. The family had Internet gambling interests based in Costa Rica, so their connections went deep.

No Nose was pacing back and forth on his veranda when Luigi first got there. He had the air conditioning and fans on high, and being on the veranda felt like a spring night in the midst of the oppressive August heat. He motioned Luigi inside when he saw him approaching. They sat in his office and No Nose gave Luigi a cigar. He leaned over and lit it, and then lit one for himself.

"It's a great cigar, John, is it Cuban?" asked Luigi while exhaling white smoke.

No Nose nodded saying, "Give me the news, Luigi, I'm all ears." Luigi updated him, explaining that *Chica* was through the Panama Canal and most probably was headed north to Costa Rica for her next stop. He had Cadillac working Costa Rican Customs and Captain Tony would start calling fuel docks in Costa Rica on Saturday.

No Nose took a long pull on his cigar and then exhaled saying, "The pigeons are getting ready to roost."

CHAPTER TWENTY-TWO

BEAU walked through the door to the Balboa Yacht Club bar dressed in tan shorts, and a white Colombia fishing shirt. His thick black hair was slicked back and still wet from his shower. His riveting blue eyes sparkled as he searched the bar for Fonda. He found her sitting at a corner table at the furthest end of the dimly lit bar. She was dressed in black Capri pants, a black scoop neck jersey top, and black heels. She looked almost unreal.

She had a wry smile on her face, and Beau broke into a grin as he walked over to her.

He extended his hand and said, "Why, Ms. Johnson, imagine running into you here."

She laughed and said, "You did read my note, didn't you, Ronald?"

"Yes, about twenty minutes ago when I was cleaning out my pockets and was looking forward to taking a long, leisurely shower. When did you get here?"

"I drove over the mountains this afternoon. It's not much of a drive, and I have an office with an apartment upstairs in Panama City, just across the America's Bridge. I work on this coast almost as much as I do on the Colon side."

"I thought you said you had an associate on this end?"

"I do, but she can handle just so much."

"Well, I have to tell you, Fonda, that this is more than just a pleasant surprise. I thought about you quite a bit on the trip over here."

"You haven't been off my mind for a minute, Ronald."

"Well, let's have some dinner," said Beau. "I hope you're as hungry as I am."

"Maybe I'm hungrier, Ronald. Let's get a table in the restaurant."

They were seated immediately and Fonda ordered fish for both of them. She asked if his crew had gone into Panama City.

"They left an hour ago, and I'm sure they won't be back until the wee hours."

He and Fonda made small talk, and she questioned him in more detail about his business interests and his life in Miami. Beau answered as generally as possible and steered the conversation back to that day's trip across the Canal. He had many questions about the workings of the Canal, and she answered all of them. Beau asked her if she had ever been to Costa Rica.

"Yes, when I was in high school. My parents took me to San Jose, and then to Quepos. We toured Manuel Antonio National Park and the neighboring rain forests. The beaches at Antonio are the most beautiful I have ever seen. We also traveled up to the Arenal volcano on our way back to San Jose and stayed there overnight. The hotel is so close to the volcano that you can see the red hot lava streaming down the mountain side all night."

"Do you think we could get together in Costa Rica, Fonda? Maybe you could take some time off and fly to San Jose?"

"Honestly, it would be impossible because of my mother."

"Then I will fly to Panama, and you can show me your country," countered Beau.

"I would like nothing better," replied Fonda enthusiastically.

They finished their dinner and Fonda again smiled wryly and said, "Would you like to see my apartment across the bridge?"

"I'm a little reluctant to leave the boat unattended. Do you mind taking the water taxi out to *Chica*?"

"Well, there'll be some dock talk, but the bartender and the waiters have already seen me with you, so what the hell."

They went back out into the humid, tropical, night and walked down to the water taxi. The moon shown on the water, and Beau couldn't hear any thunderstorms growling in the distance as the launch made its way out to *Chica*. They climbed aboard, and Beau unlocked and opened the salon door unleashing a cool blast of air from the inside. Once inside, there were no formalities. Beau kissed and embraced Fonda lifting her off her feet. He led her down the companionway stairs and into the guest cabin. They both shed their clothes and then came together and embraced at the foot of the bed. Beau kissed Fonda deeply and moved her gently against the cabin bulkhead. He kissed her sloping breasts and flicked her dark brown nipples with his tongue.

Fonda gasped and said, "Don't make me wait, Ronald."

Beau reached around and grasped Fonda's firm buttocks and gently lifted her with both his hands. Fonda reached down and guided Beau home. As he penetrated her, she began to moan softly. When the tempo started to increase she wrapped her legs around his waist and clasped her arms behind his neck. Beau started to thrust harder, pinning Fonda's back against the bulkhead.

Fonda had her tongue in Beau's ear and whispered, "Harder, Ronald, do it harder!" Beau shifted into overdrive, and Fonda tightened her arms around Beau's neck and arched up sharply. She cried out his name, and then went limp. Beau finished with her still pinned to the bulkhead. He let out a deep breath, turned, and gently rolled her onto the queen size bed. As he took her into his arms and gently kissed her, he realized that she was quietly weeping.

"Are you all right, Fonda? Did I hurt you?" whispered Beau.

"No, Ronald, just the opposite", said Fonda smiling through her tears. "I've always hoped it might be this good."

They kissed again, and then Fonda headed for the guest shower. Beau got up and walked quickly to the forward cabin's head. On a hunch, he looked through Hector's DOB kit and found the prescription vial of Viagra that he thought would be there. He took one of the little blue pills with a handful of water from the faucet. Beau was confident he could perform a second time if given twenty minutes or so. But, he doubted his stamina for a third try, if the opportunity arose, so the Viagra would be good insurance.

When he got back to the guest cabin, Fonda was lounging seductively on the bed. Beau slid in beside her and they started kissing and hugging again. Beau told Fonda that he had gotten a vasectomy years ago, if she had any worries. She said she wasn't worried, and continued to nibble on his ear. Beau wondered how many paternity suits that simple operation had saved him over the years.

Beau turned his full attention back to Fonda's flawless body. He was already becoming aroused as he rubbed her back in the dimly lit cabin.

Fonda snuggled up closer and said, "I was thinking about being with you like this all the way across the mountains, and I almost ran off the road a couple of times."

Beau laughed, "I could tell, and it was wonderful." Beau stroked her beautiful, silky smooth, skin. He worked his way down to her voluptuous backside and worked on it for a while, then began massaging her feet. Beau then swung up and straddled her legs. He kneaded her back with long, slow strokes. She moaned with pleasure as he ran his thumbs down both sides of her spine, she arched her buttocks up each time he ran his thumbs down her back, and Beau soon returned to full attention.

"I'm ready, Ronald," said Fonda in a husky voice. For the next hour Fonda made Beau glad that he'd taken that Viagra. Finally they both lay exhausted and soaked with perspiration. Beau hoped Fonda was finished for the night because he certainly was. Fonda got up and went into the guest head. When she got back in bed Fonda noticed that Beau was only on half alert.

"Quite a lively fellow you've got there," laughed Fonda. Fonda kissed him again and said, "I hate to go, but I really ought to be leaving."

Beau looked down, and thought … *Thank God!* Fonda looked over at Beau and said, smiling, "Well, it looks like I finally did him in."

"Be careful," laughed Beau. "He's only pouting because he thinks *you* don't want anymore."

Fonda and Beau lingered a few minutes more, and Fonda broke the silence with a question, "If this is your boat, Ronald, why do you sleep in the guest cabin instead of the owner's stateroom forward?

Beau never hesitated a moment and replied, "I can't sleep forward because of the little bow waves that slap the forward chines. That noise keeps me awake all night when we're at anchor."

They both took showers and dressed in silence.

Finally Beau said, "I wish you never had to leave, Fonda, I really mean it."

"I feel the same way, Ronald, but unfortunately reality has set in. Let's try and maintain contact, and maybe we can be together again soon."

"I'll call you when I get settled in Costa Rica, and we will get together."

"Before I forget," said Fonda. "Here are your three Panama exit tax receipts, at twenty dollars each," taking them out of her purse and handing them to Beau. "I took care of them on my way through Panama City this afternoon."

Beau called the water taxi, and the two of them kissed in the cockpit until the launch arrived. Beau helped Fonda aboard and watched sadly as she waved goodbye and disappeared into the humid night.

He said aloud, "Shakespeare was right, parting *is* such sweet sorrow."

Beau would do everything possible to make sure they would see each other again. But, it all depended on how tomorrow went. Beau tried to stay calm, but his mind was racing at a hundred miles per hour. He fiddled with his charts for a while and then turned in and tried to go to sleep. His alarm clock read 1:30 a.m. when the Fernandez brothers stumbled in. They sounded like they were pretty wasted, but they must have gone right to sleep because the snoring started almost immediately.

Beau woke up at his customary 6:00 a.m., only it was only 4:00 a.m. in Panama. He couldn't get back to sleep, so he went over and over the Key Largo plan in his mind. They had more firepower than he did, so surprise would be his most important ally. Beau finally got out of bed, and shrugged into a t-shirt and a pair of shorts. He turned on the engine room lights at the main breaker panel and went down to check the engines. All the fluids were good and he found no signs of any leaks. He checked the Racor fuel filter bowls and there was no water in them, just pure, clean, fuel. The bilge was dry, but he checked the automatic float switches anyway and they all worked. The generator was running smoothly and showed no signs of leaking anything. Beau closed up the engine room, went aft, and checked the rudder stuffing boxes. They both were dry. *Chica* was ready for that day's trip into the Pacific Ocean.

Beau collected his charts in the salon and made his way up to the fly bridge. He programmed the waypoints he had prepared the night before into the GPS chart plotter. When he finished he was programmed all the way to Jaco and Los Suenos. He took a last look at the paper chart of the channel leading out of the Canal Zone and into the Pacific Ocean. Then he headed below to start a pot of coffee.

While the coffee brewed, he went in and woke up Hector and Luis. They didn't look good at all. Their cabin reeked of alcohol and cigar smoke, and they had both crashed into bed with their street clothes on. As they stumbled out of their cabin Beau could see that their faces and eyelids were bloated, and their eyes were bloodshot. Beau suppressed a laugh and thought ... *they've been drinking like they were going to the electric chair today.* He chuckled to himself because they were close to right. Beau was sure he could use their hangovers to his advantage, as any impairment to their mental or physical conditions was an added advantage for him. The two of them grumbled, but they got up. Not because of Beau, but because of their fear of No Nose Cipriano. Hector had told Beau that No Nose had once killed a man who had stolen from him with a chain saw.

Beau got the two brothers some black coffee and asked them, "How was your night on the town, gentlemen?"

Hector said, "I'd like to live here, man! The hookers are beautiful and cost only a hundred dollars. Most of them could get five hundred dollars in Miami!"

Luis became animated and chimed in saying, "The food is great and the nightclubs are hot. We're coming back here sometime, for sure."

They both kept putting their heads down in their hands like they had bad headaches. Beau kept pushing them and they finally got going at 7:00 a.m. Hector slipped the mooring lines off, and Beau started *Chica* out towards the Pacific Ocean and his future.

Beau pushed the throttles up and ran out the long ship's channel at twenty-three knots. He looked to port across the Balboa causeway and was greeted with the impressive high-rise skyline of downtown Panama City. As the city and its offshore islands melted into the horizon behind him the Bertram passed a couple of sailboats and only slowed to pass over the wakes of two freighters coming in off the Pacific. Once he cleared the sea buoy he set the course for the south-southwest run out the Gulf of Panama. He pulled up his first waypoint, which left the distant Perlas Islands to port on the way to the southwest end of the Azuero Peninsula. Beau engaged the autopilot, and relaxed with his coffee. Hector came up on the fly bridge, laid down in front of the console on the bench seat cushion, and almost immediately fell asleep. Luis had retired to the forward cabin and probably was asleep also.

Beau pushed the throttles up further and soon *Chica* was running along at twenty-five knots. The Gulf of Panama was calm, and after an hour's run Beau had only seen an occasional boat on the horizon. Hector slept about two and a half hours, and then woke up and went below to relieve himself. He came back up a few minutes later with two cold bottles of water, and gave one to Beau. Beau thanked him and asked how Luis was doing below.

"He's sound asleep, and I wouldn't look for him until later this afternoon. He drank a lot of tequila last night, and I just hope he remembers what a good time he had. We are getting to old to party like the young ones, but we still try," said Hector laughing.

Beau laughed with him and then said, "Hector, I could use your eyes. There are a lot of floating trees and limbs in the water up and down this coast because of the rainy season. The trees fall in from the eroding banks and the swollen rivers sweep them out here. If we run over one it could disable the boat or even sink us."

Hector sat up in the passenger helm chair and tried to stay awake.

At 11:30 a.m., Beau was just approaching his first waypoint off the southwest tip of the Azuero Peninsula. The sea state remained as smooth as glass.

Chica was making good time and was riding the widely spaced Pacific swells like she was made for them. Actually, the Bertram 54 had a much flatter dead rise than most of the other Bertram designs and was ideal for the Pacific Ocean.

"Hector," said Beau, waking him with a start. "How about getting me a sandwich and something to drink? I bought some fresh salami, cheese, and bread in Colon."

"Okay," grunted Hector. "I could use one myself."

He returned with the sandwiches about fifteen minutes later, and they both ate in silence.

Hector continued to doze in and out of sleep. Beau had already seen two large trees floating menacingly off to starboard while Hector was dozing. He had made the turn around Punta Mala and was now running west along the wide expanse of the Azuero Peninsula towards the town of Roncador, sixty miles away. Beau checked the GPS chart and figured *Chica* was about twenty miles off shore. He had seen only two distant freighters in the past two hours. Beau's heart started pounding as he decided the time for the "Key Largo" move had come. Twenty minutes later, he spotted another floating tree off the port bow. Hector was sound asleep and snoring in the passenger chair. Beau wiped his sweaty palms on his shorts, turned the autopilot to standby, and steered *Chica* directly at the large floating tree.

When he got about twenty yards from the tree he shouted, "Ooooh … shit!" then pulled the throttles back quickly and put the engines in neutral. He wrenched the wheel over to starboard and hit the tree with a glancing blow, while the boats momentum slowed to about ten or twelve knots. The collision made a loud bang … but didn't do much damage. Hector jumped up, was thrown sideways out of his seat, and into the fly bridge coaming.

"God damn it, Hector!" Beau yelled as he put the port engine in and out of reverse and gunned it. "You weren't watching." Beau shifted the port engine back to neutral and said sternly to Hector, "Go down there and look over the transom. It feels like there are some branches stuck in the port propeller, you need to check it out."

Hector was still groggy with sleep and a little disoriented from his fall, but he hurried down the ladder and quickly moved towards the portside of the cockpit transom. Hector climbed over the transom and got out onto the swim platform. When he started to lean over to look at the propeller … Beau pushed both throttles to the maximum and held on. The big Bertram lurched forward while belching a huge cloud of black diesel smoke out of her exhaust pipes. When the smoke cleared, Beau could see Hector bobbing in the water about a hundred yards behind the boat. He then turned the boat to port abruptly and pulled the throttles back to idle sharply, and hung on again. *Chica,* rolled to her beam ends, then lurched and slowly came to a stop. He wondered how Luis had fared below, being tossed first one way and then the other.

Beau quickly scrambled under the steering console and tore the tape from the .38 revolver, then stood back up gun in hand. He could hear Hector yelling from the water behind *Chica.* Beau moved quickly to the aft fly-bridge railing as Luis staggered out of the salon door with his gun drawn. His head was bloody and his left arm hung useless at his side. Beau didn't hesitate and shot Luis right through the top of his head. Luis fell where he stood. Beau went forward to the helm and hit the throttles hard again, sliding Luis back to the transom. Beau shut the Bertram down to idle and shifted into neutral, then turned, and aimed the .38 at Luis who was crumpled against the transom. Luis looked deader than a two day old mackerel. He climbed down the ladder and retrieved the Glock. Beau checked Luis's pulse just to be sure he was dead and then scaled back up the fly bridge ladder. He put *Chica* in gear and turned back towards Hector and the floating tree.

Hector had swum over to the floating tree and was straddling it. As Beau steered *Chica* closer to the tree, Hector fired a shot at Beau on the fly bridge. It missed the fly bridge completely, but Beau heard it hit somewhere along the hull. Beau turned *Chica* and quickly motored out of range. He didn't dare leave Hector out here alive with a chance of being picked up by a passing freighter or fishing boat. He looked at his depth sounder and it read 2040 feet. He needed to dump both bodies here. In this depth, they'd never be found.

Beau quickly devised a plan of attack to finish off Hector. He would run the Bertram at high speed around the floating tree in circles starting outside of Hector's handgun range, and then slowly tighten the circle until he was in range himself. The Bertram would put up an increasingly larger wake and the tree would be tossed up and down so violently that it would be impossible for Hector to hold on and shoot accurately. Beau started turning *Chica* around the tree and quickly created a six foot confused sea. Hector had to hold onto the tree with his arms and legs just to prevent being tossed off. As the Bertram's wake got closer and closer, the tree and Hector bobbed up and down so violently that he was submerged half of the time. As Beau got close, he waited until the tree submerged, then cut the Bertram toward the tree. He pulled the throttles back to idle, and *Chica* glided past the tree at six knots just as Hector and tree bobbed up. Hector came out of the water firing wildly. Beau took a deep breath to counteract the adrenalin coursing through his veins, led him a little, and pumped three shots into his chest. Hector fell off the tree and slipped under the deep blue waters of the Pacific.

Beau took another deep breath, rested for a moment, then climbed down the ladder and opened the tuna door. He removed Luis's gold and stainless submariner and put it in his pocket. It was identical to the one he had fed to the sharks in Key West. He didn't feel at all bad about taking it as a replacement. It would serve as a reminder every time he was tempted to gamble. He pushed, pulled, and shoved Luis's heavy carcass through the tuna door and then rolled him off the swim platform into the waiting water. Beau went below and gathered up all of the Fernandez's belongings. He pitched their clothes, shoes, and toilet articles overboard, cleansing the boat of their presence. He shredded their passports, credit cards and ID's and threw them overboard. Next he cleaned the cockpit and swim platform of Luis's blood. When he was finished he returned to the fly bridge, put *Chica* back on course, throttled up, and switched on the autopilot. He drank what was left of his water and sat at the helm feeling numb.

Beau took more deep breaths and tried to shake it off. He had won and he should have felt elated, but there was no joy in it. The adrenalin was still flowing in his veins, and he started to feel cold. Beau had felt this feeling before, after firefights in Vietnam, and after covert missions when he had killed sentries with a knife to the throat. He did not feel any remorse, as it was kill or be killed. He was thankful that it had gone his way, but he did not see cause to celebrate.

The wind blowing on Beau's face helped to snap him out of it, and he remembered the shots that Hector fired at the boat. He took *Chica* down off of plane and stopped the boat, letting it run in neutral. He checked the boat for any gunshot damage and found the first bullet lodged in the fiberglass covered forward salon windshield. Beau dug the bullet out and threw it overboard. He checked out the rest of the boat and found a slug just under the port gunnel amidships, and another slug lodged in the black stripe along the port fly bridge coaming. The last one was a little close for comfort. He removed the slugs and filled the holes with a dab of white silicone. He would fix them correctly when he got to Jaco.

Beau got a cold one from the refrigerator and went back to the fly bridge.

He put *Chica* back up on plane and tried to relax. The "Key Largo" strategy had worked to perfection, with a couple of modifications. He now had a .38 with no bullets left in it, but he had Luis's seven shot, 9 mm, Glock. He thought he would hide the Glock back under the motor cowling of the Raritan guest head. He threw the empty .38 pistol overboard. That should simplify his next customs and immigration inspection in Costa Rica. Beau turned his attention to the GPS chart plotter. If he continued to run at twenty-five knots, he should arrive at Coiba Island well before dark.

CHAPTER TWENTY-THREE

A S Beau neared Coiba Island the first thing he saw was the 1400-foot mountain at its center. The island was large and encompassed nearly three hundred square miles of dense jungle terrain. He followed the GPS course right to the northeast end of the island and soon he was idling through the small passage between the small islet of Granito de Oro and the big island. The passage was less than a half of a mile wide and the water was twenty to twenty-five feet deep. There were huge rock boulders and a pretty beach on Granito de Oro. Coiba had a rock-strewn shoreline and the lush green, but forbidding looking, jungle spilled all the way down to the shoreline.

Beau stopped and anchored about four hundred yards out from the Coiba side. The Granito side had some small cottages along the tree line at the top of the beach, and Beau didn't want to be within easy swimming distance from either island. Fonda had informed him that Coiba had been a penal colony for many years, and even though the government had closed it a few years ago there were still escaped prisoners that were loose on the island. After checking out the engine room, and hiding the 9 mm automatic in the head, Beau cracked another cold one and sat back up in the fly bridge. He swept both shorelines with his binoculars and didn't see any people. But he did see many beautifully colored parrots and macaws sitting in the trees in the dense jungle. There also were fifteen or twenty frigate birds working the passage waters.

Beau decided to use the scuba mask he had Hector put with the spare parts and equipment, to check out the bottom of the boat before it got dark. He had noted no leaks when he checked the bilge, but he was anxious to check out the area of the bottom that had hit the floating tree. He stripped his shirt and shorts off and dove in off the swim platform. He swam around to the bow and dove underwater. The bottom anti-fouling paint was scratched some, but there was no serious damage. He swam aft and dove on the running gear. Some of the propeller anti-fouling paint had worn off, but that was normal after a thousand plus miles. The propellers had no dings and looked perfect. Beau looked down towards the sea bottom and was surprised to see a beautiful coral reef. There was mature coral, including large red and purple sea fans, and the reef was loaded with fish. Beau swam up to the swim platform, pulled the under mount ladder down, and climbed back aboard. He hosed himself off in the cockpit under the fresh water pressure hose and dried off with a towel in the warm afternoon sun. He put his shorts back on and started transferring the diesel fuel out of the plastic drums and into the main tanks.

Just as he was finishing the last drum, a large blue-hulled sailing ketch came around the northeast tip of Coiba and entered the Granito passage. The sailboat anchored up over by the huge boulders close to Granito de Oro. Beau could see a man and a woman handling the center cockpit ketch. They anchored her smoothly, and the ketch made a handsome sight lying in the sun sparkled water.

Beau went below to take a hot shower and locked the salon door behind him. "Better safe than sorry," as old Robert E. used to say. After the shower, he put on some clean clothes and went back out into the cockpit.

He looked through the tackle station drawers until he found a half used spool of 20-pound monofilament fishing line. He found some small hooks and some split shot in another one of the tackle drawers. Beau went inside and retrieved an empty beer can from the garbage and took a can of tuna fish from the pantry. He wound about 100 feet of monofilament line around the beer can, then tied on a little hook, and pinched on a split shot. He opened the can of tuna, picked out a few of the bigger pieces, and put one on the little hook.

Beau took several small pieces of the tuna and threw them over the side. He waited about ten seconds and then let the baited hook down in the water about ten feet. He almost instantly had a small fish on the hook. He wound the little fish in and took it off the hook. It was a small snapper of some sort. Beau grabbed a five-gallon bucket, scooped up a couple of gallons of seawater, and put the snapper in the bucket. He repeated his chumming and baiting until he had caught three small snappers about the same size.

Beau changed his rig to a bigger hook and a heavier sinker. He took one of the snappers out of the bucket and hooked it just in front of the dorsal fin. He held the mono- wrapped beer can in his left hand and let out about four feet of line that he held in his right hand. He aimed the bottom of the can where he wanted to cast, and then swung the whole snapper around his head on the four feet of mono like a cowboy with a lariat. On the third time around he let it go and the snapper flew through the air, taking 30-some feet of mono off the can. Beau let the snapper sink to the bottom and waited.

Thirty seconds later something grabbed the little snapper and almost pulled the beer can out of Beau's hands. Beau held the can out horizontally and let the bigger fish take some more line off the can. He then turned the can vertically and started winding the fishing line back on the can using his right hand as a guide. Beau had seen natives in the Bahamas and Mexico fish this way because they couldn't afford fishing rods and reels. It was slow going but five minutes later Beau put a 12-pound Spanish mackerel in the cockpit. Beau had never seen one so big. He had caught hundreds of Spanish mackerels in the Gulf of Mexico and Tampa Bay, and a really big one there was half this fish's size. Beau filleted the fish and took the filets inside after releasing the remaining small snappers back to the reef.

The sun had gone down behind Coiba and Beau decided to cook one of the mackerel filets for dinner. He coated the filet with olive oil and found a half bag of flour in with the provisions. He floured each side of the filet after adding salt and pepper. While he heated up a skillet on the electric stovetop, Beau sliced up some of the mangos, onions, and peppers he had picked up in Colon and made a salsa. He toasted up two pieces of Panamanian bread and put olive oil and garlic salt on them after they were toasted. When the skillet was hot, he poured a little olive oil in it and sautéed the filet until it was golden brown. He put it on a plate and topped it with the mango pepper salsa, sat down at the salon dining table, and ate his catch.

He washed it down with another cold one and said out loud, "I'll probably find it gets better than this … but considering what I've been through the last three weeks, *and especially today* … this will be hard to top." The fish was superb, light and flaky, the best mackerel he'd ever had.

Beau thought about the turn of events during the past week. He now owned a 54 foot sportfish, had three million dollars in cash, and by now the mafia and the rest of Florida should believe he was dead. When Hector and Luis didn't return to Miami in the next week or so the mafia might think the brother's drug deal went bad and they were killed in Mexico. The Tampa mafia would search the world for the two Fernandez brothers, but they would search in vain. Beau's luck had definitely changed. From now on, whenever he was tempted to gamble, he would just look at Luis's Rolex and remember this day. Beau suddenly felt very tired, so he cleaned up the galley, switched the anchor light on, and checked the salon door lock. He moved the Glock under his pillow, and immediately fell asleep.

Beau woke up the next morning at 6:00 a.m., daylight savings time. His Rolex glowed in the dark like it had a battery-powered light in it. He rolled over and went back to sleep. He had set the automatic coffee maker for 6:00 a.m. Central American time, and the smell of brewing coffee woke him the second time. He sat in the salon and looked out at Granito de Oro across the channel, as the sun came up over the Panamanian mountains, fifteen miles to the east. This had to be one of the most beautiful spots in the whole world.

Beau noticed some movement on the deck of the blue ketch and he retrieved his binoculars. It was the sailboat couple getting ready to dive off the stern for their morning swim. They were both stark naked. Thirty minutes later they climbed up their stern ladder, rinsed off with a hose, and dried each other off. They must have done this often because they were very fit for an older couple and had no tan lines. Beau had to laugh at himself, fifty-something and still a peeping Tom.

He made a sandwich and put it and a couple of bottles of water in a small soft sided cooler that he found in the galley. He took it to the fly bridge and started the engines. Beau came back down and pulled the anchor with the help of the windlass and secured the anchor in its chock. Then he started idling *Chica* through the center of the passage, past the blue ketch, past Coiba Island, and out into the deep blue water of the Pacific Ocean. He planed the Bertram off, and set his course to motor around the southwestern tip of Chiriqui Province and then up into Costa Rica's Golfo Dulce. His destination was Banana Bay Marina in the town of Golfito, 125 miles away. At twenty-five knots, the passage should take about five hours.

Beau starting thinking about what he would do once he got to Los Suenos. He needed to get a slip for the boat, and then go to San Jose with two duffels full of money. For now, he would leave the other one and a half million in the fuel tanks and bank it on a second trip. He would stay in one of the small, exclusive, hotels downtown that catered to visiting businessmen. He would avoid the resort hotels in San Jose, where someone from Florida who was there to fish or vacation, might recognize him. That would be the rule. Once he established some bank accounts and set up an annuity in the Cayman Islands he would apply for foreign residency. Costa Rica required a guaranteed income of fifteen thousand dollars annually to qualify. Beau would use Ronald's passport only until he could buy another identity, and he would avoid the Pacific coast resorts when thousands of Floridians were there to fish and tour the country.

Beau knew he had to sell *Chica*. Living in any of the marinas on the west coast was not an option. He would buy a smaller fishing boat, and live in a place like Tambor on the Gulf of Nicoya. He had stopped there years ago while driving with some of his buddies to Carillo for the great marlin fishing in May. There were some nice hotels and restaurants and some good-looking houses up in the mountains overlooking the Gulf. It would be close to the large port town of Puntaranes and still within a reasonable driving distance to San Jose. Tambor's hotels catered to a native Costa Rican clientele almost exclusively. Of course, in a year or two, he would be speaking good Spanish. Also, when his full beard was grown out, he would be harder to identify. At any rate, it was a beginning of a plan. A plan made easier by three million plus dollars.

Beau dodged more floating trees and logs as he made his way towards the Golfo Dulce. The picture of Hector bobbing up and down in the floating tree, firing wildly at Beau, would be forever etched in his mind.

Chica rounded Chiriqui point and entered the Golfo Dulce while Beau was finishing his salami sandwich. Beau punched in the waypoint for Golfito and started up the Gulf. There didn't seem to be much development on either side of the Golfo Dulce. He saw a few small enclaves and some beautiful volcanic beaches, some with black sand. Beau remembered the whole Pacific coast of Costa Rica was volcanic, and their beaches were white, black, and various shades of brown. The lava outcroppings located just off shore were everywhere with the lush green vegetation growing down to the water's edge. Navigation close to shore would be precarious at best.

He soon arrived at Golfito at the head of the gulf, and raised Banana Bay Marina on the VHF radio. The dock master answered and switched Beau from channel sixteen to channel ten. His name was Bruce and his English was so good that Beau suspected that he was a Gringo. He gave Beau directions to a slip, and Beau asked if he could top off his fuel on his way in. Bruce said his assistant, Gomez, would meet him at the fuel dock.

Banana Bay Marina was located in a well-protected cove, right on the main road that ran to the former downtown American section. Two hundred foot high cliffs covered with vegetation ringed the town of Golfito. The town was large by Costa Rican Pacific coast standards. It had once been a United Fruit banana town, and it had a deep-water port including a large, aging, banana boat wharf. A narrow-gauge railhead came in from the former banana plantations.

Beau had been told during one of his fishing trips there that the banana plantations were all planted in date oil palms now. United Fruit was started in Costa Rica in 1935 and left the country in 1985, after the employee's attempted to unionize. The United Fruit Company, headquartered in Cincinnati, Ohio, had warned their Costa Rican employees that if they unionized that they would pull out. It was no bluff, and when they unionized a bitter lesson was learned. The company pulled out all the banana trees from Jaco to Golfito, left Costa Rica, and planted their bananas elsewhere in Central America. United Fruit still owned the land and had planted thousands of date palm trees on the former banana plantations. The harvesting of the date palms was totally mechanized and required only a small fraction of the original employees.

Beau pulled up to the fuel dock and Gomez tied *Chica* to the dock. He handed him the diesel nozzle and Beau started fueling. After Beau finished pumping the fuel he raised the quarantine flag on the starboard outrigger.

"Where did you come in from?" asked Gomez in passable English.

"The Panama Canal," answered Beau. "Will the customs agent come to the boat?"

"No, *Senor*, first we have to call the port authority, and they will come to the boat for copies of your passport and boat documents. Bruce is doing that now, and they will arrive shortly. Then you will have to go up town to the government building to customs and immigration, but we can call you a cab. Where are you traveling to?"

"Jaco," replied Beau.

"Los Suenos Marina?" asked Gomez.

"Yes," said Beau.

"All the big sportfish boats seem to be headed there. It's first class, *Senor*."

"That's what I hear. Say, Gomez, can you take these empty drums off the boat for me? I don't need them anymore."

"Of course, *Senor,* there is always a need for clean fuel drums."

The port authority agent arrived and took Beau's passport and boat documents to the dock master's office for copying. He was back in ten minutes with the originals and a filled out form for Beau to sign. Beau signed it and was given a temporary vessel importation permit good for ninety days.

The agent cautioned Beau, "You may extend this for another ninety days at any port of entry, but beyond that you will have to go through a bonding process with a special agent. I have stapled a pamphlet explaining the permitting rules for your vessel, Mr. Santos. There are no charges for our services."

Beau thanked the agent and finished fueling. Then he moved the Bertram to his slip, taking Gomez with him to handle the forward lines on the pilings. Beau backed *Chica* into the slip and Gomez secured the bow. Gomez jumped up on the dock and Beau came down the fly bridge ladder to throw him the stern lines. He tipped Gomez a "Ulysses S. Grant" after he hooked up the shore power for him.

Beau turned off the generator and switched the Bertram's main panel to shore power. He gathered up his passport, new vessel permit, and the ship's papers and headed for the dock masters office. He was not surprised to find a blond haired, blue-eyed, Gringo sitting in the dock masters chair. He signed the marina forms and paid for the slip and fuel so he could leave as early as he wanted in the morning.

"So, where are you from, Bruce?"

"Lancaster, Pennsylvania."

"You're shitting me … you're from Amish country?" said Beau, who had expected him to answer Florida or California.

"I shit you not," laughed Bruce. "I came down here ten years ago to surf, and I never left."

"You could be in a worse place, that's for sure. Can you call me a cab to take me to customs?"

"It's already waiting outside the gate," said Bruce, smiling.

The cab ride took all of five minutes. Golfito hadn't changed much since Beau had been here last. Maybe there were a couple more small hotels and restaurants in the old American zone. The town was a typical Costa Rican, well laid out, covering a few square blocks downtown, with a church, a school, and a soccer field. The buildings and houses were clean, if not a little drab. There were chickens and an occasional pig in the streets. *Not much different than Key West …* thought Beau, laughing inwardly. The school kids were on their way home, and all of them wore identical uniforms. They looked bright and happy. Beau had been told that Costa Rica had a 95% literacy rate, which was much better than the United State's rate. The cab stopped in front of an official looking building

with a Costa Rican flag flying in front. Beau paid the cab driver five dollars and
went inside.

There was one uniformed agent dozing at a desk. Beau cleared his throat
and the agent woke up with a start.

"Can I help you, *Senor*?" he said in surprisedly good English.

"Yes, sir," said Beau. "I'd like to check myself and my boat into Costa Rica."

Beau filled out the forms, explaining that his crew had flown home from
Panama City. He declared nothing and was informed that there was no charge
except a nominal exit fee when departing the country. His passport was stamped,
and he was issued a ninety-day visa, which was extendable once. The agent,
whose name was Umberto, kept *Chica's* temporary cruising permit and said, "I'll
be down at the marina in about forty-five minutes to inspect your boat."

"Okay," said Beau. "I'll go back there directly and wait for you."

He walked outside and the same cab was still sitting there waiting for him.
Beau didn't have the heart to tell him he would rather walk, so he hopped in and
was back at the marina in no time.

The agent arrived about an hour later with a local policeman and they
inspected the boat. He took off the fruit Beau had bought in Panama. Umberto
handed Beau back *Chica's* temporary cruising permit. He also gave him a copy
of the fishing regulations, reminding him not to forget to buy a fishing license
before wetting a line.

"There is a license office at Los Suenos, Mr. Santos. Enjoy your stay in Costa
Rica."

They shook hands and Umberto and the policeman walked down the dock.
No bribes, no bullshit, what a very nice country. Beau gave the boat a good wash
down and then took a shower before he settled in for an afternoon nap.

Beau woke up at 7:00 p.m. and felt rested for the first time in three weeks.
He was hungry and decided to walk up town to stretch his legs. He put on a
fishing cap and kept his sunglasses on even though it was starting to get dark.
He walked a few blocks uptown and reacquainted himself with this pleasant
little town. Beau slipped into a quiet looking restaurant and bar called the Mar Y
Luna. He had passed up the Coconut Café and the El Pescador bar because they
sounded like tourist fisherman hangouts. He found a table in a dark corner and
sat down. There were a few locals drinking at the bar, but otherwise the restaurant was empty at this early hour. A waitress appeared and Beau ordered a bottle
of Imperial, the local beer. He looked over the menu, and when the waitress

arrived with his cerveza he ordered grilled corvina with rice and a salad. Corvina reminded him of snook, his favorite fish. His dinner arrived, and the corvina was excellent. Beau ordered another beer.

As he was finishing his second beer four sunburned Americans, fresh from a fishing charter, came in and bellied up to the bar. They were laughing and high fiving each other over the number of sailfish they had caught and released that day. The beer flowed and the group got louder and louder. Beau understood that fishing in Costa Rica, with a good captain, could be spectacular even in the off-season. No matter where you were from in the United States, fishing was usually three or four times better here. The fishing should remain excellent because the Costa Rican government had passed a law that all billfish had to be released. They had also mandated the use of circle hooks which dramatically increased the released billfish's chance of survival, by eliminating gut hooking. If Costa Rica could enforce their longliner moratorium in the near future, the fishing would continue to be spectacular for decades to come. There was an abundance of mahi-mahi, yellow fin tuna, and wahoo for the visiting anglers to bring to the dock. But the billfish were the main event.

The other thing that set Costa Rica apart from most of the world's other hot fishing spots was the consistently calm water in the coastal Pacific near the equator. Seasick prone anglers were almost guaranteed perfect conditions on their fishing trips to Costa Rica's Pacific coast.

Beau paid his check with a ten-dollar bill, and smiled to himself. The three million dollars would go a long way in this country. On his way out, he passed by the sun burned Americans unnoticed.

Beau walked directly back to the marina, and used the marina office guest phone booth to call his friend Gary Anderson. Gary's wife, Gloria, answered and Beau said, "Hello, Gloria, Seth Stone calling."

She said, "Seth, I'm so sorry about Beau. Jeb called Gary earlier this week to tell him about Beau's death and the wake. We were sorry we couldn't make it, but Gary is in the middle of a case that is being tried in court right now."

"I understand, Gloria. I know he would have been there if there was any way possible. Is Gary available?"

"I'll get him. He's in his study, and again, Seth, I'm so sorry."

Beau smiled and thought…*Well, Fuckin-A, Diddy-Bop, … the Key West ploy worked perfect and they all think I'm dead … now a'int that some shit… I'm home free!*

Gary came on the phone a minute later and Beau heard Gloria hang up the extension.

He said, "Seth, I'm so sorry I couldn't make it to Beau's wake, but I couldn't abandon my client in court."

"I understand," said Beau. "Are you all alone in your study, Gary?"

"Why yes, Seth, Gloria is watching some TV show in the family room."

"Gary, this isn't Seth … its Beau."

"My God, Beau! But Jeb called and … and."

"I know," interrupted Beau. "But I'm still alive. Seth and Jeb think I'm dead, but I'm all right. It's a long story, one I promise to tell you someday; but for now, did you get the letter I sent you?"

"Yes, Beau, I did get it, a week or so ago."

"Well don't send it. I was in some trouble with the Tampa mafia, and I had to disappear. I'm out of the country, safe and sound now, and since they think I'm dead, they'll stop looking for me. You can destroy the letter and I'd rather you didn't read it. When I get settled, I'll call you and maybe we can get together somehow."

"I'd like that Beau. Do you need any money or anything?"

"No, Gary, all I need is your friendship and silence. You're the only person who knows I'm still alive."

"You know your secret is safe with me. Call me when you're ready to meet, or whenever I can do something for you. You know I'll always be indebted to you."

"I think we're even, my friend," said Beau as he hung up. He hoped he'd see Gary again, sometime soon.

Beau went back to the boat, passing through the now busy Banana Bay Marina "Bilge" Bar, and locked himself in the salon with his Pacific Coast charts. He studied Jaco and Herradura Bay where Los Suenos was located. He would pass Quepos on the way. That was another place where he'd had an outstanding fishing trip some years ago. It had been great talking to Gary, and he really hoped he would get to see him someday.

Beau tried to go to sleep, but he stayed wide awake most of the night thinking about how his life could have turned out differently. He wished Fonda was with him and realized that she just might be his redemption. When he finally dozed off, he dreamed he was back in Vietnam, where he had been afraid to go to sleep, but was too exhausted not to.

CHAPTER TWENTY-FOUR

THE next morning Beau woke up at 6:00 a.m. Central time. He made some coffee and finished off the Panamanian bread, making toast out of it. He checked the engine room and topped off the oil in the generator. It looked like the port engine alternator could use a new v-belt, and Beau made a mental note to change both alternator belts in Los Suenos. At 6:30, he walked up to the marina office to tip Bruce before shoving off. He found Bruce drinking coffee back in his office.

"Thanks for your help, Bruce," said Beau as he handed Bruce a "U. S. Grant".

"Thank you, Mr. Santos. Do you need any help with your lines?"

"No thanks. You're here by yourself this morning and there's no wind, I can manage."

"I meant to ask you yesterday, Mr. Santos. You didn't come all the way from Florida by yourself, did you?"

"No," said Beau with a laugh, "it took me so long to get through the Panama Canal that my crew had to fly back home. They had commitments in Florida."

"The wait is even longer during the season," said Bruce shaking his head.

"Well, whatever it takes, it beats having to run around the horn."

"You got that right!" said Bruce as Beau turned to leave.

Beau pulled out of Banana Bay twenty minutes later and only looked back once, to admire the beautiful mountains. Beau ran *Chica* close to the northern shoreline and was pleased to see that there was still almost no development on the Osa Peninsula. Costa Rica had designated over half of the entire country as national parks. He finally cleared the northwest point and changed course to head along Osa's western shore towards Cano Island to the north. The coast was rocky and wild looking and was sprinkled with occasional small coves and sandy beaches. But it was the verdant green vegetation that was most spectacular growing right down to the edge of the blue Pacific. Beau soon left the Osa Peninsula behind and headed straight for Cano Island now twelve miles away. Bruce had mentioned that Cano was a national park and only a controlled number of campers were allowed on the island. He also warned Beau that during the rainy season Cano attracted particularly violent thunderstorms like a magnet.

Beau chuckled to himself and thought … *if Bruce wants to see violent thunderstorms, he ought to be in Tampa Bay in August.*

Tampa Bay was truly the lighting capital of the world, and Stone's Boatworks made a handsome living in the summer just replacing electronics damaged by the lighting hits on sailboats alone.

Cano Island soon came into view. It was as lush and rocky as the mainland, but it was quite a bit smaller and less elevated than Beau had imagined. As he piloted the Bertram past Cano, Beau thought it had a sinister look and feel about it. The water remained deep very close to the island, and Beau guessed the fishing would be very good around it. With Cano safely on *Chica's* stern Beau set a new course for Los Suenos Marina, eighty-seven miles to the northwest.

Around noon, Beau began to feel hungry. He slowed the boat to idle, then took it out of gear. He went below and made a lunch of salami and cheese rollups and took two bottles of water from the sub-zero fridge. When he came back up on the fly bridge he was astounded by what he saw. The boat was surrounded by a huge school of small yellow fin tuna and hundreds of spinner dolphins. Flocks of birds wheeled and dove at the bait. He put the boat back in gear, but kept it at idle speed. The school was moving north with him, so he switched on the autopilot and sat back and watched the show while he enjoyed his lunch. The tuna made short jumps and dashes as they fed on the gigantic bait school. The spinner dolphin took turns shooting up out of the water, like corkscrews, and then they belly flopped back in. Some of them reached four or five feet in the air. It was an awesome display of wildlife. Beau wasn't sure if the spinners were eating the bait or the smaller tunas. The whole triage moved along with a life of its own.

Beau had only seen the spinner dolphins once before while sail and marlin fishing out of Carrillo off Guanacaste Province in the northern part of Costa Rica. The captain on the Merritt 43 had his mate catch some of the small tunas on a spinning rod baited with a Clark spoon. Jimbo, the mate, with a little help from Beau, bridled the freshly caught tuna through his eye socket with a dental floss loop, then twisted a large number twelve tuna hook, attached to a 50-pound rig with a 300 lb. wind-on-leader, on top of its head and quickly returned it to the water.

The mate handed the rod to Beau and said, "Flip the clicker on and leave the reel in free spool. When something big grabs it, count to ten, then push the lever to strike, reel him tight, and hang on."

Jimbo was rigging a second small tuna for one of Beau's buddies when his clicker started to scream. Beau followed Jimbo's instructions to the letter and when the fish came tight, he set the hook. The fish really took off and slammed Beau into the gunnel. Beau recovered and headed for the fighting chair. He sat in the bucket harness and clipped the reel to the bucket harness's straps. The fish was still taking line, but was slowing down. Beau started to work the fish with short pumps of the rod, only reeling on his way down. His buddies were whooping and hollering at him, and reminding him of how bad the fish was kicking his butt. They threw cold water over his head and acted like he had a thousand pound marlin on. Beau was grudgingly gaining a little line, and a little control over the very strong fish. The captain started to back the boat as Beau made better and better progress.

Captain Bobby called down to Beau's buddies and said, "Calm down, boys! It's not a big marlin, it's a big tuna."

The line started to make large circles off the transom, as Beau continued pumping and reeling. Beau's veins stood out on his arms and his legs felt like he had just run a hundred yard dash. He worked the fish another twenty minutes, gaining more line than he lost to the game tuna. Finally he got the tuna to the surface. It was a magnificent yellow fin, well over three hundred pounds according to Captain Bobby. Jimbo gaffed it and Captain Bobby came down from the bridge and sank a second gaff in it. After a brief struggle, he and Jimbo got a tail rope on it. Captain Bobby opened the tuna door and they pulled it aboard with the help of the rest of the crew. It was a beautiful dark blue and silver, with long bright yellow crescent shaped dorsal and anal fins. The sheer size of it took what was left of Beau's breath away. Beau was too exhausted to do much else but grin, but his buddies pulled him out of the chair and took some great pictures of Beau and the giant yellow fin. Ten minutes later they were back trolling for sailfish, and Jimbo started the daunting job of bleeding and filleting the huge tuna. It was obvious he had cut up many large tunas, and twenty minutes later the fillets were cooling, in four large garbage bags, on a bed of crushed ice in the fish box. They would all be heroes in Carrillo's restaurants for the rest of their stay.

Beau looked at his GPS and he saw that he was about an hour out of Quepos. He would only see the continuous mountains, though, as the course to Los Suenos had him twenty miles off shore at that point. Beau was looking forward to fishing these waters again. He would have come back every year with his friends if the gambling losses hadn't drained most of his money. The hour dragged by slowly while Beau carefully scanned the water for any sign of floating logs.

Finally he was past Quepos and only two hours or so from Los Suenos. Beau was anxious to get there; he had studied his chart and remembered the advertising text and photos in Marlin magazine. Herradura Bay and Los Suenos looked well protected and beautiful. The property had a Spanish hacienda style Marriott Hotel, and a first class floating marina protected by a thirty-five foot high rock breakwater inside Herradura Bay. Los Suenos had trucked in a white beach, as Playa Herradura had a natural dark brown volcanic beach. The resort had five restaurants and a casino. Beau would avoid the casino.

Chica was gaining on the shoreline which was arcing out northwest towards her. Beau could see the shoreline and the town of Jaco seven or eight miles away. He followed the GPS course past Jaco and towards a high, lush green, volcanic point that jutted out a mile off shore. As *Chica* rounded the point, there it was … Herradura Bay and Los Suenos. Beau turned the Bertram and ran toward the imposing breakwater. He could see some of the bigger sportfishes' tuna towers looming above the massive rock jetty. The marina, hotel, and mountains behind the bay were all breathtaking.

Beau called the dock master on the VHF radio and asked for a slip. He was politely told that they were full, but he would be placed on the waiting list and could anchor up south of the marina in front of the hotel beach. He was also told that he was welcome to use their dinghy dock and all the other facilities at Los Suenos. Beau gave them his passport name and boat information, and idled over about three hundred yards off the hotel beach and anchored up. He decided not to fuel because less fuel in the tanks would make it easier to fish out the plastic moneybags.

Once anchored, Beau scoped the area with his binoculars, and then he busied himself extracting the inflatable dinghy and eight-horse power outboard engine from the aft cockpit lazarette. It took him close to an hour to inflate the ten-foot dinghy with its foot pump. The high-pressure floor took all the leg power he had to inflate it to fourteen psi. He wrestled the dinghy overboard and tied the bow painter to a cleat. The outboard looked almost brand new. Beau mixed some TCW-3 oil with a gallon of the gasoline he had stowed in the cockpit, fifty to one. He opened the tuna door and swung the engine onto the dinghy's transom. After filling the outboard's tank, he choked the little Johnson and started cranking it over. It almost started on the third pull. Beau adjusted the choke and pulled it a couple more times. After some sputtering and smoking it straightened itself out and started to idle nicely. He let it warm up, and then ran the throttle up in neutral before shutting it off. Beau went below and took a shower. He locked the salon door and lay down on the salon couch for a nap. Maybe he'd go in tonight after dark and have a look around.

Beau woke up and it was dark. He looked at the Rolex on his wrist and saw it was 8:00 p.m. He went down to the head, brushed his teeth, and relieved himself. He chuckled as he stood above the head. The boat had been searched three times and no one had even gotten close to finding the gun hidden under the head motor cowling. Beau had been religious about putting it back in the head any time his own head wasn't resting on the pillow above it. He didn't want to take the chance of a thief stealing it when he was ashore. Beau decided to move the cash stash from the engine room, now that he was through with customs. He retrieved the plastic bag wrapped duffels from the engine room below and rewrapped the money in smaller white kitchen garbage bags and stacked it in the galley Sub-Zero freezer behind several bags of ice. *Talk about cold cash* ... Beau laughed to himself as he stacked the money in the freezer.

Tomorrow Beau would list the Bertram with a broker at the H.M.S. Brokerage at Los Suenos. Beau knew from reading Marlin magazine that H.M.S. had international connections, and that it was the only brokerage of that kind in Costa Rica. Beau planned to take two back-to-back trips to San Jose, first transporting the "cold cash" in the black duffels, so it would look like luggage, and then depositing it in three or four different banks. Then he would return to Los Suenos and retrieve the money that was submerged in the fuel tanks. He'd hide half of it in safety deposit boxes in the same banks and deposit the rest in his newly opened accounts. On the second and subsequent trips, he would begin wiring some of the money to recommended banks in Panama and the Caymans. With that done he would leave *Chica* at Los Suenos and start getting residences set up in San Jose and Tambor.

Beau was feeling hungry and decided to give the marina restaurant a try. He put on his fishing hat, got in the dinghy, and motored into the marina. As he passed through the entrance in the breakwater he was astounded by the size of the yachts and sportfishes that were tied up at the Los Suenos docks. His

54 footer was an average to small vessel in this marina. He motored around, then past, the fuel dock and landed at the dinghy dock. He walked up the long ramp and continued along the sea wall sidewalk to the second story restaurant called, The Hook Up. It wasn't crowded, the food smelled good, and all the *Tico* waitresses were young and pretty. Beau had a cheeseburger, french- fries, and an Imperial cerveza as he watched a Yankees–Redsox game on one of the huge televisions over the bar. The restaurant had only shutters on the windows and they were open to allow the balmy night breeze and overhead fans to do their job. The view of the marina and surrounding Herradura bay was spectacular. Beau paid his check and asked the bartender about the thatched-roof restaurant he could see two hundred yards to the south. She told him the restaurant was called El Galeon and that the food was more upscale than The Hook Up's. She also said the El Galeon's bar had live music nightly. Beau thought he might try it tomorrow night, but for now it was back to the boat to lay low. He walked down to the dinghy dock and the engine started on the first pull. He noticed eight dinghies tied up at the dock as he left. Their owners were probably ashore having a good time. As Beau passed through the breakwater and back into Herradura Bay he thought … *my time to have fun will start soon, but right now it's time to lay low.* He locked himself in *Chica*, turned on some music, and quickly fell asleep.

The next morning Beau woke up at 8:00 a.m., Costa Rican time. His internal sleep clock was definitely changing for the better. He thought about Fonda and promised himself a trip to Panama as soon as he was settled. Beau put some coffee on and took a long, hot, shower. As he sat on the salon couch drinking his coffee he watched the last of the charter boats straggle out through the break-water for their run out to the trolling grounds. Beau got the boat papers together and headed for the dinghy dock. He tied up, walked up the ramp and around the sea wall sidewalk to the marina office. His slip status hadn't changed, but he had moved up on the list and should have a slip by week's end. He continued up stairs to The Hook Up and ordered breakfast. Last night's bartender waited on him and gave him a big smile. He wished he was thirty again and had to laugh at himself … *Mr. Lucky never gives up, does he?* Beau thoroughly enjoyed the large American style breakfast, and he left the cute little bartender an outrageous tip. He walked back downstairs and found his way to the H.M.S. Brokerage office and went inside.

A youngish, tall, blond haired man, who was a little on the chubby side, looked up from his desk and said, "Welcome to H.M.S., Sir. What can I do for you?"

Beau said, "I've got a Bertram 54 I'd like to sell."

"Well, you've come to the right place, Mr.?"

"Santos," said Beau.

"Mr. Santos, I'm Chip Caldwell, and I can handle your listing," said Chip while vigorously shaking Beau's hand.

Chip explained that H.M.S. had four locations in Florida, three more on the upper east coast, and two on the west coast of the United States. They listed every vessel on Yacht World, so the Internet gave them worldwide coverage.

"Why are you selling her, Mr. Santos?"

"Well, since I plan to live in Costa Rica. I want a smaller, more maneuverable, express type fishing boat with a small marlin tower."

"Good point, I can help you with that too."

"We'll get to that when the Bertram sells," said Beau with a smile on his face.

Chip copied the documentation and transfers of name letter. Then he filled out a listing contract for Beau to sign. Beau let Chip copy his passport and visa for the file.

"What should we ask for her, Chip?"

Chip looked up the Bertram in his B.U.C. book and said. "If she's in better than average condition, I'd say about $575,000."

"Ask that, but I'll take $550,000 … less your commission."

"If she surveys well, we should be able to move her for that," said Chip.

"What commission rate will you take?"

"For a boat in that price range, I'll do it for eight percent."

"That's fair. If you sell it within a month, I'll give you nine percent. Do you have room for her at your docks?"

"Not at the moment."

Beau explained the *Chica* was anchored outside the marina and he was waiting for a slip. He further explained that he needed to go to San Jose to take care of some business. But, he didn't want to leave the Bertram out on the hook and wouldn't go to San Jose until he got a slip.

"I can solve that problem, Mr. Santos," said Chip. "I'll keep my eye on your boat, and try to motivate the marina office to give you a slip. Then I'll move it for you if you're not back yet. Leave me a cash deposit or a credit card number, and I'll pay the marina for the first month's slip rent."

"How much are the slips?"

"$30 dollars a foot per month, including electric, plus a $2500 deposit. $4500 should cover it."

"O.k.," said Beau. "Do you want to see the boat?"

"Yes, Sir, I do. Why don't you go back out to your boat, and I'll run out in our launch in about twenty minutes."

Beau counted out $4500 and Chip gave him a receipt.

They shook hands and Beau said, "See you at the boat."

Beau took his copies of the paperwork and walked back to the dinghy. The little engine started on the first pull, and Beau motored back to *Chica* feeling good about how his plan was falling into place. He felt the boat would be in good hands with the almost $50,000 commission for incentive.

Fifteen minutes later, Chip showed up alongside *Chica* in a sleek 35 foot Contender with three, 250 horsepower outboards on it.

"Nice ride," said Beau as he took the bowline and rafted the Contender off of two fenders he had rigged on *Chica's* hull side.

"This is what you ought to get to fish out of, Mr. Santos. She'll run 50 miles an hour plus."

Beau just smiled and then showed Chip through the Bertram. Chip was impressed with how nice the boat was inside and out.

"She hardly looks used inside. We'll detail the outside, with your permission, when we get it to a dock."

"Do it," said Beau. "I'll drop the keys off at your office on my way to San Jose tomorrow morning."

Chip vaulted back into the Contender and motored back to the marina, giving Beau a wave and a big smile as he left. Beau knew the boat would be on the Yacht World Internet site before the day was done. As Beau watched the Contender go through the breakwater, he got a chilling feeling that someone was watching him. He shook it off almost immediately thinking …. *Who would be watching me? Everybody thinks I'm dead.*

Beau went back in the cabin and thought about his future … now that he had one. He had lost his family and friends, but at least he had the money that had eluded him all these years. He now realized that his family and friends were worth far more to him than the money. He would try to forge a lasting relationship with Fonda. He vowed to make the best of the rest of his life and hoped through some miracle he could somehow have one more chance to show them all that he was worthy of their love.

He took a deep breath and started packing a small duffel bag for his trip to San Jose tomorrow morning. He planned on renting a car in the morning and driving it over the mountains to downtown San Jose. He was planning on staying in a small, exclusive hotel. He decided not to pack the "cold cash" in the two large duffels until he was ready to go ashore tomorrow. He finished packing and stretched out on the salon couch for a siesta.

CHAPTER TWENTY-FIVE

THE next morning Seth slept in until 7:45 a.m. He showered, dressed, and left for the boatworks, stopping at the Kopper Kitchen on Central Avenue for a quick breakfast. He arrived at Stone's shortly after 9:30. His sister and her family had called from their car and were about half way to St. Petersburg. Seth called her back and offered to put them up at the beach townhouse, but Scarlett had already made reservations at the downtown Vinoy Hotel. He asked her to call him when they got in, and he'd meet them for a drink in the Palm Court Bar at the hotel.

Seth studied the Caribbean chart again, and based on the timetable he had compiled on *Chica's* movements decided to by-pass calling San Andres and jump right to the Panama Canal and Colon. He turned on his computer, keyed up the Internet and Yahoo's site. He searched their Panama Canal pages and picked the official canal page. After checking that site and "Noonsite" he had the information he needed. The canal site recommended that yachts stay at the Panama Canal Yacht Club in Colon. The Panama Canal Yacht Club web page supplied him with all the information he needed. They had dockage, a fuel dock, a restaurant, and they were close to the customs and immigration facilities. Seth called the main number and asked for the dock master.

The dock master came on the line and said, "This is Jose, how may I help you?" Seth explained he was trying to track a boat down to inform a crewmember of a family emergency and described the Bertram 54, and gave Jose her name.

"Why *Chica* was here just two days ago."

"Would she be through the canal by now?"

"It is possible, *Senor*. The captain hired an agent and a senior canal pilot. Usually that means a one-day transit, but you can check at the Balboa Yacht Club on the Pacific side of the canal. They might still be there."

"Thank you, Jose. Can you give me their phone number and the name of the dock master?"

"Of course," said Jose, and he gave Seth the information and hung up.

Seth dialed the Balboa number and asked for Roberto, the dock master.

"This is Roberto, what can I do for you, Sir?" Seth explained that he had gotten Balboa's number from Jose at the Panama City Yacht Club. He went on to tell him the family emergency story, and asked him if *Chica* was still there.

"You just missed them, Sir. They fueled up yesterday, paid their bill, and were gone this morning before I came in at 7:30."

"Did the captain have a black beard?"

"Yes, Sir, and he had two big Cubans for crew."

"Did the captain say where he was headed?"

"He asked for a weather report, but didn't indicate where he was headed," answered Roberto. "But usually 99% of the sportfishing boats go north. There is no fuel to the south, except at Tropic Star Lodge down near Columbia and they will not sell fuel to transients. North of Panama, fuel is plentiful all the way to California."

Seth thanked him and started pulling up chart and marina information for the Pacific coast.

Next, Seth figured the fuel usage from the canal to Columbia and Costa Rica. Columbia was a real stretch, but Costa Rica was easily within reach for the Bertram. Seth weighed some other facts through his mind. Columbia had a strong U.S. CIA and DEA presence throughout their country, courtesy of the war on drugs treaty. Costa Rica was politically stable. Nicaragua was politically unstable, but Guatemala wasn't, so it was also a possibility. But Costa Rica was home to tens of thousands of retired Americans, and each week thousands of American tourists visited every corner of Costa Rica. An American would not stand out or probably even be noticed in Costa Rica. Seth had been there twice over the years, once to Quepos, and another time to Flamingo. Beau had been there three or four times. They had gone for the world-class bill fishing; although he was sure Beau had also done some gambling. The drill was to fly into San Jose, which was the capital, from Miami, spend the night, and then fly out the next morning in a small plane to your Pacific coast destination. Beau might go to Quepos or Flamingo. Another marina had been built since either one of them had been there, Los Suenos Marina, just north of Jaco. Los Suenos was only a one and a half hour drive from San Jose and Jaco had no airstrip.

Seth did some more Internet research and printed it all out. He found that there were only three real marinas on Costa Rica's entire Pacific coast. The other coastal towns, such as Quepos, Jaco, Carrillo, and Tamarindo had only moorings and difficult fueling situations.

Golfito had Banana Bay Marina and was located the furthest south. Banana Bay offered transient dockage and a fuel dock. Golfito also had the first customs and port of entry office if you were approaching from the Panama Canal.

The next marina was Los Suenos, just north of Jaco. It was new and offered modern docks and fuel. Seth had seen full-page ads in the sportfishing magazines and Los Suenos looked first class.

Further up the coast, almost to Nicaragua, was Flamingo Marina. It had minimal dockage and a fuel dock. Seth had been there a few years ago and the Internet pictures looked like it hadn't changed.

It would take the Bertram at least two days to reach Costa Rican waters. Seth didn't think Beau would chance running at night up the Pacific coast during the rainy season because of the amount of large floating debris from the rivers. Seth organized the marina phone numbers and decided he would start calling the Costa Rican marinas Saturday. He didn't want to call to early and chance tipping his hand to Captain Tony and his unknown associates.

Seth checked out of the boatyard after finding Jeb in the back part of the boatworks storage shed.

"I'll see you later at the Yacht Club, Jeb. I'm going home to shower and change clothes. I'll give you a call when your Aunt Scarlett and Uncle Lon get to the Vinoy. It would be nice if we could meet them at the Vinoy and then arrive at the Yacht Club as a family."

"No problem, Dad. I'll call Lynne and let her know we'll be leaving home a little earlier. It's a shame it takes a funeral to get our family together. I haven't seen my little cousins, Rhett and Jackson, for two or three years."

"You're right, Jeb, keeping families together is getting harder and harder when they scatter to different parts of the country. Tonight is going to be a tough one, considering the circumstances. Let's you and I keep our chins up and get through it with as much dignity as possible."

On Saturday morning, Captain Tony studied Giorgio's list of Costa Rican Marinas. Starting from the south, the first fuel stop and marina was Banana Bay in Golfito. The second was Quepos, but it was just a fuel barge, as Quepos had no docks, just moorings. Forty miles north of Quepos there was a large marina called Los Suenos. It had a breakwater, floating docks and a fuel dock. The next fuel opportunity was at Puntarenas, which was a large commercial port, many miles inland at the east end of the Gulf of Nicoya. The chances of *Chica* stopping there were remote unless it was their final destination. Flamingo Marina was the next logical fuel location, and Flamingo also had docks and was on the northern Costa Rican coast near the Nicaraguan border. If Costa Rica was not their destination, Captain Tony would have to follow them north through Nicaragua, El Salvador, Guatemala, and finally Mexico.

He called Banana Bay Marina in Golfito. The dock master confirmed that *Chica* had been there yesterday and had left early that morning. Captain Tony smiled to himself, because he knew he was getting close.

He questioned the dock master about the crew and the dock master said, "There was only the captain, and he had no crew. He said his crew had left to go home from Panama City."

"Was the captain a Gringo with a black beard?"

"Yes sir."

"Did he say where he was headed?"

"He told my dockhand that he was going up the coast to Los Suenos."

"Thank you! That is his float plan destination. We were starting to get worried."

The dock master said, "Happy to be of service, Sir," and the call was over.

Captain Tony hoped that Los Suenos was going to be *Chica's* final destination. It was only an hour and a half drive over the mountains from San Jose and Santamaria Airport according to Giorgio's Internet information. Mr. C. could have his men there in less than one day from Florida.

Captain Tony relayed the latest information to Luigi via his satphone. Luigi told him Cadillac had just called and confirmed that Ronald Santos, alone, had cleared customs in Golfito. Santos had designated his final destination as Los Suenos, just north of Jaco. Luigi wondered how No Nose would react to the news about Hector and Luis jumping ship. Luigi called, and No Nose told him to come right over. He was pacing up and down on the veranda again when Luigi got there.

Luigi related Captain Tony's and Cadillac's information and No Nose said calmly, "The Fernandez brothers are probably going to fly to Mexico from

Panama City, and then will fly from there back to Miami. They could have stashed
the money in Panama, or maybe they'll stash it in Mexico. Either way, make sure
Cadillac is waiting for them at the airport. Then I want both of them brought
up here to me in Tampa. There's also a good possibility that the money is still on
the boat with the unidentified captain, who is using the Ronald Santos' passport.
We must check that situation out, too. Besides, I want that boat. Have Captain
Tony check with Los Suenos this afternoon without giving us away. If the *Chica's*
captain knows someone is looking for him, he may start running again."

Captain Tony called Los Suenos on Saturday afternoon and talked to an
assistant in the marina office. He inquired about *Chica*, a Bertram 54, and said he
was scheduled to come down from the states with some friends to fish on it. He
just wanted to make sure it had arrived.

"*Chica* arrived today, Sir, but her captain didn't have a slip reservation, so we
had to put him on the waiting list. The boat is anchored out in Herradura Bay at
the moment. We should be able to put him in a slip later this week. He's going
to check in with us each day until we have a slip available. Do you want to leave
your number?"

"Oh, no," said Captain Tony. "I'm an old friend who he hasn't seen in
years, and he doesn't know I'm coming down with the other guys. Please let me
surprise him."

"No problem, *Senor*. We will look forward to seeing you later this week."

Captain Tony called Luigi and said, "*Chica* has arrived, and she's anchored in
the bay next to the Los Suenos marina waiting for a slip. Have Giorgio print you
out the information on Los Suenos and get some men down there!"

"Thanks for the good work, Tony. I know Mr. C. is going to be pleased."

Luigi met with No Nose an hour later and showed him the Los Suenos
website printout. Luigi and No Nose hatched a plan to deal with the captain and
the Bertram at Los Suenos; at 6:00 a.m. on Sunday morning two of his Cuban
enforcers, Paco and Rafael, would be on his corporate jet on their way to San
Jose, Costa Rica. If the money was on the boat or they needed to bring the
captain back alive to Tampa, with no customs interference, it could be arranged.
No Nose sent the two Cubans because they both spoke perfect English and

Spanish. They were excellent at extracting information, and both of them were cold-blooded killers. The two pilots would stay close to the San Jose airport, and they would be ready to leave the instant that Paco or Rafael called them.

Early Sunday morning No Nose woke up, rolled over in his king size bed, and looked at his alarm clock. It was 6:00 a.m., and his plan was in motion. With the summer time change, the plane would land in San Jose at 8:30 a.m., Costa Rican time. His men would be at Los Suenos well before noon. He smiled, rolled back over, and was sound asleep again by the time the jet had taken off.

CHAPTER TWENTY-SIX

SETH woke up Friday morning still a little groggy from all the wine he drank at Beau's wake the night before. The Stone family had arrived early at the Yacht Club and formed a receiving line as Beau's friends filed into the Yacht Club's ballroom for his wake. They accepted the expressions of condolence graciously and within thirty minutes the large ballroom was full.

Jeb had started the eulogies and Beau's friends carried on from there for almost forty-five minutes. Everyone tried to keep it light, and no references were made to Beau's death in the jaws of a shark. Many humorous sailing and fishing antidotes were related, and as the mourners got past their second drink their moods became more jovial. Finally, Seth made a move to the microphone to give what would be the last eulogy of the evening.

The next morning Seth lay in bed and remembered it word for word: "You all knew Beau. He was a free spirit, a fun loving person with a lot of good traits and a few he could have done without. If you were Beau's friend, he'd do anything he could for you. He was always fun to be with, and he could turn an everyday occurrence into an adventure. He lived his life to the fullest day after day. I'll miss Beau, and not just because he's my only brother. We'll all miss his craftsmanship at the boatworks, and we'll also miss his sense of humor and infectious desire to have fun. I'll miss sailing and fishing with him, which we've done together since we were little boys. But don't cry for Beau, he wouldn't want that. Even though his last adventure ended in tragedy in Key West, remember this; most of us would have to live three full lives to experience what Beau did in one life. Whenever you think about him, let him put a smile on your face. Now the bar will be open for another hour, so let's have another drink to Beau … and let's remember the good times we had with him. That's the way *he* would have wanted it."

Seth had looked around and the whole room was crying and laughing at the same time. He remembered heading for the bar, but the rest of the night was just a blur.

He got out of bed and made his way to the shower and let the hot, thera-
peutic, water beat on his head and shoulders for quite some time. By the time
he got dressed and drove down to the boatworks, he was feeling almost human.
Seth didn't stay at the boatworks long. He thanked all the employees, individually,
for attending Beau's wake. Then he found Jeb and made sure was he was all right.

Seth had scheduled an early lunch with Scarlett, Lon, and his nephews at
Harvey's bar and grill on Fourth Street. They would leave from there to go back
to Atlanta after lunch. Both the boys were enrolled in summer soccer camps, and
according to his sister they were gifted athletes. Seth promised to come up and
watch the boys play during the fall season. Scarlett and her family were on their
way back to Atlanta by 1:30 p.m.

After they left, Seth drove back to the beach and decided to spend the rest
of the day flats fishing. He started a load of laundry before he left, and then cast
off in his Scout 17 foot flats boat. He ran down to the Skyway Bridge approach
and chummed up some white bait. Two throws of his net filled the port bait
well and he ran across Tampa Bay to Miguel Bay in Terra Ceia. He chummed the
mangroves at one of Beau's and his favorite snook holes and soon he had them
popping the white bait. He caught one snook after another until he finally broke
down and shed a tear for Beau. He hoped his hunch was right and Beau was still
alive. Maybe someday he and Beau could share some fishing time again.

Seth was up, showered, and dressed by 8:00 Saturday morning. After stopping for breakfast he arrived at the boatyard at 9:30 a.m. The boatworks was
open until 1:00 p.m. on Saturdays and Jeb was already out in the yard with a
customer when Seth made his way up to his office. He sat down and dialed up
Banana Bay Marina in Golfito and asked for the dock master.

"This is Bruce. May I help you?" said the dock master.

Seth started into the story about the family emergency and Bruce confirmed
that *Chica* had been there over night and had left early that morning. Bruce also
mentioned that someone else had called about fifteen minutes ago checking on
Chica's float plan.

"Was it Captain Tony?"

"Yes, it was."

"Oh, that's great. He's been helping me locate them," lied Seth. "Did *Chica's*
captain say where he was headed?"

"Los Suenos," said Bruce. "I'm sure you'll find him there today."

Seth thanked Bruce, hung up the phone, sat back in his chair, and said, "Bingo!" out loud.

The first part of the puzzle was solved. He paused and thought over what his next move should be. Should he tell Jeb, call the police, or go to Costa Rica himself? The whole situation was so bizarre, and so many facts were still unknown. Again, who was Captain Tony and what was behind his interest in Beau and *Chica*? Where did the two Cubans fit into all of this? Seth decided to go back to basics. He would tell no one and follow the boat.

He called American Airlines and booked an 11:30 a.m. flight to San Jose the next day. Then Seth scooped up the Los Suenos information off his desk and headed down the stairs. He found Jeb in the yard looking at a damaged lead keel on a J-105 sailboat.

"Hey Dad," said Jeb as Seth approached. "How would you fix this keel?"

"I'd pound the lead back as close to the original shape as possible with a sledge hammer, then epoxy-fill it, and batten-fair it."

"Yeah, that's what I was thinking."

"Listen, Jeb. I'm still very upset over Beau's death and I won't be much good around here for the next few days. I think I'll drive up into the North Carolina Mountains and just disappear for a week"

"Sounds like a good idea, Dad. Call me when you're on your way back and be careful."

On his way out of the yard Seth retrieved his Steiner binoculars and his night vision scope from *Tar Baby*.

Seth awoke as the big airbus started its descent into the Juan Santamaria Airport in San Jose, Costa Rica. He swallowed hard to clear his ears, and looked out at the verdant valley below as the plane descended through some patchy clouds. Ten minutes later, he was deplaning at Costs Rica's new, modern, airport. Seth was amazed at the change from the old, two gate, detached terminal that had only a few open hangers next to it. The new sleek marble and glass airport terminal had six pull up gates and articulating covered ramps. Seth shouldered his duffel off the plane and followed the signs to customs. With no need to wait for baggage, he was through customs and immigration in fifteen minutes. He walked out of customs and into a lobby where six major rental car companies had their locations.

He picked Hertz and rented a small four-wheel drive SUV. He remembered the roads as being potholed and wash-boarded, so he figured he needed something rugged. He finished the paperwork and had the agent mark a map with directions to Jaco and Los Suenos. When questioned, the agent said the roads were much improved and the trip over the mountains to Jaco should only take an hour and a half to two hours. Seth took the van shuttle to the airport Hertz lot. He was on his way to Los Suenos shortly after 1:30 p.m., Central time, in a white Toyota Forerunner.

After double-checking the map, Seth headed west on Costa Rica Route 1. He missed the turnoff to Atenas and Orotina, had to back track, and lost about forty-five minutes. He got it right the second time. After the turn off, the road went from four lanes to two, and then wound Seth through some hilly terrain and several small dusty towns. The road was lined with many neatly kept houses and small ranches. The colorful foliage was spectacular in every direction. The little towns all had a church, school, soccer field, a grocery store, and a restaurant or two. They were all orderly and neatly kept. Seth noticed entire families walking along the road both east and west. The traffic on the roads was mostly commercial trucks and buses.

Seth took the Jaco turnoff in the little town of Orotina and began his ascent up and over the Costa Rican Mountains. He had to pay close attention so he didn't drive over the side of the twisting road and plunge into the deep chasms below. There were no guardrails and the only barriers were closely planted trees on some of the more dangerous curves. Thirty minutes later Seth was driving above the clouds and starting his descent towards the Pacific Ocean and Jaco. *Going down is a little scarier than going up* ... thought Seth? He hoped the Forerunner's squealing brakes didn't fail him. He passed a burnt out hulk of a truck that had been pulled up out of a chasm and was placed alongside the road as a reminder to pay attention. He drove down a steep winding mountain stretch that ended at a one-lane bridge that had a roaring creek rushing under it. On the way back up the next mountain he passed a forty passenger tour bus going the other way.

"That could get interesting," Seth said aloud, thinking about the one lane bridge behind him.

He drove around a long curve at the top of that mountain, and there before him was the majestic, pastel blue, Pacific Ocean. As he started down the mountain he could see fifteen or twenty miles in both directions. The rugged green mountains and the coastal jungle below, bordering the aqua blue Pacific Ocean were magnificent.

He followed the black asphalt ribbon to the coastal flatlands and crossed the Tarcole River. The river was muddy and very wide. The two-lane bridge across the river was fully a half a mile long and over fifty feet above it. There were dozens of people looking over the railings at the center of the bridge. Seth slowed down but couldn't see what the attraction was. When he cleared the west end of the bridge, there was a small parking lot full of cars and buses, and a small roadside stand with a sign reading, "Feed the Crocodiles". Seth made a mental note to stop on his way back to check them out. The crocodiles he had seen on the animal channel looked twice as large as Florida's alligators.

He soon was on the coast and driving along the Gulf of Nicoya. He drove up a long hill and then dropped gently down into a green valley and past a sign that read, "Los Suenos Resort, two miles on the right." He turned right at the next sign and one mile down a small dusty road was the large imposing stone entrance to Los Suenos. Seth stopped at the guard gate and told the uniformed guard he was there to check into the Marriott. The guard saluted and opened the gate, telling Seth to turn left at the fountain roundabout. The grounds were beautifully landscaped and when Seth turned left around the fountain, he saw the Marriott in front of him and parts of the golf course to his left and right. He had copied a sitemap of Los Suenos, so he knew that past the condos to his right was the marina complex. He pulled up under a large portico and a bellman opened the door of the Toyota for him.

"Checking in, Sir?" asked the bellman.

"Yes, I am."

"Reservation, Sir?"

"No, do I need one?"

"It shouldn't be a problem this time of year. Please follow me to the front desk."

Seth followed him in to the front desk, noticing the hotel's elegant hardwood paneling and trim. The lobby and the bar beyond it were all open-air porticos and the breeze from the Pacific was cooling even this time of the year. Seth asked for a top floor room with a full marina view as he gave the desk clerk his American Express card.

"I have a room on the northwest corner, *Senor*, will that do?" said the desk clerk.

"That will be fine," said Seth as he filled out the registration card.

The clerk made a copy of his passport and handed the bellman the key to the room. The bellman retrieved Seth's duffel from the Toyota and he was informed that all vehicles were valet-parked and available 24/7 with the keys kept at the front desk. Seth followed the bellman into the elevator and up to his room. Seth tipped the bellman $10 and thanked him for his help. The room turned out to be a junior suite, with a couch, a table, and a small balcony overlooking the marina and Herradura Bay.

As soon as the bellman left, Seth unpacked his binoculars and went out on the balcony. He scanned the marina for the Bertram 54, but he could not find it. Most of the sportfishes had tuna towers, so it should have been easy to pick out. He was about to give up and take a walk down to the marina, when he noticed a group of anchored boats south of the breakwater and in front of the hotel. The beach in front of the hotel was pure white, in contrast to the brown sand along the rest of Herradura Bay. *Probably trucked in …* thought Seth, although he had seen beaches in Quepos and Flamingo that were white.

Seth turned his attention to the anchored boats and there it was the furthest one out. The Bertram 54, *Chica,* was sitting calmly at anchor with an inflatable dinghy tied up behind it. That probably meant that everybody was home. All the worry and the negative emotions from the past two weeks suddenly rushed over him. Seth shook those feelings off, and instead was glad he had followed his instincts. At least he was close to getting to the bottom of this mystery. He would remain vigilant, from the vantage point of his balcony, until somebody on *Chica* made a move.

The sun was starting to drop in the west, and Seth noticed the charter fishing boats were starting to make their way back into the beautiful bay and marina. Seth was impressed with Los Suenos. The hotel and marina were world class in size and detail. Seth never dreamed there would be anything like this in Costa Rica. He took a diet coke from the room's mini-bar and called room service. He ordered a small steak and a garden salad. Now he would settle in and wait for someone to show himself on the Bertram. The steak and salad finally arrived and Seth ate it, hungrily. By the time he finished eating, the sun was just about ready to drop below the western horizon.

Seth was sitting in a chair just inside the open doors to the balcony with the lights out, so no one outside could see him. It reminded him of some of the forward observation patrols he'd been on in the Vietnam War. You were hiding and watching for enemy movement, but you didn't know if the enemy was hiding and watching for you.

CHAPTER TWENTY SEVEN

PACO and Rafael's flight to Costa Rica on Sunday morning was uneventful until the Falcon Jet started its final approach into Santamaria Airport. The winds suddenly picked up in the valley between the mountains leading to San José, and gusted to thirty-five knots. The plane started through some of the turbulence and suddenly dropped a hundred feet. The pilot quickly increased power and wrestled the plane back up on course, but the landing was anything but smooth. They taxied into the executive jet sector of the terminal where they were unloaded and whisked through customs and immigration in a matter of minutes by a V.I.P. escort. The pilots took a cab to the Corobici Hotel which was located about ten minutes from downtown San Jose and fifteen minutes from the airport. Paco and Rafael were met at the airport by a van that would take them over the mountains to Jaco.

The Cubans had been given two prototype handguns made out of non-magnetic space age materials. They were stolen from Red Mesa Industries in Ormond Beach, Florida. Red Mesa had advertised for venture capital in a gun magazine regularly read by John Cipriano, and No Nose had responded by having Luigi Scuzzi arrange for a break-in and robbery at Red Mesa. The family's testing of the four stolen prototypes confirmed they were as accurate and reliable as Glock nine-millimeters and were undetectable when passing through airport metal detectors. The family encased the handguns in empty hairdryer shells to make their shape invisible to the baggage x-ray machines. The bullets were transported in aluminum foil lined Vitamin C bottles.

Paco and Rafael had a scenic ride across the lush green Costa Rican mountains. It reminded them of their family's homeland in Cuba. They had both visited relatives in third world Cuba, but much preferred their lives in the United States where they were born. They asked the driver why there were no guardrails, and the driver laughed and told them the trees were the guardrails. Paco commented on the fence posts surrounding the cattle farms that they passed. All the fence posts grew like trees. The driver explained that the farmers cut down small trees and cut them up into fence posts. Then they dug postholes and installed the posts, stringing barbed wire along the posts to finish the fence. But, Costa Rica's rich volcanic soil was so conducive to rapid plant growth that in only three months, the fence posts took root and started to grow again as trees.

Within an hour and fifteen minutes, the van passed a sign advertising Los Suenos Resort and Marina two miles to the south. They passed the turn off to Los Suenos and continued down the highway a few more miles to Jaco where the van driver dropped them off at the Hotel Del Mar. There was a room waiting for them and the hotel had arranged for a rental SUV that was already sitting in the parking lot.

Paco and Rafael stowed their luggage and disassembled the hairdryer shells and loaded their handguns. They had instructions from Luigi to subdue and question the *Chica's* mysterious captain, and thoroughly search the Bertram. If no answers were forthcoming they were to bring the captain back to Tampa on the jet and deliver him to Luigi. If they found the money in the Bertram, they were to dispose of the captain and bring the money back to Tampa. In either case, they were to secure the Bertram in a slip at Los Suenos Marina and deliver the vessel's documentation back to Tampa so the family could engineer a title change through its contacts in Florida.

The two hit men got in their silver KIA Sorrento and rode up the main street of Jaco, looking for a place to eat. They passed numerous bodegas, a super market called Max-y-Menos, liquor stores, bars, surf shops, discos, and a host of small restaurants.

They settled on the Sunrise Restaurant because it was crowded and advertised, "Breakfast, all day". They sat at a table next to the street, al fresco style, and watched the early surfer crowd shuffle by on their way to the beach. Both of them enjoyed watching the young surfer girls in their postage stamp bikinis.

The Cubans looked out of place in their Tommy Bahama shirts, long pants, and wrap around Richard Petty sunglasses. They neither looked like natives or tourists. Paco paid the check and left a big tip for the young waitress. He liked the way she walked and thrust out her pert little breasts. He wondered how she had stuffed her bubble butt in that small denim skirt. He thought … *if she took it off, her butt and stomach would expand at least two sizes.*

With breakfast over it was time to drive to Los Suenos and take care of business. They drove back up the highway and turned left down the road to Los

Suenos. A few minutes later they arrived in front of the massive stone guard gate.

The guard came out and Paco said in English, "We are here to look at some real estate."

The guard gave them a site map and marked the way to the real estate office that was located in the southeastern corner of the marina.

Paco said, "*Gracias,*" and drove onto Los Suenos's grounds.

They drove past the real estate office and out onto the south marina breakwater and parked west of the charter boat office facing south, per Captain Tony's instructions. Rafael raised his binoculars and swept the bay looking for *Chica*. He located the Bertram in a matter of seconds. It was the southernmost vessel anchored well off the hotel beach. The hotel looked like a rambling four story Spanish Hacienda.

"Everything about this place is first class and screams money," said Rafael.

The two of them watched the boat for a while and noticed a small gray inflatable dinghy tied off its stern. They figured whoever had come in on the boat was on it now. Finally, a man of average height and medium build came out of the salon door and looked around. He had jet-black hair and a closely cropped beard. He was darkly tanned and wore a Columbia fishing shirt and khaki shorts.

Rafael said, while looking through the binoculars, "So that could be our captain who is using Ronald Santos's passport."

They watched the captain walk through the open transom tuna door, step out on the swim platform, and get into the dinghy. He untied the dinghy and motored it towards the breakwater entrance, just west of Paco and Rafael. Paco got out of the Sorrento and tried to watch the dinghy after it entered the marina, but he lost it amongst the large yachts that were tied up in the slips. Paco finally saw him walk up a ramp next to the fuel dock and start towards the main marina building. The pair got back in the KIA and rode over to the parking lot in front of the marina building. They got out and walked to the marina office and sat on a bench across from the door. The bearded captain went by just as they sat down. He continued walking and went into the marina office.

Ten minutes later he came out and went up a flight of stairs to The Hook Up restaurant. Paco followed him up the stairs telling Rafael to wait on the bench. There was a fair amount of pedestrian traffic in and out of the marina office and on and off the docks. Rafael noticed two security officers checking and issuing fishing licenses on the other side of the walkway. There'd be no possibility of snatching the *Chica's* captain from this location.

A half an hour later the captain walked by Rafael and turned the corner and went into the H.M.S. Yacht Brokerage office.

Paco returned to the bench and said, "Our captain had some breakfast and came back down. Where did he go?"

"He went into the boat broker's office," said Rafael.

Rafael pointed out all the security in the area and the two of them agreed they'd have to take the captain in a more remote location. Thirty-five minutes later he came out of the broker's office with a manila envelope in his hand and returned to the dinghy. The Cubans watched him start the outboard and motor away. They hurried to the SUV and drove back around to their previous parking place on the south breakwater in time to see him board the Bertram and disappear inside.

Fifteen minutes later, a large center console boat with three outboards on it idled out of the marina and tied up next to *Chica*. A tall blond haired man met the captain in the cockpit and they went inside.

"Probably the broker," said Paco.

"Maybe," said Rafael.

The blond haired man had a clipboard and was taking notes. When they reappeared fifteen minutes later, they both climbed up on the fly bridge.

"Definitely the broker," said Paco.

"I agree," said Rafael. "I guess he's selling the boat for the Fernandez's".

"We need to get this guy alone, soon!"

"Maybe we can grab him tonight if he comes ashore. Otherwise, we'll have to take one of those dinghies at the small dock and pay him a surprise visit."

"We'll wait here and see," said Paco getting comfortable.

The broker left and the captain went back inside and closed the cabin door.

Around dusk, Ronald (Paco and Rafael were calling him that now), came out of the Bertram, started the outboard and headed for the dinghy dock. Paco started the car, backed out very fast, and drove the KIA around to the marina parking lot with the lights out. Paco and Rafael waited until they saw Ronald go up the stairs to The Hook Up. Then, they exited the SUV and followed him up.

Ronald sat at the bar and began talking animatedly with the female bartender. Ronald had a cerveza and appeared to order dinner. Paco flagged down a waitress and he and Rafael ordered grilled chicken and rice, and two coffees. Ronald took his time eating dinner, obviously preferring to talk with the comely bartender rather than concentrating on eating. Paco and Rafael ate their dinner quietly, trying to appear oblivious to Ronald's presence. They were just finishing when Ronald abruptly stood up, paid his tab with cash, and walked downstairs.

"Follow him," said Paco. "I'll pay the check and catch up. He can't go far on foot."

Rafael got up and followed Ronald slowly down stairs. Ronald got to the bottom of the stairs and walked out towards the parking lot and then turned right down a sidewalk leading to the El Galeon restaurant, a couple of hundred yards south. Rafael kept his distance and followed fifty yards or so behind him. Paco came out of the marina complex and spotted Rafael on the sidewalk and walked briskly in his direction. They both watched Ronald saunter through the front door of the El Galeon and disappear inside.

Paco and Rafael waited for five minutes and then walked into the bar. The Galeon was full of visiting fisherman drinking and listening to the three-piece band. Ronald had taken the last seat at the end of the bar. Paco and Rafael slipped into two chairs at a table in the very back of the room. They ordered two cervezas and watched Ronald's back as they talked.

"We'll snatch him when he goes back to his dinghy," said Paco. "Finish your beer and then walk down to the dinghy dock. It's dark in front of the ship's store and brokerage office, so wait in the shadows there. I'll follow him out of here and close on him quickly when he gets near the brokerage office. Walk out of the shadows and ask him to light your cigar. That will throw him off guard, and give you a chance to stick your gun in his face. I'll stick mine in his back a few seconds later. The only security they have at night is a guard in a closed shack at the main ramp by the office, and the guard in the golf cart who patrols the parking lots. There's no one near the dinghy dock end."

Rafael finished his beer and walked out of the El Galeon bar and headed for the dinghy dock. He walked around the main office complex and ducked in between the brokerage office and the ship's store. He stood in the shadows and waited. A half an hour later, he saw a man walking towards him along the seawall sidewalk. It was Ronald.

Rafael waited until he was almost to him and then he stepped out of the shadows with a cigar in his left hand and said, "*Senor*, can I trouble you for a light?"

Ronald was startled and took a step back and said, "No sir, I'm sorry, but I don't smoke".

At that moment, Paco came up behind him and shoved his pistol into his back and said, "Not a sound or you're a dead man".

Rafael pressed the barrel of the pistol in his right hand against Ronald's cheek and told him to put his hands behind his back. He complied and Paco tightened a large plastic tie wrap around his wrists. They quickly pushed him down the ramp to the dinghy dock and put him in the dinghy. Paco got in and continued to hold the pistol in Ronald's' back. Rafael got in and started the outboard.

They pulled away from the dock and Ronald said softly, "Who are you?" Paco shoved the pistol harder into Ronald's ribs until he winched in pain.

"Not another word, Ronald, not until you're spoken to," said Paco.

Beau thought he might be in deep shit when he was called Ronald. He had not gotten a good look at either of his captors, except he knew they were Hispanic. They rode the rest of the way to the Bertram in silence. Beau was puzzled. Were these guys local thugs who got his name from someone inside the marina office, or were they from Tampa? When they arrived at *Chica*, Beau was hoisted, unceremoniously, out of the dinghy. The big Hispanic took Beau's keys out of his pocket, opened the salon door, and pushed him roughly inside.

The big Hispanic sat him down in one of the chairs and said, "You asked who we are. To answer your question, Ronald or whatever your name really is, the Cipriano family sent us down here to bring back the three million dollars that you and the Fernandez brothers stole from them. The sooner you show us where it is, the easier we'll make it for you." With that said he hit Beau across the face with the back of his hand, knocking Beau and the chair to the floor.

Beau yelped and the big one said, "That's just a sample of what's going to happen to you if you don't talk. It will get as nasty as it has to, Captain. We might even cut your *cojones* off!"

Beau lay on the cabin sole and his face smarted from the blow the Hispanic had delivered. But it only took Beau a few seconds to realize what had happened, and he felt stupid for not seeing it coming. Somehow, No Nose had discovered that the Bertram, Ronald Santos, and the Fernandez brothers were one and the same. Then they had tracked the boat down, and they thought he was an unidentified accomplice of the brothers and Ricardo Cabeza.

"You've got the wrong man," growled Beau tasting blood in his mouth. "My names not Ronald, I'm just a delivery captain doing what I was hired to do."

"Bull shit," said the smaller Hispanic. "So where are the Fernandez brothers?"

"They got off in Panama City with four large duffel bags and their suitcases. They said they were headed back to Miami."

"What are you doing here with their boat, and why are you using Ronald Santos's passport?" asked the big one.

"They wanted me to deliver it here so it could be sold. Hector said that Ronald Santos lives in Fort Lauderdale. They made me use his passport, and they want me to sell the Bertram posing as the owner. When it sells I'm supposed to wire the money to a bank in Mexico and take a five percent cut, plus expenses."

"What's your real name, Captain?"

"Jimmy Williams," answered Beau.

"How did you get mixed up with the Fernandez brothers, Jimmy?"

"I'm a customer, I bet on football with their book. But I'm a charter-fishing captain, and I normally run a sportfish out of Miami Beach Marina. July, August, and September are my slow months, so this delivery and the sales commission is big money for me this time of the year."

The two Cubans pulled Beau off the salon floor and sat him back in the chair.

Beau piped up and said, "Look, there's $7,000 or $8,000 in the top drawer of the guest cabin bureau. Hector and Luis gave that to me for expenses."

"Where's the passport?" said the big one.

"It's in the same drawer with the cash. The boat papers and brokerage contract are there also."

The big Hispanic made a move to the guest cabin and came back with a stack of hundred dollar bills, Ronald's passport, and all the boat papers.

"It's all here, Rafael, maybe Jimmy is telling us the truth."

I'll call Wall-to-Wall and have him check Capt. Jimmy out, Paco," said Rafael.

Paco and Rafael ... thought Beau ... *they must be two of Cipriano's Cuban hit men. I've got to get to the Glock in the head.*

"Come on, boys, I'm just a working stiff like you guys," said Beau.

"We'll know soon enough, Jimmy," said Rafael.

Rafael pulled a sat phone out of his left front pocket and went out in the cockpit to make a call. He was back in five minutes.

Rafael said, "Wall-to-Wall says to keep this guy on ice until he calls me back. He's going to have Cadillac check him out to see if he's telling the truth. I told him about the eight grand and the brokerage contract. Meanwhile he says to search the whole boat for the three million.

The two of them started tearing the boat apart looking for the money. They started forward and worked aft. They pulled out all the drawers, and looked in every cabin, locker, and cubbyhole. They checked the galley cabinets, refrigerator, and freezer. But, they didn't unload the bags of ice. Paco went through the engine room and came out a greasy mess. Rafael checked the fly bridge, the cockpit freezer, the bait well, the lazarette, and then finally gave up. The two of them straightened up the salon enough so they could sit on the leather couch.

Paco said to Rafael, "Now, we'll just wait for the boss to call back."

He raised the antenna on his satphone and propped it against the starboard salon window.

Beau breathed a little easier, at least he had bought himself some time and he hadn't been beaten up too badly yet. His nose was bleeding and he thought it was probably broken. Paco told Beau to get up and go forward. He guided him down to the guest cabin and told him to lie on the bunk.

Beau asked, "Can I take a piss first?"

Paco nodded his head and said, "all right."

Paco cut the tie wrap around Beau's wrist with a switchblade he had in his pocket. As Beau got up off the bunk, he felt the pistol barrel in his back again. Paco marched him into the head and kept the barrel pressed in his back while Beau relieved himself. *So much for pulling out the Glock and turning the tables ...* thought Beau. Paco had Beau put his hands behind his back again and he slipped on another tie wrap and pulled it tight.

"Lie down on that bunk and don't move a muscle," said Paco, as he tie-wrapped Beau's ankles together. "If you have to move, call for me."

As soon as Paco left the cabin Beau started working his feet and legs through his manacled wrists. He could almost get his hands over his butt and under his thighs. He kept working quietly and slowly made a little progress. He knew that when the call came in from the man they called Wall-to-Wall the beating and worse would resume.

CHAPTER TWENTY EIGHT

S ETH shifted his position in his chair looking out over the balcony. The sun had disappeared into the Pacific Ocean and dusk was settling in. He leaned forward and trained his binoculars on the Bertram as it bobbed gracefully in the remnants of the afternoon sea breeze. Suddenly, the Bertram's salon door opened and Beau walked out into the cockpit like he didn't have a care in the world. Even in the failing light Seth could tell he was all right. Beau had grown a full beard and he needed a haircut. He was wearing a green fly-fishing shirt and a pair of tan shorts. Seth was elated to see him alive and well. But, he wondered where the two Cubans were. And he also wondered if maybe this whole caper was all Beau's idea. Seth watched as Beau slowly took in the whole harbor scene. He was very relaxed and didn't look the least bit nervous. The whole thing still didn't make any sense to Seth. For some reason Beau wanted the whole world to think he was dead.

Beau locked the salon door, got into the dinghy that was tied behind the Bertram, and started the outboard engine. He cast off and ran towards the breakwater on full plane. He throttled the dinghy down at the entrance to the marina, and Seth lost him behind the large yachts that were tied up in their slips. He was obviously headed for the fuel or dinghy dock on the north side of the marina.

Seth thought ... *the obvious thing for me to do is to just to hustle down there, confront him, and find out what the hell is going on.*

Seth started to put his binoculars down, when he caught some sudden movement out of the corner of his left eye. It was a silver SUV backing out of a parking space down on the south breakwater at an excessive rate of speed. The SUV had also not turned on its headlights. As the SUV skidded to a stop, it immediately peeled out in forward still not showing any running lights. Seth switched to his night scope as darkness fell, and watched the silver SUV race around to the parking lot in front of the marina complex. The SUV parked in the front row, but nobody exited the vehicle.

Switching the night scope back to the north side of the marina, Seth got a glimpse of Beau walking around the seawall towards the main marina building. He could see an illuminated sign on the second floor of the building that read, The Hook Up. Beau went up the stairs to The Hook Up, which was listed as a casual restaurant and sports bar in the Los Suenos hotel guide. Two minutes later two men got out of the silver SUV and walked up the stairs to The Hook Up.

Now Seth was really scratching his head; no Cubans on the Bertram, but two men that were staked out on the breakwater watching the Bertram, and who were obviously very interested in Beau. He seriously doubted that they were any kind of law enforcement, and he thought they were probably there as a result of Captain Tony's research. Seth knew that just the fact that the two men were watching and following Beau was in itself sinister, but he still had no clue to what was really going on.

He decided to play a waiting game, but first he would take some steps to gain more of an advantage. He knew that the two men were following Beau, but no one knew that he was there. Seth took the steak knife from his room service dinner plate, wiped it off, and slipped it in his pocket. He left the room and rode the elevator downstairs to the lobby. Then he walked, casually, out the north side exit between the lobby and the bar. He followed a sidewalk that wound through the manicured grounds towards the marina. He entered a long vine covered trellis section of the walkway, and followed it until it ended near the entrance to the El Galeon restaurant. Seth walked the rest of the distance in the dimly lit parking lot and stopped behind the silver SUV. He looked up and down the parking lot and sidewalk and didn't see the security guard in the golf cart, anywhere. Then he walked up behind the SUV and slit both of the rear tires. He quickly retraced his steps and was back up in his hotel room in less than ten minutes.

Seth focused his night scope on the parking lot and saw no movement anywhere. He settled in the chair that he had moved out onto the darkened balcony and concentrated the night scope on The Hook Up area. Thirty minutes later Beau walked down the stairs and made his way up the sidewalk towards the El Galeon. Seth could hear the music wafting through the air from the El Galeon all the way up on his balcony. Sure enough, when Beau was half way there the smaller of the two stalkers was on his tail. Beau went inside and the stalker waited outside until his larger companion hustled up. Then they both went in. Seth had gotten a good look at the both of them while they stood under the front entrance lights at the El Galeon. They were definitely Hispanics, and both of them wore Hawaiian shirts and long pants, with the shirts worn, outside, tropical style. Seth had noticed that every other male guest in the resort, that he had seen, was dressed in shorts, as it was 93 degrees at night and humid. These two guys were not tourists or locals. They were dressed for San Jose where the temperature was 82 during the day and 68 at night, year around. About thirty minutes later the smaller man came out of the front door of the El Galeon, and walked back towards the marina office complex and disappeared into the darkness. In the last hour that Seth had been watching he had not seen the security guard in the golf cart, which he had noticed earlier, even once.

Twenty minutes later Beau came back out of the El Galeon and walked back to the marina entrance. The larger Hispanic was fifty paces behind Beau, and was closing on him fast. Even though Seth was using his night scope he lost track of them once they entered the marina complex.

Ten minutes later Seth caught a glimpse of a dinghy moving in the yacht basin. When the dinghy cleared the breakwater he got a better look. There were three men sitting in the dinghy. Beau was sitting in the bow with the large Hispanic behind him. The smaller Hispanic was running the outboard. They idled all the way out to the Bertram. Seth watched the two Hispanics haul Beau roughly out of the dinghy. Beau appeared to have his hands tied behind his back. A minute later the three of them disappeared inside the salon door. Seth could see some movement inside the Bertram's lighted salon, but he was too far away to tell what was happening.

Beau was obviously in trouble, and Seth didn't know what the reasons were or exactly who the players were. But it was his brother, and it was time for Seth to make a move to sort it all out. He put his binoculars and night scope in a small kit bag he had brought along, and put his passport and wallet in the room safe. He kept the purloined steak knife in his short's pocket. Seth locked the room, went down to the front desk, and asked that the Forerunner be brought up front.

Five minutes later he drove out the front gate and turned right towards Playa Herradura's public beach. He arrived there minutes later, parked as far north as possible, and locked the SUV. Seth looked around and the beach area appeared totally deserted. Not wanting to take any unnecessary chances, he opened the hood and pulled off the coil wire and put it in the kit bag along with his hotel room and SUV keys. Seth walked north along the water's edge until he came to a rocky creek mouth that emptied into the bay. The creek was a natural boundary between the public beach and Los Suenos. Seth retrieved his night scope from his kit bag and focused it out on the *Chica* in the bay. He could see the smaller

Hispanic talking on a satphone in the fishing cockpit. He finished his conversation and folded the sat phone's antennae down as he made his way back inside the salon.

Seth took his shoes off and stowed them in the kit bag, along with the night scope. He took his Columbia fishing shirt off and put it in the bag and then zipped it up. He hid the bag in among some large boulders at the creek mouth, then slipped quietly into the warm Herradura Bay water, and began to swim slowly out to the Bertram. He hated to swim at night, because of the bull sharks, but he had no choice. He took his time to conserve his energy and twenty minutes later he reached up and grabbed *Chica's* swim platform. All he could hear was the droning sound of the Bertram's generator. He rested for a good five minutes and then pulled himself silently up on the swim platform. He peeked up over the transom and really couldn't see anything but the tops of two heads sitting inside the salon. After another five minutes went by the smaller man got up and walked across the salon. He said something to the larger man and picked up a satphone and started for the door.

Seth ducked down behind the transom and held his breath. He heard the salon door open and close, and he could hear the man walking across the cockpit sole in his street shoes. Seth could smell the cigar as soon as the man lit it. The Hispanic took a couple of puffs and then walked aft and sat down on the transom facing forward. Just as he sat down the satphone rang. He answered the phone saying, "Yeah, Boss ... We searched every inch of the boat ... no money ... nobody ever heard of him, huh? O.K., we can do that ... yeah, sure, I have a camera in my cell phone. Luigi ... let me make sure I've got this all straight. Mr. Cipriano wants us to kill Capt. Jimmy, blunt force like he hit his head and fell overboard ...Yeah, we got a little dinghy; we can take him out a half a mile and dump him. Then we take pictures of the brokerage contract and the boat papers. We wipe our prints out of the boat and bring you the eight grand and the Ronald Santos passport ... Right, leave the boat out on the anchor for the brokerage agent to handle and put the dinghy back at the marina dock. All right, we should be back in San Jose tomorrow morning. We'll see you tomorrow afternoon in Tampa."

Seth listened to the phone call and when the small Hispanic mentioned the name Cipriano the situation started to fall into place in his mind. The two Hispanics were Tampa mafia. The Tampa mafia was after Beau, alias Capt. Jimmy. Money was involved and they had decided to kill him in the next few minutes. Seth had no time left to make a decision. The small Hispanic flipped his cigar over the starboard side and started to get up off the transom gunnel.

Seth silently took a deep breath, reared up and caught him in a chokehold. The Hispanic struggled but to no avail. He dropped the phone in the water and tried to pull his gun out of his waistband. Seth gave his throat a violent jerk and the gun fell harmlessly in the water. When the smaller man's air was gone, Seth twisted his head until he heard his neck snap. His Airborne Ranger hand-to-hand combat trainer would have been proud of him. Good technique was important, but the element of surprise was the biggest factor. Seth lowered the dead man to the deck, and climbed over the transom. He needed to get in position in case the dead man's partner came looking for him.

While checking out the cockpit, Seth spotted a fire extinguisher mounted behind the flybridge ladder. He crawled over to the ladder and took the fire extinguisher off of its bracket. Seth checked the gauge and the needle was solidly in the green. He stood up and peeked into the salon and saw the larger Hispanic sitting on the L-shaped couch. He was reading through a stack of papers on the coffee table. The large Hispanic was at least forty pounds heavier and four or five inches taller than Seth. He also looked at least twenty years younger. Seth spotted his pistol sitting on the coffee table next to the stack of papers. He was obviously tired as he yawned and stretched his arms several times as Seth watched him. Beau was nowhere to be seen, and Seth guessed he was tied up in one of the forward cabins. The salon was disheveled like it had been thoroughly searched, and only minimally straightened up. Seth hoped he could surprise the larger man, and get enough of the fire extinguisher foam in his eyes to blind him before he could reach his handgun. If Seth couldn't get to the gun first, he would try to hit him over the head with the heavy metal extinguisher. The Hispanic rolled his neck and started to leaf through the papers in front of him again. Seth figured if he just walked in through the door normally the Hispanic would think it was his partner coming in from his smoke.

Seth clenched the steak knife between his teeth, pirate style, and pulled the safety pin out of the extinguisher handle. He opened the door slowly and moved towards the larger man who casually glanced up.

His eyes suddenly got wider and he started to say, "What the fu …" just as Seth let him have it in the face with the fire extinguisher.

He screamed with pain and tried to wipe the stinging foam out of his eyes. Seth slid across the foam-covered coffee table on his knees and hit the screaming man a glancing blow on the side of his head with the extinguisher. The gun was lost in the foam that covered the table and couch. The Hispanic shook his head, grunted like a feral pig, and launched himself blindly at Seth. He got a hold of Seth around his waist and tried to roll him to the salon floor. Seth managed to extricate the steak knife from his clenched teeth and buried the knife in the Hispanic's back. Seth tried to twist the knife, but the handle broke off at the hilt. The large man screamed in pain as he rolled on the floor and pummeled Seth with his fists. The Hispanic got a grip on Seth and hurled him across the room. Seth landed in a heap, with the wind knocked out of him. The Hispanic groped in the foam for his gun and came up with it. Seth rolled weakly behind a leather chair and tried to catch his breath. The Hispanic still couldn't see and fired wildly in Seth's direction. Seth heard the second shot hit the salon wall inches above him. The large man wiped his eyes with his left hand and looked around the salon for Seth.

Seth pushed the leather chair out in front of him and gathered himself to make one last charge at the huge Hispanic. He'd either knock the wind out of the bigger man or take a bullet. In mid air, he heard two shots ring out almost simultaneously. When he contacted the Hispanic, he was already falling backwards. Seth landed on top of him and the huge man didn't move. Seth rolled off and looked behind him.

Beau was standing at the top of the companionway stairs holding a smoking Glock automatic pistol with both hands. Tie wraps held his wrists and ankles together, and he said with a huge smile on his face, "I wondered who was causing all of that commotion up here, but I didn't think it was the Cavalry riding in to save my sorry ass."

Seth slowly got up, limped over to Beau, took the 9 mm Glock out of Beau's hands, and gave him a big hug.

He spoke softly in Beau's ear as he hugged him, "You've got a lot of explaining to do, asshole, but I'm glad you hopped on up here when you did."

Seth got a kitchen knife and cut the tie wraps off of Beau's wrists and ankles.

"How did you get your hands in front of you, Beau? When I saw them take you out of the dinghy, they had them tied behind your back."

Beau said, "They put me on a bed below and tie wrapped my ankles after smacking me around a little. I made up a story to buy me some time and they were checking it out with the Cipriano family in Florida. I have been keeping the Glock hidden behind the motor cover on the Raritan head. I knew I had to get to it before the return call came in and they found out my story was bullshit. I figured that the Glock was my only chance, so I worked my wrists down under my butt a millimeter at a time and stretched everything out slowly. Then I slowly worked my feet and legs through. It's amazing how loose you can get when you work on it for over an hour, and you know you're going to die if you don't do it. The tie wrap cut my wrists up pretty bad though, look at the blood. By the way, where is Rafael?"

"That must be the cigar smoking one I surprised in the cockpit. I was hiding on the swim platform when he took the phone call from the Cipriano family in Tampa. They told him to kill you. We better bring him inside."

They covered both the dead Cubans with bed sheets, and straightened up the salon.

"Let me get my wrists cleaned up and bandaged and I'll tell you the whole story from the beginning," said Beau as Seth sat down in the leather chair in the salon.

It took almost an hour for Beau to relate the events of the past three weeks. Seth had many questions during the course of the story and Beau answered all of them without hesitation. Beau was amazed by Seth's intuition, observation skills, and relentless pursuit of the Bertram.

Seth told Beau, "I just couldn't buy the shark tank thing, although the Key West Police even sent me your Rolex with the regatta inscription engraved on it."

"Give it to Jeb."

"I already did. He took your death pretty hard. I'd tell you what was said about you at your wake at the Yacht Club … your friends filled the whole ballroom … but it would give you a big head."

"It probably had more to do with the free food and drink, than me," laughed Beau. "But seriously, Seth, I want you to take at least a million of the three million that's hidden on this boat. It's the least I can do."

"Beau, I think it was brilliant of you to hide half the money in the fuel tanks, and even more brilliant to use your buddy Gary, in Ohio, for insurance. I think you outsmarted the Fernandez brothers at their own game. You know I've always thought you were smarter and more resourceful than me, except with women and gambling. But this whole thing is wrong from the start. I don't want any of the money, Beau. It's dirty money. I don't like why you're in this situation, and I don't like the fact that you can't go back home. I only came to find you because you're my brother, and I can see now that there was no other way out of this for you. But, six people are dead, and even though you're alive, our family has lost you. I won't pontificate further, but you know what got you into this mess in the first place. I hope you've learned your lesson from all of this. Take the money and buy yourself a new identity as soon as possible. The Cipriano family might be looking for Ronald Santos' passport to pop up somewhere so don't use it. We'll only keep it in case we get stopped on the way to San Jose. You'll be safe because they think Beau Stone is dead. I'm not going to tell Jeb or anyone else that you're still alive. I might come down here fishing in a year or two, if you've straightened out. I'd like nothing better than to spend time and go fishing with you like we did when we were growing up on the creek. Contact me through Gary Anderson when the time is right. Now let's get the money out of the fuel tanks and figure a way to make this Bertram and the two dead Tampa guys disappear."

Seth and Beau took the inspection port lids off the top of the fuel tanks and fished the plastic wrapped bundles of bills out. They rebagged it in new garbage bags and loaded it in the inflatable dinghy along with the "cold cash" that they had loaded into the two black duffels. Beau packed his remaining clothes and belongings in another garbage bag and put it in the dinghy.

Seth had figured a way to torch the Bertram and still give them time to make it ashore before it blew. He took the dinghy gasoline can and shook some gas over the salon furniture. Then he soaked some dishtowels with some of the remaining gas and made a wick by stuffing them in the nearly empty gas can. He set it next to the coffee maker and removed the coffee pot. Seth set the automatic timer for twenty minutes and laid the end of the gas soaked wick on the bare electric burner. When the coffee maker turned on the gas soaked towel would soon catch fire and the fume-laden salon should explode in a huge ball of fire. The Bertram would burn to its waterline and sink. The two dead bodies would be incinerated and the engines would melt in the intense heat. There would be nothing left to salvage, and any investigation would turn up nothing. No Nose Cipriano would write off Paco, Rafael, and the mysterious captain Jimmy Williams, as being killed in the *Chica's* explosion and fire. No Nose would continue to search for the Fernandez brothers and his three million dollars in vain.

Seth and Beau climbed in the dinghy started the outboard, and quietly idled toward Playa Herradura in the dark. Seth looked back at the now dark *Chica* and could only hear the sound of the generator exhaust.

Back at the beach, Seth retrieved his kit bag from amongst the creek boulders, put his shirt and shoes back on, and then quickly loaded the money and outboard engine into the Forerunner. Beau deflated the dinghy, and the two of them were just loading it into the rear hatch of the Toyota when the first explosion went off. The Bertram's salon windows were blown out and the boat was engulfed in flames. Within seconds the fire turned into a raging inferno that lit up the water, beaches, and mountains around the bay with an eerie glow.

Seth quickly replaced the coil wire, and jumped in the driver's seat. He turned the key, and the Forerunner's engine sprang to life. As Seth backed out to the road, a second explosion rocked the Bertram and blew the flybridge thirty feet into the air.

They drove through the gate into Los Suenos, waved to the guard who was on his walkie-talkie, and proceeded to the Marriott. Seth left Beau in the SUV and went up to his room. He collected his passport, money, and duffel bag. He glanced out the balcony door at *Chica*, which was now burning all the way down to the waterline. He went down to the lobby and left the room key at the empty front desk with a note; "Unexpectedly called back to San Jose. Run my charges on my American Express imprint. Thanks, Mr. Stone." There were no hotel personnel anywhere in the front part of the hotel, as everyone was out on the ocean side veranda watching the Bertram burn.

Seth pulled out of Los Suenos and headed for San Jose. They drove in silence for almost twenty minutes.

Finally Beau said, "We need to ditch the dinghy and outboard engine."

"I already know the perfect place to do that. It's about ten or fifteen minutes from here."

The sun was just coming up when they started over the bridge across the Tarcole River. The road was deserted at that hour and Seth stopped the Forerunner in the middle of the bridge.

"This is where we lose the dinghy. Jump out and we'll throw it over the rail and into the river."

The dinghy fell fifty feet into the fast moving river and was instantly attacked by two 20 foot crocodiles that appeared from below in the muddy river water.

"Holy Shit!" said Beau. "They're huge."

Seth threw the outboard over the rail and it disappeared into the river with a splash. They quickly jumped back in the Forerunner and exited the bridge area.

Beau said, "If anyone ever fell off that bridge, they wouldn't have a chance in hell of making it to shore."

Seth laughed and said, "Right on, brother. Nobody is going to go anywhere near there."

They drove back over the mountains and Beau was amazed at their beauty. They made small talk and soon passed the San Jose airport. Everything important had already been said. Twenty–five minutes later, they were in crowded, downtown, San Jose.

Seth drove to the center of town, found a luggage store, and parked. Beau went inside and returned with three more large duffels. He put the fuel tank money in two of them and his clothes in the third while Seth drove to the Amstel Hotel, which was located several blocks away. Seth had stayed at the Amstel on his last trip to Costa Rica. It was a small, quiet, upscale hotel, which catered to South American and European businessmen. Duffels full of "samples" would not cause any stir at the Amstel. Seth told Beau to stay in the car when they got to the hotel. Seth checked in and had the bellman take all of the duffels out of the SUV, except his, up to the room. He came back out fifteen minutes later and handed Beau the room key and a photocopy of his passport and visa.

"Beau, use my ID until you can buy a passport and a new identity. Just say you lost it or it was stolen and luckily you always travel with a copy. Go across the street and get some lunch, and then go in the side entrance of the Amstel and straight up to the room. Shave off the beard and wear your hat and sunglasses in the Amstel. We look alike except for the hair color. Maybe you should dye your hair? Actually, do that today. As soon as you get new ID, change hotels and deposit the money as you had planned. I suggest you keep that Glock with you at all times."

"Thanks, Seth, I'll be in touch after I get settled."

"Have Gary call only at my townhouse, not at the boatworks. If something happens to Gary, send me a postcard from the country you're in to the townhouse with just a phone number on it, nothing else, and I'll call until I get you."

Beau started to say something else, but Seth interrupted, "There's nothing left to say, Beau. We've said it all. The rest is up to you. We're both alive, so let's make the best of what time we have left."

They shook hands and Beau reached over and hugged Seth saying, "I love you, brother."

Seth said, "If I didn't love you, Beau, I wouldn't have followed you here."

Beau got out of the car and closed the door. Seth pulled away from the curb and headed for the airport. Beau watched the white Forerunner drive away until he lost it in the city traffic. Seth never looked back.

EPILOQUE

CHIP Caldwell stood on the south breakwater at Los Suenos and looked out to where the Bertram 54 had been anchored the day before. The Bertram, Ronald Santos, and his commission were gone in a puff of smoke. Everyone at Los Suenos was buzzing about the explosions, the fire, and the sinking of the Bertram. Chip was distraught about the $50,000 commission that was lost. He would have put half of that money in his pocket. At least he still had the $4,500 cash deposit in the company safe.

Maybe this afternoon when the sun got high, he'd ride out there on the Contender with his dive gear. If he could find the dinghy's outboard and get it running … he could salvage another eight or nine hundred dollars out of the deal.

Made in the USA
Charleston, SC
05 February 2014